October 2004
For Rich.
Hope this do
high respect for the Kennedy's.
Get well soon — The Snack

House of Sugar

Bay of Pigs –
  The CIA/Mafia Assassination
    Conspiracies

Cuba
1960-1963

A NOVEL BY
Sheldon Burton Webster

This book is a work of fiction. Places, events, and situations
in this story are purely fictional. Any resemblance to actual persons, living or
dead, is coincidental.

ISBN: 0-7596-8571-1 (e-book)
ISBN: 0-7596-8573-8 (Paperback)
ISBN: 0-7596-8574-6 (Hardcover)
ISBN: 0-7596-8572-X (RocketBook)

This book is printed on acid free paper.

1stBooks - rev. 11/20/02

Also by Sheldon Burton Webster,

- *The Betheaden Road*

- *The Voyage of the Encounter*

Dedicated
to the
Officers and Men
of
La Brigada 2506

Prologue

The United States Government's intelligence service partnership with the Mafia began during World War II when the OSS recruited Mafia chieftain Lucky Luciano for "Operation Underworld" to assist the Office of Naval Intelligence in fighting saboteurs on the New York waterfront. Luciano, the founder of the National Commission or Syndicate, was serving a thirty-to-fifty-year sentence in Dannemora Federal Prison for forced prostitution and racketeering. At the time of his conviction in 1936, Luciano controlled the heroin distribution in the United States. His imprisonment had dealt a major blow to the Syndicate's drug operations.

By participating in Operation Underworld, Luciano was allowed to resume active leadership of the Commission from his new jail cell at the state prison in Albany. The ONI successfully used the Mafia gang's anti-sabotage surveillance on the New York docks to eliminate the Nazi saboteurs. Luciano, the inmate, was also responsible for recruiting the Sicilian Mafia to help with General George Patton's Seventh Army invasion of Sicily in July of 1943.

After the War, the greatest criminal talent of his time was rewarded for his military intelligence service by being deported from the United States to Italy where he quickly rebuilt his international heroin syndicate.

In his book, *The Politics of Heroin in Southeast Asia,* author Alfred W. McCoy best describes the Luciano postwar heroin operations:

"The narcotics syndicate Luciano organized after World War II remains one of the most remarkable in the history of the traffic. For more than a decade it moved morphine base from the Middle East to Europe, transformed it into heroin, and then exported it in substantial quantities to the United States—all without ever suffering a major arrest or seizure. The organization's comprehensive distribution network within the United States increased the number of active addicts from an estimated 20,000 at the close of the war to 60,000 in 1952 and 150,000 by 1965."

Drawing upon the OSS/Luciano partnership successes, in 1947 the newly formed CIA engaged the Corsican Mafia as enforcers to eliminate the striking Socialist dock unions in Marseilles that were crippling the fragile French postwar economy. The operation went as planned and the Communist union leaders were assassinated, allowing France to remain a free nation. Luciano established the clichéd "French Connection" out of the Port of Marseilles as his international distribution center for heroin shipments entering the United States through Mafia-controlled Havana.

From its inception, the CIA ignored the Mafia's illicit narcotics trafficking for a percentage of the drug profits, which were deposited into a labyrinth of secret bank accounts scattered around the world. Without congressional knowledge or oversight, these funds were used to fulfill presidential political favors and campaign promises by overthrowing unfriendly governments considered adversaries to Wall Street and State Department foreign policies. Unwittingly the CIA had become the standing president's enforcer.

Throughout the Cold War, the control of the world's opium supply translated into billions of dollars in hard currency, which became one of the underlying reasons for the United States involvement in Southeast Asia.

When the United States placed pressure on the Turkish government to abolish opium production by 1967, the world's heroin supply had already begun shifting from the Middle East to the Golden Triangle of Southeast Asia.

The CIA had in 1950 become secretly involved in the Indochina narcotics scene by providing support for Chiang Kai-shek's Nationalist Kuomintang, or KMT, Army that had retreated from China's Yunnan Province into northeastern Burma. To harass the Chinese Communists, the CIA re-armed and supplied the KMT ragtag forces to invade southern China from bases in the Shan States. After three failed invasion attempts, the KMT troops came under the leadership of General Li Mi, who became a warlord monopolizing the opium trade with support provided by the United States Government.

The defeat of the French Vietnamese Expeditionary Corps at Dien Bien Phu in 1954 brought a Communist threat for control of the Golden Triangle where seventy-percent of the world's opium supply was being produced in the rugged mountains of Burma, Thailand and Laos. For the United States anti-Communist

Thai, Lao and South Vietnamese allies who depended heavily on the opium trade to stay in power, pilots from CIA Air America began flying raw opium out of the Golden Triangle to the refineries in Vientiane and Saigon to finance the Laotian Government and the Hmong Mercenary Army under the command of General Vang Pao.

Fidel Castro marched into Havana on New Year's Day 1959 and immediately closed the Lucky Luciano international narcotics-smuggling operations along with Meyer Lansky casino concessions operated by Tampa Mafia chieftain, Santo Trafficante, Jr. When the Eisenhower Administration reduced the Cuban sugar import quota, Castro retaliated by establishing the National Institution of Agrarian Reform, turning the large landholdings of the Hershey Corporation, United Fruit Company and others into cooperatives for the Cuban people. The nationalization of American interests placed great political pressure on President Eisenhower to protect American investments. The once pro-Castro American press that had helped put him in power, turned to labeling Fidel Castro: "The Communist Regime that Threatens the Western Hemisphere."

After the Democrats won the Presidency in 1960 in an election filled with hard-line anti-Communist rhetoric and election fraud controversy, the Kennedy Administration reluctantly implemented the Eisenhower Administration plan by approving the CIA-trained Cuban exile force for the invasion of Cuba.

And this is where our story begins—with events leading up to the April 1961 invasion at the Bay of Pigs by *La Brigada 2506.*

ACKNOWLEDGMENTS AND AUTHOR'S NOTE

This is a book of fiction, a story told by the characters whose lives I have interwoven with history in the CIA's failed Bay of Pigs invasion of Cuba, the CIA/Mafia conspiracy in the assassination of President John F. Kennedy, and the botched attempts on Fidel Castro's life. In telling the story, certain liberties have been taken with the historical events that were kept classified by the United States government until 1997. Recorded conversations of the real individuals have been interposed with the voice of the fictional characters to make this story of human tragedy and failed foreign policy come to life. I also made an exerted effort to correctly report times, dates, and places during the early 1960s when the events took place.

A special thanks is extended to Grayston L. Lynch, the legendary CIA covert actions officer and retired Special Forces captain who led the Cuban *La Brigada* into the Bay of Pigs; and to Lt. Col. Joseph L. Shannon, USAF Retired, the training officer of the exiled Cuban Air Force and the sole surviving American pilot to fly combat at the Bay of Pigs, for their interviews. The assistance of retired Army Special Forces Colonel John T. Goorley and other contributing veterans of the United States Armed Forces is greatly appreciated.

I thank Mark A. Ginzo, a Cuban expatriate who fought with Ernesto "Che" Guevara in the revolution before defecting to the United States and becoming a lawyer-turned priest. I am also indebted to the many Cuban-American expatriates and Cuban nationals who treated me not as an adversary but as a friend in their candid interviews while I was researching this book. Many thanks go to my fellow writers: Carl "Doc" Kirby, Carolynne Scott, Caryl Johnston, Bob Wilbanks and Michael D. Shrader, now deceased. And, with all my heart, I thank Alice Helms, who labored diligently and patiently to edit my many drafts of the manuscript.

I read the following sources to help me accurately write this book:
Robert E. Quirk, *Fidel Castro*, New York, W.W. Norton & Company, 1993
Evan Thomas, *The Very Best Men*, New York, Simon & Schuster, 1995
Ronald Kessler, *Inside the CIA*, New York, Simon & Schuster, 1992

Alfred W. McCoy, *The Politics of Heroin in Southeast Asia*, New York, Harper & Row, 1972

Sam Giancana and Chuck Giancana, *Double Cross*, New York, Warner Books, Inc., 1972

Peter Kornbluh (Editor), *Bay of Pigs Declassified: The Secret CIA Report on the Invasion of Cuba*, New York, The New Press, 1998

Victor Lasky, *It Didn't Start with Watergate*, New York, Dial Press, 1977

Harrison Livingstone and Robert Groden, *High Treason*, New York, Carroll & Graf Publishing, Inc., 1989

Tom Kuntz and Phil Kuntz (Editors), *The Sinatra Files*, New York, Three River Press, 2000

Shelby L. Stanton, *Green Berets at War*, Nanato, California, Presidio Press, 1985

Peter Wyden, *Bay of Pigs, The Untold Story*, New York, Simon & Schuster, 1979

Leslie Bethell (Editor), *Cuba: A Short History*, Melbourne, Australia, Cambridge University Press, 1993

Albert C. Persons, *Bay of Pigs: A Firsthand Account of the Mission by a U.S. Pilot in Support of the Cuban Invasion Force in 1961*, Jefferson, North Carolina, McFarland & Company, Inc., 1990

Ovid Demaris, *The Director*, New York, Harper's Magazine Press, 1975

Michael R. Beschloss, *Taking Charge: The Johnson White House Tapes, 1963-1964*, New York, Simon & Schuster, 1997

Seymour M. Hersh, *The Dark Side of Camelot*, Boston, Little, Brown and Company, 1997

Grayston L. Lynch, *Decision for Disaster: Betrayal at the Bay of Pigs*, Washington, Brassey's, Inc., 1998

F. Clifton Berry, Jr., *Inside the CIA: The Architecture, Art & Atmosphere of America's Premier Intelligence Agency*, Montgomery, Alabama, Community Communications, Inc., 1997

Lewis Carroll, *Alice in Wonderland* and *Through the Looking Glass*, New York, Grosset & Dunlap, 1974

Christopher Andrew, *For the President's Eyes Only*, New York, Harper Perennial, 1996

Victor Marchetti and John D. Marks, *The CIA and the Cult of Intelligence*, New York, Alfred A. Knopf, 1974

Jonathan Kwitny, *The Crimes of Patriots*, New York, W.W. Norton & Company, 1987

Warren Trest and Don Doddy, *Wings of Denial the Alabama Air National Guard's Covert Role at the Bay of Pigs*, Montgomery, Alabama, New South Books, 2001

Jim Garrison, *On the Trail of the Assassins, My Investigation and Prosecution of the Murder of President Kennedy*, New York, Sheridan Square Press, 1988

S. B. W.
Birmingham, Alabama
July 2002

Cuba
1960-1963

"I will break the CIA into a thousand pieces."
President John F. Kennedy

"And ye shall know the truth, and the truth shall make you free."
Gospel according to St. John. Inscribed in the lobby of the CIA Headquarters
CIA Director Allen W. Dulles

"The politicians and the CIA made it real simple.
We'd each provide men for the hit…"
Mafia Boss Sam Giancana

"Oswald had been an instrument very well chosen and well prepared by the
extreme right wing, by the ultraconservative reactionaries of the United States,
for the defined purpose of getting rid of the president…"
Fidel Castro

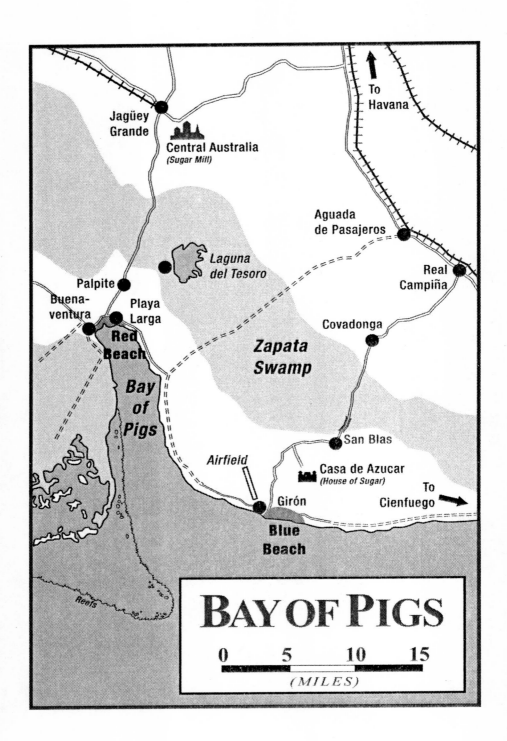

Jagüey Grande

Central Australia
(Sugar Mill)

To Havana

Aguada de Pasajeros

Laguna del Tesoro

Real Campiña

Palpite

Buena-ventura

Playa Larga

Red Beach

Covadonga

Zapata Swamp

Bay of Pigs

San Blas

Airfield

Casa de Azucar
(House of Sugar)

Girón

Blue Beach

To Cienfuego

Reefs

BAY OF PIGS

0   5   10   15

(MILES)

Cast of Characters

The Mafia

Exner, Judith Campbell—Las Vegas showgirl and mistress to Mafia boss Sam Giancana. Met President-elect Kennedy in Las Vegas in 1960 and later admitted to sleeping with him in the White House while serving as a courier for the Mafia. Relationship with Kennedy ended on March 22, 1962 when FBI Director J. Edgar Hoover held private luncheon in the White House and warned the president of fraternizing with the Mafia.

Giancana, Momo Salvatore—Alias Sam Gold known also as Moony or Sam by the Mafia. The Chicago Black Hand godfather was also the National Commission chairman of organized crime for the United States. He rigged the 1960 presidential election in Chicago and West Virginia, thus delivering the White House to Kennedy. The close associate of entertainer Frank Sinatra was a self-confessed co-conspirator with a rogue cell of CIA officers in the assassination of President Kennedy. Giancana was murdered in his suburban Chicago home in June of 1975 five days before he was to testify before Senator Frank Church's Senate Intelligence Committee investigation of the CIA and FBI. His murder was never solved but many clues point to a CIA/ Mafia hit.

Marcello, Carlos—Mafia godfather of New Orleans organization deported to Guatemala by Attorney General Robert Kennedy in April of 1961, confirming the Kennedy Mafia double-cross. Smuggled back into the United States by CIA pilot David Ferrie, Marcello continued to operate in hiding until his empire collapsed after his imprisonment in Texarkana in June of 1983.

Rosselli, John—Alias John Rawlston also known as Johnny. The former Al Capone underling served time in federal prison for extortion in the Hollywood movie industry. The boss of Las Vegas for the National Commission was a loyal lieutenant to Sam Giancana. While under FBI witness protection, Rosselli disappeared five days prior to being called to testify before the Church Committee. A year later in August of 1976 fishermen found his body in an oil drum off North Miami Beach. Like Giancana, his murder has never been solved but suspicions point to a CIA directed assassination.

Trafficante, Santo—Known as Joe. The former Mafia chief in Havana ran the Syndicate's narcotics operations from Tampa, Florida. After Giancana and Rosselli murders, Trafficante was known by the mob's adage: "If you want to know who done it—look for the last man standing." Trafficante remained untouchable in his international drug trafficking operations in Latin America and Asia until his death of kidney failure in 1987.

The CIA and its Agents

Alabama Air National Guardsmen—Eighty members of the 117th Tactical Reconnaissance Wing under the command of General Reid Doster trained the Cuban exile air force in Nicaragua as CIA contract civilians. LTC Joseph L. Shannon was the exile air force training officer who flew the final mission at Bay of Pigs and survived. Killed in action where Major Riley Shamburger, Captain Thomas W. Ray, Wade C. Gray and Leo F. Baker.

Banister, Guy—Former Special Agent in charge of the Chicago FBI office and Deputy Commissioner of the New Orleans Police Department. Banister operated Guy Banister Associates, Inc., in New Orleans as a front for the CIA's Cuban Revolutionary Council (C.R.C.) to train anti-Castro guerrillas. As a sponsor for the Kennedy assassination, Banister was the handler for CIA pilot David Ferrie and also was responsible for making Lee Harvey Oswald appear to be Communist to cover his connection with the CIA.

Bissell, Richard Mervin, Jr.—Senior covert operations officer responsible for the Bay of Pigs, Operation ZAPATA. Bissell was a former Yale economics professor who fathered the Marshall Plan to rebuild Europe after World War II. He was responsible for the development of the U-2 intelligence-gathering surveillance aircraft. Bobby Kennedy fired Bissell for Operation MONGOOSE's failure to assassinate Fidel Castro. In February of 1962, he left the CIA after being awarded the Medal of Freedom by J.F.K.

Cabell, Charles P. —Retired Air Force General who served as deputy director of the CIA under Allen Dulles. He was the air boss for Operation ZAPATA and fired by President Kennedy afterwards. His brother, Earle Cabell, was the Mayor of Dallas, Texas when Kennedy was assassinated.

Dulles, Allen W. —OSS legend appointed by President Truman as the architect for founding the Central Intelligence Agency. He served as the agency's third Director of Central Intelligence (DCI) from February 26, 1953 to November 29, 1961. Dulles was know as the "Great White Case Officer" for disregarding the agency's chain of command and dealing directly with the agents in the field. He was fired by J.F.K. on November 29, 1961 as a result of the failed Bay of Pigs. Afterwards he was appointed to the Warren Commission by L.B.J. and given the responsibility for handling the investigation of the CIA's involvement in the Kennedy assassination.

FitzGerald, Desmond—Former Wall Street lawyer and Army captain who fought with the Chinese in Burma during WW II and later served as CIA chief of the Far East Division. After Richard Bissell's dismissal, FitzGerald was appointed by Robert Kennedy to head the ultra-secret Special Affairs Staff (S.A.S.), the successor to Operation MONGOOSE whose mission it was to assassinate Fidel Castro. Under pressure from the Kennedys, and against advice from his CIA counterintelligence, FitzGerald personally recruited Cuban turncoat Rolando Cubelas for the assassination. He was noted for his use of *Alice's Adventures in Wonderland* metaphors for keeping his colleagues off balance. In 1965 he was appointed Deputy Director of Plans responsible for CIA covert operations.

Lynch, Grayston L.—Retired United States Army Special Forces Captain turned CIA officer who ran the field operations at the Bay of Pigs. After the invasion, Lynch was assigned to the Cuban Task Force Special Operations Division (SOD), code named JM/WAVE. The largest CIA station in the world was leased from the University of Miami and located on what is now the present day Miami Zoo. The United States secret war against Cuba was waged until JM/WAVE was closed in 1967. Over 2,126 covert operations were conducted with orders "set Cuba aflame."

McCone, John A. —Director of the CIA from November 29, 1961 to April 28, 1965. Appointed by President Kennedy to replace Allen Dulles, he had no prior intelligence experience.

Oswald, Lee Harvey—CIA operative and scapegoat arrested for being the "lone gunman" in President John F. Kennedy's assassination. Mafia lieutenant Jack Ruby murdered the former United States Marine, who was fluent in Russian and held a top-secret security clearance, in Dallas, Texas on November 24, 1963 while the world watched on television.

The Politicians

Eisenhower, Dwight David—34th President of the United States, (1953-1961). Ike was a Republican and former supreme Commander of the Allied forces in Europe during World War II. He directed the CIA to formulate a plan to remove Fidel Castro from power after he nationalized American investments in retaliation for sugar quota import reductions to the United States.

Johnson, Lyndon Baines—36th President of the United States, (1963-1969). L.B.J. was a Democrat from Texas who became president upon Kennedy's death. He was reelected for a full term in 1964 and did not seek reelection in 1968 due to the division in the nation over his handling of the Vietnam War. He died January 23, 1973.

Kennedy, John Fitzgerald—35th President of the United States, (1961-1963). J.F.K. was a Democrat from Massachusetts whose administration suffered severe political setback in April 1961 after the CIA Bay of Pigs invasion failed to over-throw the Cuban government. Kennedy was assassinated in Dallas, Texas on the afternoon of November 22, 1963. Chief Justice of the Supreme Court Earl Warren was appointed by President Johnson to investigate his death. Certain findings of the Warren Commission were sealed from the public until 2033 for national security reasons.

Kennedy, Robert Francis—Attorney General of the United States, (1961-1964). The younger brother of President John F. Kennedy was responsible for forming the Special Affairs Staff—a secret CIA operation to assassinate Cuban dictator Fidel Castro. R.F.K. never testified before the Warren Commission on his brother's death. He was assassinated in Los Angeles in June of 1968 by an alleged Mafia hit while campaigning for president.

Nixon, Richard Milhous—Vice President of the United States, (1953-1961) under President Eisenhower. John Kennedy defeated the Republican presidential candidate from California in the 1960 election that was marred by election fraud that was never investigated by the Justice Department.

The Cubans

Batista, Fulgencio—Dictator of Cuba; 1933-1940; President, 1940-1944; Dicta-tor, 1952-1958. The Batista regimes were known for corruption and close associa-tion with the American Mafia. Fidel Castro ousted Batista from power on January 1, 1959.

Castro Ruz, Fidel—Cuban Maximum Leader from 1959 to the present. Castro came to power with the help of CIA supplied munitions and *The New York Times'* favorable press coverage by *Times* reporter, Herbert Mathews. The Cuban leader has survived nine United States Presidents and numerous CIA assassina-tion plots.

Castro Ruz, Raúl—Younger brother of Cuban Dictator Fidel Castro and the Minister of the Revolutionary Cuban Armed Forces.

Cubelas, Rolando Secades—Code name, AMLASH. The turncoat Cuban major was recruited by Desmond FitzGerald to assassinate Castro at a meeting in Paris in October of 1963, a month before Kennedy's assassination.

Guevara, Ernesto "Che"—Legendary Argentine medical doctor who became a myth for social revolutions around the world. The Bolivian Army executed Che on October 9, 1967 in the mountainous village of La Higuera. To confirm his death, the CIA cut off Guevara's hands, packed them in dry ice, and shipped them to CIA headquarters in Langley, Virginia. His severed hands were later returned to Havana and now are on display in the Museum of the Revolution.

Valdés, Ramiro—Head of the Cuban Interior Ministry's security police, the Directory of General Intelligence (DGI).

Varona, Antonio de—Former Cuban Prime Minister under Batista and Minister of Public Works under Castro. He was an outspoken member of the Cuban Revolutionary Council (C.R.C.)—the exile government formed by the U.S. to take power after the overthrow of Fidel Castro. During the Bay of Pigs invasion, members of the C.R.C. were held incommunicado at the secret Opa-Locka airfield in Miami.

Chapter One

Fontainebleau Hotel, Miami Beach

Sunday, September 25, 1960

His name was Axial Hanson, a master of skullduggery when it came to CIA covert operations to overthrow foreign governments. He had registered two days ago using his alias, Alex B. Hudson, and was patiently staking out the entrance to the hotel from his guest room when a black Lincoln with Tampa plates pulled under the porte cochere and stopped. His spirits lifted when the driver opened the back door for the short bald Italian. *Trafficante! I'll give you dogs enough time to sniff each other's asses before ole Nine-fingers goes down and joins you grease balls.*

Hanson was preparing for his three o'clock meeting with the leaders of the National Commission to be held in the Boom Boom Room underneath the hotel lobby. The organized crime chairman, Sam Giancana, known as "Mooney" for being the meanest of Chicago's "Little Italy" Black Hand Mafia, would be in attendance. He was registered under the name of Sam Gold and was having lunch downstairs with Johnny Roselli from Las Vegas who was a guest at the Kenilworth Hotel under the alias, John Rawlston. The third gangster was the man Axial Hanson had just seen getting out of the Lincoln—Trafficante, the don of the international narcotics trafficking syndicate.

1

Hanson lit a Chesterfield and glanced down at the "Parade" supplement to the Sunday *Miami Herald* featuring Giancana and Trafficante's pictures on the FBI's Ten-Most-Wanted List. *Those two hoods are almost identical twins,* he thought, letting his mind race while he waited. *J. Edgar would go ballistic if he knew the CIA had planned this meeting with gangsters the FBI doesn't have a clue on how to capture.*

At times like this, Axial Hanson liked to think back to his good old days after the war when he was an FBI special agent on the organized crime desk in Chicago. He had worked with Bob Maheu, his friend and a former agent who had arranged this meeting with the Commission through his private detective agency in Washington where Howard Hughes was only one of many influential names on his client list.

Colonel Sheffield Edwards, CIA Director of Security, had selected the right man when asked to recommend someone to serve as the case officer for the Mafia to operate under deep-cover as a civilian in Havana. "This is the most sensitive covert action *ever* and Hanson is as tough as they come," Edwards had informed the CIA Director, Allen Dulles. "His peers on the clandestine staff know next to nothing about the reclusive maverick's personal life except that Mr. Coup, or Nine-fingers as he is called by the Mafia, is from a prominent Westport, Connecticut family and was Skull and Bones at Yale. He's a very peculiar man, a confirmed bachelor who is a strong advocate of sexpionage."

The man they were discussing had indeed graduated from Yale, class of 1938, and gone to work for the Bank of Boston before he joined the Army. After Officer Candidate School he had served with the First Division in the invasion of North Africa, where he had gotten wounded in the hip. While recovering he had volunteered for the Office of Strategic Services and operated with the French resistance, becoming a Jeb team leader. When Allen Dulles formed the CIA in 1947, one of the first officers the new director recruited was Axial Hanson.

In November 1952, Dulles assigned Hanson to Operation TPAJAX to work with British Intelligence in undermining Iranian Prime Minister Mohamed Mossadeq's left-wing regime that nationalized the Anglo-American Oil Company. When the August 1953 coup nearly collapsed, the quick-thinking young officer saved the day by personally intervening with the Iranian military to back the

Shah—his heroic act quickly turned into legend within the Directorate of Plans. Axial was then assigned the following year to mastermind the Guatemalan government's overthrow that became a CIA textbook case for coup d'etat success, earning Hanson the nickname 'Mr. Coup.'

Axial walked into the bathroom to comb his hair before meeting with the Mafia chieftains. The forty-three year old covert operations officer smiled at his image and said, "Nine-fingers, what you need is time in the Havana sun, you good looking son-of-a-bitch. This is a great chance to kiss-up to Mr. Dulles by knocking off Fidel's ass."

He finished brushing his teeth, thinking about the picture of the woman the DCI had shown him in their briefing last week in Washington. Allen Dulles had asked, "Axial, do you by chance remember the Englishman Allenby Woodson during the war?"

"Yes, of course—the correspondent with the BBC with the handlebar mustache."

"Well, I reckon I've spotted the perfect spy," Dulles had said with his good-natured chuckle. "I want you to recruit Sir Allenby's daughter. He gave me this picture of her while I was his guest at the East India Club in London last week. Miss Woodson has been assigned to the BBC Havana bureau and her father thinks we need an agent in the foreign press for propaganda against Castro's government, and I agreed."

That British broad is one hunky-dory looking piece of ass, Axial Hanson was thinking as he finished getting dressed.

The hotel management had closed the Boom Boom Room for the afternoon and the lone bartender looked bored as he watched the waves off the Atlantic through the crack in the drawn curtains. He had a clue that the tall and elegantly dressed Johnny Roselli was the former Al Capone underling who had served three years in federal prison for attempting to extort payments from the Hollywood movie industry. After his release he operated the Sans Souci Casino in Havana for National Commission founder Meyer Lansky during the days of corrupt dictator Fulgencio Batista. The debonair gangster who ran Las Vegas noticed Giancana's hairpiece was off-center while watching him tap his fingers impatiently. "Roselli, what the fuck we doing here? You best not be wasting my time. *Capisce?*"

Roselli smiled at the short, squatty man seated across from him and contemplated straightening his toupee before changing the subject. "Heard anything from Sinatra lately?"

Giancana lit his cigar and chuckled. "Nice job, Roselli, you and Frankie setting up my whore Judy Campbell as Jack Kennedy's mistress. She'll be fucking him in the White House, and we'll be listening."

"Thanks, Mooney. Now if we can only get Jack elected we've got him by his balls."

"Jack *will* be elected, *capisce?*" Giancana snapped, looking up when Santo Trafficante came barging through the door unannounced. "Holy shit, look what the dogs done drug up. What you doing here, Santo?"

Santo Trafficante, the former mob drug chieftain in Havana, took off his madras sport coat and shook hands. "What kind of deal you guys got cooking that couldn't wait until Monday?" he asked as he sat down next to Roselli and faced Giancana's cigar.

"What *fucking* deal, Johnny? I hate surprises, *capisce?*" Giancana whispered, leaning across the table at them.

"Relax, Mooney. Look, you guys, Axial Hanson from the CIA is gonna meet us here at three o'clock and I didn't want to say nothing about it over the telephone."

"*What?* What's so damn important that I gotta fly down here and miss the Bears' game?" Giancana asked when Trafficante butted in.

"Them bastards want more than their ten percent off our dope trafficking?"

Giancana snapped his fingers, "Hey bartender, get off your ass and bring my friend here a vodka tonic."

"Mooney, the greedy bastards got their cut of two hundred million last year. Must be that the slush funds they got stashed are running out now that we've been kicked out of Havana."

Giancana nodded, "Yeah, Trafficante, you're right, them fuckers know how to spend the dough, and we gotta serious problem with our dope shipments since Castro…"

"Hold it!" Roselli said, holding up his hands. "It hasn't got anything to do with our money laundering deal with them CIA guys. I'm telling you straight. I got a call to have lunch with Bob Maheu at the Brown Derby in Beverly Hills a couple of weeks ago...early September."

"What the hell's Maheu got to do with it?"

"Maheu & Associates gotta big job for us, Mooney, with the government and he's using Nine-fingers as our go-between with the G-men and..."

Trafficante's eyes widened. "You kidding? If Kennedy gets elected he'll make Bobby attorney general, and we're all fucked."

Giancana leaned across the table. "Not so loud. That dumb ass over there behind the bar has got ears. Let Roselli finish."

"Listen to me, Mooney. Bobby Kennedy was a real pain in the ass in the McClellan committee investigation. He's after Hoffa and the teamsters big time. Now, what you gonna do about it?"

"Shut the hell up, Santo. Let Roselli finish," Giancana ordered. "I didn't come down here to discuss Bobby Kennedy. After thirty months what did the McClellan investigation and the FBI pin on us anyhow? *Nothing!* Not one of our guys went to jail."

Roselli agreed. "Okay, as I was telling you, Maheu...well listen to this shit. He told me that the CIA wants a *contract* on Castro. Since I ran things in Havana okay, Maheu told me I was his man to arrange the hit if the Outfit wants to open back up in Cuba."

Trafficante's voice shot across the table at Roselli. "*Fuck* Castro! Bobby Kennedy is the guy who needs to be hit."

"Shut up, *capisce?*"

Roselli nervously combed his silver-gray hair before intervening, "Okay, hold it you guys. Let me finish. See, I go to New York on the fourteenth of September to meet this guy at the Plaza Hotel. Jesus Christ, it turns out to be ole Nine-fingers himself! I met him once at a cocktail party at Maheu's house in Washington and..."

"Wait a fuckin' minute. This CIA shit bugs me."

Giancana looked at Santo and laughed. "You dumb shit. I've been doing business with Nine-fingers for years. So what's the big deal? What you got us into, Johnny?"

"Nothing yet," Roselli sighed. "I told them I'd talk it over with you guys. They offered me a hundred fifty grand plus expenses to make the hit. I told them that I had partners and I wanted my partners in on it. They guaranteed me the G-men won't screw with our other operations in Havana once we hit Fidel. You guys want in or not?"

The gangster from Tampa stood up and took off his tie. "Yeah, I'm interested. But the CIA isn't the last word anymore; it's the fucking FBI guys. Bobby and the McClellan committee got Hoover on our asses after he looked stupid saying the Mafia didn't exist."

"You're right," Roselli added, "but unfortunately the McClellan investigation convinced the whole world the mob is alive and well."

"No shit, Roselli. Hoover's declared war on 'La Cosa Nostra' as he calls us. But that ain't nothing. Mooney, what the hell we doing about Bobby if JFK makes him attorney general?"

"Guys, I've got that all under control with Joe Kennedy, *capisce?*"

"I don't know, Sam," Trafficante said as he sat back down. "Bobby Kennedy thinks we'll roll over and stick our heads up our asses if you don't do something to stop him."

"Forget it, Santo. What you guys think then about this Castro deal?"

"What the hell, Roselli, let's party in Havana," Trafficante said rubbing his hands together. "The Tropicana, with all them naked broads. This job don't come with no guarantees, does it?"

"Hell no, it don't," said Giancana relighting his cigar. "Let's get serious here for a minute. What are you guys really thinking?"

Trafficante raised one cheek of his ass and farted. "Bang—gangland-style killing, Mooney. Just like Chicago in the good ole days, done by some Cubans who used to work for me as enforcers. Gotta appear to be an inside job by the Cubans."

"Santo, you're a rotten-smelling fucker," Giancana said fanning the air. "How the hell you gonna find a Cuban to kill Castro? Number one, you ain't, and number two, if you do, them Cubans will screw it up."

"Yeah, Sam's right. Chicago style isn't the call here," Roselli agreed, looking toward the bar and raising his hand to catch the bartender's attention. "Let's have another round and plan this thing out."

The drinks came, and Roselli waited. "Okay, I've spent half my life with these guys. Cubans are funny, sneaky little bastards. Poison is the only way."

"Poison Castro? You trying to be a comedian or something?" Giancana asked, looking in the mirror and straightening his toupee.

"Hell yeah, that'll work, Mooney," Roselli bristled. "Castro, the son-of-a-bitch eats like a hog. That's the way to hit him, if we've got the right poison."

"Like I've been saying all afternoon, gents, Bobby's still the problem. If Kennedy gets elected you can bet your ass Bobby is the next attorney general. Them bastards and the FBI will put the heat on our Cuban operation and all the others, big-time."

"Santo you sound like a damn busted record," Giancana hissed. "That shit ain't gonna happen. I've cut a deal with Joe Kennedy, see?"

"What kind of deal?"

"Ole man Joe came crying to me at the Ambassador East a couple of months ago saying that Frank Costello and the New York mob had a contract out on him."

"What the hell for?"

"Playing high and mighty like he's God, I guess. Got a big head after buying off Roosevelt and getting appointed as chairman of the SEC, then ambassador to England. Costello called in a mark from Joe's bootlegging days and wanted him to front a piece of property in New York City for the boys. Ole Joe turned his back on Costello, saying he wanted to distance himself from the mob now that Jack was looking presidential. Bad mistake, Joe. *Bad* fucking mistake, Joe Kennedy."

The bartender looked up as the room filled with laughter. "So what did you do, Mooney?" Roselli cackled.

Giancana blew a perfect smoke ring and gave it time to disappear in the stale air. "I called Costello to Chicago and got it all worked out nice and easy."

"Why the hell do you know that Jack is going in as president?" asked Traffi-cante. "He's got to beat Tricky Dick Nixon first."

"You make me laugh. I'm rigging the fuckin' Chicago election and spent a wad buying votes in West Virginia—a half mil of my own cash on them inbred son-of-a-bitchin' hillbillies in places like Logan County, *capisce?*"

Roselli finished off his drink and nodded. "Yeah, Mooney will get our man in the White House."

"You bet your ass. As Joe Kennedy told me: 'Mooney you can sit in the fuckin' Oval Office if you want to, but just please don't let them kill me.'"

"Okay, that's all fine and dandy," Trafficante acquiesced, "but there's got to be more in it to hit Castro than a lousy one-fifty grand and the heat off our Havana operations, Mooney."

"What I'm saying is that the heat is off every one of our fucking operations when Jack's elected."

"Then I've got my old gambling racket back in Havana!"

"Keep the gambling, Johnny—Pocket change," Trafficante said, sticking out his lips like a fish out of water. "I want my dope shipments from Marseilles coming back through Havana. Makes shipping Miami, New York, New Orleans a lot easier."

Johnny Roselli felt he had a consensus. "Okay, it will teach Castro and his Communist assholes to screw with us. So, you guys in or out?"

"I'm in," Mooney said, "but you handle the negotiations, Johnny, in case there's a double-cross."

"Sure, relax. You're the backup man and Santo is the courier to Cuba. Here comes Nine-fingers now."

Axial Hanson took off his sunglasses when he entered the bar having changed into a tan seersucker suit and white buck shoes. He limped over to the three men seated at the table, nodded and opened his briefcase. Lighting a Ches-terfield, he watched the threesome's eyes widen. "It's one hundred fifty-thousand in circulated hundreds if you want to count it, Sam. It's been awhile since we've done any business."

"Yeah, in Tehran, 1952. You doing all right, Nine-fingers?" Giancana asked as he shook Hanson's right hand missing the little finger cut off by the German Gestapo.

Hanson smiled. "Thank you for making the arrangements, Mr. Roselli. It's good to see you again Sam."

"You met our associate here, Santo Trafficante?"

"Only by his reputation, Sam. Saw yours and Mr. Trafficante's names on the FBI's Ten-Most-Wanted list in today's Miami paper." Angling his head toward the silver-haired mobster, Hanson asked, "Why did Mr. Roselli's name get left off?"

Sam Giancana's voice stiffened. "Yeah, Hoover has a hard-on for us after the McClellan hearings. Is that a problem with the CIA doing business?"

"No, hell no. It's hunky-dory with the Company. All that I want you to do, gentlemen, is knock off Fidel Castro."

The room fell very quiet until Roselli finally asked, "You guys got poison strong enough to kill him?"

"Yeah, we got poison strong enough to kill an elephant," Hanson laughed. "Our department of dirty tricks just developed a pill containing botulism. It left no signs in an autopsy performed on the monkey when they tested it."

"That's the stuff. You guys get us the poison and we'll take it from there."

"Hunky-dory, Sam. I'll meet you gentlemen at the Havana Hilton on the first of December. I'll be registered under the name Alex Hudson."

"What's wrong Nine-fingers? You don't trust us or something?"

"Sure I trust you. We've done business before in Iran, remember? But let's just say that I love the hell out of Havana," Hanson replied, sliding his briefcase toward Giancana and shaking his hand.

Hanson had left his Buena Vista apartment complex in Miami, and flew to Havana checking into the Hilton for the Thanksgiving holidays. He decided to go to the pool to catch some sun before pursuing his secondary mission of recruiting a foreign agent in the Havana press corps to spread disinformation against Castro's government. It was better than dealing with his hoodlums, who had already called and said they were going to be a week late.

Holly Woodson had arrived in Havana a year before Castro's 1959 New Year's Day takeover. It had been a busy assignment for the twenty-four-year-old auburn-haired beauty whose job was to cable weekly reports on the Revolution's domestic and political news events back to London. She spent a lot of time at the Hilton casino, and the El Floridita bar in the heart of the old city was her nightly hangout. Holly was looking forward to her visit home for the Christmas Holidays and marking her calendar when her phone rang.

"Hello, Miss Woodson. This is Axial Hanson, an old friend of your father from the war. I'm in Havana working for the Gibraltar Steamship Company out of Miami. Our new president, Thomas Cabot, former president of United Fruit, is coming to Havana. I would like to meet with you to arrange an interview. There's a very confidential and newsworthy story Mr. Cabot wants reported in the press. What about six o'clock in the Turret Lounge at your hotel this afternoon for a cocktail?"

Hanson arrived at the Hotel Nacional wearing a freshly pressed white linen suit and placed his tan Panama hat with a black band on the table. He smoothed his neatly trimmed mustache and wet his lips while he admired the postcard view of the Malecon and the Havana Harbor captured in the sunset. He lit a Chesterfield and ordered aged rum, neat with soda. He waited while listening to the band playing a rumba, and patted his white bucks to the beat of the tambourine.

Holly had left her corner suite still angry over the phone conversation she had with her father confirming his relationship with Axial Hanson. His crisp English voice still burned her ears. "Holly, my dear, don't let this upset you, but I am thinking of libel action against Billingsley for slandering you. The barman at the East India Club informed me that my dear fellow BBC director is furious with me for using my Board influence to promote you from your administrative position to the foreign press corps. Billingsley was overheard saying, 'At least Havana is a good out-of-the-way place for Sir Allenby's daughter,' mind you."

"That's nothing, Father."

"Hear, hear me out, please, Holly. 'Yes, indeed, a bloody foreign correspondent is no job for a woman to be in,' it was reported that my Judah colleague Wimple replied back, my barman, Jason, informed me—mind you."

"Oh, Father, I'm used to that sort thing by now."

"That is not the point. Billingsley was then quoted as saying, 'For dear sake, I do hope she doesn't have a bloody affair with Fidel Castro like she did that poor professor Clive Langford at Lady Margaret Hall at Oxford. What an embarrassment to the BBC and Buckingham Palace!'"

Can you imagine that old fool Billingsley saying that? Holly thought as she got off the elevator. *If my name was Harold Woodson, and I was having an affair with Professor Langford's wife, I would be the bloody chauvinist hero.*

Hanson stood to his full six feet when he saw her get off the elevator and cross the dance floor with the rhythm of the bongo drums in the movement of her hips. The moment Holly brushed her auburn hair out of her eyes, Axial Hanson knew—like Allen Dulles had said—they had found the perfect spy.

"So you are Sir Allenby's daughter?" he asked with a suspended half smile as she turned her back and sat down.

"Yes, Mr. Hanson, and you're a friend of my father," she replied in a self-assured British accent that revealed her upper-crust background.

"An acquaintance would be more accurate. I met your father a couple of times at the Ritz Hotel in Paris after the war. He was doing a story on the OSS and sharing a drink with Ernie Hemingway when he interviewed me."

"Oh yes. You were in the OSS, were you, Mr. Hanson?"

"Worked with French resistance serving as a Jed team leader."

"What is a Jed, might I ask?"

"Oh, just an OSS saying that originated in Jedburgh, Scotland, where, in the old days, they'd hang you and then ask questions. Yes, something like that, I suppose."

"You're being too modest. When I inquired about you, my father said that being a Jed after working with the French partisans is the most prestigious title in the western intelligence community."

"I thank him for saying that. Speaking of titles, how is Sir Allenby these days? He must be awfully proud of your blossoming career at the BBC."

"He's very well, thank you for asking. But living up to my father's expectations is quite frightening at times, especially since my older brother Harold was killed during the war."

"Legends *are* hard to follow, Holly. Does your father ever visit you here or see his old friend Hemingway?"

"No. Now what's your story, Mr. Hanson?"

"Will you please call me by my alias, Alex Hudson?" Hanson asked taking a look around to make sure they would not be overheard. "I am actually an officer of the Central Intelligence Agency, and your father's old friend, Allen Dulles, wants to offer you employment as one of our agents here in Havana. There is a first-class ticket to Washington waiting for you at the Pan Am counter at the airport if you would like to investigate this offer. We have also arranged for Sir Allenby to fly over to meet with us, and the two of you can spend Christmas in New York as our guests."

"I'm a journalist, not a spy, Mr. Hudson. Thank you for the kind offer but…"

"Let's not get too hasty, Miss Woodson. Your father, I'm sure, would be very proud for you to at least accept Mr. Dulles' invitation to meet him in D.C."

"No thank you."

"Miss Woodson, I hesitate to inform you, but this was Sir Allenby's idea."

***

It was a cold December day in downtown Washington as Allen Dulles watched Sir Allenby help his daughter off with her coat in the private dining room of the Alibi Club. *What a stunning woman*, the CIA director was thinking as he pulled out Holly Woodson's chair. *Yes, I've found the perfect spy, thanks to Mr. Coup's fine recruiting in Havana.*

The two men kept Holly entertained with tales of bygone days as they embellished each other's heroic escapades during the war. After coffee and dessert, Mr. Dulles suggested that they adjourn to his South Building office in the CIA complex on E Street for a friendly chat about Holly's future.

The gray-haired director took off his signature tweed sport jacket upon entering his office. His white brush mustache was clamped to the stem of his pipe as he cleaned the fog off his gold-rimmed glasses. The director got directly to the point. "Holly, for your assistance as a journalist in stopping the spread of Communism in the western hemisphere, I am willing to offer you one thousand dollars a month plus five hundred dollars for incidentals to come to work for us. Of course, an unlimited expense account is thrown in, I reckon," Dulles said in his jovial manner puffing on his pipe.

Holly didn't flinch at the generous compensation that was exactly four times the amount she was making with the BBC. "Nice of you to make the offer, Mr. Dulles. Two thousand dollars a month and a thousand for niceties would be my fee for keeping check on Fidel and his cronies."

The director rocked back in his chair, too shocked to respond to the counter offer. *That is an obscene amount to pay a twenty-five-year-old woman, even for my agency with its budget of hundreds of millions.*

Holly lit a cigarette before crossing her legs and pulling down her skirt. Dulles sucked on his pipe and stared at her realizing her father was very astute in recommending her potential as a spy. Getting the American press to cooperate in foreign intelligence propaganda in Havana had been a big problem for the CIA. Finally he said with a sigh, "Yes, Holly, that's fair enough, I reckon."

Holly smiled at her father who was beaming with approval when Dulles added, "You should be very proud of her, Sir Allenby. She is like her father, a tough negotiator. Now, Holly, there's an eight-week international studies course at Georgetown University—our crash course in intelligence-gathering techniques, which starts after the first of the year."

Sir Allenby chuckled to himself at his daughter's gall, but the joviality quickly faded. If his son and wife had survived the London bombings, Harold would be in Holly's place and his daughter could be safely back in London having his grandchildren. The slender Englishman twisted his handlebar mustache saying, "Thank you, Allen, might I recommend that Holly obtain the approval of the British Home Secretary and M-16 since she is a British subject." Then as an afterthought he added, "If you like, my dear, I will arrange a short leave of absence for you at the BBC when we arrive in New York for our Christmas holiday."

Chapter Two

Chicago

November 8, 1960

Sam Giancana jumped up on the table and shouted, "Get Frankie on the phone," when the returns came in with a paper-thin margin electing John F. Kennedy the thirty-fifth president of the United States.

"Now we got our man in the White House and, just like Joe Kennedy said, we'll be running the fucking country," the cigar-smoking gangster bragged to Frank Sinatra on the long distance call from his Villa Venice Supper Club on the outskirts of Chicago. In the back of his mind, however, he still feared the new president would appoint his younger brother as the next attorney general of the United States.

When he hung up from his call, it occurred to Giancana that if JFK put Bobby in charge of the Justice Department, it meant one of two things: Bobby would either put pressure on J. Edgar Hoover to back off his war on organized crime, or he would use his army of FBI agents to destroy the National Commission.

That shit ain't going to happen, he thought, phoning the home of Chicago City Mayor Richard Daley, "Mayor, this is Mooney. I want you to call Jack Kennedy tonight and tell him congratulations. My Commission expects his administration to have a change in policy toward organized crime. Appointing Bobby Kennedy as attorney general wasn't what I had in mind."

The next afternoon Sam Giancana called an emergency meeting of the Commission at the Ambassador East Hotel. "We've been double-crossed!" he screamed in a violent rage after all the Syndicate's chieftains had assembled in Chicago. "Bobby has been appointed as attorney general to erase all Joe Kennedy's markers with the mob. My name is at the top of the list, and you guys are next in line. Now, what the fuck are we going to do about it?"

On December 27th bitter cold winds whipped across Lake Michigan from a fierce storm, bringing in the early frigid night. Giancana was in his favorite hangout, the Armory Lounge, when the *CBS Evening News* aired the Attorney General-appointee Bobby Kennedy and FBI Director J. Edgar Hoover jointly announcing the new administration's "war on organized crime." In a matter of seconds Giancana's phone was bombarded by calls from Costello in New York, Jimmy Hoffa in Detroit, and Marcello in New Orleans. He thought he had heard from everyone except Johnny Roselli in Las Vegas when Santo Trafficante's call came through. "I tried to tell you at the Fontainebleau back in September, and you goddamn wouldn't listen, Mooney! Whatcha doing to take care of those double-crossing Kennedy bastards?"

Giancana slammed down the receiver and immediately picked it up again to call Frank Sinatra in Las Vegas. He was insane with rage at his liaison with the Kennedys and the man who had assured him that Jack was under his thumb. There was no answer in his room at The Sands Hotel, so he called Sinatra's Cal-Neva Lodge at Lake Tahoe.

"The fucker is never at home!" he shouted, dialing CR 4-2368, Sinatra's unpublished listing in Beverly Hills, hoping for a miracle.

The housekeeper answered on the fourth ring. "I'm sorry, Mr. Giancana, Mr. Sinatra is in Washington planning the president's inaugural gala venue at the Washington Armory."

Giancana threw his whiskey glass across the bar. "Somebody get Roselli on the phone!" he shouted, ordering a fresh drink and storming around the bar until

Roselli was on the line. "Johnny, I'm getting the goddamn runaround from Frank. Where the hell is Sinatra? It's a fucking double-cross. He's been spending my money and he's got to produce."

"I just talked to him in D.C.," Roselli replied. "If Frankie can't deliver, I want him to tell me that the load's too heavy."

"He better make it, because after this administration goes out he'll have a headache."

"I said, 'Frankie, can I ask one question?' He said, 'Johnny, I took Sam's name and wrote it down and told Bobby Kennedy, this is my buddy. This is my *buddy*. This is what I want you to know, Bob.' Between you and me, Frank saw Joe Kennedy three different times. He called him three times—Joe Kennedy, the father."

"When he says he's gonna do a guy a little favor, I don't give a shit how long it takes, he's got to give you a little favor," Giancana screamed back.

"I know. Don't worry," Roselli cowered. "When he gets moved into the White House, Kennedy will be banging Judy Campbell on a regular basis and we can get any information we want out of her."

* * *

Standing six-foot-four in a muscular 220-pound frame, the lieutenant was the perfect Army recruiting poster except for one thing—he was wearing Cuban fatigues missing his insignia as a First Lieutenant in the Army of the United States. A floppy jungle hat covered his thinning blond hair bleached white by the tropical sun, pulled down now on a broad face anchoring his granite jaw. It was a face featuring intense blue eyes that seemed to dance with energy when he spoke in his slow Texan twang. The officer's only flaw was a busted nose, a constant reminder of his West Point football-playing days.

Tex Morris as he was called, inhaled the thin air of the high Sierra Madre Mountains on Guatemala's west coast where he was assigned to Camp Trax, the CIA's secret training facility for the Cuban exiles. The remote Helvetia coffee plantation covered five thousand acres of mountainous terrain rising to eight thousand feet. From the headquarters compound the distant plume of the Santi-aguita Volcano could be seen drifting lazily in the stiff tropical wind.

Tex had heard the word as he passed by the communication shack that John F. Kennedy was his new commander-in-chief. He swaggered into the makeshift headquarters to greetings from Colonel Jack offering him a steaming cup of coffee. The Marine amphibious specialist began his orientation briefing to thirty-eighth American military cadre who were called to attention: "At ease men and take your seats. This morning we will begin training our *Guats*, as the Cuban exiles are called. Everyone here goes by their first name including the officers. We have approximately six months to train *La Brigada* for an amphibious inva-sion. Some of the Guats have previous military experience, some don't. Tex here is my training officer, and we have a lot of work to accomplish in a short time. This mission started out to train a small band of four hundred Guats as saboteurs and guerrillas to infiltrate Cuba. It has escalated into training a fully conventional amphibious invasion force of fifteen hundred men to serve as a cadre for the six thousand political prisoners to be liberated at the invasion site."

"The unit has been designated *La Brigada* 2506, in honor of the serial num-ber of our first training casualty who fell two thousand feet to his death a few days ago. Conditions here are not the best, but we will have to make do. Are there any questions? If not, you're dismissed. Tex, I need to see you."

"Yes sir, Colonel Jack."

"I'm told there's a lot of political infighting amongst the Guats, and a rumor of a rebellion by a few. Keep me informed and go kick some ass."

***

Rivulets of sweat dripped off Colonel Jack's Budweiser can that sat on the bar in the makeshift Officer's Club as he was having lunch. Outside the screech of mud-caked brakes broke in the noonday heat of January 26th as CIA's Guatemala Chief of Station, Bob Davis, burst through the door. "Got bad news, Jack."

"Now what's up?"

"The Cuban Revolutionary Council is arriving here tomorrow to investigate complaints that you're mistreating your Guats. Just got a message from Bissell himself. Axial Hanson and the director's special assistant, a kid named Walter Elliot, will be flying in with them."

"Damn it!" the colonel swore, "The last thing I need is a bunch of Cuban politicians coming down here trying to tell me how to do my job. What does Bissell think? How should I handle it?"

"You're hearing only part of your problem, Colonel. I had dinner in the Presidential Palace last night with the Guatemalan president. Ydigoras is raising hell about your Guats going AWOL and causing a ruckus by visiting the prostitutes in Guatemala City. We're supposed to be keeping this operation quiet, for Christ's sake, and you got drunk Guats running wild all over the whole country."

"What's this *you* bullshit? When there's a problem, it's always my problem and not yours. What in the hell do you brilliant Company guys suppose I should do about the AWOLs? Court martial the bastards under the UCMJ? Shoot them for desertion?"

"Calm down," Bob Davis said with a sigh sinking a church key into the top of his beer can. "Okay, remember we're in this thing together. Politically, this could turn into a can of worms. Whatever you do, make damn sure we don't lose support from the White House. Kennedy is real fucking shaky on the whole operation, and we don't want to lose him. Hasn't signed off on the mission's final go-ahead. These CRC guys, you know, can raise a big flap back in Washington."

"Okay. I'll handle it then, but you better back me up."

"That depends on your plans."

The colonel's face reddened. "You dipshit! Get the hell out of here and go tend to business in Guatemala City, and tell the Guatemalan president I said to kiss my ass. If he didn't like Guats why the hell did he invite the Cubans down here in the first place?"

The chief of station slapped the colonel on the back, "Okay, Jack, but remember this is politically sensitive stuff. Let me know if I can be of assistance."

"I'll take care of it," the colonel snarled sliding off his stool and heading toward the door. "Where's Tex?" he asked when he watched Davis' jeep drive off.

"He's still got Guats on the firing range, trying to get 'em qualified," the XO replied, listening to the distant sound of small arms fire.

"Damn, that Texan is a go-getter. Send my jeep down to get him, *pronto*."

Fifteen minutes later Tex hustled into the Officers Club in muddy fatigues and found Colonel Jack at the bar waiting impatiently. "Grab a beer, Tex, and let's have a talk. Working the hell out of the Guats, aren't you, son?"

"Well, sir, I've got a few men who still have not qualified. I'm planning to keep them on the firing range until they do or we run out of ammo. They *will* all be qualified, sir."

"Attaboy, Tex. I didn't bring you up here to discuss training. We got bigger troubles than Guats who can't shoot."

"What's that, sir?"

"Bob Davis, Guatemalan chief, just left. We've got a bunch of Cuban politicians coming down here from Miami—Revolutionary Council guys. They'll be investigating the way we're running this operation."

"Yes, sir."

"The Cubans are accompanied by two CIA officers—fellows named Hanson and Elliot. Do you know which Guats are the troublemakers, or have any ideas on how I should handle this?"

"The CIA give any specifics, sir?"

"Not much, bitching about living quarters, food, and bullshit. And that's not all; the president of Guatemala is raising hell about the Guats going over the hill and hitting the whorehouses in Guatemala City."

Tex leaned closer to the colonel. "Sir, we've got just a handful of Guats who are the problem. I know who they are, and if you will grant me permission, sir, they won't be around when the politicians arrive."

"Okay. What's your plan? No, don't tell me. I'd rather not know. You guys handle it. What the hell am I paying you for anyhow?" the colonel chuckled, finishing off his beer.

"Yes, sir. I'll take care of it, sir."

"Just do it then, and cover your ass when it comes to the CIA second guessing what you're up to."

"Yes, sir. When do they arrive?"

"Tomorrow at 1500 hours, and I want you at the airstrip as their escort."

"Yes, sir. Colonel, know what will eliminate your AWOL problem and improve morale with the Guats?"

The colonel sighed. "Give the whining bastards liberty in the presidential suite at the Fontainebleau Hotel in Miami?"

"Well, excuse me for saying so, sir, but these Guats are no different from any other soldiers. Their brains are in the head of their pricks after months in the jungle, sir. We need to get them laid as a reward for busting their ass, sir."

Colonel Jack laughed. "Just how in the hell do you expect us to get these guys laid? There's nothing fuckable in fifty miles short of jungle monkeys, for Christ's sake!"

"I can take care of that, too, if you like, sir, when Walter Elliot arrives, if he's the goofy-looking fellow I'm thinking about."

"You know Elliot?"

"Yes, sir. Remember I met him in D.C. when the CIA recruited me. He's weird little guy. But first I've got to take care of the fuckups, sir."

"Right."

"Sir, may I recommend scheduling a twenty-mile forced march starting at 0500 tomorrow morning? When *La Brigada* gets back their asses will be dragging, sir, if you know what I mean."

The colonel smashed his Budweiser can and smiled. "Consider it done, son."

"Thank you, sir. Request permission to get back on the range, sir."

"Carry on, cowboy."

By midnight that night, Tex and a handful of his senior Special Forces NCOs had rounded up the Cuban dissidents and placed them under guard at a remote site in the mountains. He had his men remove the Cubans' combat boots to prevent them from escaping. Before reveille the next morning, Tex spread the rumor among the brigade that the dissidents had been sent back to Cuba and turned over to Castro's secret police in Havana as infiltrators.

Reveille was held at 0400 hours the next morning. Tex stood before the formation backed by his twenty-seven Special Forces NCOs. *"La Brigada!"* he shouted. "Are you ready to liberate Cuba from Fidel?"

"Si, señor Tex!" the fifteen hundred men of *La Brigada* screamed back at him before they were dismissed for chow.

Chapter Three

White House

January 29, 1961

On his first Sunday in the White House, President John F. Kennedy was in the Oval Office nervously awaiting a CIA top-secret briefing on plans to overthrow the Cuban government. Reviewing his notes with occasional glances at his charts, General David Gray, the liaison between the Pentagon and the CIA's covert operations, tried to ignore the young president's restlessness and his attorney general's complaints about being inconvenienced by the afternoon meeting.

While they waited, Secretary of State Dean Rusk and Defense Secretary Robert McNamara were chatting between themselves and trying to ignore Bobby Kennedy as the Oval Office filled with the tension of men trapped in the hold of a sinking ship.

At the precise hour, the man known in the CIA as "The Great White Case Officer" limped in on a cane and sat down apart from the others. A much younger man entered with the CIA Director and remained standing. "Good afternoon, Mr. President, gentlemen," Allen Dulles said with a jovial laugh that seemed hollow. "This is my special assistant, Walter Elliot."

Dulles quickly took attendance. The president's key advisors were all present, and he hoped his timing to sequester the new president on a Sunday afternoon, when he would rather be napping, would expedite the invasion's approval.

The DCI straightened his bow tie and fumbled in his tweed sport coat for his tobacco pouch. He then took a long time packing his pipe, looking first at one man and then the other, before holding his lighter close to the bowl, the sucking sound grating the men's nerves like fingernails on a chalkboard.

The architect of the CIA's plan to dispose of Fidel Castro grew skeptical as he sensed the defensive postures of his audience, especially the president. *Does Jack Kennedy have the balls to make Operation Pluto a success?* he wondered.

The CIA had finalized the plan during the twilight of the Eisenhower presidency. It was Ike's plan, not Kennedy's, and former Vice President Richard Nixon had loved it. Dulles knew that if the new president's father had not arranged for the Chicago Mafia to steal the 1960 election for his son, this meeting would have been held with President Nixon. This was precisely why the young president had not fired him as the Director of Central Intelligence.

Richard Bissell, the CIA's Director of Covert Operations and the man responsible for the execution of the invasion, was intentionally absent. Dulles hoped no one asked for the former Yale economics professor who had received world recognition for devising the Marshall Plan to rebuild war-torn Europe. Bissell knew too much, and to avoid cross-examination by the president it was best that he was absent. *The less the president knows the better*, Dulles was thinking as he laid his tobacco pouch on the table and fogged the air with a cloud of smoke. It was now time to make his pitch for Operation Pluto.

Walter Stewart Elliot III was awed by being in the Oval Office in the presence of the President of the United States and his top advisors and witnessing history in the making. *Damn, what unbelievable power these guys have*, he thought, hoping his excitement did not make his heart jump out of rhythm.

The Director's assistant had been stricken with rheumatic fever at the age of four. It started with a sore throat, followed by inflamed joints in his knees and ankles. He was rushed to the hospital where the finest Boston pediatricians diagnosed his illness. Then, at the age of six, he was stricken again, an occurrence that happens to one out of every four victims of the disease. After receiving massive doses of penicillin, young Walter was left with a mitral valve prolapse, or heart murmur—the failure of the valve to properly close with each heartbeat. From that day on, Walter had lived with the inconvenience of having a dysfunctional heart.

Margaret Chamberlain Elliot, a stately woman blessed with brains but not beauty, closely monitored her son's heart condition. She confined him to the mahogany-paneled library of their Boston mansion where the boy read for hours on end, developing a keen interest in world politics, history, and current affairs. In his quest for knowledge, Walter became infatuated with the powers of Alexander the Great, Napoleon, and Adolph Hitler—men who arose from obscurity to shape world history. A host of intellects from MIT and Oxford, including foreign politicians and dignitaries, came to tutor Walter at home.

Mrs. Elliot was not at all surprised when Walter, at the age of twelve, scored 158 on the Stanford-Binet IQ exam administered by a child psychologist in New York. Becoming the youngest Junior Mensa inductee into the prestigious Greater New York Mensa, Walter Elliot became widely acclaimed within the internationally renowned society for being in the top two percent of the world's IQs.

While other boys were outside playing baseball and developing physically, Walter remained confined, exercising his mind and harboring a harsh resentment for his frailty. Having missed interaction with other children until he was sixteen and left to attend Yale University, the sickly teenager had developed into an idealistic dreamer with secret aspirations to someday make his mark on world history.

Walter Elliot took off his wire-rimmed glasses and squinted at the squirming president realizing he had taken his first step in achieving that lifelong ambition. He also knew after his three years with the agency that the only man in the United States government Allen Dulles was accountable to was President Kennedy. *This is awesome*, he thought, trying hard to conceal his excitement. *I'm in the same room with the two most powerful men on earth. World history is being written this afternoon and I'm witnessing the overthrow of the Cuban government.*

Walter was wearing his signature Ivy League dark tailored suit, white Oxford buttoned-down shirt, a conservative striped tie, and wingtips. He glanced at General Gray's spit-shined cordovans. *What a waste of time. If the military utilized the time spent shining things to improving their minds, they wouldn't be so ignorant,* Walter thought, still harboring resentment for not being able to take the Naval Academy physical. He had turned this inferiority complex into an intellectual superiority that was often manifested by controlled arrogance and sometimes by outright snobbery. This delighted Mr. Dulles, who often reminded Walter that he was the spitting image of his deceased father.

Winston Porter Elliot had served with Allen Dulles in the OSS during World War II. In the spring of 1944 while stationed in Switzerland, they recruited a German intelligence officer to plan the failed assassination of Adolf Hitler. After the war, Dulles' brilliant success earned him the title of America's "spymaster," and President Truman assigned him as the architect for the improved agency that would replace the OSS. The National Security Act of 1947 formed the Central Intelligence Agency to fight the Cold War against the Communists. Deputy Director Dulles was appointed *The Company's* third director in February 1953, long after Winston had returned to civilian life as CEO of Elliot Silver, Inc.

Father would have been proud to see me in the Oval Office with his old friend Allen, Walter thought, recalling his father's story of Mr. Dulles' affair with the famed American spy, Mary Bancroft. He could hear his father's deep voice quoting Dulles: "Mary, we can let the work cover our romance and our romance cover the work as long as we have Winston Elliot to cover both."

It was Winston Elliot's Yale-OSS-good-old-boy-network that put his son's career on the fast track from the day he arrived at CIA headquarters aided by being a member of the Skull and Bones secret society. Mr. Dulles had met Walter at his father's funeral in Boston on the Wednesday after Thanksgiving during his senior year at Yale. He had felt very sorry for the young man whose father had committed suicide over the financial demise of the family's silver business. Dulles felt compelled to ask Walter to fly to Washington for an interview during his Christmas vacation.

Allen Dulles was in his usual jolly mood and well into his second scotch before lunch at the CIA-frequented Alibi Club, a small exclusive men's club in a narrow red brick building near the White House. Walter was awed at being the guest of the CIA director in the private club his father had so often and fondly spoken about. His host glanced about the room for uninvited listeners and lit his pipe.

"Walter," Mr. Dulles began, "how I miss the great times your father and I shared. He was a magnificent OSS officer, possessing a special knack for figuring things out when no one else could. He and I damned near assassinated Adolph Hitler, I reckon."

"Yes, sir. I've heard the story many times. What an incredible role the two of you played in world history."

"Yes, Walter, it was. Now that I reflect back on it, I have often wondered if it would have been different—and I hesitate to say this to you..." Dulles chuckled, taking a sip of his scotch. "I tried my damndest to convince your father to join me in forming the CIA— you know?"

"No, sir. Father never mentioned that."

"Nor should he because he had this deep family commitment to his father and your mother to return to Boston and run Elliot Silver. I always admired him for doing that."

"Yes, sir. Unfortunately, Elliot Silver is doomed and he didn't realize it, especially with the resurgence of the Japanese competition after the war. I'm sure if he had it all to do over again he would have taken you up on it."

"Yes. Yes, possibly so. I see a lot of your father in you. I would like very much for you to consider pursuing a career in the intelligence community. Espionage runs in your Skull and Bones pedigree. I reckon you're going to join Elliot Silver after you graduate?"

"Not if this is a job offer, Mr. Dulles."

"Yes, indeed it is. Do you have a clear conscience about not pursuing your family's business?"

"Sadly, sir, there's no business left to speak of. Elliot Silver is dying a slow, painful death. With the foreign competition, there's nothing that I could do even if I stayed. The Board hired a new CEO to attempt to turn things around. I only hope for Mother's sake that he can keep it afloat or sell it. Thank you for your offer, Mr. Dulles, but I have a medical problem which would..."

"What's the problem?"

"I was stricken with rheumatic fever as a child, leaving me with a mitral valve prolapse—or heart murmur."

"Does it bother you now?"

"If I physically exert myself it feels like my heart will pound a hole in my chest, a medical condition called tachycardia. I also have irregular heartbeats or palpitations at night."

"Don't worry about it. I'll get a waiver on your physical. I need your brains, Walter, not your brawn. You'll attend intelligence training down at Camp Perry, known as 'The Farm', and I will waive the physical part, like jump school and jungle training at Fort Gulick in the Canal Zone. We have plenty of muscle at the Company to support a Mensa like you," the director chuckled, ordering another drink.

Walter Elliot's career as a civilian trainee began the week after he graduated *magna cum laude* from Yale University. After completing basic school and serving for a year in various staff positions at the CIA headquarters, Allen Dulles made Walter his special assistant, grooming him in the secretive ways of the intelligence community where people spoke in riddles and became so paranoid they trusted no one. It was a riddler's game, and with his quickness of wit and intellect the young Elliot excelled at the intelligence jargon of putting things in *Alice in Wonderland* prose or *Dick Tracy* comic strip gobbledygook, to his boss' delight. Walter Elliot's dream was to one day receive the presidential appointment to the directorship of the Central Intelligence Agency. *Nothing is going to get in my way*, Walter was thinking when the president leaned forward in his chair. "May we get started, Mr. Dulles?"

General Gray began his briefing by holding his audience spellbound for the next thirty minutes. The new president and his advisors were astonished to hear that the CIA was already training a group of Cuban exiles at a secret base in Guatemala for a World War II-type amphibious invasion at Trinidad. "Are there any questions, gentlemen?"

President Kennedy immediately asked, "General Gray, what is your committee's assessment of the likelihood for success of the operation?"

"Mr. President," the former associate professor at West Point began with a voice brimming with self-importance, "our feasibility study reveals that the Trinidad Plan has a 'fair' chance of success. Another beachhead would require the Cuban expatriates to have United States air and sea support. Our opinion is that without it there is only a twenty percent chance for success."

"Twenty percent?" Attorney General Bobby Kennedy and Robert McNamara exclaimed simultaneously.

"Yes, gentlemen. If it's not Trinidad, its only twenty percent," the general said with a snarl.

Dulles calmly smoked his pipe and watched the president gaze out the window at the slate gray sky, looking like a man who had just lost his lover. The wind-driven snow was drifting around the White House as Kennedy tapped nervously on his desk. This would be his first major decision as commander-in-chief.

John Kennedy knew he had won the presidency on the tough anti-Communist rhetoric in his platform. Richard Nixon was a staunch Communist-basher and had campaigned very strongly "to have Castro's Communist dictatorship ninety miles from our border eradicated." The Kennedy campaign had stolen Nixon's rhetoric and the election by promising the American voters he would oust Fidel. The president now faced the difficult decision to either proceed or cancel Operation Pluto.

We are in an all-out nuclear arms race with the Soviet Union, the president was thinking as his advisors waited silently for his decision. *Americans live in fear of a nuclear attack by the Russians, fallout shelters are being built across the nation, and our schools are having bomb drills. If we invade Cuba, it will appear to the world that we're the aggressors picking on our poor Latin neighbors. The Soviets will have a propaganda field day with that. This thing could lead to a nuclear war if it backfires.*

The president looked over at the stoop-shouldered man who was indirectly asking him to invade Cuba. If he did so and failed it would be a political disaster. The president was unwilling to take the political risk. "Gentlemen, let me make this quite clear. No American forces are to be directly involved. If you can accomplish Castro's overthrow without our direct involvement, like you did in the overthrow of President Arbenz in Guatemala in 1954, then come up with a plan to do it without our direct military intervention. I want the invasion moved from Trinidad. It looks too American. Is that clear, Mr. Dulles?"

"Give us the go-ahead to wipe out Castro's air force before hand. It is still my strong recommendation you reconsider using Trinidad for the invasion site. It's close to the mountains and there's a political prison there, Mr. President," Dulles replied with an air of insubordination to the man twenty years his junior. "If not Trinidad, it's still our assessment that we can eliminate the Cuban air force on the ground and gain air superiority without using U.S. air power."

There was a skeptical murmur that ran through the Oval Office when the President asked, "How do you plan to achieve that?"

"We have eighty experienced B-26 bomber personnel from the Alabama Air Guard under General Reid Doster in Birmingham as contract civilians. B-26s are the same type aircraft the Cuban and other Central American air forces fly. We've removed all U.S. insignia and repainted the fuselages with Cuban markings. As we speak, the Cuban crews are being trained in a secret air base in Nicaragua."

"Okay, your plan calls for an uprising by the Cuban people. Is that realistic?"

"Most certainly, Mr. President. We have saboteurs already in Cuba to create havoc if the invasion lands in Trinidad, where there are six thousand political prisoners that I mentioned that will be released and used as an army. Propaganda broadcasts from our transmitters in Key West and Swan Island will incite the populace. Once the beachhead is established, we'll have the support of the Cuban people, and Castro is doomed, I reckon."

"Yes or no, Mr. Dulles? Does the CIA really think that the Cuban people will revolt against Castro?" the president asked again.

Short, rapid puffs of smoke from Dulles' pipe hid his face, giving the appearance of a steam locomotive pulling out of a station.

What a diversion, Walter thought, catching his boss' eye momentarily.

The kid's brilliant, Dulles thought winking at Walter. *He can transcribe from memory verbatim notes of this meeting for the files, I reckon.*

Dulles lifted his foot to ease his gout remembering when Vice President Nixon was the White House action officer for Special Group 54-12—the coordinator of CIA and military intelligence. The director glanced at General Gray and hoped the Joint Chiefs had not forgotten with the change of the administration that the invasion had already been sanctioned. *If Dick Nixon had gotten elected this would be a done deal, or even better, the invasion should have taken place before Eisenhower left office*, Dulles thought, letting out an audible sigh.

"I'm waiting for an answer, Mr. Director."

"Yes" came with a humorless chuckle. "Our evaluation is that they will, Mr. President."

"Good. If that's the case then come up with a plan that will appear to the rest of the world that the Cubans acted on their own," the president ordered. "The CIA did an exceptional job in deposing President Arbenz in Guatemala without a lot of bloodshed."

"Thank you, Mr. President. We have designed this operation after our Guatemala model. I must say we learned much from our involvement in the overthrow of the Jacob Arbenz government. It was accomplished with a handful of exiles and a few surplus P-47 fighters flown by American CIA pilots. Disposing of Arbenz was in the best interest of the United States, especially after he tried to nationalize the United Fruit Company."

"Yes, well good luck with Castro then. We have a lot of U.S. investments in Cuba at risk, especially our sugar-related industries. Hershey Corporation, for example, and Coca-Cola, United Fruit—they all gave heavily to my campaign and have a huge stake in Cuba."

"I realize we have billions at stake in Cuba, Mr. President. If Castro is allowed to remain with his Communist beachhead, the entire Western Hemisphere is threatened. You will have fulfilled your campaign promise to get rid of him."

"Castro has to go!" Bobby inserted with a juvenile laugh.

"Very well then, gentlemen," Kennedy said, shooting a sharp look at his younger brother. "Provide training, logistics, and communications, whatever they need, but come up with a modified plan for no direct involvement by our armed forces. I want a quiet invasion at night that will tell the world the Cuban people have acted without the United States. Is that clear?"

"Yes, Mr. President," Dulles replied, disappearing again behind his smokescreen.

"And remember, gentlemen, I reserve the right to cancel this thing right up to the end," the president said, getting up. "By the way, how's construction on your new CIA headquarters at Langley coming?"

"We're on schedule and looking forward to your dedication speech in September. By then Fidel Castro will have faded into Cuban history and we will have only the Soviets to worry about." Dulles laughed struggling to stand up on his sore feet.

Goose bumps ran up Walter's spine. He was working for the most powerful man in the United States who could overthrow foreign governments at the drop of a hat. *What finesse Mr. Dulles has to manipulate the president,* he thought, assisting his boss out of the Oval Office. He looked back at the president huddled with his advisors feeling the strings of seductive power of one day controlling the reins of the CIA.

Chapter Four

Camp Trax, Guatemala

January 27, 1961

The reduction of power changed the C-54's engine rhythm as the plane lost altitude on the flight from the CIA's Opa-Locka, Florida airfield to the secret runway on the Helvetia coffee plantation. CIA pilot Buck Persons fought the swirling winds to keep his bouncing plane stable on its terrifying approach to the airstrip on top of a 6,000 foot ridge that ended abruptly at the side of the mountain. There were more power reductions before Walter Elliot heard the flaps go down, followed by the thump of the landing gear as the plane banked on its final approach.

Buck Persons watched the smoke plume on his right blowing off the Santiaguita Volcano to get the direction of the wind. When he could see the white crosses clearly in the German pioneer cemetery on his left, he had been told, it was time to touchdown. "Hold on, we've got a hard landing!" Buck announced to his passengers over the intercom just as the plane slammed into the runway and bounced.

Walter fought to remain calm feeling the adrenaline rushing through his body as his pulse quickened. With clinched teeth, he got a white-knuckled grip on the canvas bench running the length of the cargo hole, and prepared for another bone-jarring jolt. He held his breath as the wheels screeched and the engine roared when the pilot reversed props and jammed on the brakes, bringing the plane to an abrupt

33

halt at the very end of the strip. Walter Elliot gasped for breath, feeling his heart ricochet around in his chest like a racket ball as he managed to regain his composure.

Persons, a corporate pilot for Harbert International in Birmingham, revved the engines and taxied to the tarmac, very pleased to have made it down safely. Walter was busy scraping a hole in the painted windows of the C-54 so he could see the jeeps and men in fatigues waiting for them on the runway when he heard Buck apologizing to his passengers as he passed by.

"Damn, that was hairy!" Walter shouted over the Cuban politicians jabbering away in Spanish behind him.

Buck flashed him a sheepish grin. "Big airplane, short runway."

Axial Hanson who had remained calm as a cucumber began laughing hysterically. "What you bitching about, Elliot? You're in Guatemala in one piece, aren't you?"

Hanson, you're an adrenaline junkie, Walter thought as he told himself: *Settle down, Walter, at last you're out of Washington so don't confirm that you're a rookie by acting like a dumb ass.*

Walter glanced over his shoulder when he heard Antonio Varona, the former vice president and leader of the Cuban senate, shouting at Persons, when he got to the back of the plane. "You are a very reckless pilot, señor."

That Señor Varona is a pain in the ass, Walter thought as he grabbed his gear and stepped to the door when the hot humid air fogged his glasses. In a split second the CIA officer was picking himself up off the tarmac six feet below.

"Get a parachute next time, Elliot, and you won't bust your ass and look like a fool," Hanson yelled down to him from the door of the plane.

"Welcome to Guatemala, you clumsy weirdo," Tex said to the special forces NCOs standing with him who burst out laughing watching Walter scramble around on the tarmac gathering up his gear. "That's the CIA for you, men, fucking up by the numbers. I bet those dudes shit in their mess kits after that landing. Okay, knock it off, here come our dignitaries from Washington, so shape-up and stand tall," Tex ordered, bringing things down to a quiet snicker as the group from the plane came forward.

Tex raised his voice as the screams of the tropical birds announced their arrival, "Welcome to Camp Trax, gentlemen. Glad you made it safely."

"*Right*," Walter replied as he set down his duffel bag.

"You okay, Walter?"

"Yes, I'm fine, thank you, lieutenant" Walter replied, brushing off his pants and pulling down his bush hat to shade his eyes from the afternoon sun. "These glasses are killers," he muttered, taking out his handkerchief and cleaning the lenses.

"Yeah, they say any landing you walk away from is a good one," Hanson added, making Tex's men burst into laughter all over again.

"Call me, Tex, gentlemen. First names only down here in the jungle—for security reasons. You sure you're alright, Walter?"

"Yeah, Tex. Meet Axial from the Cuban Government Task Force/Miami, and these gentlemen are representatives of the Cuban Revolutionary Council," Walter said, making the introductions of the CRC members.

"Welcome to Camp Trax, gentlemen." Tex began in Spanish, firmly shaking each man's hand while watching the Cuban politicians surveying the vacant camp and mumbling among themselves.

"Everyone speak English? Okay, good. Now gentlemen, Colonel Jack, wants me to escort you over to the mess where we have a roasted hog for dinner. I will brief you afterwards on how *La Brigada*'s training is progressing."

"No, Señor Tex," Antonio Varona blurted out, his dark eyes dancing with hostility behind black-framed glasses. "We have come to visit our men, not to feast on roast pig while our soldiers are eating garbage." Gesturing wildly around with his hands, he shouted, "Where are our men? Take us to them immediately."

"*La Brigada* is on a twenty-mile hike so hold on here a sec," Tex replied, stepping closer and glaring at the Cuban politician's baldhead. "I need to get you a sombrero for this tropical sun."

"Don't worry about this head of mine when our men are starving."

"Who told you that? We all eat from the same mess here at Camp Trax. Your men do the cooking, not the Americans. You will see that if *La Brigada* is starving, I'm also starving. Now, let's go see if we're having roast pig or garbage for dinner.

Please, Señor Varona, be my guest and ride with me," Tex said slapping Varona on the back good-naturedly, watching the others shuffle their feet with their eyes combing the ground as if they were searching for lost money.

Varona's jaw slackened as he looked around, searching out his companions for support. "That is not the report I have received," he said with sweat beading on his forehead.

Walter joined Varona in the back seat of Tex's jeep and the CRC leader was smiling now. The CIA Officer jabbed his glasses up the bridge of his nose, taken aback by how quickly and firmly Tex had defused the Cuban leader's hostility. *Maybe I misjudged Tex,* he thought, liking Tex's firm but diplomatic manner. *He's not a stupid jock, that's for damn sure,* Elliot was thinking, making mental notes for his report to Dulles. *I'll use Tex to my advantage and keep him well clear of Hanson.*

Walter Elliot was trying to forget how stupid he must have looked falling out of the airplane as the jeep crossed the little bridge and drove up the hill to the Camp Trax mess hall.

It had been a full day, and Walter was doing most of the talking in the deserted O Club bar as he poured the Texan another heavy-handed shot of bourbon from a bottle he had brought down for Colonel Jack. "Lookit, Tex, what's the real situation here? Operation Pluto depends on keeping these Guats, as you call them, ready for the invasion. Level with me, off the record, just between the two us. What's wrong with the Cubans' morale?"

Tex glanced at the CIA officer and yawned. *What a measly four-eyed goofy-looking son-of-a-bitch you are, Elliot. Why in the hell should I waste my time talking to an asshole that falls out of airplanes?* Then Tex laughed to himself. *It'll be easy to snooker this goofball into getting my Guats a whorehouse.*

Walter stood up, put his hands in his pockets, and rocked back and forth on his heels. "Lookit, I know you guys don't appreciate us coming down here and screwing with your operation, but this is damn important. I can understand your reluctance to speak freely, but hell, man, time is of the essence."

"Roger that. I've got to hit the rack."

"Hold it. I will assure you this is all off the record. Confidential. We still haven't sold President Kennedy on Operation Pluto and a lot is riding on my report. The interest of the United States foreign policy, and certainly with regard to the Soviet intervention in the Western Hemisphere, is pending on what I say. Your mission's success hinges on the two of us, as stupid as it might sound, convincing the president to sign off on this thing. By the way, you did a heck of a job this morning defusing Varona."

"Walt, you're preaching to the choir. I'm just a peon. You should be talking to the colonel."

"Hanson's tried that. Colonel Jack is a difficult man to communicate with, especially if he thinks we will make him look bad. Lookit, I am just like you, the junior officer and besides..."

"You're talking to the wrong guy."

"No, damn it, lookit. It's my first time out of Washington and I need your help in getting the real facts for the DCI. You *do* know I am the Director of Central Intelligence's special assistant, don't you?"

Tex took a drink of whiskey and nodded when Walter leaned over and said in a whisper, "By having direct access to the DCI, I'll get you a choice assignment after this operation is finished in a few months."

"Really, now?"

"Yes. Really now. Listen to me."

"Shit. I've got to get some sleep."

"Yes, yes, I know. I can get you assigned wherever in the hell you want to go–Europe, Bragg, you name it. I can make that call."

"Okay, Walter. If that's the case, where the hell can I go for some real combat experience?"

Walter sat down before looking around the empty bar left only with the sounds of the tropics and the lingering smell of stale beer and cigarettes. "Let's just say there is the 'land of the million elephants and the white parasol,' as they call the land of Siam."

"Cut out the fucking riddles."

"Okay, to be more specific, Laos."

"And just where in the hell is that?"

37

"We're on the same page here then?"

"What the hell is this, Walter? Can your scrawny little ass get me into some real combat so I'm first in my West Point class to get a Combat Infantryman's Badge?"

"Yes, and take it easy on the insults. Just a few days ago I was privy to General Lansdale's memo to the president on unconventional warfare in Southeast Asia. We have clandestine paramilitary operations going on in Laos as I speak—war between the U.S.-backed Lao Army using Hmong tribesmen fighting against the Pathet Lao Communist guerrillas. Now, that's about as much classified information as your military ears are ever going to hear. Top Secret stuff."

"So, you can get me something more exciting than nursemaid to a bunch of Guats in the middle of this frigging jungle? Like a real combat assignment? I'm talking *real* combat—no cowboy and Indians."

"Yes, in the Laotian highlands we're training approximately nine thousand Hmong under the command of Lieutenant Colonel Vang Pao to fight the Pathet Lao. Command and control for the Hmong is out of CIA Chief of Station Vientiane, the Laotian capital. Presently we have *only* nine Special Forces personnel in Laos. How would you like to be number ten?"

Tex took a sip of his whiskey. *I'm thinking the wormy little bastard's on the level.* "Okay, I'm in, Elliot, if you're guaranteeing me one of those slots, roger?"

"You've got my word on that, Tex. Now let's get started, with your help I have a situation report to write."

"Look at me, you four-eyed fucker. You tell one soul I told you this and I'll kick your ass, roger?"

"I said take it easy on the insults. We're a team working toward the means to an end. I'll make sure you get reassigned to Vientiane as soon as you get the Guats ready to ship out."

"What we need here at Camp Trax is a good old-fashioned Mexican whorehouse, like you find in Juarez across the border from El Paso. You've been there, Walt?"

Walter squirmed in his chair. At twenty-three he was still a virgin. "No," he replied, "but I've been to the red light district in Amsterdam where the ladies of the night displayed themselves in windows. What's so special about Mexicans?"

"You're missing my whole point. Like all soldiers, my Guats' brains are in the heads of their dicks. We've got to get them some women down here so they pay attention to their training and stop whore hopping in Guatemala City. Pussy is a helluva motivator, real strong stuff."

Walter took out his notepad. "Yes indeed, it *is* very strong stuff. It got Adam expelled from the Garden of Eden," he said, laughing for the first time.

"Spare me the Sunday school lesson, will you, partner?"

"Sorry, you're saying establish a bordello here at Camp Trax at taxpayers' expense? Come on now."

"I'm serious."

"And how should we staff it? Prostitutes from Guatemala City?"

"Shit, Walt. What in the hell do they teach you guys in the CIA? With our strained relations with the locals, the last thing we need is more involvement with the Guatemalans to compromise the security of the mission."

"You're correct. Lookit, you've made an excellent point. Where would you recommend we find them?"

"Costa Rica. Never been there, but some of my men tell me the women are beautiful, especially in San Jose."

"Wow. This will be a real difficult concept to pitch to Mr. Dulles. Perhaps impossible. You think this is the *real* solution to the problem, do you?"

"It's the *only* solution. You get us a bunch of Costa Rican whores down here and I'll have these Guats ready for the invasion. You'll be a hero for getting the Guats back to work and the politicians off your boss' ass."

"That I can do, Tex," Walter smiled confidently. *How can I convince Dulles to build a whorehouse at Camp Trax? First, I'd have to pull a major coup d'etat by undermining Hanson's assessment of La Brigada's poor performance being the result of laziness and a lack of will to fight.* Walter stood up, "Thanks a million, Tex, I'll get your orders to Laos cut when I return. Be patient, it takes a while."

***

By the time Walter Elliot and Axial Hanson returned to Washington after dropping off Antonio Varona and the other CRC members at the Opa-Locka airfield in Miami, Walter had devised his plan. Hanson's report, which he had read on the plane from Miami, would have to go through Richard Bissell before reaching Mr. Dulles' desk. He had written his own clandestine situation report to place in the hands of the DCI before hand.

"Good morning, Mr. Dulles," Walter said upon entering the director's Washington office before seven on a cold, blustery January morning two days later. It was again time for Walter to speak in riddles to his boss.

"Well, Walter! Surprised to see you in so early. What do you have to say for yourself after going on your first hunting trip afield? Any chiggers?" The director chuckled.

"Only fleas, sir. The dogs are scratching themselves to distraction, or should I say into desertion—in military terms, 'going over the hill' over the fleas."

"You got those dogs some flea powder, I reckon?"

"No sir. Instead I'll recommend we get them some bitch dogs in heat for company, sir. The bitches will make scratching fleas passé, making the Guats obedient, well-trained hunters, sir."

"Where could you buy some bitch dogs?"

"I understand Costa Rica should provide a reliable supply."

"Why so far?"

"Using bitches from Guatemala would cause trouble with their local handlers jeopardizing security."

"Are you planning on feeding our bitches Purina Dog Chow from Washington?"

"It's an immaterial cost, sir, considering our investment to date has run into the millions."

"Yes I know, don't remind me. What about a doghouse for our bitches?"

"To be built by the Guatemalans at our expense. No major problem to have a kennel erected ASAP outside of the town of San Philipe."

"Walter, how did you improvise your solution to solve our flea problem?"

"By observation and human intelligence, sir. I'm convinced it's the right solution."

"Yes, it makes sense to me. Nice job. Now go over to Bissell's office and let him become the dog trainer, like you're Joshua slipping into Jericho. I'm having dinner with him tonight at the Alibi Club; so convince him to pitch the bitches as his idea in case these bitches take a bite out of somebody's ass. We don't want it to be ours, savvy?"

"Right away, sir," Walter replied before leaving for Bissell's office at Quarters Eye, the shabbiest of temporary buildings around the reflecting pool facing the Lincoln Memorial.

In New York, Antonio Varona and his Cuban Revolution Council representatives were still skeptical of *La Brigada*'s treatment but had no real evidence to make it a further issue. Their destiny lay firmly in the hands of the CIA's chief of Operation Pluto, Richard Bissell, who was waiting impatiently for final approval for the invasion from President John Kennedy. He looked up when Walter walked into his office. "Mr. Bissell, I'm out of order, but I have a plan…"

* * *

"By God, you've done it, son!" Colonel Jack shouted when the plane landed at the Retalhuleu airbase fifteen miles south of Camp Trax in the valley forty kilometers from the Pacific Ocean. He handed Tex his binoculars. "Look at those fillies getting off that plane!"

"Thank you, sir," Tex replied as be watched the Costa Rican prostitutes emerging from the C-54 and climbing into the awaiting bus.

"Now, Tex, what I have here is a serious need, by God, for a camp morale officer for our little House of R&R. Somebody's got to control these whores and set up the standard operating procedures, and I know just the man for the job."

Tex grinned. "Who did you have in mind, sir?"

"The man that got them here. So go get them set-up and make damn sure they're off limits to the American cadre."

Yeah, right, Colonel, Tex thought, looking forward to his first date in two months. "War's hell, Colonel. I'll have it all organized and an SOP written by 0800 tomorrow morning."

41

"I'm not saying that order applies to lieutenants, cowboy," the colonel laughed, watching Tex jump into his jeep to escort the ladies to their newly constructed quarters.

Tex's jeep driver pulled ahead of the bus before it turned off the main highway to San Felipe and onto a narrow lane. He was a handsome figure standing in the courtyard of the bordello complex with its shiny tin-roofed stucco buildings smelling of fresh mortar. The two buildings were lined with private rooms entering from the porches with a bar and dance hall in the rear of the main structure. Tex was thinking what a helluva mess it would cause if the press discovered the CIA's use of American taxpayers money to build it when he heard the bus cross the bridge and watched it slowly come up to the top of the rise and stop in front of him.

Their eyes met as Teresa Ortiz led her girls off the bus. "Where to from here, soldier?" she asked in perfect English.

The Costa Rican beauty was wearing khaki pants and a white blouse that emphasized her small waist and her perfect five-foot-four body. "Let's go in the bar, Señorita," Tex replied, grabbing her bag and ordering his men to bring the ladies' luggage and stack it on the porch.

"Are you in charge?"

"Yes, and who are you?" Tex grinned, smelling her French perfume when she brushed her hair from her grayish green eyes. She tilted her chin downward to take a closer look at him over the rim of her sunglasses.

"Señorita Teresa Ortiz."

"My name's Tex," he replied, turning to address the entire group. "Now listen up, ladies. Give me your attention. Orientation will begin in fifteen minutes in the main salon of the *Casa de*...what was your name again?"

"Teresa Ortiz."

"Casa de Teresa is now the new name of this joint. By the colonel's orders you, Señorita Ortiz, are the Casa's Madame, and you ladies are directly under my command."

"Thank you, John Wayne, but I am already in charge – *Duke* and these girls are my employees."

An hour later, the house rules had been established and posted on the bulletin board on the porch and the girls had been assigned rooms. The sergeant was on his way to headquarters to type the SOP for two daily shifts for men earning either a red or green coupon to come down from Camp Trax for their reward. On the entrance to the lane off the main highway a guard had been posted beside the sign: OFF LIMITS TO UNAUTHORIZED PERSONNEL.

Tex had finished attending to details and lay down on the bunk in Teresa's corner room in the building nearest the stream. It was evening now and the sun was sinking quickly behind the Sierra Madre. The Santiaguita Volcano in the distance was belching smoke, and a cool breeze was blowing through the open windows.

"What in the hell do you think you're doing, John Wayne?"

"Well, I just figured I'd sample a little bit of the inventory, if you're in the mood," Tex said with a laugh as he unbuttoned his fatigue jacket.

"Look, asshole, get the hell out of here. If you want to get laid, go fuck one of the girls. I'm working for the Company just like you are. Now, I've had a long day. *Out!*"

"No offense, Teresa. I'm sorry, Jesus, if you need anything, just give me a shout," Tex mumbled, feeling his face flush as he walked to the door. "I'll check on you tomorrow, gal, when you're in a better mood."

Tex drove a jeep down the following night from Camp Trax. He was freshly shaven and had purchased a bouquet of flowers in San Felipe on the way. "Oh, how thoughtful," Teresa smiled, placing the flowers in a glass jar for a vase. "Teresa, what's a good looking gal like you doing running a whorehouse when you're beautiful enough to be married to the governor of Texas?"

"In Costa Rica it's a legitimate business, not like the States where sex is considered dirty by a bunch of hypocrites who go to church with their families on Sunday and cheat on their wives on Monday night. Besides that, the money's good, and sex makes people happy. My girls are happy. They make a lot of money. Costa Rican girls are the only women in the world who do not ask their customers for payment until they are sure they are satisfied."

43

"Yeah? No kidding. Well, that's not so in Mexico. Mexican whores want it up front. But for a classy, educated gal like you, don't you think whoring is a little degrading?"

"I'm a businesswoman damn your ass. Let me ask you this? Why are you a mercenary?"

"To get rid of the damn Communists, Teresa. We Americans have the responsibility of protecting the free world against the commies. Those pinkos plan to take over the free world, Costa Rica included—freedom is a mighty sacred thing."

"Freedom's sacred, the hell you say? *Whose freedom?* The Latin Americans or the American fat cats on Wall Street who exploit Latinos? Whose freedom are you talking about here?"

"Just a sec. Calm down gal."

"You asked for it, mister asshole. Greedy shareholders of the United Fruit Company are the imperialists who have suppressed Central American countries for centuries, and most recently in Guatemala when your CIA overthrew our government for the Wall Street fuckers. You Yankees must think Latinos are stupid!"

"Who told you all that crap?"

"My father was a minister in the Guatemalan government of President Arbenz before he was killed in 1954 by your CIA-backed coup."

"I'm sorry about that, but I had nothing to do with it, Teresa. What I meant to say is that you are capable of doing much more than you are doing."

"Why do you think I'm doing what I'm doing? My girls are down here making the Cuban exiles happy. They bring smiles to their lonely faces. You mercenaries are trained killers and puppets for the American capitalists and Wall Street tycoons. I saw no smiles on the corpses that you mercenaries killed when I fled Guatemala City as a girl."

"Okay, gal. Look, I said I'm sorry…"

"No, as you Americans say, don't try to butter me up. You keep going on about your business of being a CIA mercenary killing innocent people for your American crooked politicians that suck up to big business to finance their political campaigns. I will go on running my Key Largo, making my customers happy and making money. How much money do you make working for the CIA?"

"Not enough for the crap I have to put up with. Why hell, I'm not in this shit for the money..."

"The CIA is paying me thousands of dollars to bring my girls down here from Costa Rica, and I'll be making a hell of a lot more money than you will when I get back to San Jose when this job is finished. You know what I do with most of it, mister big guy?"

"I have no idea."

"I send it to my aunt in Guatemala City and she feeds the children in the orphanages who are living in a hell that was caused by the civil war the CIA started when they overthrew our government for United Fruit. *Thousands* have died. So is it not degrading for you to kill thousands of innocent people? What is better? Killing people and making no money, John Wayne, or making lonely men happy and making big bucks for starving orphans in Guatemala?"

"Okay, gal, let's forget it."

"Why don't you just get the hell out of here, Tex?"

A week had passed and Tex came once again down from Camp Trax into the valley. Maybe it was his note of apology that had gotten him in her bedroom along with the bottle of rum. *The Bacardi is working. I can't believe she's finally willing,* he thought as he undressed to the sounds of Latin music playing on his portable GE transistor radio.

"Duke?" she asked, taking a sip of her rum and Coke.

"Yes ma'am," Tex replied softly as he unfastened her bra.

"How long have you been here?"

"Seems like forever until you showed up."

"Me too. I hate this place, but it will all be over soon now."

"How did you learn to speak English like an American?"

"My mother was forced to be a housekeeper to feed us after my father was killed. She worked for an American in San Jose. Señor David Horseman was an attorney who practiced law in California and Costa Rica. We lived six months in each country and he would take us with him to San Diego. I went to grade and high school and to San Diego State for two years before he died in a car accident."

"Gal, you've had a tough life," Tex said pulling her to him.

45

Teresa pushed away, panting after a lingering embrace. "You like my body?" she smiled, modeling her bikini panties in the candlelight and pouring them another drink.

"You're stacked like Bridgett Bardot. Now come here and lie down, my Teresa with the most beautiful tits south of El Paso. Come on over here, gal. You've got my prick harder than a branding iron."

"Duke, you naughty boy. You horny Americans always wanting to fuck, not make love to a woman. I'll teach the Duke how to make love to a Latino tonight, very slowly so it lasts for a long, long time."

She turned up the music before lying beside him. He could feel the heat from her smooth body and taste her hot breath as she nibbled at his lips before thrusting her tongue deeper inside. She rubbed his muscular chest and kissed his nipples, slowly working her way down his belly. "You are so hard," she groaned as Tex Morris watched red lava flowing down the side of Santiaguita in the distance.

***

In the last week of March a group of officers arrived unannounced from the Joint Chiefs of Staff to determine the combat readiness of *La Brigada*. After a briefing by Colonel Jack they spent two days sitting around camp playing gin rummy and drinking Bacardi and Coke. "This is, after all, a CIA operation, and the Pentagon wants very little to do with its success or predicted failure," the officer in charge joked as they got on a plane back to the Pentagon.

Once they were gone, Tex rushed down the mountain to San Felipe to reopen the Casa de Teresa and to his bewilderment found it abandoned. He rushed inside and was pleased to find a note on Teresa's dresser. "Duke, you can reach me at the Key Largo Bar in San Jose, I'll miss you."

Tex Morris jumped back in his jeep and roared up the mountain to find Colonel Jack typing the final paragraph of his Camp Trax After Action Report:

With the establishment of the brothel, the military effectiveness of *La Brigada* readily obtained combat efficiency. The Cubans were told that the CIA's plan will bring a massive uprising against Castro at the time of the invasion and that both air and naval support from the United States will be available if needed. They listened excitedly to the nightly propaganda broadcast by Swan Island radio that encourages the Cuban people to revolt. If the liberation of the political prisoners at Trinidad is successful, I am confident that the brigade will meet its primary objective of securing a beachhead and be successful in the overthrow of the Castro government.

Colonel Jack looked up when the bewildered Special Forces lieutenant walked into his office and saluted. "Let's get packed up, cowboy. Out training mission has been accomplished, it's time to get the hell out of here."

Chapter Five

Washington D.C.

Thursday, April 13, 1961

Allen Dulles seemed quiet and reserved, not his usual jolly self, to his secretary of many years, Mildred Cole. He spent long hours in his office staring out the window at the cherry blossoms on the Washington Mall, smoking his pipe and saying little. The gray-haired spinster also noticed that Walter Elliot seemed depressed as he walked by her desk.

Walter glanced at the Great White Case Officer staring out the window at the rain and wondered if he was reminiscing about the grand old days in the OSS in Switzerland with Mary Bancroft. Or was he worrying that the Cuban invasion was going to be a disaster.

Dulles was worried about just that. President Kennedy had just changed the invasion to the Bay of Pigs that would turn Operation Pluto into the biggest fiasco of his long and illustrious spy career. It was now time to rattle riddles with his special assistant after making up his mind to distance himself from the inevitable by being absent from Washington on D-Day, Monday, April 17, 1961.

"Mildred, please have Walter step into my office for a second," he said. *Today seems like a Dick Tracy type of day*, the director was thinking as Walter shut his office door.

"Good morning, sir," Walter said, standing erect and looking very serious.

Dick Tracy motioned for him to take a seat. "Well, Junior, you came up with a masterful plan for training our Pluto mongrels in Guatemala, I reckon. Now they're ready for the hunt, I'm told."

"Thank you, Mr. Director. It was nothing, only my perception of the male canine predisposition to breed bitches. It was a natural solution, sir."

"Yes, nature has its powerful forces." Dulles chuckled, making Walter smile for the first time. "Well done, Junior, getting those bitches for the Guats. No more training problems after that. Sam Catchem's perception was that it was his idea, but I give you the credit now that it was a success."

"Let Mr. Bissell go on thinking that, sir."

"*Now,* for the perception of the deception of Ivan; there's a place distant where Dick Tracy shall reside during the Pluto invasion. Sam Catchem will be handling the case from the Quarters Eye precinct station."

"Yes, sir. Should Junior make any plans to travel with Mr. Tracy in order to deceive the Russians, sir?"

"No, Junior," Dulles replied, his voice coming in a monotone from behind a cloud of pipe smoke. "Dick Tracy will be accompanied by Miss Trueheart. You remain here to capture the sensation from the precinct station. Reside there until the case is resolved. Stay there twenty-four hours a day. I'll blink you on the quarter at the Quarters when I need the scoop. Ensure that Dick Tracy doesn't sustain a detached retina by Chief Brandon giving Pluto the no go, which I think the president might just do at the final moment."

"Yes sir," Walter replied. "If the president gives a no-go, I will immediately notify you. Sam Catchem doesn't have a hang-up with Junior hanging around the precinct during the Pluto raid, does he?"

"He thinks it's his idea for you to be there, I reckon. He needs the quickness of your mind. So go, it's almost time. Remember, Sam Catchem must be shadowed in my absence. Savvy?"

"Yes, sir," Walter replied turning to leave.

"Oh, by the way, pick me up at 9 P.M. Monday night at the roost and brief me on all the details."

"Yes sir, 9 P.M. Monday night, Mr. Tracy," Walter replied with a smile, before returning to his office to organize his desk before leaving for Georgetown to pack.

Mildred Cole entered Dulles' office while he was repacking his pipe with his feet propped on his desk. "Mildred, go ahead and notify the roost to file my flight plan and be standing by for a ten o'clock takeoff."

"Yes, Mr. D," she replied, handing him a folder. "Here's your Young Presidents Organization speech and your itinerary for Puerto Rico. Shall I call Mrs. D?"

"Please. Tell her I will pick her up in twenty minutes and ring for my driver. I'm about ready," Dulles said as he stood and walked over to the coat rack.

"I'm worried about Walter. He seems to be extremely uptight, awfully troubled about something, more so than usual. Have you noticed?" Mildred asked, helping her boss on with his raincoat.

"Well, from what I read in *The Wall Street Journal*, Elliot Silver is now in bankruptcy. He and his mother are the sole shareholders, I reckon. Very close to the Widow Elliot, that boy is. Poor lady has lost her husband's fortune."

"Yes, it's a shame, poor dear. All of this on top of Mr. Elliot's death. Have you spoken with her lately?"

"Only briefly at Winston's funeral several years ago. She's quite a tyrant, a very domineering woman in her time. We never got along. I went so far as to tell Winston one night at a bar in Geneva that he should divorce the bitch."

"What a wicked thing to say, Mr. D!" Mildred laughed, shaking her head. "I'll say this for young Elliot, he's the smartest of all the young men that I've seen in the nearly forty years I've been in this town, except of course for you, Mr. D."

"Thank you," Dulles chuckled, "but I'm not nearly in the league with Walter. He was a Mensa inductee as a kid, you know."

"And has such social graces."

Dulles nodded in agreement opening his black leather briefcase and placing the file neatly on top. "Mildred, I am neither young nor very smart, I reckon, or I wouldn't have gotten talked into this Pluto Operation by Dick Bissell."

"Yes, Dick has created a real problem for us. Have a pleasant journey and don't worry, Mr. D, and I'm sure things will work out," Mildred replied as she watched her boss hobble out the door. *That's my Mr. D*, she thought, returning to her desk.

The master at placing blame on someone else while he is off to Puerto Rico at taxpayer expense with the Cuban situation about to explode.

Dulles' pilots were waiting at the CIA hanger at the Friendship Airport in Baltimore when he arrived. In a matter of minutes, Allen Dulles had distanced himself from any involvement with the invasion of Cuba as Walter finished packing and rushed out of his Georgetown apartment for Quarters Eye. He nearly ran over the postman on the stairs.

"If you're Walter Elliot, I've got a registered letter you need to sign."

"You bet," Walter replied, signing the green postal form and shutting the door. He held the large brown envelope from the Boston Federal Bankruptcy Court for a moment, dreading to read the bankruptcy judge's order to sign over his 2,270,000 shares of Elliot Silver common stock to the court within ten days.

"Damn!" Walter swore with the harsh realization that the shares that once had a book value of thirty dollars per share were now just worthless paper. One hundred years of his family's fortunes had dissipated at a stroke of the pen of the bankruptcy judge. He threw the envelope into his briefcase and grabbed the phone.

In Boston his mother's phone rang for the third time. He glanced at his watch and hung up before the fourth ring. *No time to get involved with mother now,* he thought as he shut his front door and ran to his car.

Walter Elliot drove across the Arlington Bridge when he suddenly had the urge to throw the envelope into the Potomac. *Why get upset?* he asked himself. *I had known this day was coming for years. Now I'm just like all the rest of the young professionals in D.C.—stinking broke. Unfortunately, Elliot Silver caused father's suicide and its demise will destroy mother as well.*

Walter was not exactly broke. His trust account at First Boston had a balance of well over three hundred and fifty thousand dollars, but his inheritance wouldn't be available for another ten years, at age thirty-three. *What do I need money for anyway, my $500 a month salary is quite adequate to live on.*

Money to live on was not the point. His real loss was the power and prestige that real money brings. *People who aren't born wealthy don't understand that,* Walter was thinking knowing he would have to go about regaining his wealth and prestige using his position with the CIA and his brains.

51

As Walter Elliot rounded the Lincoln Memorial he began to eulogize the slow, anguished demise of Elliot Silver. The oldest silver company in the United States was finally dead, leaving only an abandoned, decaying, sprawling factory on the outskirts of Boston. One of his earliest childhood memories was visiting the plant with his grandfather during the war while his father was overseas. He still recalled the nasty smell of sulfuric acid and all those noisy machines making him cry. He recalled his grandfather consoling him before the whistle blew, and everything becoming quiet, then the next shift beginning the racket again and making him start crying all over.

While his father was in Switzerland, he remembered going with his mother on the train to New York, staying at the Plaza Hotel and having lunch with the president of Tiffany and his wife. *Poor mother would brag about my brilliance, embarrassing me to death. The bankruptcy will kill the soul of the most wonderful woman on earth. Damn the Japanese, the greedy unions, and the manipulators of the silver market that caused us to lose it all,* he thought. *I should have made more of an effort to call her before I left the apartment. Mother is going to be terribly upset with me.*

Father had seen it all coming, but mother would never have let him sell the company. He never had his heart in the business in the first place. If Dad had stayed with Dulles, he'd be running Operation Pluto today, and he'd be proud of me.

The DCI is on his way out of town for a purpose. He knew this operation was flawed, so he left town to put the monkey on Bissell's back. Is it paranoia, his age, or the gout that has gotten the old man down? Or is it a way to evade the disaster ahead? How lucky I am to be part of it.

Lucky? Walter Elliot asked himself thinking of the court order to sign over what once was sixty-eight million of his inheritance. *There's got to be a silver lining in this cloud,* Walter thought, laughing at his play on words. Being in the war room with the CIA Director of Covert Operations for the overthrow of the Cuban government was tremendous luck. This was his chance to make a name for himself he thought as Dulles' warning came back to him. "Be careful, Junior, and remember, stay a fly on the wall. If Operation Pluto fails, you don't want to be associated with the losers because Kennedy will make sure their heads roll."

Walter ran up the steps of the drab two-story temporary building that was surrounded by a chain-link fence to secure Quarters Eye, the CIA command and control for the invasion. The rain had stopped and the sweet fragrance of cherry blossoms floated in the light breeze off the Potomac. He was leaving behind his frustrations over Elliot Silver's bankruptcy locked in his briefcase in the trunk.

The tension inside the war room was brutal as a dozen men in shirtsleeves were feverishly at work, partially hidden under a thick blanket of cigarette smoke. Their intensity hit Walter with the reality that hundreds, if not thousands, of people were about to die on both sides. He rubbed his burning eyes as they slowly adjusted to the dark, looking for Bissell in the crowd of men shouting over the chirping of the crypto machines. The hair on the back of his neck stood up as he saw the large map of Cuba stretched across one wall and the red telephone to the White House on the desk waiting to ring.

Bissell, like a God, walked out of the smog. "Stow your gear and get in here on the double. I need you to help man the commo desk, Walt," ordered the tall, slightly stooped DCO, pointing his finger to the dormitory wing.

"Yes sir," Walter replied to the man he greatly admired before running down the hall and throwing his suitcase on the first empty army cot. He glanced up at the barred windows and noticed that the green paint was peeling off the walls of what would be his home for the next six days.

* * *

At the White House, President Kennedy was struggling with whether to make Operation Pluto a "go" or "no go." It became obvious to Walter the moment he took his seat at the commo desk that things were not yet settled when he glanced up at Dick Bissell, who was reading a communiqué from the Secretary of State. "President Kennedy is demanding to know the status of the Cuban exile government to replace Castro," the DCO sighed. "Walt, let's send the White House the following communiqué."

Elliot nodded, feeling the pressure of sending his first coded message to the president of the United States: "CIA planners have established creditable Cuban Revolutionary Council, CRC, government-in-exile now in seclusion. New government will accompany the exile forces on invasion to establish provisional government once military foothold in Cuba is established. Got that, Walter?"

"Got it, sir," Walter replied, reading back the message.

"Good job. Hanson? Where the hell's Axial?"

"He's down the hall taking a leak."

"Get Hanson for me on the double."

"What the hell's up now, Dick?" Hanson asked, walking into the war room wiping his hands with a paper towel.

"Get your public relations man in New York, Lem Jones, to prepare a communiqué for the Cuban Revolutionary Council to broadcast from Radio Swan when the invasion takes place. The CRC will declare themselves the provisional government until elections can be held after Castro is jailed or killed. Then get all the Cubans rounded up at the Statler Hotel so we can fly them down to Opa-Locka, and keep them incommunicado until after the invasion takes place," Bissell replied quickly lighting a cigarette.

"You want the CRC locked up at Opa?" Hanson laughed.

"Damn right! Under armed guard, if necessary. The last thing I want is those tin-horn Cuban politicians spouting off at the mouth and screwing up my operation."

Jesus Christ, Walter was thinking, making a mental note to tell Dulles that the CRC was being locked up at the CIA's base in Florida. *That guy, Varona we took to Guatemala is going to be really pissed.*

Chapter Six

Puerto Cabezas, Nicaragua

April 14, 1961

It was now Friday afternoon, and *La Brigada* had boarded six tired, rusty freighters on lease from the United Fruit Company. The ragtag armada was standing by for sailing orders in the stifling tropical heat. Time was running out, and still no word had arrived from the White House on the final "go" or "no go" for the invasion when Gray Lynch came into the radio shack on the command ship *Blagar*.

Back in Washington, Walter Elliot was a busy man at the Quarters Eye communications desk authenticating the incoming transmissions: Dozens of nonstop messages between the Havana underground, the Opa-Locka airfield, Radio Swan, the Happy Valley secret airfield in Nicaragua, and the United States Navy had to be coded, decoded, and encrypted. He grabbed Information Report No. CS-4/141,402 received from Gray Lynch at Puerto Cabezas and immediately decoded it.

"Imperative that the fleet sails by 1600 hours to make D-Day ETA. Immediate confirmation on sailing orders requested."

"Mr. Bissell! You need to act on this one, sir. It's from Gray Lynch!" Walter shouted, his words bringing quiet to the war room.

"Right, Walt," Bissell replied after reading it. "Why in the hell can't Kennedy make up his damn mind? Get the White House on the horn, pronto. I must speak with the president, so don't take any crap from the staffers."

Walter picked up the hot line to the president and shouted, "Red Light," bringing quiet to the room with everyone looking at Bissell. "Good afternoon, Mr. President," said the DCO in a clear and calm voice. "Sir, I respectfully remind you that it is now time to fish or cut bait, sir. What I mean, sir, it's the go or no go deadline.

"No later than 1300 hundred. The fleet must sail to make their new invasion ETA…"

"The fleet could be diverted as late as noon on Sunday the 16th of April if necessary…"

"Very well, Mr. President," Bissell said hanging up.

"What the hell did he say?" Hanson cried out.

"Elliot, get a message to Gray for the fleet to sail immediately. Tell him that the President will give the final go or no go at 1600 hours on Sunday, April 16th. No, belay that. Just tell him to get the hell underway and forget the rest."

A loud cheer filled the room. "Now, Axial, does that answer your question?"

"You bet your ass, Mr. DCO. Do we want to have the Special Forces cadre at Bragg to fly to Opa in case we need them for backup?"

"Not a bad idea, but the president ordered no U.S. personnel are to be involved. Gray's got Tex on board the *Blagar* with him."

Hanson put his forefinger to his lips. "Hey, keep that quiet. Tex is really on board the *Blagar*?"

"Yeah. Gray needed him."

"Dick, you said no active-duty personnel are supposed to be involved in this damn thing."

Bissell shrugged. "Who said he's involved? Gray wanted him to serve as special service officer to organize the ship's library."

"That's not funny. This is a terrible breach of security. What the hell happens if he gets captured?"

"Gray gave me his word that he would keep him on board the *Blagar*, so don't worry."

"Don't worry—the hell you say! If he *does* make it back you know how those cocky Special Forces bastards like to run their mouths. This is a hell of a security risk and I'm making a note to make damn sure that doesn't happen!"

General Cabell, Deputy Director of the CIA, and the air operations officer, spoke up. "Good idea, you make damn sure you do that, Hanson. By the way, when will *La Brigada* be told that President Kennedy has changed the invasion from Trinidad to the Bay of Pigs?"

"Not until they're out to sea, and then we will change the name of the operation to Zapata," Bissell replied.

Colonel Hawkins, who had been given only four days by the president to re-write the invasion plan, turned white with anger. "*What?* Dick, we've got to tell those people on the ships *now*! They've got to get ready. You people have no concept of what it takes to pull off a night invasion of this magnitude without the right planning and intelligence. This is suicide, and I told the president so in my memorandum. I believe I made it clear that the only way the Bay of Pigs could possibly succeed was with absolute air superiority."

"Okay, colonel. Take it easy," Bissell replied. "As soon as the fleet's under way I'll send the word for Gray to make the change. Gray has the Zapata operation plan for the new beachheads on board the *Blagar* with orders not to open them until he's at sea."

"Thank you very much," the colonel sarcastically replied. "There's a hell of a lot of difference in landing in Trinidad where Castro is hated by the locals and there are six thousand political prisoners to be set free. *La Brigada* could easily escape into the mountains and set up guerrilla operations if the invasion faltered."

"I'm missing something here," Hanson butted in, "what the hell are you guys talking about?"

"Kennedy ruled out Trinidad as being too obvious a landing site for U.S. participation and there might be civilian casualties. We had to come up with a less conspicuous beachhead. He insisted that the landing be made in the middle of the night to give the Navy time to withdraw undetected into international waters."

57

"*What?* No one told me about that! Where in the goddamn hell is the Bay of Pigs?" shouted Hanson, walking over to the Cuban map.

"Security. Need-to-know basis, *Mr. Coup,*" Bissell replied, his voice dry, "just Colonel Hawkins and the deputy…"

Colonel Hawkins pointed to the map. "Southern coast near the Zapata Swamp. A vast mangrove swamp where the locals are fearlessly loyal to Castro, we were told by intelligence initially. The locals are called *carboneros* and *macheteros* and make their living making charcoal and cutting sugar cane. Castro built roads across the Zapata Swamp and an airfield for his special project, *Villa Playa Giron,* a tourist center on the beach at Playa Giron."

Hanson's face flushed with anger. "Need to know, Dick? Didn't you read the *New York Times* headlines this morning? The whole fucking world knows what's going on by now."

"Everybody but those poor bastards on the ships," the colonel snarled, joining Hanson at the map, We *must* maintain air superiority from the airfield at Playa Giron if they are going to have any chance."

"Let's take it a step at a time, gentlemen," Bissell said calmly. "General Cabell, when is the first air strike to be launched?"

"Don't worry about that," Hanson interrupted. "This is D minus 3. We have plenty of time."

"Negative, gentlemen," General Cabell replied, "the President, acting upon recommendations of the State Department, has ordered that we strike the main fields in Cuba to destroy Castro's air force at dawn tomorrow."

"*What?*" Hanson and Colonel Hawkins shouted.

"That's the order from our Commander-in-Chief, gentlemen."

"*My God,* General! Why not wait until D-Day? We'll blow our element of surprise. Why not hit Havana simultaneously with the invasion?"

"Hawkins is right, I promised the exiles they wouldn't face hostile air," Hanson added.

"Now just hold it, gentlemen, this wasn't our idea," Bissell interrupted. "Two B-26s with Cuban pilots will fly from Happy Valley and land in Miami as defectors. The president wanted it this way to give the appearance that it was mutinous Cuban pilots that bombed Havana."

"Jesus Christ! Why not just send Castro a telegram and tell him he has two days to prepare before the invasion?"

"Yeah, Colonel Hawkins is right. That will give him plenty of time to round up the Cuban underground too!" Hanson added, pouring another cup of coffee.

"Look, we'll have U-2 surveillance," Bissell replied. "If we don't knock out the Cuban planes on the first run, we can follow up with a second or third mission to finish the job."

"I don't know about that," General Cabell snarled. "Elliot, get a message off to General Doster at Happy Valley to launch eight B-26s tomorrow morning in time to strike their targets at dawn in Havana, San Antonio de los Banos, and Santiago de Cuba. Coordinate the air strike over Cuba with another two planes acting as decoy deserters to land at Miami International afterwards. Got it?"

"Confirmed," Walter replied, jumping when Colonel Hawkins slammed his fist on the table.

"Eight? Only eight planes, General, *sir*? We've got twenty-three of the old relics. Why not launch them all and do the job right?"

"Look, Colonel, I'm the air chief here," the four-star general, snarled. "Two planes must be used as decoys, and the rest are to be held in reserve and flown to the airstrip at Playa Giron to give close air support for the invasion."

Walter handed Bissell Information Report CS-4/141,437 that had just been received from Havana. "Here's some positive news, Mr. Bissell. Our saboteurs in Cuba are already at work setting fire to the nationalized Hershey sugar mill this morning, and a bomb just exploded in the Encanto Department Store in downtown Havana."

"Okay. That's good. Glad something around this damn operation is positive."

At the White House, a visibly shaken John Kennedy had hung up the phone after speaking with Bissell and placed his hands over his face. "Should I call the CIA back and abort this thing, Dean?"

The secretary of state frowned and lowered his voice. "That is your decision, Mr. President. But remember the Guatemalans have all but kicked us out of their country. Where the hell are we going to send *La Brigada* and what do we do with them once they get there? What if they resist disarmament? Create havoc? They are the most effective armed forces in Central America at the moment, Mr. President. We sure as hell can't bring them back to the United States. It would be a disaster to have fifteen hundred Cubans running around Miami telling the world that the Kennedy administration had betrayed them in their fight against the Communists."

"Yes, you're right, and thanks, Dean. I still have until noon on Sunday to mull this thing over," Kennedy sighed, slumping down in an armchair and staring aimlessly at the wall map of Cuba.

At the Happy Valley airstrip in Nicaragua, General Reid Doster, commander of the Alabama Air National Guard, read the decoded message from Quarters Eye and his face reddened. "What in the hell are those stupid sons-of-bitches thinking in Washington? They're giving Castro a wake up call on D minus 3?" he shouted in his heavy southern drawl.

General Doster looked out the window at his B-26 bombers bearing the Cuban star. His pilots and maintenance crews from Birmingham had been training the Cuban pilots in Nicaragua for months now. What once seemed like a realistic air operation to support the invasion fleet had suddenly evaporated. The General turned to his operations officer, Lieutenant Colonel Joe Shannon, a soft-spoken WWII fighter pilot, to give the order: "Prepare to launch tomorrow at 0100 hours. Two aircraft will hit the airfield at Santiago de Cuba, two will go to San Antonio de los Banos, and two will hit the San Antonio air base in Havana. Take two planes and shoot some holes in them to make it appear as though they've been in a fight. Coordinate their landings at Miami International to make it look like they'd hit the Cuban targets."

"You're kidding me, General, aren't you, sir?" Lt. Col. Shannon asked with a questioning look. After reading the general's disgust, he followed his orders without waiting for a reply.

* * *

It was now 0800 hours on April 15th and Walter Elliot had been at his commo desk in Quarters Eye since one o'clock that morning. The first message came in from the B-26 raid on Havana and was being decoded. Information Report CS-4/150,800 from the CIA officer stationed in Havana was quickly handed to Dick Bissell, who read the message to his staff. "Initial assessment of air strike on Havana field has destroyed fifty percent of the aircraft on the ground and ignited fuel dump. City covered in thick black smoke and populace in panic. Castro broadcasting to prepare for invasion, placing all military units and militia on full alert along with the DGI."

"Well," Bissell said, rubbing his unshaven chin, "the decoy planes should be landing in Miami at any moment now, so standby."

As planned, the two B-26 bombers from Nicaragua landed at Miami International Airport at twelve minutes before the hour, the left engine of one being shot out by its pilot with his pistol from the cockpit before landing. The press swarmed the two pilots who made brief rehearsed statements of their attacks and desertion before being whisked away by the CIA to Opa-Locka for a flight back to Happy Valley.

As their plane took off, United States Ambassador Adlai Stevenson stood before the General Assembly of the United Nations in New York. His wristwatch showed two minutes before his 10:30 address to the world denying Cuban Foreign Minister Dr. Raul Roa's allegations that the Americans were responsible for the air attacks on Cuba at 6:30 that morning. Outside, the chants of *"Cuba Si, Yankee No"* came from the protesters marching in front of the UN building.

Just as the ambassador took his place at the podium, Captain Rafael del Lagas of the Cuban Air Force requested landing instructions from the Miami International tower and taxied his Cuban Air Force B-26 to the edge of the field. The Cuban deserter was more surprised than the U.S. Custom agents who rushed to meet him when he parked his plane next to the two bogus B-26s from Nicaragua and cut his engines.

The defector climbed out of the cockpit as the press swarmed his plane, shouting questions in Spanish while carefully examining the aircraft. The CIA B-26s had plastic noses, and the Cuban plane's nose was made of metal and was missing a blue stripe painted along the cockpit for friendly identification.

The two CIA officers who were returning from Opa-Locka after dropping off the Cuban pilots heard the landing reported on their car radio. They rushed back to the airport, barking instructions to secure the area as a reporter from the *Miami Herald* shouted: "The first planes are nothing but a bunch of phony hocks! Their machine guns haven't even been fired!"

In New York, Ambassador Adlai Stevenson had been caught in one of the biggest diplomatic lies in American history.

At 11:06 A.M., President Kennedy suddenly rushed out of the reception lounge on the eighth floor of the State Department where he had been addressing a group honoring "African Freedom Day." The elevator took him down to the Secretary of State's offices. "What's up, Dean?" the president snapped as he barged into the room.

"I have Adlai on the phone from New York, Mr. President. He's absolutely livid about being made a fool of in his address to the General Assembly this morning. With the Cuban pilot's defection our planes from Nicaragua are known phonies. Ambassador Stevenson is threatening to resign, Mr. President."

"That does it! All future air strikes on Cuba are hereby canceled as of now. Understand? Every damn one of them! Let me speak with Adlai," Kennedy ordered.

The phone conversation between the UN secretary and the president lasted for five minutes; time enough for the president to prevent the Ambassador's resignation. Kennedy then headed for the White House where Jacqueline and the children were packed and waiting. The marine helicopter flew the first family to Glen Ora, their home near Middlesburg, Virginia, to relax and golf for the remainder of the weekend.

Back at Quarters Eye the president's phone rang, activating the flashing red lights above the map of Cuba. The war room became ghostly quiet, leaving only the monotonous drone of the cryptograph machine. *Is the president calling to cancel the operation?* Dick Bissell wondered as he grabbed the receiver. "Bissell speaking.

Yes, Mr. Secretary," he said to Dean Rusk in his office at the State Department. "Yes sir, we have been informed of the Cuban defector landing a plane in Miami...But Mr. Secretary...Mr. Secretary, it is essential that we have additional air strikes to destroy the remainder of the Cuban air force. Yes, I understand. Can we meet with the President? Then I want to have a meeting with you as soon as possible. We still have time to sort this thing out."

Bissell hung up, leaving his hand on the receiver, too angry to move when he heard General Cabell ask, "What's going on here, Dick?"

"We're preparing for a mop-up strike in Havana to finish the job," Hanson interrupted.

"Oh? I don't recall permission for multiple strikes. I think we need to take that up with the President," snorted the knickers-and golf-cap clad general who had just returned from golfing at the Chevy Chase Club.

"The General is right, gentlemen, we don't have permission," Bissell sighed. "General, be prepared to brief the Secretary of State on our air operations in his office at 1800. The president has just ordered all future air strikes on Cuba canceled. Have you got any U-2 reports yet?"

Axial laid the report on the table. "Twelve of Castro's eighteen aircraft have been destroyed. He's got two T-33 jets, two Sea Furies, and two B-26s left. If we don't get permission from the President to finish the job, the Guats are screwed."

Chapter Seven

San Blas, Cuba

Sunday, April 16, 1961

You pompous bastard! Luis Benes was thinking as he glared across the Plaza de Armas at the aristocrat standing in the shade of the belfry of Our Lady of the Assumption Church with his son, Manuel. *No, Luis. You're the bastard,* the mulatto told himself ordering his second *aguardiente* in the open-air Bar Habana when he heard the tolling of the noon bell.

Luis took a drink of the clear cane liquor and stared across the plaza at the Don of San Blas dressed in his white linen suit with a Panama hat covering his black hair with traces of gray at the temples. *Carlos Garcia Rangel, you treat me like shit. I can't help it if my life's been cursed by the sins of Papa and his Negrito mistress who died giving me birth. I have nothing, and with the same father I am entitled to half the Hacienda del Azucar. Today justice will come, and I will see that you burn in hell.*

Don Carlos watched his son counting the chimes resounding down upon the hostile crowd gathering under the giant majagua tree that anchored the corner of the plaza. "Father Lopez, tomorrow our lives turn into a living hell," Don Carlos said to his priest after the twelfth toll had faded away.

The old hooked-nose padre gave a fleeting glance across the plaza to the crowd gathering in front of the Bar Habana. "Castro's Revolution will pass, Don Carlos. God sees to it that all things political pass with time."

"No, Father, this time Fidel Castro *defies* God. I just pray to live to see the day Manuel tolls the bell our family cast in Spain with a pound of gold and silver to give it a heavenly tone."

"Of course, Don Carlos. Next year Manuel will be old enough to ring the bell," the priest replied, smiling down at the husky, green-eyed twelve-year-old.

"This church has been the foundation of our family for generations."

"And it shall remain so, Don Carlos," the priest quickly replied, stepping up to help Eduardo, the acne-faced altar boy, tie the bell rope when Manuel sneaked up behind him.

In the Bar Habana, Eduardo's father, Gonzalo Martinez Azanza, poured his customer another drink. "Luis, what will you do when Castro confiscates Don Carlos' hacienda and gives it to the *macheteros*?"

Luis' grayish eyes narrowed. "It's also *my* land, Gonzo," shouted the light-skinned mulatto with pronounced Spanish features on a clean-shaven face that stood out in a crowd.

"You're a dreamer, Luis."

"And you're an asshole for saying so, Gonzo."

The bartender threw himself over the bar shouting across the plaza, "Eduardo! What the hell are you doing, son?"

Eduardo grabbed Manuel on the steps of the church and wrestled him to the ground, saying low so the Don couldn't hear: "You rich little bastard, I'll teach you to slip up and pinch my ass you sneaky little shitass. Castro is going to give us all your papa's land and then Maria will have to be a whore to make enough money for you to eat."

Manuel struggled free, striking Eduardo in the face, and from across the plaza Luis Benes heard Don Carlos scream: "Eduardo Martinez! Pick on someone your own size or I'll run you back to Havana!"

Gonzo threw down his towel and ran out into the plaza shouting, "Turn my son loose, Don Carlos."

"You best shut up, Gonzo, and get back in here or Carlos will have your ass," Luis laughed as Eduardo ran across the plaza smirking at the Don before ducking into the safety of the Bar Habana.

"Papa! Don Carlos attacked me!" the boy's voice cracked above the profane chatter of the drinkers defending Cuba against the American invaders.

Luis brushed the flies off his drink and turned on Eduardo like a pit bull: "Shut up, you stupid bastard, if you fuck with the Don, he'll kill you." The mulatto then asked, "Gonzo, did anyone ever tell you that you've got a fool for a son?"

Gonzo shrugged, hugging his son, as Luis Benes returned to his drink.

On the steps of the church, the old priest could be seen gesturing with his hands in an attempt to calm the Don. "I don't know what has come over Eduardo," the priest kept saying while ringing his hands. "It must be all this political unrest. Eduardo is a troubled boy from a bad background in Havana."

"No, Father, Eduardo is a *punk*."

"I must work harder with him. His mother's dead."

"I heard in Havana that she was a whore who gave him to Gonzo for a piece of ass. I'll speak to Gonzo this afternoon. I don't want to ever see Eduardo ringing this bell, Father. *Never*," Don Carlos said putting his hand on Manuel's shoulder. "Now, let's go find your sister, son."

They searched the plaza in the hot sun and found Maria and her youngest brother waiting in the shade of the church, having missed the fight. "Can we go home now, Papa?" the four-year old called out as they approached.

"No, Alfredo. We must listen to Castro's speech first," his father replied, watching as his macheteros filed out of the Bar Habana and gathered under the sheltering shade of the majagua tree.

From inside the bar, Luis was keeping a close eye on the Garcias through the open window when he heard the drummer beating out a cadence for the San Blas garrison marching into the plaza from their barracks. Luis took his drink and walked to the door when the crowd went wild applauding the soldiers and chanting, *"Death to the Yankees! Yankees go home!"*

Don Carlos applauded politely before rubbing his growling stomach and feeling for the revolver in his belt. *Castro, I hope the Yankees kill you,* he was thinking when he realized Maria was watching him. "Maria, you are so lovely, just like Mama," he smiled and said.

"And you are the handsomest father in all of Cuba," Maria replied, bringing a faint smile to her father's face before his dark thoughts returned. *Look at the carboneros, you rotten bunch of Socialists, cutting marabu trees and burning them into charcoal and carrying the sacks to Cienfuegos for mere pesos. You are poisoning my macheteros who work hard cutting my cane. If I leave before hearing Castro, Luis and the carboneros will call me a Yankee sympathizer.*

Don Carlos watched the black-shawled women shepherding their children away from their men dressed in white guayaberas that contrasted nicely against their black skin in the shade of the majagua tree. The sun burned down on the backs of the soldiers standing at ease in front of the Soviet army truck with the loud speaker, waiting for Fidel's speech. Don Carlos took off his Panama hat and was wiping sweat with his handkerchief when Luis stepped out into the heat. Looking over at Don Carlos, he smiled weakly and waved.

Catching Luis' eye, the Don began thinking, *what's going on, Luis? I'm sorry that we didn't share the same mother, but you are lucky to be my bastard brother. Without my hacienda you would be starving like the rest of these carboneros. I made you my superintendent and bought you a new Chevy truck with a radio. What the hell else do you want, an air-conditioned one? Luis, will I be able to trust you to complete the harvest when the trouble comes and I have to leave?* "I am very angry..."

"About what, Papa?" Maria asked, taking her father's hand when Manuel laughed, "Eduardo shoved me down after mass."

"That Eduardo is a creep, Papa."

"Don't worry, your brother hit him with a good right jab," Don Carlos said ruffling his son's hair. "I will speak to Gonzo about the punk."

"Papa," Manuel said, casting his eyes down to the ground, "Eduardo said Castro would take our land...and...Eduardo said Maria would have to become a whore to make money for us to eat. It's not true, is it, Papa?"

"Papa!" Maria gasped, covering her mouth, seeing her father's face turn white with anger. "Quiet! I will take care of Eduardo this afternoon!" Carlos snapped hearing the militia being called to attention.

"Maria, the Cuban people have suffered greatly. They've been oppressed by the Yankees who propped up corrupt politicians like Batista, and by the Spanish from the very beginning. But is that my fault?"

"No, Papa. Of course it's not your fault."

"The *Negritos* are crazy for thinking Fidel will make their life better."

"Will he, Papa?"

Don Carlos looked down and admired the innocent face of his daughter with beautiful dark eyes like her mother – her question lingered. *Will he, Papa?*

"Will he?" the Don of San Blas asked with a shrug of his shoulders. "No, Maria. *Never!*"

In his own mind, Don Carlos felt, like his forefathers before him, that he provided his macheteros work, quarters, and credit at the Bar Habana and his stores. All their lives depended on the sugar harvest; it was the Cuban economy. He knew too that Fidel Castro's Revolution had changed all for the worst.

If I was a poor Negrito I wouldn't be fooled by Fidel, Don Carlos was thinking, lighting his cigar to stifle his hunger and looking at his half brother across the plaza. *Luis, when I leave for Miami I'm depending on you to complete the harvest so that we all can eat.*

Carlos shot an angry look at the men standing under the majagua tree. *Negritos, can Castro give you land? Yes, but it is my land he will give you. My family's land, a grant from the King of Spain. Can Castro unshackle you from the Yankee imperialists that control Cuba's economy? Hell no! Castro will only make all our lives more difficult by destroying the American sugar market.*

Don Carlos watched as the crowd outside of the Bar Habana grew restless. He felt their envy of his vast wealth and power as master of the Hacienda del Azucar and knew it would never change. In his heart he knew Luis felt the same.

He took a long draw on his cigar. Havana had been bombed yesterday morning, according to the Cuban newscast. If the Yankees overthrow Castro, his family's life and Cuba would remain unchanged. *Please, God. Kill Fidel for the sake of Cuba!* he prayed when he heard his youngest son whine, "Papa, I'm hungry."

"We will go soon, Alfredo."

"Will the Yankees bomb San Blas too?"

"No, Manuel. There is nothing in San Blas to bomb, only sugar cane and carboneros." Don Carlos laughed for the first time. One of the wealthiest men in Cuba smiled weakly at Maria, who took her youngest brother's hand. *What handsome children I have,* he thought, taking a long draw on his cigar, and exhaling into the hot air.

"The Yankees will probably invade Havana, son," Carlos continued when Fidel Castro's powerful voice came blaring from the PA system, bringing wild cheers from the crowd. The militiamen snapped to attention and were given parade rest as Castro's voice drew in the crowd like metal shavings to a magnet.

"The United States sponsored the attack on Havana because it cannot forgive us for achieving a Socialist revolution under their noses," Castro raved to the crowd of ten thousand at the graveside funeral of the air raid victims in Havana. "Let us face the enemy with the conviction that to die for our country is to live, and to live in chains is to live in shame and disgrace."

San Blas and all Cubans were listening. *"War! War!"* came the background chants over the speakers from the Havana crowd, when the San Blastions in the Plaza de Armas picked up the chant. *"War! War!"*

Castro's voice resounded through the plaza, echoing off the buildings, "The Yankees are trying to deceive the world, but the whole world knows that the attack was made with Yankee planes piloted by mercenaries paid for by the United States Central Intelligence Agency."

The crowd grew hostile when Castro's speech ended with these somber words: "The invasion of Cuba by the Yankee imperialists is imminent!"

Don Carlos felt his guts knotting inside as he was thinking, *and they will kill you too, Fidel, you son-of-a-bitch.* Then he watched the soldiers break ranks, discharging their rifles into the air and sending Alfredo crying into his arms. "That's it! Let's go home," Don Carlos ordered as the crowd began shouting, *"Cuba si! Yankee no! Yankees go home!"*

Across the plaza, Luis stood in the door of the Bar Habana with Gonzo, both men smoking cigars and laughing as they heard Manuel deviling his younger brother by saying, "Alfredo, you crybaby. The soldiers are shooting holes in the sky, stupid."

"Stop it, boys" the Don ordered, leading his children up the steps of the church where Father Lopez was standing with folded arms, his cassock drooping loosely off his stooped shoulders like a scarecrow's gown.

"There is something of great importance that I must discuss with you this afternoon, Father."

"What is it, my son? Eduardo?" The priest asked cupping his hand to his ear so he could hear.

"No, I'll take care of that situation later. I will return at three this afternoon after we have eaten and the demonstration has stopped."

"I will be waiting," the priest replied, reading the anger in Don Carlos' eyes and ruffling Manuel's hair. Father Lopez could not keep from smiling when he overhead the older boy asking,

"Papa, do we have a Central Intelligence Agency?"

"Castro has secret police, the Directory of General Intelligence, or DGI," Don Carlos replied unlocking the black Olds 98 to the fragrance of new car leather.

"Do you hate Yankees?" the boy asked, running ahead to beat Alfredo to the front seat of the car.

"God says hate no one," Carlos replied, starting the engine and switching off the Havana radio just as Eduardo came running by with his arms out like he was an airplane.

"You creep!" Manuel shouted out the window as they passed him by. "Papa, Castro can't really give our land away to Eduardo?"

"No, so stop worrying. I'll take care of Eduardo this afternoon."

The family rode in silence toward the Hacienda del Azucar under a hazy Cuban sky with only the sounds of the car's tires crunching gravel. The smell of charred cane came through the open windows as the patchwork of partially harvested fields sprouting stubble shimmered in the strong midday breeze.

Manuel watched his father's eyes focusing on the road ahead as he chewed angrily on his cigar. The boy loved to see the standing cane waving in a glistening sea of silverish green. *These lands will all be mine someday if what Eduardo said about Castro is a lie,* he was thinking when he heard his sister asking, "May I go back to San Blas this afternoon with you, Papa?"

"Not this afternoon, Maria. I have business to discuss with Father Lopez that will take a long time, and with all those crazy soldiers, it's not safe in San Blas for my fifteen-year-old señorita."

"What are you going to do to Eduardo?"

"Leave it to me," her father replied as he turned down the long drive to the Casa de Azucar lined with towering eucalyptus trees.

"Can I go, Papa? Can I?"

"No, Alfredo. We're home now," Carlos sighed, admiring his beloved Casa de Azucar, standing in the shade of towering royal palms swaying in the coastal breeze.

"Alfredo, you're so stupid," Manuel said punching his brother in the stomach. "If Maria can't go, why can you? She's bigger than a little four-year-old sissy!"

"Stop hitting me, Manuel. I'm almost five!"

"Stop it, you two! If you misbehave in front of the servants, you will spend the afternoon in your rooms."

"I'm sorry, Papa, watch out for Blanco!" Manuel shouted as his white Fox Terrier came bounding down the drive to greet them.

The car approached the grand two-story mansion built in 1764 on the highest knoll of the six thousand acres King Charles III of Spain had granted to Don Frandio Garcia Lopez for his service to the Crown after Spain regained Cuba from the British. European master craftsmen and local carpenters and masons took four years to complete one of the finest villas in all of Cuba, a monument to the architectural splendor of the colonial era.

The car stopped at the curved steps leading to the veranda of the pale yellow villa with a red tile roof and turquoise shutters to protect it from hurricanes that blew in from the east. The soothing sounds of water splashing from the fountain in the

71

center of the circular drive harmonized with the cheerful chatter of the servants and Blanco's welcome.

Carlos got out of the car admiring the elegant gardens that were best reviewed from the eighty-foot round stone tower where his forefathers had monitored the slaves working in the fields that spread in all directions. He loved to climb to the top of the spiral stairway and peer out at the glistening waters of the Bay of Pigs to the south and westward to the Central Australian smoke stacks. In the distance was the domed bell tower of his beloved Our Lady of the Assumption Church in San Blas.

From the veranda, the Garcias entered into the coolness of the reception gallery. In the sanctuary of its thirty-foot ceiling, a blue-skied mural of guardian angels protected their home against evil.

Trailing footsteps echoed off checkered Italian marble into the great hall. From its cathedral ceiling hung a grand crystal Barcelonan chandelier lighting the archways and mosaic-lined yellow walls delicately decorated in ornate gold-trimmed molding. The villa's treasures included priceless seventeenth-century antiques and the finest renaissance art.

Through two massive oaken doors the family entered the formal dining room to the tantalizing aroma of roasted pig with rice, beans and fried sweet bananas. The children stood behind their assigned places at a table set with elegance and fresh flowers as the servants withdrew to the kitchen, and all was quiet. It was at times like this that Don Carlos missed his wife greatly. He looked out sadly at her empty chair and place setting at the end of the long table and was thinking, *I know you are with us, Maria, my love.*

"What a feast you have prepared!" Manuel said as Chef Gerardo entered from the kitchen, wiping his hands on his apron.

"Thank you, Señor Manuel, are you hungry?"

"Very!" replied the boy as he held the chair for Maria.

"Manuel, say the blessing then so we can eat," Don Carlos said with a parting nod to the chef.

* * *

At his Havana apartment Fidel Castro had finished lunch with his most trusted advisors, brother Raul and the Argentine doctor, Ernesto "Che" Guevara. The funeral for Saturday's air raid victims was still very much on the dictator's mind as the men sat in the small kitchen with cigars and cognac. Dressed in combat fatigues and armed with pistols, they cursed the Americans and the CIA, with Fidel dominating the conversation.

"The defense of Cuba from the immediate invasion now rests in our hands," Castro reminded his confidants.

"All military units and militia are on full alert," Raul boasted. "Our soldiers are ready for the Yankees…"

"Where do you think the bastards will make their landing?" Che interrupted, "Here in Havana?"

"You two are not thinking correctly," Castro said matter-of-factly.

"How so?" Raul asked, with a quizzical look on his face.

"The Yankees have already invaded. Right under our noses."

"Impossible!"

"Yes, an invasion of terrorists, here on Cuban soil, and the two of you are not smart enough to realize it?"

"Fidel, what are you saying?" Che asked holding up the amber bottle of L'art De Martell, "More cognac?"

Castro held his glass to the bottle. "Remember what we did in the Sierra Maestra?"

"Of course, we remember," Che laughed. "We were young guerrillas with a thirst for freedom that overthrew Batista."

"Yes, but there are now urban guerrillas—Cubans who are in important positions that the Yankee CIA has recruited as terrorists to oust us. Urban guerrillas *are* the most dangerous kind."

"But we have our DGI, brother."

"Damn it, Raul. The CIA has undercover counter-revolutionists that they will now draw upon to help overthrow the revolution."

"That's true," Che agreed. "The list we have of the counter-revolutionists must be dealt with at once."

"Now you're thinking correctly."

"I will have our secret police and militia arrest them at once," Raul interjected, reaching for the telephone.

Fidel caught his arm. "Wait a minute. We must have a plan. The most dangerous ones must be arrested first. Those men with power, the directors of the National Sugar Association, men like Don Carlos Garcia Rangel. The Association is against our agrarian reform and are Yankee sympathizers with much power over the people. Arrest these men first and then go down the list. Keep a close watch on Bishop Masvidal for he organized the Catholic Federation against us."

"Consider it done!" Raul shouted, grabbing the phone and calling the headquarters of the DGI. "Let me speak to Major Ramiro Valdés."

Castro's orders were being followed in Havana as the Garcia family gathered in the music room for Maria's Sunday recital. Her delicate fingers glided across the ivory keys of the grand piano, bringing Strauss' *Blue Danube* to life. *She's becoming an accomplished pianist. Her mother taught her well*, Don Carlos thought as he smoked a cigar and sipped his coffee.

Manuel fidgeted; the recital was the hardest part of his Sunday ordeal. *First mass and then having to sit and listen to Maria*, the boy thought gazing out of the window, wishing he could shoot his .22 rifle before his father left. He would have to settle for a game of baseball with the boys down in the quarters. Maria finally finished with a curtsy and applause as Manuel rushed upstairs to change his clothes.

"Come, Blanco," Manuel called from his red Schwinn Phantom as he raced down the road past Luis Benes' house with its tin roof. He waved to the black car going up the driveway as he raced to get to the ball field. The boy's New York Yankees baseball cap was pulled down low, shading his eyes from the sun, when he took to the mound pitching with the controlled heat of a major league pitcher.

Chapter Eight

Afternoon

April 16, 1961

Don Carlos felt the refreshing coolness from the heat of the afternoon as he entered the side door of the church to the fragrance of incense burning from the noon mass. "Good afternoon, Father," he called out, trying not to startle the old priest seated at the table.

"Hello, my son," the priest replied, looking up with a glazed softness in his eyes after his troubled morning as he sat cassockless finishing his lunch. "Come sit, Don Carlos," he said, motioning with a frail hand "Now tell me what is troubling you. Is it the Yankee invasion, the harvest, or Eduardo?"

Don Carlos shrugged lightly. "I'll take care of the punk."

The priest nodded as Carlos took a seat at the end of the table, choosing his words carefully, "I'm gravely concerned for my life now that the Yankee invasion is imminent. But it is not the Yankees I'm afraid of."

"You're not afraid of the Americans?"

Don Carlos chuckled. "No, it's Fidel Castro who threatens my life."

"Nonsense!"

"But it's true. Castro thinks of me as a counter-revolutionist and has me under DGI surveillance at all times my brother-in-law in Havana has told me. This is a threat not only to my life and property but to my children's lives as well."

75

"But, Don Carlos, Fidel Castro will defend our country against the Yankee imperialists. Our people love Fidel. You saw their demonstration in the plaza after his speech."

"Yes, I saw it, and it was disgusting."

"*Si*, but he built the new highway to connect San Blas to the outside world. Before we could cross the swamp only by boat and we had no bus service…"

"No, Father, he built the highway from Real Campiña so he could get to Giron, his favorite fishing spot, where he built an expensive lodge with poor people's money. I saw Castro fishing in Giron only a few weeks ago. He looked at my new car and spat on the road."

"Perhaps, but the people say he is the prophet of the poor and will free Cuba from the Yankees."

"The people are poor, but what Castro says to the people is rotten lies," Don Carlos shouted, his voice echoing in the quietness of the church.

The priest held his finger to his lips. "Why do you feel so threatened?"

"Castro is a Socialist. He will take my properties and redistribute the land to the people. He has already done so with the land owned by foreigners."

"I think not with your land."

"Do you know much about the National Institute of Agrarian Reform that Castro formed last May after the Revolution came to power?"

"So what about it?"

"He mandated that all foreign ownership over thirty-three hundred acres be redistributed back to the people in eighty-two acre tracts. The revolutionists say they will subsidize the new owners to grow sugar cane, but so far they have done nothing except lie to our people. This was the first step and just the beginning of the land redistribution—first the foreign-owned properties, next we wealthy Cubans."

The old priest looked around cautiously before speaking. "Bishop Masvidal has officially denounced the totalitarian methods of the government and has called for respect for private lands."

"The bishop is right."

"He is, but the peasants have been suppressed for centuries. Now they are saying it's time they have their own land. I am sorry to tell you this."

"I'm not here to plead my case against land reform. You know I am a director and past president of the National Sugar Association. We have fought against the foreign companies that have controlled Cuba's sugar production. We have fought for the Cuban people by getting the best price in the international market. Yet Castro says that the members of the Association are counter-revolutionaries."

"I am not a politician, my son. I am your priest, and I was *also* your father's priest, and I gave mass for your grandfather's funeral when I first arrived from Spain almost fifty years ago. You and your family have long been good to the people of San Blas and to this church your forefathers built. What is it you want from me, Don Carlos? I pray to God each night that this will all go away."

"Father, today the winds of change blow across our island—misdirected evil winds from Castro's Havana, in my opinion. When the land is redistributed there will be no method of sustaining the production of the sugar by farming small plots without fertilizer or equipment. Cuba's sugar harvest will be a terrible disaster. Insignificant production will cause our economy to collapse since the sugar harvest is the life of Cuba. Yes, the workers will have land, but can they eat dirt?"

"I hear what you have said. What is it that you want, my son?"

"Nothing at all for me, Padre. Nothing! Only your help in protecting my children should something happen to me."

"Your children are safe in the Casa de Azucar. Why worry?"

Don Carlos watched the priest take a drink of the red wine with the cheese he was having for dessert. Carlos felt a deep love and respect for this man who had meant so much to him during his life. He was feeling guilty now for wondering whether the old man was naïve or becoming senile.

The Don began again, trying to be patient, "No, my children will not be safe at the Casa de Azucar. We must have a plan for their evacuation to Havana if Castro has me arrested, like his brother Raul has threatened. Remember my sister's husband still has his post as the Colombian ambassador."

"Yes, I remember officiating at the marriage of Roscena and Ambassador Valdovinos. The Casa de Azucar was decorated like it was a royal wedding. I pray they are well."

"Yes, very well. My chef, Gerardo, has been instructed to bring the children here to the church if something happens. Promise that you will see them safely to Havana to the Colombian Embassy if I'm arrested. Roscena will know what to do."

"I think you worry too much. They are strong children. God will take care of them after they have gone through so much with their mother's illness."

"Do you promise me, Father?"

"Yes, I promise. Now go and rest. It's Sunday—our day for rest."

Don Carlos reached into his shirt pocket and pulled out a white envelope. "Here are five thousand pesos for any expenses. Remember, Fidel Castro will destroy everything that stands in his way, even the Catholic Church if it threatens the Revolution."

How right you are, Father Lopez thought as he walked Don Carlos to the door. "I promise. Now I will go and pray for you and your family."

The priest heard Don Carlos' car start and then kneeled before the altar carved of cedar to exalt the Eucharist, embossed in ornate iconography encrusted with gold leaf. Sputtering candles left from the noon mass were slowly dying, leaving a dim gold light symbolic of the divine life. "Oh merciful Father, give the Catholic Federation the strength to protect our Church from Castro and the guidance and strength to do thy holy will in these troubled times. I pray in the name of the Holy Ghost. Amen."

Don Carlos drove slowly through the Plaza de Armas spotting Eduardo. "Come here you skinny bastard!" he shouted out the window.

The boy sprinted to the Bar Habana and disappeared inside as Don Carlos gunned his engine, sliding to a sharp stop. He slammed the car door and charged inside shouting, "Gonzo, where is Eduardo?"

It was late in the evening and the Garcia family gathered around the kitchen table eating leftovers. Chef Gerardo had gone to play dominoes with Luis in his house and the other servants had been given the night off to be with their families. "We have had an interesting day," Don Carlos said, smiling to his children, hiding his feelings for their mother, which always seemed the hardest on Sunday evenings. "Maria, put Alfredo to bed now, and then you and Manuel do your homework."

"I don't want to go to bed," Alfredo whined as his sister led him away to a taunting face from his brother who went into the library with his books.

The sun had disappeared below the horizon and the wind had died. In the distance an occasional bull crocodile's bellow echoed up from the vast Zapata Swamp. Carlos loved the sounds as he went into the large library and poured a brandy before lighting his after-dinner Partagas. It was from this room that he managed his hacienda as his forefathers had done for two hundred years before him. "Start studying, Manuel," he ordered.

"Yes, Papa," replied Manuel, gazing out the tall windows at the fireflies and wishing his mother was there to help him with his arithmetic.

"You must get up early. It's a long drive to Cienfuegos."

Manuel nodded, took a seat behind the massive wooden desk, and opened his math workbook. Nearly thirteen now, he looked forward to finishing the seventh grade and starting the summer vacation. His father would take him each morning to oversee the workers and to baseball games in Havana on the weekends. *Only one more year and I will attend the Havana Academy*, he thought, unable to concentrate on his homework. *Only the wealthiest of Cuban families send their sons away to school.* "Papa, can I take Blanco to the Havana Academy?"

"No way. Now study."

The evening passed with the antique grandfather clock in the hall chiming each hour until Manuel counted to the strike of nine. "Do I have to go to bed now, Papa?"

Don Carlos Garcia grunted from his leather armchair and kept reading the *Havana Bohemia*. While the boy waited for an answer, he studied the darkened mahogany walls that were permeated with the smoke from generations of fine cigars. He was still waiting for the dreaded order that came each night at the stroke of nine when Don Carlos folded the newspaper and Manuel read the headline: *FIDEL PUTS MILITIA ON FULL ALERT AFTER YANKEE BOMBINGS.*

79

Someday I will be running the hacienda from behind this desk, smoking Partagas cigars and reading the Bohemia just like Papa, he thought when his father lowered his newspaper with a deeper frown on his forehead. He was taking slow, deliberate draws of his cigar, exhaling slowly out the corner of his mouth.

The sights and sounds of the demonstration in the Plaza de Armas and Castro's words were now haunting the Don of San Blas. *"The Yankee invasion is imminent!" How much time do I have before I must leave?* he asked himself. Realizing he was ignoring his son, he quietly laid the paper aside and leaned back in his chair.

The boy glanced around the library at the thousands of leather-bound volumes of Shakespearean classics, history, and scientific journals on the agricultural practices of cultivating sugarcane. He wondered how many of these books Papa had read, having no idea that the Don was thinking not about the books but if Luis could be trusted to take care of the harvest when he fled.

Will Luis turn on me like all the rest? Should I talk to Luis tomorrow? Can he be trusted to manage the hacienda until the Yankees oust Castro? That is the risk I have to take since Luis considered this land rightfully his.

Don Carlos cringed at the thought, not really wanting to tell Manuel to go to bed. "Good night, my son," he finally said, reaching over and kissing the boy lightly on the forehead. "It's your bedtime, and don't forget to let Blanco out and brush your teeth."

"Good night, Papa. I love you."

"I love you, too, my son." *What a fine young man he is growing into, and what a pity his mother did not live to see it,* he thought, returning to the *Bohemia.*

Manuel paused on the steps of the veranda to wait for his dog to return, and for the first time felt frightened by the thoughts of the Yankee invasion. *It will be far away in Havana,* he told himself seeing his father snuff out his cigar and slowly shake his head. *I hate the Yankees for what they are doing to Papa.* Blanco came in and Don Carlos heard the sounds of their feet scampering up the stairs.

The walls of Manuel's bedroom were decorated with posters of a Spanish matador facing a charging bull along with the Havana Creoles, and New York

Yankees in their pinstripe uniforms. From his balcony he could see all the way to the Bay of Pigs when the moon was full, but tonight, only the distant lights of the fishing village of Playa Giron could be seen as he knelt and said his prayers:

"Now I lay me down to sleep. Almighty God, bless my Papa, and don't let him worry about Castro or the Americans. Bless my little brother Alfredo, and my sister Maria too. God bless the Yankees and let them win the World Series. God bless Blanco and don't ever let Blanco die. And God, please bless Mama up in heaven tonight. I pray in the name of the Virgin Mary. Amen."

Manuel and his dog pounced into the canopied bed.

In the quietness of the dark room he lay patting his dog curled beside him. The boy felt his father's sorrow along with his own loneliness, which came each night when he turned out the lights. It was not the darkness that he was afraid of, only the loneliness that it brought.

He drifted off to the sounds of his mother's piano downstairs. He rose slightly, realizing it was only the wind chimes on the veranda and that his mother would never play her piano again. He drew the light blanket to his chin and fell into a deep slumber.

Again, Manuel Garcia dreamt of his mother's death. He remembered how strong she had been, never complaining right up until the bitter end. Into his dream came the words of his father on that Christmas morning after Father Lopez administered the last rites, as the family gathered around Maria Garcia's coffin in the great hall. "Your mother is in heaven now and she watches over us each day while she plays for the angels. So my children, never let her down."

Downstairs it was now Maria's time to be alone with Papa. Don Carlos dreaded the thought that it would soon be time for Maria to go away to the music conservatory at the University of Madrid. After her mother's death she had become the surrogate mother for her brothers, and Don Carlos had depended heavily on her for that.

"Papa, what did you say to Eduardo?"

Don Carlos shrugged lightly. "I took care of Eduardo. If he so much as speaks to you let me know."

"Yes, Papa," the girl blushed, glancing at the floor.

"Oh, Maria, my beautiful daughter. Each day you remind me more of your mother, God rest her soul. It's you that I am worried about. Are you happy? You have so many responsibilities with the villa and with school. You're doing a wonderful job with your brothers."

"This house is nothing for me. We have such good servants who take care of the domestic chores and Gerardo is the greatest chef. It's you that we're all worried about, Papa. It's the Americans, isn't it?"

Don Carlos took a long draw on his cigar. *Fidel Castro is destroying my way of life, not the Yankees. They need my sugar. I will be safe with them. How can this possibly be happening to me now? Last year my wife died at thirty-seven, and now Castro destroys everything. When should I tell Maria about my plans for my children's evacuation?*

"Maria, Fidel Castro will cause our family more trouble than the Yankees ever will."

"How so?"

"Castro will try to take away our family's land someday, but don't worry about it tonight," Carlos said, and getting up and walking to the arched doorway, he turned off the light.

"Papa, what did Eduardo say?" the girl asked as they entered the hallway.

"Maria, *never* mention his name again to me; only, that is, if he should ever bother you. Is that clear?"

"I'm sorry."

"There is nothing to be sorry for, I love you so much."

"I am worried about the Americans. What will we do?"

"We will go to bed and say our prayers and get a good night's rest. Tomorrow will be a busy day."

In the Bay of Pigs only a few miles away, a young American Army officer stood on the afterdeck of an approaching ship as the lights went out in the Casa de Azucar. Don Carlos lay awake, thinking of the DGI's investigation and his warning to Father Lopez that morning at the church: *"Father Lopez, tomorrow our lives turn into a living hell."*

Chapter Nine

The Bay of Pigs

April 16, 1961

The surplus Navy LCI *Blagar* was making a steady eight knots in light seas with Lieutenant William G. Morris standing on the fantail searching the dark Caribbean waters for a glimpse of the Cuban coast. His guts were knotted, having never been in combat before. *I better not drop the ball this time,* he thought, remembering having gone from hero to zero after missing the winning touchdown pass that would have given West Point a perfect 1958 season. How he dropped the "Pitt pass" would be a question Tex Morris would be asked for the rest of his life.

It was H-hour minus 3, and he couldn't stop thinking of Gray's orders: "If you get captured, blow your brains out."

The lieutenant realized that he was risking his life in complete anonymity—without fame, fortune or glory—to become a corpse without campaign ribbons or medals to mark his early grave in a place called the *Bahia de Los Cochinos* or Bay of Pigs.

Tex nervously paced the deck, dressed in Cuban fatigues absent of American rank or insignia, which made him a spy the second he stepped ashore. His floppy hat covered his face, which was smeared with camouflage grease, leaving only the whites of his eyes visible in the dark. If Lara Jane Morris could see her son now she would have thought he was a mercenary steaming up the Congo on the *African Queen* and not a Special Forces officer of the Army of the United States.

Tex was having a hard time conquering his fears. By sunrise he could be an unidentified body floating in the surf being eaten by crabs. By sundown he could very well be dead in this covert Cuban invasion code-named "Operation Zapata," which was known only to the president and top officials at the CIA and Pentagon.

He ran over Gray's orders once again to make sure he had it right. "Tex, it's critical you take San Blas by surprise and capture the local militia. If I give the order, blow the bridge to cut off Castro's counterattack from the north. Hold San Blas until the paratrooper reinforcements are dropped at daybreak at Covadonga. Hold your position until the 4th Battalion relieves you and then fall back to the beach. Don't get captured."

"What if I do?"

"Get captured?" asked Gray Lynch, the CIA officer whose mission it was to ensure Operation Zapata succeeded. "Don't, and that's an order. No Americans are taking part in this operation. Absolutely none! Roger?"

"Roger."

"This whole operation depends on capturing the bridge at San Blas," Gray said again with urgency in his voice, "The airfield at Giron cannot be overrun by a counterattack or we lose our air cover. San Blas must be taken and held until the 4th Battalion's armor secures the railroad at Real Campiña twenty clicks inland. B-26s will be arriving at the airfield at daylight. If things break down, I'll give you the order to blow the bridge across the Zapata Swamp canal to stop a counterattack."

Tex Morris strained to see the first signs of the island. *Simple damn mission. Take eight Cubans I've never trained with and take San Blas by daylight. Well, at least my guys have experience raiding Cuba, and Gray says they're the best he's got. Why Kennedy changed the beachhead from Trinidad to the Bay of Pigs beats the hell out of me.*

The fear in the lieutenant's gut told him that the chances for accomplishing his mission during the next twenty-four hours were slim. *One American and fifteen hundred Cuban exiles against Castro's forty thousand men. Damn! These are worse odds than Davy Crockett had at the Alamo. This time Number 88's not going to drop the fucking ball.*

The fluorescent dial on his wristwatch glowed H minus 3. He leaned over the railing, peered down into the phosphorus sparkling in the wake, and heaved his guts out.

Tex wiped his mouth and glanced around to make sure he was alone before taking a deep breath of the salt air and reevaluating his odds. *How many defenders at San Blas? How many will have to be killed? Will our landing on Blue Beach at 0100 go undetected? I'll need a lot of luck to move eight miles inland undetected and capture the enemy sleeping.*

Then Tex asked himself *the* question that hit him the hardest: *Why in the hell am I doing this? Liberating Cuba from Communist Castro is one thing, but is a Communist Cuba worth dying for?*

Tex was having second thoughts now as he scanned the horizon at the silhouettes of the invasion's blacked-out transports and U.S. Navy destroyers steaming in formation. It reminded him of a scene from *Guns of Navarone,* and he knew he played a major role in this picture show. The lieutenant also knew the movie, "Operation Zapata starring Tex Morris from Odessa, Texas," would never be seen in the marquee lights at the Rex Theater back home.

Tex watched as the *USS San Marcos* majestically appeared out of the dark and began moving up the convoy from astern. Harbored inside the LSD's huge open well deck were the CIA's landing craft for the Cuban invasion. In a few hours, *La Brigada 2506* that Tex trained in the jungles of Guatemala would launch their invasion to overthrow Fidel Castro. *I might be scared shitless, but Tex Morris is an American soldier, damn proud of taking part in the liberation of Cuba.*

Gray Lynch left the ship's bridge and climbed down the ladder to the radio shack. The bull-necked ex-commando in his early fifties carried wounds from Normandy, the Battle of the Bulge, and Heartbreak Ridge in Korea. He was the CIA equivalent of an unofficial military commander for the Cuban exiles. Unconventional warfare was the profession of the Spanish-speaking ex-Special

Forces captain just back from having served his last tour in counterinsurgency in his country's "secret war" in Laos.

"Contact the *San Marcos* and confirm the landing craft rendezvous with *Blagar* at 0100 hours to switch out American for Cuban crews," Gray ordered, having made up his mind he was going ashore to inspect the beaches before H-hour. If he didn't like what he found, he would abort the invasion.

Gray glanced at his watch. *I hope all of the arms we smuggled to the Cuban underground from Key West have gotten into the right hands. If Morris gets captured or killed my ass is grass, but it's a risk I have to take.*

Gray knew the operation had problems before the president changed the beachhead from Trinidad to the Bay of Pigs. You don't fight in three wars without getting gut feelings when things are going to get screwed up. War is unpredictable at best, and without the six thousand political prisoners in Trinidad he had no army to fight with, yet the president and the CIA ordered the invasion to take place.

Where's my man, Tex? Gray was thinking as he made his way aft. They had met only a few days ago in the Bar Estrella in the stinking Nicaraguan port of Puerto Cabezas when the *Blagar* joined the invasion fleet. Tex had just flown in with the brigade from the CIA's secret base in the Guatemalan mountains where he had spent the last six months training the Cuban exiles.

De Oppresso Liber, to liberate from oppression, was the bonding motto of the two Special Forces officers the night they met. It went unspoken that they were members of the most elite fighting force on the planet. "Gray is the name and kicking Commies' asses is my game," Gray had said as he extended his hand. "I wasn't in port for two seconds before hearing you were in charge of the finest whorehouse south of El Paso!"

"Thank you, sir. It's a pleasure to met you, Mr. Lynch."

"I've been at this game for a while and I'll be damned if I ever heard of the Company financing a brothel. No wonder the men call you *El Grande.*"

"Yes, sir. Didn't have anything to do with it, sir."

"Cut out the sir shit and just call me Gray like all the rest of these bums around here," Gray said, laughing. "Let's grab a beer. We gotta talk."

Gray was amidship now making a final check of the men and equipment. The fact that he was about to violate a direct order from the president was giving him heartburn. *Screw the son-of-a-bitch*, he decided. *Kennedy is covering his political ass and couldn't care less about how many of these Cubans get killed.*

Tex was still on the fantail and wished he could pick up the phone and call Teresa Ortiz who was probably in San Jose running the Key Largo. He was thinking about the Casa de Teresa in the coolness of the Guatemala mountains, and how many times they had made love. *My God, maybe Teresa is right,* the lieutenant was thinking, remembering her Latin passion and how good their last night had been before she suddenly disappeared.

Max, his Bravo fire-team leader, walked up and placed a hand on his shoulder. "*El Grande,* my friend. How are you?"

"A little nervous."

"Who the hell's not nervous?" Max replied. "For the past six months, after training at this closed Navy installation south of New Orleans, I nearly pissed in my pants running guns with Gray for the underground out of Miami."

"No kidding?" Tex asked, watching the medium-height man with a very long and very tanned face with the moves of a boxer—light on his feet and always a step ahead of the others. *The perfect squad leader,* he had been told by Gray when he introduced them yesterday.

"You in the Army or Marines?" Max asked after a long silence, "and what are you doing here?"

It was the lieutenant's story and he wanted to tell it—perhaps as a confession, or perhaps just to kill time before a captive audience as H-hour was quickly approaching. "I'm in the Army. I could have played football at Texas or A&M and gone home and run my dad's drilling supply company instead of being a military officer."

"Some guys are made for the military, some of us aren't. I'm a lawyer. Graduate of NYU, and was practicing in Havana when Castro's secret police tried to arrest me as an enemy of the Revolution. I was lucky to get to Miami. Four days in the Florida Straits with nothing to eat and little to drink. I swore if God would let me live, I would return to kill the son-of-a-bitch. Thank you, *El Grande*, for joining *La Brigada*."

"You've really got a case of the red-ass for Fidel, don't you?"

"Some people would say that, especially when I know there's a good chance the son-of-a-bitch will kill us tonight."

Tex let out a nervous laugh that made his stomach roll. "I can remember my dad saying at the VFW picnics that my great granddaddy died with Davy Crockett at the Alamo. Of course, he's a bullshitter, so I doubt if it's true. But I do know he fought Rommel in North Africa with General Patton. I wish I could call him up right now."

"You Texans are fighting and lying son-of-a-bitches!"

"Roger that, and don't leave out humping women, partner. I guess I was just born to follow my family tradition. Senator Johnson got me an appointment to West Point."

"Oh! You are a West Pointer and know the vice president?"

"Yeah, but don't mention it. We aren't supposed to talk about that shit out here. You know, my dad and Johnson are asshole buddies. In Texas politics money talks and bullshit walks, and dad has plenty of both. Now, my mom, she raised hell about me joining the Army, but when we flew to Washington to have lunch in the senate dining room she got okay with it. We spent two nights at the senator's house and I met his daughters. I remember mom telling me later that if I had a lick of sense I'd forget about the Army and marry one of the Johnson girls."

"Now I know why you're here, *El Grande*. Johnson wanted to keep you away from his señoritas."

"*No way!* Anyhow, I got an infantry commission. Graduated number ninety-eight in my class, if you can you believe that for a ball player who started at end for three years."

"You're 'the lonesome end?' The all-American from West Point?"

"No," Tex laughed. "That was a fellow named Bill Carpenter, and we went 8-0-1 in '58 and beat the shit out of Navy 22 to 6. Would have had a perfect season except I dropped the damn ball in the end zone in the 14-14 tie with the University of Pittsburgh. God, I hated screwing up Coach Blaik's perfect season."

"It takes eleven players sixty minutes to win a football game, Tex. Just like this invasion, a lot of teamwork."

"Well, I've been catching hell for it ever since, especially in infantry basic at Fort Benning, and jump school and ranger training. Everywhere I go in this man's Army somebody says, 'Hey, aren't you Number 88, the guy that dropped the Pitt pass?'"

"I don't know anything about your Army, just hitting the beach and dropping off guns out of Gray's speedboat. Did you say you were a ranger, Tex?"

"Special Forces."

"Ooh! I see, Señor West Pointer, Special Forces guerrilla killer!" the lawyer laughed.

"Cut it out! We aren't supposed to talk about that shit. Tell you what…"

"Lie to me, *El Grande.*"

"This is no lie. There was this blond hostess at the Fort Benning O Club I was screwing. Most determined woman I ever met on getting married, so I slipped out when I got my orders for Bragg. I'll never forget *Sea of Love* playing on the radio when I cleared post with all my junk in the trunk of my Ford ragtop. Signed in with the duty officer at the Special Warfare Center at Bragg. And you know what, Max?"

"Keep lying, *El Grande.*"

"No shit! I went directly over to the 82nd O Club annex and met this gal that was stacked like a brick shithouse and we went over to her place…"

"*El Grande,* stop worrying about that Pitt pass. You're *La Brigada*'s hero, building them a whorehouse in Guatemala."

"I didn't have shit to do with it. It was the doings of a little wormy guy named Walter Elliot. But I did have twenty-seven of the best NCOs train your guys into one lean, mean, fighting machine. I wish I had my troops with us tonight. Hell, Max, I guess I'm the only man on this ship that's never been shot at before."

"Yeah, but don't worry, soon it'll happen. Just keep your head down and don't try to be a hero."

"No hero. Right, Max," Tex said, with his mind playing back the voice of General Yarborough, the commandant of the Special Warfare Center. "Lieutenant, I've cut you TDY orders to the Pentagon. Report at 0800 hours tomorrow morning to the Chief of the Office of Personnel Operations. Here, take your 201 file along with you when you go."

"May I ask what this is all about, General?"

"Can't discuss it with you, Tex, but Special Warfare asked for and got my best first lieutenant. Good luck, son."

"First Lieutenant, sir?"

"Step over here," the general ordered, opening a small blue velvet box and pinning on the silver bars.

Tex recalled the Southern Airways DC3 lumbering up to the gate at National Airport in Washington later that same afternoon. A cold north wind blew against the wool trousers of his Class A uniform bloused over his spit-shined Cochran jump boots as he walked off the plane. He was on his way to the officer's guesthouse at Fort Belvoir, Virginia.

The next morning, he made his first visit to the Pentagon's sprawling thirty-four acres of what seemed like a rat's maze and signed in with the duty officer. After clearing security, he was delighted to see the familiar face of Chief Warrant Officer Roy Johnson from the personnel section at West Point, who greeted him with a grin. "What's up, Chief?" Tex asked as they walked toward the administration section.

"I've been in this man's Army for over twenty years, lieutenant. You Special Forces guys are doing some really off-the-wall stuff lately," Johnson replied in his Mississippi drawl as he double-checked Tex's file. "You still catching hell, number 88? You know, I was at that game when you dropped the Pitt pass in the end zone."

"Roger, Chief. They didn't put that shit in my 201 file, did they?"

"No, but I'm thinking about it," Johnson said with a straight face, before flashing Tex a big grin.

Fifteen minutes later they were in the Pentagon Special Warfare branch talking to a lieutenant colonel who reviewed his file before dismissing Johnson. "Okay, lieutenant, go in and report to the colonel in the conference room."

To Tex's surprise, a United States Marine Corps colonel with brown wavy, close-clipped hair was seated at a mahogany conference table. He reminded Tex of a Hollywood movie star whose name he couldn't remember. Seated next to the colonel was a young man in a business suit.

Tex snapped to attention and saluted. "Lieutenant William G. Morris reporting as ordered, sir."

Colonel Jack Hawkins, a lean officer with a chest full of medals from World War II and Korea and the paramilitary chief of the CIA Cuban Task Force for the invasion, returned his salute. "At ease, lieutenant. Meet Walter Elliot from the CIA and have a seat."

"Good morning, Mr. Elliot," Tex said, getting a weak handshake from the man who looked like a college freshman. *So this gimpy little fucker is what a live CIA guy looks like*, Tex thought as he sat down.

The colonel finally finished a meticulous review of his personnel file before handing it to Mr. Elliot, who read it in less than thirty seconds and shoved it back.

"This conversation is classified top secret. Do you understand?"

"Yes sir."

"Lieutenant Morris, we are looking for a Special Forces officer with your training experience. The Special Forces Warfare Center tells us that in the past year you have been doing a damn fine job down at Fort Bragg. You're the man for the job, we think."

"Thank you, sir."

"I'm told that you're fluent in Spanish."

"I was raised in Odessa, Texas, sir. I've been conversant with the Mexicans since I was born. Took couple of years of Spanish in high school and passed the Special Forces Spanish language course. But I'd be the first to admit that my conversational Spanish is a far sight better than my writing."

Colonel Hawkins glanced over at the CIA officer, who looked bored. The colonel thought for a moment, sizing up the soldier who sat erect, confident and alert, yet relaxed, appearing older than twenty-two. "You have any questions for the lieutenant, Mr. Elliot?"

Morris is your typical dumb jock, Walter had been thinking. *West Pointer, no imagination, lots of brawn but little brains, well programmed to blindly follow orders. If he's the colonel's choice, he'll be fine with Axial Hanson.* "Lieutenant, do you have any wedding plans anytime soon?"

"No sir."

The colonel glanced back at Mr. Elliot, who touched the rim of his glasses and gave a slight nod. Hawkins had spent four months preparing the Trinidad plan for the invasion and he could not afford to select the wrong man.

The colonel finally nodded in approval: *Morris will be the right officer.* "Okay, Lieutenant Morris. You are assigned to a top-secret operation for the CIA. You will be working for me and have a training section of twenty-seven Special Forces NCOs from Bragg under your command. You will receive no written orders and be assigned on indefinite temporary duty status here at the Special Warfare branch. Go with Mr. Elliot. I want you to get changed into civvies. Do you feel comfortable with this assignment?"

"Yes sir. Thank you, sir."

"Damn good answer, mister. I'll give General Yarborough a call personally and thank him for sending me the right officer," the colonel said leaning back in his chair. "You're dismissed, and may I remind you again, lieutenant, this is a top-secret mission. Open your mouth and I'll have your ass. Understand?"

"Yes sir, colonel," Tex replied, snapping to attention, trying to wipe the grin off his face when Mr. Elliot stood up and knocked over Colonel Hawkins' briefcase.

The Lieutenant's watch showed 2330 hours when Max drew him back into the conservation. "What happened to you then, Tex?"

"I spent the afternoon in a shabby World War II barracks in the CIA compound on the Washington Mall with this nerd Elliot who didn't say much, just stared holes in me like I was some kind of military freak. Took me to the shrink for a psychological exam. And you know what? Son-of-a-bitch asked if I was a queer."

"Well, are you, big boy?"

"Screw you, Max! Then after a couple of hours Elliot came in with a set of Sears work khakis and a plane ticket to Miami. That afternoon I was in a rundown building on the old Navy air base at Opa-Locka near the Miami airport. The very next day I flew to Camp Trax in the Guatemala mountains to start training you guys."

Max was no longer listening. *This kid's scared stiff,* thought the seasoned gunrunner who had done this many times before. Max was fighting that emptiness a man gets just before he goes into combat even though the night was just right—no moon and calm seas. "What did Gray tell you about going in?"

"Just not to get captured. I'm scared shitless, man."

"You always are, no matter how many times you do it. Gray's counting on us. He's afraid the 4th will get bogged down and not take Real Campiña on time."

"There's not much chance we will make it unless the locals revolt. If they don't, the Navy and the Marines had better step in and bail us out."

"Don't worry, *El Grande,* the Cubans hate Castro, and there's always lots of 'ifs' in an invasion. Gray's right. Don't get captured, and if you do, blow your head off, it will be a better way to die than if Castro gets ahold of you."

"Roger that."

"My *amigo,* Hugo, is running the boats, so get back to the beach and he will get you back to the ship."

"You don't think we're going to make it, do you, Max?"

"I'm a lawyer and no one is paying me to make predictions, *El Grande,* so let's just go out there and take San Blas and everything will be okay. There's the coast. *Buena suerte, mi amigo.*"

"Good luck to you too."

"You guys ready?" Gray asked, walking up.

"We're ready," Tex replied.

"I'll never forget the morning we hit Omaha Beach on D-Day, 2nd Infantry Division, and I've never been so scared."

Tex turned and looked at his mentor. "Were you really?"

"Yeah, and I'll tell you something else. I'm scared as hell right now. I'm going in after you guys to inspect the beach."

Gazing out at the low dark coast of Cuba for the first time, the smell of the island came with the salt air, bringing Tex Morris the inner peace that suddenly overcame his fear. "Gray, if I die in San Blas, remember my parents live in Odessa. Tell my dad I didn't drop the ball."

"Don't, then, Number 88. Now let's shove off."

Chapter Ten

Battle of San Blas

April 17, 1961

Manuel Garcia slid into home plate at Yankee Stadium to the roaring cheers of thousands of New Yorkers. "What's wrong, Blanco?" the awakening boy muttered as he sat up in his bed with the pinstripes of his dream vanishing to the vicious barks of his dog. "Papa! Papa!" he cried out, hearing the distant thunder of high explosives and seeing the skies over Playa Giron illuminated with tracers through his window.

Down the hall, Don Carlos was blasted out of a fitful sleep by the explosions and the cries of his son. He ran up the watchtower in his nightshirt for a better view of the battle of Playa Giron three miles to the south. "Oh my God," he gasped, rubbing his eyes with disbelief seeing tracers crisscrossing the night sky. "The Yankees have invaded us!"

Don Carlos bolted down the steps and into the villa. "Children! Get up! Get the boys up, Maria! The Yankees have invaded! We must leave at once!" he shouted, ringing for Gerardo before slipping on his trousers and dashing into Manuel's room.

"Go where, Papa?" Manuel asked as he followed his father down the hall toward Alfredo's room with Blanco still barking.

95

"Go get dressed, Manuel. *Hush* Blanco! Put on your school clothes, son, and hurry."

"Are the Americans coming to kill us?" cried Alfredo, tears streaming from his sleepy eyes.

"No. Stop crying and be brave," his father ordered. "Maria? Are you dressed yet?"

"Almost, Papa. What should I do next?"

"Get Alfredo dressed quickly. Pack your suitcase and Alfredo's, the small ones, and then help Manuel pack his."

Gerardo ran up the stairs, still in nightclothes, his dark eyes terrified with fear. "What's happening in Giron?" he gasped.

"The Yankees are invading. Now go pack the children some sandwiches and something to drink. Quickly. We've got to go."

"Si, señor, will the Yankees bomb the casa?"

"Go! Go! I don't know, Gerardo. We have no time to waste. When you're finished packing the food, bring my car around front and don't turn on the head-lights."

"Si, señor."

Don Carlos ran to his room to finish getting dressed, grabbing his snub-nosed .38 revolver and slipping it into his belt. He glanced out the window at the sight of the battle and then rushed to get the children, making sure they had their suitcases. "Come quickly, children, downstairs," he ordered, yelling at Blanco to stop barking as he went.

Gerardo had pulled the car in the circular drive, its engine idling and the lights turned out, "I am taking the children to San Blas. Turn off all the lights in the villa and go warn the macheteros to stay in their quarters. I will be back in one hour. Go get Señor Luis up to meet me for breakfast."

"Si Señor. I hope he's not in Cienfuegos at the casino."

"Just find him right away."

"Where are we going, Papa?" Manuel asked as he put his suitcase in the trunk, and then stooped to pick up Blanco.

"No, Manuel. Blanco must stay with Gerardo."

"But Papa, *no!* The Yankees are coming! I must take him! Oh, please let me take Blanco," cried the boy clutching the dog to his chest.

"Gerardo and I will take care of Blanco," his father said softly, taking the dog from the boy's arms and placing him on the ground. Blanco sat on his haunches whining, seeming to sense something bad was happening to his world.

As the Olds pulled away in the dark, Manuel stuck his head out the window. "No Blanco! Stay! Feed Blanco, Gerardo, please." His voice trailed away as the Casa de Azucar faded into a framed backdrop of exploding ordnance in the distant sky as the car turned up the drive with Maria asking, "Papa, where are we going?"

"Are you coming too, Papa?"

"Children, quiet for a minute. Quiet, everyone, please!"

"Turn your lights on," Manuel said.

"I don't want to be detected on the road to San Blas by the Americans. Now listen, children. I am taking you to San Blas to Father Lopez. He will see that you get safely to your Aunt Roscena at the Colombian Embassy in Havana. Maria, you are very familiar with the place?"

"Yes. We've been there many times. Why the embassy?"

"You'll be safe there. Neither the Americans nor Castro can touch you while you are in the safety of the embassy with Aunt Roscena."

"Papa, come with us," Manuel begged, leaning over the front seat, putting his arm around his father's shoulders as the car turned toward the San Blas highway.

"I will come later. Now remember, boys! *Manuel*—are you and Alfredo listening to me?"

"*Si,* Papa."

"Do exactly as Maria and Father Lopez say. She is responsible for the two of you and Manuel you best not pick on your brother. Do you understand, my brave sons?"

"Who are the Yankees?"

Manuel, without thinking, smacked his brother on the head. "Who are the Yankees? Alfredo, you are so stupid!"

"Stop it, Manuel, or I will take off my belt," Carlos ordered.

"The Americans are the Yankees, Alfredo."

97

"That's better, now, Maria, before I forget, take this and put it inside your bra."

"What is it?"

"It's two thousand U.S. dollars and some pesos."

"Why dollars? The Americans are invading."

"I know, but their money is good in all countries. Go ahead, put it away."

* * *

Hugo Sanchez commanded the first attack wave of LCMs headed for Blue Beach. Tracers from the *Blagar's* 50-caliber machine guns streaked overhead, raising the hair on his neck as the landing craft vibrated underneath him. He was wondering if Tex Morris and his men got through the enemy lines when the boat struck the beach, and the coxswain revved the diesels. "Drop the ramp," Hugo ordered, as the men of the 4th Battalion charged into the knee-deep water screaming, *"Adelante! Adelante!"* The Bay of Pigs invasion had begun with *La Brigada* on Cuban soil at Playa Giron.

An hour earlier, Tex and his men had been put ashore in a black rubber boat powered by an 18-horsepower silent outboard. They waded onto the deserted beach beyond the intersections of the bypass roads on the east end of Giron.

The squad slipped into the woods, bypassing the town, which, to their amazement, was illuminated with streetlights running along the beach. They crept past the Giron barracks, where a hundred militiamen were asleep, and made their way to the San Blas highway undetected.

So far, so good, Tex thought, checking his watch as he signaled for his men to move out. *The landing couldn't have gone better if we had rehearsed it a hundred times.*

It was still five hours before daylight and the patrol had advanced along the Giron highway through dense underbrush that opened up to fields of partially harvested sugar cane. Armed with M3A submachine guns and moving in a wedge, they advanced in an overwatch formation with Tex behind the Alpha fire team. Max brought up the rear with his Bravo team armed with the two BARs. Suddenly, behind them, the sky lit up with tracers and the percussion of high explosives. The invasion of Cuba had begun making contact with the enemy possible at any time.

The men were spread three meters apart and moving rapidly, their silhouettes visible in the weak light on the white surface of the chert highway. Only the sounds of their feet and heavy breathing broke the silence. *Eight miles is a lot of real estate to cover before first light*, Tex was thinking, setting the pace with a double time shuffle and hoping no one came up from behind them, fleeing Giron.

In his pocket, Tex had an ESSO road map of the area that was better than nothing. He recalled Gray's intelligence briefing from the Cuban underground that estimated the strength of the San Blas garrison at forty militiamen. They were quartered in a two-story barracks on the far side of the village, fifty yards from the causeway bridge across the Zapata Canal. The enemy was armed with a few Soviet submachine guns, but mostly with M52 Czech bolt-action rifles. He had to take them sleeping. The element of surprise was critical. If any vehicles came up the highway from Giron, he had ordered his men to stop them, even if it meant killing the driver and commandeering his vehicle.

Ahead, the highway took a hard turn to the right and it was time for a breather. Sentries were placed up and down the road and the rest of the men gathered inside an abandoned building. "How we doing, men?" Tex asked, dropping his heavy pack filled with twenty pounds of C4 plastic explosives and taking a long drink from his canteen.

The men were sweating profusely under their heavy loads, but morale seemed high by the sounds of their eager replies. "Okay guys, this is the halfway point. Anybody having trouble keeping up?"

"Tex, will you order us a Casa de Teresa from Washington when we capture San Blas?" Max asked, bringing forth laughter.

"We'll have our hands full, *mi amigo*. I'll take care of it when we're in Havana."

"You going all the way to Havana with us, Tex?"

"San Blas first. Now switch fire teams on the point and give the men with the BARs a rest. Here, I'll take one of them. Let's get ready to move out. Remember, we have to stop all vehicles coming up from the rear. Any questions?"

"How we doing on time?" Max asked.

"We're doing okay. Let's move out."

Twenty minutes up the road, Tex heard the roar of a vehicle long before he could see it or tell in which direction it was traveling. The men had heard it too as they broke to opposite sides of the highway and took up positions in the ditches. The sound grew louder. *Where the hell is it coming from?* Tex wondered, rising to his knees and realized it was slowing down to his right, perhaps twenty meters ahead. "Sounds like a car, but where the hell is it?" he whispered, straining to see the vehicle that had nearly stopped. "Keep down, but be ready to take it out," Tex ordered as the black phantom swung into the highway just ahead of them and roared off, kicking up a cloud of dust.

"Hold your fire!" Tex shouted, as he stood and drew a bead with his BAR on the car's disappearing taillights. His trigger finger tightened. Split second decisions—*shoot or don't shoot? Have we been detected? Should I take a chance and let the car pass?*

Tex lowered his weapon, putting on the safety. "Move out," he ordered, with the fading sound of the car pumping fresh fear into his guts.

Inside that car, Manuel marveled at his father's ability to drive without headlights. "Papa, how do you know how to keep the car between the ditches?" he asked, holding onto the seat.

"I drive with my eyes on the horizon, so don't be nervous. I've driven this road a million times. We'll be at San Blas soon."

"Please, go with us, Papa," Maria pleaded.

"Don't worry. I will meet you in Havana at Aunt Roscena's. She will take care of you until I can get there."

"Bring Blanco, Papa! Please bring Blanco!"

"I will try to, Manuel. Blanco will be just fine with Gerardo. Be brave, now," Don Carlos replied, thanking God that he was driving in the dark so his children couldn't see the tears welling up in his eyes.

Ten minutes later the car slowly entered the sleeping village to be greeted by dawn and the lonely bark of a stray dog. Crossing the Plaza de Armas, its tail-lights cast a red glow on the back entrance to the church when it stopped. "Stay here for a minute and stay quiet," Don Carlos whispered. Feeling for his pistol, he eased open his door and walked quickly toward the church.

"Father Lopez," he said, rapping on the door as the stray dog came up whining for food. "Father Lopez," he said again, slowly turning the doorknob with the tired hinges squeaking as it opened. Hearing the priest snoring, he struck a match and shouted, "Father Lopez! Wake up!"

"What? Who's there?"

"It's Carlos. You must get up! Quickly, the Americans have invaded Playa Giron."

"Don Carlos? Is that you, my son?" asked the priest with a yawn.

"Yes, Father. Light your lamp quickly. I have the children in the car. We must get them to Havana at once."

"What time is it?"

"Nearly three in the morning. I will bring the children inside. Are you dressed?"

"Yes, bring the children, I am getting up. Dear God, the Americans have invaded us?"

Inside the church the children gathered around the table in the priest's stale quarters with the kerosene lamp casting spooky shadows on the polished marble floor. "Padre, can you get the children to the train in Real Campiña by ten this morning?"

"If the bus is on time."

"What time does the bus leave from San Blas?"

"The bus will leave here at nine o'clock. Plenty of time to make the train to Havana if the bus is still coming."

"Yes. The bus goes from Real Campiña to Giron and back daily, right?"

"That is the route."

God, Don Carlos thought. *The bus will not go to Giron because of the fighting. Do I risk taking the children the last twenty miles to catch the train? No. Too risky. It would be best to let the priest take them.*

"Castro's DGI are at the station in Real Campiña. They will be looking for my car. Be careful, the police do not suspect you."

"We will leave as soon as it is daylight."

"You have the money I gave you?"

"Of course. If the bus is not running, I will make sure they are safely on the train somehow. What is happening in Giron now?"

"I don't know. The sky is on fire with the shelling," Don Carlos replied, gathering his children to say goodbye. "I am going back home now, you are safe here with Father Lopez. Do exactly as he says."

"No, Papa, don't leave me!" young Alfredo cried, grabbing his father's leg.

"Be brave and do as Maria says. Don't worry, I will come to Havana as soon as possible, my son."

"Papa, I love you, *please* bring Blanco."

"We all love you, Papa. Be careful," Maria said without crying, pulling her brothers away.

Thank God this car can fly, Don Carlos thought, flooring the accelerator of the Olds 98, determined to get back to his villa before the DGI's arrival. Gripping the steering wheel, he was desperately trying to clear his mind of the children he left behind.

As the car sped through the night, Carlos was making plans for Luis to oversee the hacienda after his escape to Miami. The secret police would be coming at any moment and he needed to leave before daylight. He would ride his horse along the beach to Cienfuegos and, from there, hire a fishing boat to take him to the Grand Caymans or Jamaica. He would call Havana from Cienfuegos before he left to make sure the children were safe. *Don't forget the passport, and God...don't let Luis betray me.*

Don Carlos kicked the Olds into passing gear, having no way of knowing that the patrol was taking a five-minute break in the ditches up ahead.

Tex emptied his canteen thinking San Blas was at least another hour when he heard the car coming down the highway, only this time it was headed south toward Giron. "Vehicle approaching. Do you hear it? Stay down! I'll take it out."

From the sound of tires churning gravel, the vehicle was coming at an incredibly high speed. Tex flipped off the safety on his BAR just as the black phantom streaked by, spraying gravel like a Texas twister, kicking up a blinding cloud of dust. "My God, it's that same car!" Tex shouted, swinging around and firing four bursts of rapid fire into the car's taillights.

"Damn it, I missed him. He must have been doing a hundred," Tex shouted, shouldering the weapon for another try, before thinking there was no need to waste ammo, when he heard the car slowing down.

"No, I think you got him," Max whispered. "Yes, he's stopping. Where did you shoot?"

"I just shot into his rear, into the dust. Shit, I don't know!"

"Listen, the car stopped. Do I go and finish him off?" Max asked matter-of-factly.

Chapter Eleven

San Blas

April 17, 1961

The bronze cross atop the domed tower was visible on the three-tiered belfry of the Our Lady of the Assumption Church and appeared soft beige in the morning's first light. This was a bad sign to Lieutenant Tex Morris, who quickened his pace to an airborne shuffle. As they approached the village, Tex felt an anxiety attack strike. *This is just another training exercise*, he had been telling himself for the last four hours, except this time people were going to get killed.

Who was that driver? Did he alert the garrison? Was he a messenger from Giron? I hope to hell I killed him. Damn! I should have let Max go back to check it out. Whoever he was, he was up to no good or he wouldn't have been driving like a bat-out-of-hell with his lights off. If the garrison has been alerted, we're out-gunned six-to-one.

Ten minutes later, the patrol was crouching in the ditch of the highway, some fifty yards from the village of twenty buildings anchored by a church in the middle of the plaza. Tex took out his binoculars, scanning the barracks for sentries, and was pleased to find San Blas sleeping except for a stray dog that roamed the deserted streets scavenging for food.

"Okay, men, listen up," Tex whispered, wiping the sweat off his face. "It's 0500 hours and I'm going to take Alpha fire team and slip down this ditch to the swamp. We're coming in the back door of the barracks and hopefully will catch them asleep. Give us ten minutes to get into position. Then Bravo moves into the village and takes up positions surrounding the front of the barracks in the plaza by the church. If it turns into a firefight, be damn careful not to shoot us."

Tex turned his back to the village and sketched a map in the sand. "Here's the barracks. It's the two-story building located to the right of the church on the main street leading out of town, and the back door to the swamp should be about here."

"So, Bravo comes in from the main road into the village?"

"Roger, Max. Now remember, we want to capture the militiamen, not kill them."

"They're our brothers and will fight Castro only if they are alive," Max whispered.

"Okay. Synchronize your watches. It's 0503 hours. At exactly 0515, Max, move into your positions. We're hitting the back door at 0520, so be ready. Any other questions?" Tex asked, looking around at his men and feeling calm and very much in control now that it was down to the real thing.

"We'll disarm the militiamen and interrogate them," Tex continued. "If they'll join us and we can trust them, that's okay with me. If not, tie them up and hold the prisoners in the barracks or the jail, if there is one."

"They will fight with us. They are our brothers."

"I hope so, Max. After we secure the village perimeter, I'll set the demolition charges on the bridge. I want one man up in the church belfry pronto for a lookout."

"I'll go," Max volunteered, when the distant sounds of approaching aircraft sent a rooster flying up on a post, announcing dawn with a loud cock-a-doodle-do.

"Let's go," Tex grunted, adjusting his backpack. "That must be the 1st Battalion paratroopers now. Move out before the whole damn town wakes up."

* * *

In Washington, it was a quarter past six Eastern Standard Time, and Dick Bissell and General Charles Cabell were leaving Secretary of State Dean Rusk's office at the State Department. Their pleadings for a second air strike to destroy the remainder of the Cuban air force were reflected by the general's heavy sigh as he slammed Bissell's car door. "The secretary is one hard-headed man to deal with when he's made up his mind."

"Yeah, especially if he has the president's ass to cover."

"*You* said it, Dick, not me."

"Well, at least we got the air strikes reestablished over the beachhead, and if the invasion goes as planned our B-26s can land and refuel and maintain air superiority from the Giron airstrip."

"They can't without air support from the jet fighters off the *Essex* to knock out the remainder of Castro's air force."

"What's left of it after our initial raids?"

"From the U-2 photos, two T-33 jet trainers and the same number of British Sea Fury fighters and B-26s appear airworthy, that's about all," Cabell sighed.

"Well, that's not that bad, is it?"

"Yes, it's plenty bad without cover from the Navy A4Ds. The 26s don't have a chance against the T-33s if they are armed, or the Sea Furies either. Besides, the 26s don't have tail gunners to make room for extra fuel for the six-hour flight from Nicaragua. They'll be sitting ducks I'm afraid, and it's all a damn pity when we could have eliminated the rest of Castro's planes on the ground. All President Kennedy had to do was give the order."

"What time did the secretary say the president would be returning from his weekend at Glen Ora, General?"

"Ten o'clock this morning, and you had better be waiting for him on the White House lawn with your hat in your hand when the chopper lands. This thing is about to unravel and damn quickly if we lose air superiority."

"Right," replied Bissell, hurrying up the steps to Quarters Eye and bursting into a war room full of confusion. "What's the situation, Elliot? Just the important stuff."

"This is the latest poop, sir. Urgent request by Gray for air support from the *Essex*. Castro's planes just shot down two of our B-26s and sank much of the brigade's fuel and ammunition when the *Rio Escondido* exploded."

"Jesus Christ! They sank the *Rio*? Get me the White House on the horn and see if I can talk to the president at Glen Ora. We've got to have air cover."

* * *

A short blast of machine gun fire followed by shouting in the street sent young Manuel Garcia scrambling for cover under the table in the church where he had fallen asleep.

"Outside with your hands up!" shouted a voice in Spanish with a slow Texas twang followed by two more blasts of gunfire.

"Don't shoot! We surrender," a second voice pleaded.

"Keep your hands up and move it!" the first voice countered to the sounds of the Bravo team running forward in the street.

"Maria," Manuel whispered, "where *are* you?"

"Stay down, children!" the priest ordered in a whisper, crouching beside Manuel, who was now reunited with Maria and Alfredo under the table.

"Who's the officer-in-charge?" the foreign voice asked.

"I am Lieutenant Relondo Silas of the Cuban Army, señor. I'm the commander of the garrison of San Blas, and you have made a very bad mistake."

"Shut up, Silas! Search the barracks and make sure no one is left hiding," ordered the first voice. "Get two men on the perimeter of the village, Max. Lieutenant Silas, get your men in formation, hands on top of their heads."

"Sergeant, have the men fall in and do as the Americano says."

"Okay, Max, see if you can talk 'em into joining *La Brigada* if you like, but make it snappy," Tex ordered as he watched the garrison forming.

Max stepped forward: "*Amigos*, my name is Maximiliano Cassio Cortez. I was a lawyer in Havana before the Revolution. We are soldiers from the Cuban exile *La Brigada*, which landed last night at Playa Giron to liberate Cuba from the Communist, Fidel Castro. Don't be afraid. We are your comrades-in-arm in the

107

fight for freedom against the Socialists. Any man willing to join *La Brigada* step forward, and we will return your rifle and welcome you as our comrades."

Tex read the sober faces of the soldiers standing barefoot in nightshirts with their hands resting on the top of their heads. Their unshaven faces portrayed anger and resentment with every pair of contemptuous eyes staring at Max as if to say, *"to hell with you."*

As they stood humiliated, not a man uttered a single word as Max began again. "What's wrong, my amigos?" he asked, his voice higher. "Are you still asleep? *La Brigada* is here to liberate our country!"

"If you are here to liberate Cuba, why is your officer an ugly American?"

Max glanced over at Tex. "This man is big and ugly all right, lieutenant, but he's our amigo."

Silas spit on the ground. "No! He's a Yankee imperialist mercenary. The Yankee warplanes bombed Havana Saturday, killing many Cubans. We'll fight to the end with Fidel and protect Cuba from the bastards. *Death to the invaders!*"

"Don't listen to Silas," Max shouted, "Men, step forward in the name of a free Cuba."

"Any man breaking ranks will be court-martialed and shot for treason," the Cuban officer barked, turning his head, looking for movement in the ranks.

"Shut up, you Communist bastard!" Max screamed, slapping the lieutenant making a loud startling whack. "These men are my brothers, they can think for themselves. Now who will step forward and join *La Brigada* for the liberation of Cuba?"

The militiamen stood steady, their eyes straight ahead still wearing the resentment of being held captive in their underwear as Max made his final plea. "Our 4th Battalion will be here by noon. You will see then. We have tanks—many tanks—and the Cuban garrisons in Santiago de Cuba and Trinidad have already joined *La Brigada*."

Tex dropped his eyes to the ground sensing Max's anger and frustration building, when he caught a man's reflection on the balcony above him mirrored in the puddle on the street. He dropped to the pavement with his weapon belching fire, spewing spent shell casings on the ground, as the bullets riddled the enemy like he had grasped a high-voltage line. Tex watched him sink to his knees, dropping his rifle, as the gunfire echoed in the Plaza de Armas and then died away, spreading the stench of gunpowder in the early morning breeze.

"I got him!" Tex shouted, scrambling up as the dying soldier raised his fist in final defiance. *"Viva Fidel!"* he gasped, his voice trailing off as he fell from the balcony with a heavy thud.

The militiamen, cowered by the gunfire, rose slowly and looked in shock at their fallen comrade's body lying still and pale before them in a puddle of blood. A young soldier cried out, making the sign of the cross. "Jose! The American has killed Jose Onis!"

Tex ducked back into the doorway standing at the ready and shouted, "That's it, Max. Lock the prisoners in the barracks and get that body off the street, men. Max, up in the bell tower on the double."

Jesus I killed him, Tex thought, glaring down at Jose Onis' dark eyes staring hauntingly skyward and seeing the blood oozing from five bullet holes in his undershirt. The corpse exhaled a ghastly moan when the Cubans picked him up, trailing blood on the pavement in passing.

Grabbing his machine gun by the sling to keep it from shaking, Tex picked up the rifle and jacked open the bolt. "Dumb bastard, his rifle wasn't even loaded, thank God, or I would be dead," he said, handing the rifle to Max and walking away.

"Father, will the American now come to kill us, too?" Maria whispered, clutching one arm of each brother as they crouched together under the table when the door to the church burst open.

"What do you want?" Father Lopez asked, his joints creaking as he stood. "This is a place of worship, the house of God."

"Which way to the bell tower, Padre?" Max asked.

Father Lopez pointed through the sanctuary to the front of the church and motioned for the children to stay down.

"Padre, the dead soldier outside they called Jose Onis. You need to administer his last rites," Max said with the sound of his voice echoing off the tall arched lateral vaults of the sanctuary ceiling as he ran through.

All was quiet now with the first traces of sunlight creeping through the open door. The prisms of light lay softly on the floor, and through the opening a light breeze brought with it the stench of spent ammo. Alfredo began crying. "Shut up or you'll get us killed," Manuel whispered, then gasped when the shadow of a giant appeared on the floor, blocking out the sunshine.

"What do you want?" Father Lopez asked. "This is a church…"

"Relax, Padre," Tex interrupted. "We'll only be here for a short time. Why are the children on the floor? Get up, you kids," he said softly in Spanish, pulling the chairs aside. "No one will hurt you guys."

Manuel slowly stood, pushing Alfredo and Maria behind him. His eyes hit the buckle of the giant's web belt, and then slowly moved up into the blackened face of the scariest man his young eyes had ever seen. "Señor, you leave my brother and sister alone."

Tex dropped to one knee, laying his machine gun on the floor, and removed his pack. "Where are your parents?" he asked, looking in the boy's eyes.

"They are both dead, señor. Please, don't you kill us," Manuel's voice said breaking.

"No one will kill you," Tex laughed taking a chocolate bar out of his pack. "Want some candy? How old are you, señorita?"

Maria dropped her eyes and didn't answer as Manuel retreated behind the table. "Leave my sister alone, señor," he said, through clinched teeth.

Poor kids are scared shitless, Tex thought, grabbing his machine gun. "Keep the children inside, padre, and tell your people in the village to do the same and no one will get hurt."

"How long do you plan to stay?"

"That depends, Padre," Tex grunted, retrieving his pack and heading for the belfry, leaving the chocolate bar lying on the table.

"Anything happening up here?" Tex asked, seeing the southern sky over Giron covered with a blanket of thick black smoke from the burning *Rio Escondido.*

"All's quiet for the moment," Max pouted. "Those cowards."

"Yeah, I know." Tex sighed taking his binoculars and searching the highway running across the Zapata Swamp until it disappeared into ground fog. "Keep a sharp lookout to the north while I get Gray on the radio and let him know we've accomplished our mission. Then I've got to go down and wire the bridge."

An hour later the once-gentle breeze was blowing stronger and Max's anger was still burning as he paced around with his machine gun slung over his shoulder. "Tex, what's wrong with these stupid cowards? Why did they not join *La Brigada?*"

"I guess there are two sides to every fight."

"Bull shit, Tex. What time were the 1st Battalion paratroopers making their drop?"

"At daylight. Something has screwed up or they would be here by now."

"The people in Real Campiña will welcome us with open arms when we arrive, I assure you."

"Sure," Tex replied, scanning for any sign of a counterattack coming down the highway from the north. "I'll keep a close lookout. Go down and get some grub and check on the men, and don't screw with the prisoners."

"Don't worry. Those cowards are not worth it."

Tex watched the priest and Max cross the Plaza de Armas and enter the barracks where the soldier's body had been placed. The sun was now high in the sky and the wind was gusting. If Tex Morris had not just killed a man, it would have been a perfect day.

The lieutenant was wondering if the poor bastard they called Jose had a family—a wife and kids, a mother who would be furious that he had killed her son. It was either kill or be killed, and Jose Onis forgot to chamber a round and came out the loser.

Lara Jane Morris back in Odessa would have hated that he killed another mother's son, but he didn't have to tell her. She would have hated it a lot worse if Jose Onis had not forgotten to jack in a round. Maybe what Teresa said about soldiering versus whoring was right, now that he thought about it.

Tex took a drink of water from his canteen. *It's kill or be killed; that's just part of it. Before this day is over, it won't just be Jose Onis who has bit the bullet.*

The priest had administered the last rites to Private Onis and, with a crowd of parishioners following, was making his way back across the plaza. He stopped outside the Bar Habana and Tex couldn't make out what he told his parishioners. The Bar Habana had just opened as Father Lopez returned to the church, letting in the stray dog and finding Maria pacing the floor.

"Father, how are we going to get to the train?" Maria asked, nearly in tears, hearing the people in the plaza angrily discussing Jose Onis' death. Peeping out the cracked door, she could see the crowd casting resentful glances at the exiles guarding the barracks.

"No bus will be coming today, children. We will have to take the donkey cart to Real Campiña."

"What? Padre, that will take us hours."

"It's our only way unless we call upon Gabriel to swoop down from heaven and fly us there," the old priest laughed. "Feed your brothers, Maria, and I will be back very soon so that we can leave."

"I want to go home," Alfredo whimpered.

"Shut up, crybaby! We are going to Havana, and that is that!"

"You told a lie, Manuel. Papa is not dead, liar, liar."

"Stop it!" Maria snapped as the voice of the American boomed across the plaza from the belfry above.

"Max! Get Max. The 4th Battalion is coming with our armor!"

Max ran from the barracks through the open door of the church and up the steps. To the south a column was closing quickly on the highway from Giron, trailing a great white cloud of dust against the heavy black smoke of the burning ship.

"Thank God they made it," Tex calmly said, lowering his binoculars to the sounds of aircraft closing in.

Slowly the two specks grew larger in the sky to the south. "What are they?" Max asked.

112

"I don't know. Looks like B-26s. Yeah, they're our Invaders."

"Jesus Christ! Look!" Max shouted, pointing north to a cloud of dust lifting off the highway from Real Campiña, "Here comes the whole Cuban Army!"

"My God! You're right, Max. Our paratroopers were supposed to hold them. It's a horse race to see who gets here first. Alert the men."

Alfredo was clutching his sister's hand and watching Manuel feed the last of the chocolate bar to the dog lying on the floor begging for more. The priest heard the commotion outside and said, "Keep down boys, I think we're in real trouble now."

Closing from the north, the Cuban 117th Militia Battalion's sixty-vehicle convoy with a force of nine hundred men raced toward the Bay of Pigs. The B-26s had spotted the column and came in low over the belfry of the church, their engines making a deafening roar at two hundred feet. Tex watched as the planes started their strafing run on the Cubans.

The first plane's twenty-millimeter cannons blasted away, trailing white smoke in its wake as the convoy's lead vehicle exploded in a fireball. "Give 'em hell!" Max began screaming as he watched the instantaneous chain of explosions march down the column. Cuban soldiers could be seen diving for cover, escaping the deadly chatter of the plane's fifty calibers as the counterattack halted a mile north of San Blas.

Tex grinned and slapped Max on the back watching the bombers make a slow, lumbering turn over the swamp for another attack.

"More! More!" Max screamed, holding up his machine gun and jumping with excitement.

The lieutenant glanced back to the south, relieved that the 4th was nearing the village lead by an M-41 tank. "Thank God!" Tex shouted, "the 4th beat the bastards here."

Tex turned when suddenly there came screaming out of the sun two Cuban T-33s swooping down on the slow-flying B-26s like hawks closing in for the kill of a dove. "Oh shit! Look yonder, Max!" Tex shouted, as the jet's 20-millimeter cannons riddled the lead B-26's fuselage causing the plane to explode in mid-air.

"Bail out!" the lieutenant screamed as the burning wreckage came crashing down into the swamp beyond.

The second bomber broke off its attack, trying desperately to escape into the sun. The Cuban pilots gave chase, their cannons hammering away until the B-26 Invader's port engine caught ablaze trailing black smoke. Tex Morris cheered as the pilots skillfully crash landed their crippled plane into a cane field and crawled out of the wreckage. Then to his horror, he watched as Captains Pete Ray and Leo Baker of the Alabama Air National Guard were surrounded by the enemy and executed on the spot.

"You cowardly bastards! You'll never take me alive," Tex shouted as he trained his binoculars on the American pilot's corpses being loaded into a truck. The Cuban planes broke off the engagement and banked hard to the north for Havana, their jet engines screaming in a victory roll, leaving Tex with the sickening feeling that he was about to meet the pilot's fate.

Below, the clattering tracks of the tank and armored trucks maneuvered into the village, taking up positions on the flanks and in the street directly below the belfry. While their engines idled, the commander got out of his jeep, looked up at Tex, and saluted.

There was a moment of calm in San Blas, broken only by the distant secondary explosions of bombed vehicles on the Real Campiña highway. It was high noon and there was no tolling of Our Lady of the Assumption's bell as Tex gave the order, "Max, go down and show the 4th commander the way up here on the double."

"Padre, tell the people to evacuate the village," Max said as he ran out of the church. "This place is going to catch hell."

Eduardo Martinez watched from the door of the Bar Habana with his father, his face bleeding from freshly squeezed zits.

Chapter Twelve

D-Day, Bay of Pigs

Monday, April 17, 1961

"Oh my God!" the driver screamed, slumping down in his seat, as shattered glass from the rear window showered the car's interior. Don Carlos floored the accelerator when the second barrage struck the engine block, barely missing him and silencing the Havana radio station.

"You son of a bitches!" he swore when the car starting swerving dangerously out of control while he pumped the dead accelerator and fought the wheel. *Don't touch the brakes or the taillights will come on,* he thought as his fishtailing Olds plowed into the ditch.

Carlos jerked open his door and rolled out, drawing his pistol as he went. The rancid smell of motor oil simmering on the hot manifold hit him in the face as he held his breath, wondering if his assailants were coming to finish him off. The car's punctured radiator slowly hissed out of steam, leaving only the sounds of the crickets and fear to accompany him.

There was someone coming down the road, but he thanked God that it was only the distant sounds of the battle of Giron. He shrugged, feeling blood trickle down his face while his heart slowly receded from his throat.

Standing on rubbery legs, he once again strained to see if his attackers were coming to find his corpse. Stuffing his pistol in his belt, Carlos wiped the blood off his face with his handkerchief and began walking home. *Thank God the children are safe with Father Lopez in San Blas or they would have just been killed.*

Don Carlos felt that whoever ambushed him knew he had left home and he didn't think it was Castro's secret police. There was too much confusion with the Yankee invasion for the police to be worried about him now. *Could it have been Luis,* was the thought that ran through Carlos' mind. *Luis could have had time to lay the ambush after I left for San Blas!*

Surely to hell, Luis wasn't involved, Carlos thought, starting his slow jog toward the Casa de Azucar, three miles away. It was much shorter to cut cross-country and navigate off the villa's tower, looming on the horizon. He was running now, stumbling and falling in the dark as he went. *At least my shortcut takes me away from another ambush,* he thought, trudging into the first traces of dawn.

The sun was well above the horizon by the time the exhausted Don arrived at the Casa de Azucar. His blackened shirt trailed a stream of sweat as he ran up the spiral steps of the villa to Blanco's welcoming barks. Gerardo hustled out of the kitchen almost tripping over the dog. "Don Carlos! Where have you been? My God, look at you!"

"I'm okay, Gerardo. I'm a mess but alive." Don Carlos replied laying the pistol on the kitchen table and patting the dog. "Good boy. Down. *Down*, Blanco."

"The children? Are they safe with Father Lopez?"

"Yes. Where is Luis?"

"He went to look for you on his horse when you did not return. Where is your car?"

"Which way did he go?"

"I don't know. Señor, where is your car?"

"I was ambushed on the San Blas highway. I'm lucky to be alive. My Olds, it's shot all to hell, goddamn them. Did Luis say which way he was going?"

"No, señor. I assume up the San Blas highway."

"Oh my God! They will ambush Luis, too."

"The Yankees?"

"I think so, Gerardo. You must go and look for Luis!"

The chief wiped his hands nervously on the apron before nodding his head. "Your breakfast is waiting, señor. Luis has already eaten. Come and eat, you look exhausted."

"I need a drink of water and my coffee before you leave."

Gerardo disappeared into the kitchen and returned in a few seconds, handing Carlos the glass of water with the look of a man who had just encountered a ghost. Then a weak smile painted his worried face as he ran to the window, hearing the distant sound of galloping hoofs. "Don Carlos, look! Thank the almighty, Luis is back."

Carlos had already run out onto the veranda as Luis dismounted. Gerardo looked on in disbelief as the men embraced, giving short whacks on each other's backs. The Don peered up at his half-brother with tears in his eyes. "Luis, you're alive! You're alive!"

Don Carlos fought to regain his composure by draping his arm around Luis' shoulder as the two men walked back inside. Carlos' life was unraveling before him. He was relieved to know that Luis had not tried to kill him in the ambush. The man who had disgraced the Garcia family for nearly half a century was stepping up to help when he needed him the most. Don Carlos glanced at his brother and was feeling guilty that each day of his life Luis had hidden his anger, hurt, and pride and never hinted that he was a member of the family when they were children growing up.

Carlos shook Luis' hand. "Thank you for going to look for me, I was just about to go look for you."

Luis' eyes swept the floor—*I bet you were, you liar.* Rejected by both his family and the macheteros, he belonged to no one, having lived his life alone in a small villa instead of in the Casa de Azucar. Lately, he had spent his free time drinking at the Bar Habana with Gonzo instead of consuming anything he could find to read on the raising of sugar cane.

Luis looked up—*Your bitch of a mother sheltered you from me, Don Carlos. I had to work in the fields and she let me go to school only through the sixth grade. I was allowed into the Casa de Azucar only once in my entire life to attend my father's wake before his funeral twenty years ago. I had to self-educate myself by having Gerardo sneak books out of the library. I was his eldest son and rightful heir to this goddamn place. Now, Carlos, today justice will finally prevail.*

Don Carlos led Luis through the villa feeling lucky, at this dark hour, to have his brother he could trust. With Luis managing the hacienda, the harvest would be saved. His mind snapped back when he heard Luis say, "My God, Don Carlos. I found your car and I was sure you were dead!"

"But it was you, Luis, that I was worried about. As I said, I was just going to look for you."

"What happened? Where are the children?"

"They are in San Blas with the priest."

"Your beautiful new car has been shot to hell. Was it an airplane?"

"No! The Yankees, I think, with machine guns ambushed me. Forget about the damned car, I'll get a new one. Let's get something to eat."

Don Carlos grabbed Luis' arm as he walked into the kitchen. "Let's have breakfast in the dining room. We have much business to discuss."

"*Gracias*, but I've never eaten…"

"It's okay. Serve breakfast in here, Gerardo."

Luis entered the formal dining room for the first time in his life and took a seat to the right of Don Carlos. Gazing out the open windows his thoughts turned bitter. *So many damned times I have seen Carlos and our father dining in this entire splendor through these windows. Now when Carlos really needs me, I'm allowed inside and fed some scraps like I'm his dog.*

"Luis, are you listening? I said I have to leave at once. Castro's secret police will be coming to arrest me at any moment now."

"Oh, sorry, I wasn't listening. Yes, you must leave at once. Do you want me to take you in my Chevy back to San Blas and to Real Campiña and see if we can locate the children?"

"No! Are you crazy? I just almost got killed on the Real highway!"

"Of course. What was I thinking? Which way do we go then?"

"I go alone along the beach to Cienfuegos on horseback. The police will not think of following me. *Listen!* Whose planes are those? Are they Castro's or Yankees?"

"Who knows? Let's eat before they bomb us," Luis laughed, "we must not die on an empty stomach. Or shall we have a rum just in case?"

"This isn't the time to be funny, Luis. But why not have a short one from our late father's private reserve? Why not, brother?"

The men's eyes met and lingered like two lovers. It was a relief to Don Carlos for his words to have finally been spoken. Yes, he had finally gotten around to calling Luis 'brother' after nearly fifty years. It was the right time to say it, since he might not have the chance to ever say it again.

Luis knew Carlos had said it because he needed him to harvest the crop and run the hacienda until the Americans killed Fidel Castro. He leaned back in his chair and dropped his eyes in deep resentment at the words that had just been spoken, feeling the same shitty abuse that had always been part of his life. *Now you call me 'brother,' brother, now that your ass is in a crack and you're desperate. Why was I not your brother before? Did you call me brother at Christmas? At our father's funeral or our sister's wedding? Never. Only now when Castro's police are coming to arrest you, you two-faced bastard.*

"Gerardo, pour us a rum from Papa's Bacardi Select and leave me the bottle. Oh, bring my cigars too."

The chef of forty years glanced at Don Carlos seated in the formal dining room with the mulatto and raised his eyebrows. *Señora Garcia would turn in her grave if she knew about this*, he thought as he poured the rum. He then dismissed himself and stood outside the door to hear the clinking of fine crystal as Luis raised his glass. "To your health, my brother."

"*Salud*," Don Carlos replied, as they silently drank, neither man looking at his brother. For Luis the soothing richness of the aged rum felt warm in his stomach as his dream of becoming the next master of the Casa de Azucar seemed to be turning into a reality. Inside the Don, the rum burned at his guts like the fires of hell. Gerardo stood outside the dining room door still shaking his head before he rushed off to fry some eggs.

119

After breakfast, the two men discussed the status of the harvest in detail before adjourning to the library. Don Carlos sat at his desk and wrote a formal power of attorney naming Luis Benes as hacienda manager with Gerardo signing as witness. Detailed instructions were given for selling the crop and at the designated price. Finally a letter was written to the bank president in Havana authorizing Luis' signature on the bank account.

"Do you understand everything the way I want it?" Don Carlos asked, sealing the envelope.

Luis nodded. *I am now officially the Don of the Casa de Azucar, you asshole—my dream has come true!* "Yes, I understand everything, Carlos. Leave now, the DGI will come at any moment."

"No, tonight after dark. Have Gerardo saddle my horse. Let's go up the tower and have a look at the fighting in Giron."

"Let's fix another rum first."

"Yes, of course, why not brother. Our optic nerves will see better if we have another one and how's your cigar?" Carlos asked, slapping his brother's back with a laugh as they poured with a heavy hand.

Both men were breathing heavily ten minutes later when they reached the top of the steps to find the southern sky covered in clouds of black smoke from burning ships. Carlos trained his binoculars on the San Blas church belfry and wondered if his children had reached Havana. He suddenly gasped as an artillery shell blasted away the belfry, sending a plume of white smoke gushing skyward.

"My God! Look, Luis!" Don Carlos shouted, handing over his binoculars. The men stood in a rum stupor, watching the distant artillery duel destroying San Blas.

"Are you sure the children are out of there?"

"I hope so, but…I hope…I don't know."

"Should you go to San Blas and see?"

"It would be dangerous! I could get killed. Luis you go for me!"

"Of course I will go. *Now* leave before the police arrive to arrest you."

"I cannot possibly leave until I know for sure my children are safe in Havana. Be careful, Luis, and hurry. Here, take the binoculars and a horse and stay off the roads. My God, Luis, my children! Hurry back, please."

"Okay, but you must leave now, Carlos. I will find out about the children and call Roscena."

"*No*! I am not leaving until I'm sure they're safe in Havana."

Chapter Thirteen

Zapata Swamp

17th of April

The haloed sun burned a hole in the afternoon sky as an uneasy calm fell over the swamp. The old priest pushed the skiff through the stagnant, brackish waters with a pole while Manuel paddled in the bow and swatted mosquitoes. Father Lopez had been crossing the Zapata Swamp in a skiff for years before Castro built the new highway. *I can navigate my way in the dark*, he thought, as the sounds of the Cuban regulars on the highway preparing for battle filtered through the mangrove trees.

Manuel caught glimpses of artillery pieces being moved up the burning column of wrecked vehicles a hundred yards away. He paddled with strong strokes through the pungent stench of high explosives when suddenly the priest stopped poling. "My children, just in case we get separated, the priest in Real Campiña is named Father O'Brien. He's the redheaded Irishman you have seen with me in San Blas, Maria. Get to Real Campiña and Father O'Brien will gladly take you to Havana."

"Are you going to leave us?" Manuel asked.

"No, of course not. We just need to have another plan."

The priest's voice was smothered by a blast from the Cuban artillery shelling San Blas from the highway. Manuel stopped paddling to watch the muzzle flashes as the deafening percussion of the big guns vibrated in his chest. In the distance he watched as the first shell scored a direct hit on the belfry of Our Lady of the Assumption, sending a plume of smoke skyward. "Father!" Manuel screamed. "Castro's soldiers have blown away our bell!"

Maria, crouched with Alfredo in the bottom of the boat, raised up and shouted, "Shut up, Manuel, you idiot and paddle faster."

"Just do as Maria said and keep paddling," the old priest ordered, turning to see his most sacred possession being reduced to rubble as tears streamed down his leathery cheeks.

"I hope they killed the giant ugly American," Manuel angrily replied, glancing over his shoulder in time to witness the flashes from *La Brigada's* M-41 tank and 75mm recoilless rifles returning fire from their positions in the village. The screaming incoming rounds of 4.2-inch mortars exploded on the highway, shooting clouds of black and white dust skyward and making the earth tremble as the battle for San Blas raged on.

In the stench of the humid air, the sounds of the distant shelling slowly died away leaving only the brutal heat and the swarms of mosquitoes to keep the refugees company.

"Why is God punishing us?" Maria cried out to the priest who was silently asking that same question of the Divine.

It was late in the afternoon when they reached the northern shore of the Zapata Swamp. Exhausted, Father Lopez pulled the skiff out of the water with the children's help. Wiping his brow, he glanced at the sunset, "We had better get going, children. It's getting late."

"Where to, Father?" Maria asked as she picked up their suitcases.

"There is a carbonero who lives just up the trail. We can find shelter for the night in his hut. Tomorrow I will get you to Real Campiña by ten o'clock to catch the train to Havana."

"I'm thirsty," Alfredo whined.

"You're scared, too, aren't you, sissy?"

"Stop it, Manuel! Act your age or I will tell Papa and he will whip your butt!"

"I'm sorry," the boy replied, picking up his suitcase and the sack of food. He held his head high, not wanting Maria to know how miserable he felt leaving Blanco behind. *This isn't make-believe, the fighting was real. I can't wait to tell Papa I've been in a war,* the twelve-year-old was thinking. Manuel Garcia's chest filled with pride with every stride having single-handedly faced the giant to protect Maria and Alfredo. *I hope the direct hit on the belfry tower blew the American all to hell.*

The overgrown trail dimmed in the failing twilight and gave way to a small opening on a slight rise ahead. In the middle stood a squalid hovel built of thatched palms—the house of Pedro Vargas, an outcast from San Blas known as "San Lazaro the leper." The old priest and the children struggled into the clearing, exhausted.

"Pedro!" Father Lopez shouted in a hoarse voice that echoed in the vast emptiness of the swamp. *The chance of the children catching leprosy is much less than being eaten by crocodiles,* he thought as he waited.

"I don't like this place," Alfredo whined, grasping his sister's hand and slapping at the mosquito on his forehead.

"You baby!"

"Manuel!" Maria snapped, sharply jerking her brother's hair. She jumped when a bull crocodile bellowed sending the children into a huddle and the wild pigs on the edge of the clearing squealed when the priest shouted louder, "Pedro! Are you here?"

"Who are you and what the hell do you want of me?" responded a gravelly voice slurred by *aguardiente*. San Lazaro took a drink of the distilled sugarcane juice cut with water. He glared out at the intruders, exhaling the foul breath from what was left of his nostrils as he waited for an answer.

"It's Father Lopez from San Blas."

A loud hideous cackle burst forth from the hovel and into the firefly-filled dusk. "Are you Jesus coming to heal this Lazarus? You're not afraid of catching leprosy?"

Father Lopez advanced and let himself into the hut while the children stood frozen in their tracks.

"What's leprosy?"

"A disease that rots your flesh, Alfredo, you dummy."

"Can I catch it?"

"Quiet you two," Maria whispered, trembling with fear as she crept closer to hear the men's voices inside the hut.

"No, Pedro. We are only passing to Real Campiña and need refuge for the night. How are you?"

"Rotten. Come and see for yourself, old man of God. Why in the goddamn hell are you crossing the swamp with three children instead of taking the highway?"

"Pedro, may God forgive you. Now light a lamp and try to show some common decency in the presence of the children."

"God pardoned me with his curse alright," the leper replied as he struck a match lighting the kerosene lamp. The untrimmed wick burned yellow at the edges, casting a flickering light onto Pedro Vargas' decaying face as the priest made the sign of the cross and closed his eyes. The children gasped, turning away after seeing the filthy and decomposing face out of a horror movie glaring at them.

Manuel examined the dark lesions where two scabbed cavities of a nose sucked in the foul air with the raspy sound of a man with tuberculosis. He caught Vargas' dark, beady eyes molesting Maria's body, and stepped between them when San Lazaro grunted, "*Dios perdone?* The hell you say, you old fool."

The barefoot leper took a drink of cane liquor then staggered, catching himself. Manuel flinched at seeing the man's toes were eaten away on one foot by the disease, leaving nubs wrapped in unsightly rags. In the flickering light, the "L" branded on Pedro Vargas' forehead twenty years ago marked him a cursed man quarantined in the swamp to slowly decompose.

"Maria, my child, do you have food left?" Father Lopez asked, as the girl reluctantly placed the suitcase down in the corner behind Manuel, dragging Alfredo along.

"Only enough for one meal and some breakfast," she replied, looking down to avoid the leper's stare.

"Good. Eat lightly then. Save some for tomorrow and get ready for bed."

Maria edged closer to the priest, catching a whiff of San Lazaro's stench as he stepped outside to relieve himself. "Is it safe here, Father?"

"Safer than the swamp with the crocodiles and wild boars. Eat and go to sleep. And don't forget to say your prayers."

The smoldering fire was piled high with green branches to smoke out the mosquitoes. Maria lay on the mat spread upon the dirt floor next to her brothers, having warned them repeatedly to keep their hands out of their mouths. Father Lopez's out-of-cadence snoring harmonized with the labored breathing of the noseless leper.

The occasional squeal of the leper's pigs was answered by the eerier grunts of the wild boars from the swamp. Terrified that there was leprosy in the air, Maria took shallow breaths before finally drifting into a restless slumber after praying as she had never prayed before.

The stench of San Lazaro's breath abruptly woke Maria Garcia. Her eyes adjusted to the dark to find to her horror the form of the naked wretch squatting over her with an erection harder than the horns of the devil resting only inches from her face. *Can I ignore him?* she thought, holding her breath as San Lazaro's filthy hand slowly massaged her breasts while he stroked himself.

Trembling, she shoved his callused hand away, whispering, "Stop it, San Lazaro! I mean it!"

"You want to be difficult?" San Lazaro hissed, abruptly forcing both of his hands inside her blouse and gripping her tender nipples, twisting them painfully between his forefingers and thumbs while hunching like a dog.

126

"Stop it!" the hysterical girl screamed, and pushing and clawing at her attacker, she struggled to her feet.

"What's the problem?" Father Lopez mumbled, getting up.

"Shut up, padre, and go back to sleep," the leper ordered as he grabbed Maria's throat.

"Pedro! Leave the girl alone!"

"Go to hell you old fool! San Lazaro wants this tender young body."

"Manuel!" Maria screamed, as San Lazaro pinned her against the center post of the hut when Father Lopez grabbed the assailant by his arm. "In the name of God, let the child go and make yourself decent!"

"Go to hell, old man. I am *God*. I'm getting some of this tender young pussy, you damned old fool," San Lazaro shouted, shoving the priest to the floor and kicking him in the face.

"God forgive me," Father Lopez whispered, grabbing the *aguardiente* jug on his way up and striking San Lazaro on the side of his face, driving him to his knees. Maria was screaming, kicking to get free when there came the swish of the razor-sharp machete slicing the air with the sound of a knife splitting an overripe melon. The priest's frail body crumpled, his dying gasp drowned out by the children's screams at seeing his head tumble and roll across the floor.

Manuel grabbed Alfredo, dragging him into the corner of the hut from where he could see Maria's struggling silhouette, still in the grasp of her naked attacker. Petrified, he forced himself away from Alfredo frozen in the fetal position.

San Lazaro dragged Maria down to the mat, ripping off her blouse while his wicked cackles harmonized with the squealing of the hogs. "Settle down. This is going to feel *r-e-e-eal* good, you little bitch," he said throwing the girl on her back, pinning her hands over her head before mounting her screaming, twisting body.

Manuel crawled forward until his hand struck the priest's severed neck and he jerked it back covered with hot blood. He felt again, groping in the dark for the machete before finding the cold sticky blade, and grabbed the handle.

Like a matador's *estoque*, he rose, and with all his might thrust the machete under San Lazaro's left shoulder blade. He felt the blade strike the heart as San

Lazaro gasped and collapsed on top of Maria, who screamed and shoved the corpse away before springing to her feet.

Manuel wiped his hands on his pants. "Are you okay?" he asked, hugging his sister who was putting on her torn blouse. "The criminal is dead."

"We've got to get the hell out of here, Manuel!" Maria cried, as Alfredo grasped her legs, refusing to let go until she picked him up and kissed him. "It's okay now, baby."

The first traces of daylight were taking the hard edges off the mangroves as the children tiptoed over Father Lopez' headless corpse. The swift decapitation had left the priest's eyes staring blankly skyward. Manuel froze, making the sign of the cross. "Cover the Padre with a blanket," Maria ordered before seeing San Lazaro's body, machete still embedded, was blocking the door.

Manuel jerked the machete out of the body and stuck the blade into the dirt. "Be careful, don't dare touch the dead son-of-a-bitch."

"Okay, Manuel, you lead the way and I'll carry the baby."

"I can't take the machete and all this stuff!"

"Leave the suitcases behind then, let's get the hell out of here," Maria cried, as they fled gasping and stumbling down the abandoned path into the eerie shadows of the early morning light.

The sun had pierced the mangroves when they came into a small clearing, and Manuel froze in his tracks. Twenty yards ahead stood a massive wild boar rooting for grubs. The beast cautiously raised its enormous black head, its razor-sharp tusks glistening in the sun as it sniffed the air, releasing a low guttural grunt. *"God!* Don't move!" the boy whispered when the animal caught their wind.

Maria let out a blood-curdling scream as the animal pawed the earth then lowered its head and charged with lightning speed.

128

Chapter Fourteen

17 April 1961

The high-pitched scream ended in a tremendous explosion that blasted Tex Morris out of a sound nap on a pew in the sanctuary. Debris and dust from the belfry rained down from the direct hit, leaving a huge opening in the roof and filling the air with choking dust as he struggled to get up. Through the smoke the golden glare of the exposed altar signified that the divine light had somehow miraculously saved the young officer's life.

He stood in a daze with his ears ringing and blood dripping from his nose. "Max! Max! Where in the hell are you?" he shouted, running forward toward the glistening altar, looking up into the haunting eyes of the Virgin Mary staring down at him. "Well, I guess Maximilian got his," he said to her.

"Almost, but I had to go to take a crap," Max shouted, running up, kicking back timbers from the collapsed roof. "Are you okay?" he asked, stopping dead in his tracks when his body was encased by the golden glare from the sun off the altar. Dropping to his knees Max crossed himself, whispering, "Thank you God for sparing me."

"Holy shit! Get down! Incoming mail!" Tex yelled, as both men hit the floor. The artillery round exploded outside in the plaza, toppling the altar and smashing the carved cedar into smithereens.

129

"Let's get the hell out of here!" Tex ordered.

* * *

Walter Elliot took the Company's black Chevy sedan to meet Mr. and Mrs. Dulles at the Roost on their return flight from Puerto Rico. The plane was exactly on time, touching down at 9 P.M. on Monday, April 17th, at the CIA's private hanger at Friendship Airport in Baltimore. Walter rehearsed his briefing and was nervous in breaking the bad news to the DCI that the conditions in Cuba had deteriorated. *Why had Mr. Dulles not called to check on Operation Zapata?* Walter had been asking himself for several days now.

The plane's door opened and the DCI preceded his wife down the steps into a chilly spring night, where greetings were exchanged. Mr. Dulles then suggested that his driver take Mrs. Dulles home in the Chevy so that he and Walter could have a chat while Walter drove.

When the two men were alone in Dulles' Cadillac, Dulles began idle chitchat about the Puerto Rico weather and the Young President's Organization meeting. Walter thought it was very strange that he wasn't talking in riddles when the DCI casually asked, "Well, Walter, how's Operation Zapata going?"

"Not very well, sir. Not very well at all."

"Yes," Allen Dulles replied, with a quizzical expression on his face.

"*La Brigada* is holding on by its fingernails."

"And?"

"Air support from the Navy has not been approved yet, or at least at the time I left. The Guats have lost air superiority. It's turning into a real flap, sir. A total mess."

"Oh well."

"As a matter of fact, sir, the second air strike on Saturday was scuttled."

"Why did they do that?" Dulles calmly asked.

"I was not informed, sir. Mr. Bissell and the General were over at the State Department most of Sunday night. I'm not sure what took place. I can only speculate and would rather you speak directly with Mr. Bissell," Walter replied, turning onto P Street and stopping in front of Dulles' home.

"Come in and have a drink."

"Yes sir," Walter replied, relieved to be giving his detailed briefing at last.

The two men entered the library and Dulles poured himself a stiff Scotch. "Have one, Walter?"

"No thank you, sir. I'm going back to the war room."

"Walter, do you know Constantine Caramalis?"

"Only that he's the prime minister of Greece."

"Yes, very good of you. I will be attending a reception at the White House tomorrow night. Caramalis will be arriving in Washington tomorrow afternoon and I have a meeting with him and the president beforehand. Please get me his psychological profile from the Directorate of Intelligence and brief me at ten in the morning. I'm a little tired and won't come in until then."

"Yes, sir," Walter sighed. *My God, here we are in the middle of the Bay of Pigs invasion with everything going to hell and Dulles wants a briefing on Caramalis!* "What about Zapata? Mr. Bissell is expecting me back tonight on the communications desk."

"Yes, of course, give Dick a hand over there. He needs it, and I'm confident you're doing your usual first-class job. Be back with the scoop on the Greek by 10 A.M. please."

"Yes sir, I will, but…"

"No buts."

"I was only going to say that if *La Brigada* does not get tactical air support from the Navy, then this…"

Dulles shook his head and reached for his pipe. "That's in the hands of Dick and the president, I reckon. There is nothing more I can do about it, and the less I know about it the better. By the way, how's your mother doing?"

"Not well, sir. Thank you for asking. She will probably have to sell her home in Boston to raise enough money to live on and cover her legal expense. Elliot Silver is in chapter 7."

"Is that liquidation?"

"Yes sir."

"That will be dreadfully unpleasant for you and your mother, I'm sure," Dulles replied. "Thanks for retrieving us, Walter. Now until tomorrow at ten."

"Yes sir. Do I return to Quarters Eye after I brief you on the prime minister? I'm sure I'll be asked."

"Most certainly, if it is not already over by then. See your job through there. Good lesson for a brilliant young CIA officer on how an operation is not to be run. But remember; don't get too close to it. Like I've said, some heads are going to roll. Good night, Walter."

"Good night, sir." *Does the director know something I don't know?* Walter thought as he got into the car. *From some other source perhaps? Sounds like Dick Bissell just got hung out to dry.*

By the time he arrived at Quarters Eye, Walter Elliot was very cautious when he entered the war room.

***

At dark the shelling stopped on the 18th of April and Tex was in the Bar Habana, which had miraculously escaped damage. "How's your ammunition holding out?" he asked the major.

The major took a drink and shut his eyes. "Low, very low, *El Grande*. Why haven't the Americans given us the air support they promised?"

"I'm sure it's been requested. You had better get your men ready for a frontal attack across the bridge. I'd blow it except I haven't got word from Red Dog One yet."

"But not tonight, and I don't think Castro's men will attack."

"Why not?"

"Because it's late and they're tired and hungry. Mañana, we will attack in the early morning."

"Okay, then let's consider hitting them after dark. You have the armored trucks and your men are still fairly fresh."

The major shook his head. "No, they're too tired, and it's too risky."

"We're all tired, but we need the element of surprise, especially using the armor to lead the assault. Castro's men are sitting ducks stuck on the levee. They can't flank us because of the swamp."

"Yes, I know, mañana, we will attack then."

Tex placed his hand on the major's shoulder. "Okay, it's your war, major. I'm just here to give support."

"Then call the American warships to give us naval support and air strikes, for God's sake, *El Grande!*"

"I would if I could, but I can't. If the brass in Washington knew I was here I'd be court-martialed."

Max burst into the bar waving the radio in his hand. "Tex, come quickly!"

"What's up?"

"It's Gray. He wants you right now."

Tex took the radio and walked outside and keyed the mike, "Red Dog One, Red Dog Two, over."

"Cowboy, give me a status report. Over."

"Roger, Red Dog One. Stand off. Enemy dug in on highway levee with artillery blocking our advance. Our tank is dead and the major refuses to counterattack. Ammunition critical. Air cover critical. Over."

"Roger, Red Dog Two. Do you have the bridge wired?"

"Roger. She's ready to blow, Red Dog One."

"Instruct Max on how to detonate it. Roger? Over."

"Roger."

"Then get the hell on back to the beach. Out."

"What about my men? Red Dog One. Over."

"Leave them there to fight with the 4th and get back to the beach. Over and out."

Tex keyed the mike, starting to protest. It was Gray's orders and he knew what he was doing. *It's a hell of a hike to Giron*, Tex thought as he looked toward the flatbed Soviet truck parked in the plaza and smiled knowing how to hot-wire the ignition.

Tex returned to the bar to find Max drinking a beer with the major. "Well, gentlemen, I've been ordered back to the beach. Max, you keep the radio and when Gray gives the order blow the bridge."

The major's eyes danced with anger. "Why are you leaving *El Grande?*"

"Orders are orders. Good luck gentlemen," Tex replied as he headed toward the door.

"Hey! *Americano*! Who pays for the beer?" Gonzo shouted.

Tex stopped and spun around. "Here's for the fucking beer," he laughed walking over to the bar and knocking Gonzo flat on his ass with a savage lick to the jaw.

He could still hear Max laughing when he got the Russian truck started.

Chapter Fifteen

D Day + 1

Tuesday, April 18, 1961

The wild boar flashed his razored tusks, lowered his great head and charged, closing the twenty yards in a split second. Manuel stood his ground, raising the machete, and like the matadors' *estoque* he had often seen used in the Havana bullring, and at the precise second, thrust the pointed blade into the eye of the charging beast. The momentum of the five hundred-pound boar drove the blade into its brain, and with a deathly squeal, the boar fell dead at their feet.

That had been two hours ago. After catching their breaths, the children continued running up the trail that led out of the mangroves, onto a fertile plain, and into the heat of the morning sun. They stumbled onto a windmill turning slowly in the cloudless sky and drank their fill of water from the spout before collapsing exhausted on the ground.

"We have got to wash the blood out of our clothes before we catch leprosy," Maria said, standing and stripping to her panties.

"Yes, before we are seen too," Manuel replied, taking off his bloody shirt. "Did San Lazaro hurt you?" the boy asked, seeing his sister's naked body and feeling a sense of arousal before looking away feeling ashamed.

"No."

"He deserved to die. Could you feel him dying, Maria?"

"Oh, Manuel! You were so brave. You saved us from San Lazaro and the wild boar. Thank God!"

"The boar was nothing, but I would kill San Lazaro every day of my life for ever touching you."

"Don't ever mention his name again. Someone in the Revolution might try to say we murdered him and the priest when they find the bodies."

"Oh, damn! We should have buried them, Maria."

"No! Stop it! Promise, the both of you, on Mama's grave, never to mention this terrible thing."

Manuel grabbed his brother's ear, "I promise, I promise. Did you lop off the Padre's head too, Manuel?"

"No, San Lazaro did. I'll slap the hell out of you if you ever say that again."

"No, don't hit me, or I'll tell Papa!"

"Stop it you two!" Maria shrieked, consoling the little one. "It's okay now, we're safe, Alfredo. Do you understand what I just said?" Maria asked, returning to the trough, while Manuel stole glances at his sister's naked breasts as she washed herself. "Here, wash your blouse again, Maria, and get dressed. I'm climbing the windmill to see where we are."

Moments later, Maria heard Manuel cry out from above, pointing northward, "I can see the sugar mill smoke stack in Covadonga. We can catch the bus to Real Campiña from there. Hurry, we have to find Father O'Brien. Let's get out of here before someone sees us."

"Oh my God, Manuel! I've lost the money Papa gave us—it must have fallen out of my bra when I was attacked."

"What will we do, Maria?"

"You must go back and find it, and hurry. We will wait for you here."

"Maria, keep the machete."

"No, are you crazy—there are more wild boars. Now run."

On board the *Blagar*, Gray Lynch was listening to the radio traffic that San Blas was under heavy artillery attack. Early Tuesday morning, he had a moment of hope when the radio reported that the 4th Battalion was counterattacking to the north. Five hours later it had failed and now he heard the battalion was withdrawing from San Blas back to Blue Beach. "Red Dog Two. Max, did you blow the bridge? Over?" he kept shouting into his radio.

Reduced to a pile of rubble by the 122-millimeter howitzers and the 185-millimeter mortars, San Blas was quiet. Gonzo and Eduardo came out of the Bar Habana's cellar, where they had weathered the shelling. To their amazement the bar was the only building besides the heavily damaged barracks still standing in a village of ruins.

The 4th Battalion had run out of ammunition and retreated, leaving booby traps that killed two soldiers of the Cuban 117th Militia when they entered the village at 1000 hours and liberated the San Blas Garrison locked in their barracks.

Lieutenant Silas searched in the debris of Our Lady of the Assumption, hoping Father Lopez was still alive so he could say mass over Jose Onis and the others. At noon, he ordered the wooden coffins of the dead placed inside the Bar Habana out of the tropical sun until a priest could be found.

The lieutenant was forming his men into ranks when the soldiers of the 117th began shouting: *"Fidel! Fidel! Death to the invaders!"*

The formidable figure of a cigar-chomping Fidel Castro, brandishing a 45-caliber pistol stood in the turret of the lead tank as the column came to a squeaky stop in the Plaza de Armas. Castro ordered Silas and his men to mount up and the column moved out to drive *La Brigada* from Giron. San Blas stood deserted except for the stray dog scavenging in the rubble and Gonzo and his son shouting and waving the soldiers onward.

When the column approached the riddled Oldsmobile on the highway south of town, Castro ordered a halt and dismounted. "I know whom this car belongs to!" he shouted, pacing around it several times before looking inside and feeling the driver's seat. "He must still be alive," he said, checking his hand for blood before stepping back for a panoramic view of the bullet-riddled wreck.

"Whose car is this, *Commandante*? Your amigos?"

"No, Ramon. It belongs to Don Carlos Garcia Rangel, the master of the Hacienda del Azucar over there," Castro said, pointing toward the villa's tower in the distance. "The Don is an anti-revolutionist and the one I am most certain is responsible for directing the Yankee invasion at Playa Giron. Go arrest him at once."

"Si, *Commandante*. Where do we find this Don Carlos?"

"Did you look in the car?"

"There is no man in the car."

"Well, then he must be at his casa. Over there by the tall tower is his villa. He must have directed the mercenaries from the top."

"Si, *Señor Commandante*."

"I saw him driving this fancy Oldsmobile in Giron last month when I was inspecting the construction of the villas. I have reports of him being in Havana and leaving the Colombian embassy. He's a past president of the National Sugar Association who speaks out against the Revolution's agrarian land reform. The Don has been under surveillance as an anti-revolutionist for some time now. Arrest him. What are you waiting for?" Castro shouted as he mounted his tank.

"What's his name again?" Ramon asked.

"You never listen! His name is Don Carlos Garcia Rangel. Do I have to write it down?"

Ramon locked eyes with his sergeant, "Take some men and go to the villa by the tall tower. Arrest the owner, Don Carlos Garcia Rangel, at once and take him to the Central Australian for interrogation."

A sergeant and two privates spun their Toyota landcruiser around, kicking up a cloud of dust that trailed black in the wind off the burnt cane field.

The Don paced the floor of his library wondering if his children had escaped the battle of San Blas. He wished for a telephone to call Roscena in Havana since he had not heard from Luis last night. *Has Luis turned Judas and deserted me?* he wondered, realizing for the first time that he had made a mistake by not heeding Luis' pleas to flee to Cienfuegos.

Don Carlos knew his time was running out as he removed the portrait of his forefather, Don Frandio Garcia Lopez that concealed the family safe. He turned the combination, known for over two hundred years only by the masters of the Hacienda del Azucar, and took out his passport and inspected it closely. Then he removed a faded parchment envelope bearing the 1763 seal of Charles III containing the land grant deed to the Hacienda del Azucar that transferred title. On the last page of the faded parchment, Don Carlos took his fountain pen and, as his forefathers before him, started to transfer title before putting the pen down. *No, it's not time yet,* he thought. *Manuel's still too young.*

Carlos then placed the deed in a larger envelope addressed to his sister at the Colombian embassy in Havana along with a note to hold it for safekeeping. Blanco's ears perked up—his growls turning into furious barking at the sounds of intruding footsteps running down the hallway. The soldiers stormed into the room just as Don Carlos sealed the envelope and placed it on the side of his desk. "I'm unarmed!" he shouted, holding up his hands and glancing down nervously at their rifles.

"Are you Don Carlos Garcia Rangel?" shouted the sergeant over Blanco's barking.

"I am. You have no right to intrude. Get the hell out of my villa."

"Shut up! Fidel has ordered your arrest. You are going with us, señor," he ordered, drawing his pistol.

"You have no right to arrest me…"

"Shut up and turn around," the sergeant interrupted, shoving Don Carlos against the wall.

"Hell no you don't!" Don Carlos shouted, shoving the soldiers who stepped forward with a rope when Blanco lunged forward and sunk his teeth into the sergeant's leg.

"Damn perro!" the victim shouted, kicking the dog loose and firing a single shot into its head. Don Carlos watched in horror as Blanco flipped about on the floor before falling dead.

"You swine!" the Don screamed as his hands were bound. "You bastards will pay dearly for killing my son's dog."

"No, you are the one that will pay for helping the invaders. You are a prisoner of the Revolution now, so let's go, you traitor."

Galloping across the burnt cane field after keeping San Blas under surveillance all night, Luis saw the green army vehicle speeding away from the Casa de Azucar. He pulled his mount to an abrupt halt, training his binoculars on Don Carlos in the back seat.

"*Buenas!*" Luis shouted so loud it made his horse rear up. *Carlos' love for his children has cost him dearly. Now I am the rightful Don of the Casa de Azucar. What happens if my nephew never reaches Havana?* Luis was thinking, spurring his horse into a gallop toward the villa to search for the deed to the hacienda.

Dismounting, he ran up the steps into the library and stepped over Blanco lying on the floor. "Ha! Is this what I think it is?" he whispered, carefully opening the envelope and removing the faded parchment. Seeing that title to the Hacienda del Azucar had not been transferred to Manuel, Luis danced like a man spared from the gallows, shouting over and over between drinks of rum, "I'm the Don of Casa de Azucar! Don Luis! Don Luis!"

He quickly placed the envelope in a bottom drawer hearing Gerardo coming down the hall to investigate.

* * *

In Washington it was four PM on Tuesday, April the 18th. From the faces of the advisors assembled in the cabinet room off the Oval Office waiting for the president, it looked like midnight.

President Kennedy was behind closed doors in a meeting with his top advisor, Arthur Schlesinger, and having misgivings of appointing the aging Dulles as CIA Director. "It was a mistake from the beginning to put Dulles in the administration," the president said. "Dulles is a legendary figure, and it's hard to operate with legendary figures."

"You rightly took your father's advice in appointing him. Like Hoover, who wiretapped you with Nazi spy Inga Arvad when you were in Naval Intelligence,

140

Dulles knew the political favors you received from Giancana in the Chicago election. You had no choice…"

The president cut his eyes at his advisor with a scornful look.

"Yes, of course, Mr. President. Who do you consider a likely candidate for Dulles' replacement?"

"Bobby. He's wasted in the Justice Department as attorney general. If I can't trust my brother, who can I trust?"

"No one, Mr. President."

"I'll get Fidel Castro if it kills me."

"We will, Mr. President, but Bobby isn't the right choice for CIA director."

"And why not?"

"If things get all fouled up again, whom could you blame it on? Bobby Kennedy?"

"Yes, you are right. We need an outsider—a Republican would be even better."

This is not a pretty sight, Walter Elliott thought when he walked into the cabinet room turned emergency command center with Director Dulles and Axial Hanson. The young officer surveyed the massive conference table littered with crumpled notes, overflowing ashtrays, and half-empty coffee cups. U-2 recon photos of the Cuban invasion stood on an easel half hidden in cigarette smoke.

The president entered looking drawn and worn, trailed by Schlesinger. Everyone stood and remained standing when the president began to speak with a condescending Bostonian accent. "There are to be no statements to the press, gentlemen, that do not back my judgments all the way on this thing. Is that entirely understood by everyone? The CIA, Mr. Dulles?"

"Yes, Mr. President," Dulles replied, followed by a mumbling of compliance from the others. The president glared directly at him and opened his mouth to fire him, but stopped short, motioning for Bobby to follow him out of the room.

What type of man could put his political image above the lives of those men dying on the Giron beaches? Walter asked himself. From the way the president looked at the CIA director, he knew his days were over, along with Bissell, Hanson and God knows, maybe his.

Kennedy will pay a hell of a price if he sacks the Great White Case Officer to cover his ass, Axial Hanson thought as the hair on his neck bristled. The CIA officers left the cabinet room to return to Quarters Eye feeling very dejected.

It was six hours later and Dick Bissell stood unshaven and haggard in the war room. Across town at the White House the president, dressed in black tie and tails, was hosting the annual congressional reception in the East Room of the White House. John Kennedy, seemingly unconcerned over the fate of *La Brigada*, mixed and mingled with the congressmen and their wives at the gala.

To Walter Elliot the state of emotions and composure of the men in Quarters Eye was rapidly disintegrating as he watched Mr. Bissell surveying the situation board. "Damn it," Bissell swore, turning to Hanson. "We must persuade the president to send air cover from the *Essex* or this is the end of the fucking road."

"And how do we do that?"

"It's time for the president to have a fresh report. Elliot, get the White House on the phone and set up a briefing immediately."

Walter picked up the phone and dialed Kenneth O'Donnell, the president's appointment secretary and was placed on hold. Bissell impatiently paced the floor as O'Donnell left the East Room reception and took the call. "Mr. Bissell *must* have a meeting with the President! That's the earliest. Okay, Mr. O'Donnell, Mr. Bissell will be there."

"What time, Elliot?"

"Midnight, sir. Do you want me to accompany you?"

At two minutes before twelve, Walter Elliot followed entering the cabinet room for the second time that day. President Kennedy stood apart from Vice President Johnson who Walter overheard asking Robert McNamara and Dean Rusk, "What the hell is goin' on down yonder?"

Bobby Kennedy came in with a fresh drink of Scotch. Before the Vice President received an answer, he had joined the other cabinet members dressed in tuxedos at the conference table. The Joint Chiefs of Staff stood in the corner in dress uniforms, their chests draped with rows of service medals and you could tell from the look on their faces there was about to be war. The strong smell of liquor and cigars permeated the air as the politicians and military men turned their attention to the President calling the meeting to order.

Bissell began his plea, "Mr. President, this is a moment of desperation. We must have air cover or all is lost."

Admiral Burke spoke up. "Let me take two jets and shoot down the enemy aircraft…"

"No," President Kennedy quickly interrupted.

"What about unmarked jets to fly cover, with orders not to engage…"

The president shook his head, his face reddening.

"If we bring in one destroyer to provide fire support to evacuate the beach…"

"Burke, I don't want the United States involved in this!" Kennedy snapped.

"Hell, Mr. President, we *are* involved!" the Admiral firmly replied, shocking his fellow officers.

Walter shook his head seeing that the president and Bissell were going in two different directions. *Bissell still desperately wants the operation to succeed. Kennedy is thinking only of political damage control and ways to minimize the impact of failure on his presidency. What a crock of shit!*

So on into the early morning of Wednesday, the 19th of April, the two sides argued while the men of *La Brigada* were running out of ammunition and were surrounded. By the time the CIA officers left the cabinet room, the failed Bay of Pigs was quickly passing into history.

* * *

The lieutenant ditched the stolen Soviet truck four miles down the Giron highway; it was safer to go the rest of the way on foot. It was 0800 hours on the morning of the 19th of April when he heard the planes approaching—two B-26s, friendlies.

Lieutenant Colonel Joe Shannon and his wingman, Major Riley Shamburger of the Alabama Air National Guard, were making a final desperation sortie to give the men pinned-down on the beach some relief after all the remaining Cuban air crews were either dead or too exhausted to fly. "You got a boogie on your tail,

Riley," the colonel shouted as a pair of Cuban T-33 fighters swooped down upon them.

Major Shamburger shouted back that his plane had been hit and was on fire. Shannon watched as his plane erupted into a fireball from a direct hit from the enemy's cannons and crashed into the water, taking the lives of the Major and his co-pilot, Wade Gray.

Joe Shannon's fighter-pilot instincts from World War II made him turn into the path of the oncoming jet which pulled up into a vertical climb to escape the B-26's eight 50-calibers. Shannon dropped down low to the water and banked into the rising sun at full throttle to escape his attacker. Tex heard the engines of the lone B-26 drone off into the distance, relieved that the pilot had escaped Shamburger's fate. Shannon had risked his life in a gallant and heroic attempt to save *La Brigada* while the aircraft carrier *USS Essex,* with its jets that could have changed the course of the battle, steamed in formation with its escort destroyers only forty miles away.

Tex walked slowly toward *La Brigada*'s beachfront bungalow headquarters on Playa Giron. Exhaustion was taking over. It was 0900 hours and each step felt like his boots weighed a ton trudging though the sand. There was a temporary lull in the artillery barrage, and the smoke-filled sky, for once, was clear of Castro's planes. Tex crouched twenty feet from the surf and watched Hugo Sanchez beach his LCM and drop the ramp.

"*Hola, El Grande*! Can you help us?"

"You bet," Tex replied, seeing that the boat was filled with ammunition boxes salvaged off the sunken *Rio Escondido.*

"Never thought I'd see you standing, my man!" Hugo laughed. "Let's get this shit off-loaded and I'll run you out to the ship before we're overrun. I'm low on fuel."

The Special Forces officer had been trained to never leave a comrade behind. But as he looked around him, he knew the situation had become hopeless when the last of the ammo was unloaded. Tex Morris hung his head with shame at the thought of leaving his Guats to fight and die alone as he boarded the LCM.

With the wind in their faces, Hugo pointed to the sunken ships and destroyed equipment that littered the beach. "Look at this damn mess, *El Grande*. Why in the hell doesn't the Navy give these poor bastards some air cover so we can get them out?"

"Damned if I know, those shit-heads back in Washington have fucked us."

"*La Brigada* has fought against overwhelming odds for hours. It looks like they will keep on fighting to the bitter end."

"It's still not too late," Tex sighed, pointing to the superstructure of the American destroyers in the distance.

"If Kennedy would only give the order for air cover we could at least pull out the survivors!" Hugo shouted when the beach exploded behind them into a massive barrage from the Cuban artillery.

"That's all she wrote," Tex said, feeling the burden personally for America's failed promises to the men he had trained and was now abandoning as the LCM pulled along side the ship.

Tex boarded the *Blagar* and scampered up the ladder to find Gray Lynch in the ship's message center. The small cramped compartment was an inferno of mass confusion as the unscrambled messages from Washington piled up in the corner and continued to pour in unanswered.

Gray Lynch was shirtless and sweating profusely. His voice, raspy from shouting over the radio, was barely audible for a man who had been awake now for seventy-two hours, subsisting on black coffee. He looked up, shook his head, managing a weak smile. "Welcome back on board, cowboy. Thank God I'm not going to have to explain what happened to you when the shit hits the fan in Washington."

Tex grinned and glanced up at the situation board on the bulkhead. "Shit's hit the fan, all right," he replied, seeing the red arrow swooping down through San Blas to Blue Beach. "Didn't Max blow the bridge?"

"Hell no. The 4th ran out of ammo and retreated to the beach."

"Aw, hell, Gray. I gave Max specific orders to blow it."

"Max would have, but he's dead."

"Max got it?"

Gray released a sigh of exhaustion. "It wouldn't have made any difference if Max had blown it or not. Castro's forces poured in on the back roads from Playa Larga to outflank us here and here," he said, pointing on the map. *La Brigada* is out of ammunition and there'll be no air or naval support coming from Kennedy."

"Kennedy's hung them out to die?"

"Yep," Gray grimly replied over the static-crackled radio transmission of the *La Brigada* commander, Pepe San Román. "Tanks closing in on Blue Beach from the north and east. They're firing directly at our headquarters. Right on the beach. Send all available aircraft now!"

Tex was scanning the beach with his binoculars when he heard Pepe's final transmission, "I have nothing left to fight with. I'm destroying my radio. I can't wait for you."

"They're finished," Gray said, recording 14:32 hours in the log. "Let's get this tub the hell out of here and see if we can organize a rescue for survivors," he said, as the two men watched the beach erupting like the grand finale of fireworks on the Fourth of July. The murderous bombardment took its toll on Tex Morris as he brushed away tears of anger, choking out a closure. "My poor Guats are all dead."

Gray reached over and placed a firm hand on the lieutenant's shoulder. "I'm proud of you, son. Damn proud of you. You accomplished your mission. Too bad this mission is top secret. No one can ever know what you did or I would put you in for a Bronze Star."

Tex managed a weak smile, wiping the tears from his eyes. "Thanks, Gray, but all I did was kill some poor bastard named Jose Onis and knock the hell out of a little creepy barkeeper in a joint called the Bar Habana. That's about all."

"In this business it won't be the last guy you kill, so forget about it. You got the job done as far as I'm concerned."

The ship was headed out to sea, leaving the carnage of the Bay of Pigs in its wake along with its place in history. "Know your next assignment, Tex?"

"Back to Bragg to wait for orders that Elliott promised me to some place called Laos. But first I'm paying a surprise visit to a certain Costa Rican señorita for some well deserved R&R."

"Laos? The Land of a Million Elephants and a White Parasol. I was an A-team leader of the first SF units in-country, so tell Vang Pao hello for me. Have fun, son, and cover you frigging ass," Gray said, his voice only a whisper. "Thanks again, and remember, you haven't been on this mission. The first tin can that comes alongside, you're out of here, cowboy."

"I'll keep my mouth shut, Gray. Heads are going to roll, aren't they?"

Chapter Sixteen

Bar Habana

Wednesday, April 19, 1961

Burned out carcasses of Cuban army vehicles were being cleared off the Real Campiña highway and the bridge was still wired for detonation. No delivery trucks would come today, and the Bar Habana had run out of beer and rum. The *aguardiente* was almost gone, causing grave concern for the bartender suffering a case of the short-man syndrome. The cocky little man had been humiliated twice publicly in the past few days and was now rubbing his swollen jaw, nearly broken by the American they called *El Grande* when he walked out on his bar tab.

Gonzo was still livid over the disgrace he and Eduardo had experienced last Sunday afternoon in the Bar Habana, when it was packed with macheteros and carboneros. Rethinking it all, he had no choice but to obey the Don, who was armed, and could have killed him and gotten away with it.

The bartender had arrived in San Blas from Havana after being fired from the Hotel Nacional where he had stupidly and foolishly shorted the liquor inventory, trading whiskey to a pimp for sex with his stable. When Roselli got the numbers, he placed a contract on Gonzo's life for two hundred dollars.

148

Gonzo fled with his illegitimate son, Eduardo, on the first bus for Giron, where he heard Castro was building a tourist resort and he could find work. The bus broke down in San Blas, where fate reintroduced him to the Don, a long-time regular at the Nacional casino where Gonzo had served him during his monthly National Sugar Association Board meetings.

Standing in the Plaza de Armas, Gonzo had pleaded his case for the injustice he had received from the American Mafia and asked the Don if he could work at the Casa de Azucar.

Don Carlos took one look at his tall, acne-faced son and shook his head. "Gonzo, if you like, you can open a bar over there in that abandoned building I own. We will be seventy-five/twenty-five partners, and you make damn sure none of that Mafia trash from Havana follows you here or you will wish Roselli had killed you a thousand times."

Late last Sunday afternoon, Don Carlos had charged into the smoke-filled bar like it was the *plaza de toros* with the blood vessels on his face protruding like a raging bull. The customers parted as he charged the bar screaming for Eduardo. "What's wrong?" Gonzo asked, as all fell silent.

"Where is that skinny bastard?" the Don shouted, grabbing Gonzo by his shirt and jerking him across the bar as the crowd formed in a large semicircle around them.

"Eduardo!" Gonzo called out, "come here at once!"

The boy appeared in the doorway, his pointed face painted with horror at the sight of Don Carlos clutching his father's collar and dangling him on his tiptoes.

"Get your ass over here, punk," Don Carlos shouted, motioning with his head.

"Do as you're told, boy," his father ordered. "What's the matter, Don Carlos? What is it? What has the boy done?"

Don Carlos shoved Gonzo aside; grabbing the boy by the arm, he pinned him against the bar. In a flash, his pistol was between the startled youth's eyes. The metallic click of the revolver cocking sent murmurs of trepidation rumbling through the crowd.

"This punk has insulted my daughter. I am going to put this gun in his mouth and blow off his pimply face," Carlos said, forcing the barrel against Eduardo's quivering lips until he cried out and opened his mouth.

"God, no! Don Carlos! Please don't," pleaded Gonzo, watching helplessly as his son swallowed the barrel.

"I'm sorry, Señor Don Carlos," came the boy's barely audible apology as his terror-stricken eyes rolled from side to side searching desperately for salvation.

"No! Don Carlos, no! Please, señor, don't kill my boy. He's my only son," Gonzo cried out bringing grumbles for a pardon rippling from his patrons.

"Shut up all you bastards!" Don Carlos shouted, shoving the pistol deeper into the boy's gagging mouth. "Can you taste the lead in these bullets, Eduardo?"

The crowd stood silent, expecting at any second for the pistol to erupt until Don Carlos finally relented, "Okay punk, I will not kill you this time, but if there is a next time, you are dead meat." He then glanced around the bar seeking confirmation for his acquittal.

Dropping the pistol's hammer brought sighs of relief from the gallery as he slowly pulled the barrel out, laughing sadistically. "Gonzo, now teach this bastard son of yours not to ever insult my daughter again."

"What do you want me to do, señor?"

The Don pulled off his wide black belt, waving it like a bullwhip above his head before throwing it at Gonzo. "Take down his pants and whip his ass until it bleeds. I'll tell you when to stop, but pour me a Bacardi 8 *Anos* first," he ordered, leaning against the bar and using his handkerchief to clean the gun of Eduardo's slobber.

"Please don't, Papa. Please…" the boy pleaded, as he slowly turned his back to the crowd and dropped his trousers. The first lick fell with a dull whack.

Don Carlos threw down his rum and poured another. "Give me the damn belt," he ordered, to the sound of the belt cutting the air with a nasty hiss. Time and again it fell with a sickening crackle, tearing into the boy's flesh until Eduardo dropped to the floor, his body turning spastic. Don Carlos kept up the beating until the bar turned bloody and the boy could scream no more.

Gonzo looked out at the rubble of San Blas and shook his head. *Thank God I still have Bar Habana, but what good is a bar if a man has no honor or respect left? Don Carlos has destroyed all that. If it is the last thing on earth I do, I will get even with the rich bastard. I will not take dishonor to my grave,* he was thinking when Eduardo came limping through the door.

"Eduardo, how do you feel? We *will* get even, don't you worry."

"I'm hurting, Papa. Mostly my pride."

"The beer truck won't run from Real Campiña today and we're out. Take a skiff across the swamp to get a fresh supply of *aguardiente* from San Lazaro, and don't stick your fingers in your mouth. These soldiers coming and going on the highway are thirsty. We'll make a fortune."

"Papa, I saw Father Lopez leave on Monday in the skiff with Maria just before the shelling started."

"Are you crazy? Forget about Maria and get moving."

"Where can I find a skiff, Papa?"

"Get going! There is one tied under the bridge and don't forget to take these empty jugs."

"*Si*, Papa," Eduardo replied, walking gingerly out the door. *I will fuck Maria Garcia someday,* he was thinking as he skirted the shell craters in the plaza, *and when I'm finished, I will cut her throat.*

Gonzo wiped the long bar with a dirty towel and watched his son as he limped across the Plaza de Armas. At that moment he hated Don Carlos more than the *Americanos* that had destroyed San Blas. *I will ask Luis when he gets here where he thinks Father Lopez was going with Don Carlos' spoiled brats?*

* * *

When the early morning bombing of the Havana airfield had taken place on Saturday, BBC correspondent Holly Woodson had witnessed the attack from the cocktail lounge atop the Hotel Nacional. She was as surprised as everyone else as she telexed her Havana bureau chief, Charles Parker attending his mother's funeral in Manchester, England. Within the hour, Holly was instructed to report live to BBC London by telephone and then cable her reports over the UPI and the AP wire services to *The London* and *New York Times*.

That afternoon Parker cabled additional instructions to make preparations to send a film crew to cover an invasion if it occurred. "Under no circumstances are you to accompany them, Miss Woodson," were his orders.

To bloody hell with you, Charles Parker. I've got conflicting orders from Axial Hanson, she was thinking as she tuned in Radio Swan. She glanced at 3:44 A.M. on her watch when the Revolutionary Council bulletin hit the airways calling for the Cuban armed forces to revolt: "Take up strategic positions that control roads and railroads! Take prisoners or shoot those who refuse to obey your orders..."

This is it, by Jove, Holly was thinking when the telephone rang. "There is an invasion at Playa Giron on the Bay of Pigs," reported the caller, an unidentified CIA informant. Holly hung up and alerted her cameraman, Sam, and within the hour she was headed with her film crew for Giron in the bureau's Range Rover.

Holly was thinking back now to the end of Batista's dictatorship when Castro took power on New Year's Day 1959 and kicked out the Mafia. The young woman had fallen instantly in love with Havana and the Cuban people, who were amazingly sensual—always touching and looking directly into her eyes. The hearts of the people on this dance-crazed island were filled with emotional intensity, music and laughter, quite different from the stiff, formal Englishmen.

Those bloody Yanks are going to screw up this beautiful island, she was thinking, as they raced through the early morning hours for the Cuban southern coast. Holly felt an adrenalin rush like she had never felt before. Her fear of being a spy in a war was nothing compared to her anger at Charlie Parker's orders not to cover the invasion. "Being a war correspondent is a man's job," he had told her along with everyone else at the BBC except her father, Sir Allenby.

The BBC might fire Holly Woodson, but she would prove to Charles Parker that she was capable of doing anything he could do. The loving daughter would also prove to Sir Allenby that she could live up to the expectations of her brother, Harold, who was killed with his mother in the London bombings. *Holly is fin-*

ished with shit assignments reserved for the woman, she told herself with a sudden flashback to her days at Oxford University.

Holly was thinking now of Clive Langford, her tutorial professor of history at Lady Margaret Hall who had encouraged her to become a journalist like her father. What a wimp he had turned out to be after deflowering her on the banks of the River Cherwell one spring night in her junior year. After a steamy six-month romance of making love in the most bazaar places, Holly became pregnant.

Professor Langford panicked at the news. Riddled with guilt and fear for his professorship, he confessed to his wife. What a stir it had created when the short, stodgy Mrs. Langford went to Ellan Quigley, the college secretary, and demanded that "the little tramp" be expelled.

Holly suddenly found herself being thrown out of the only women's college at Oxford University by the wife of the man who had told her he loved her and was going to marry her. Sir Allenby had intervened and threatened to expose the scandal in the press if his daughter was not reinstated. Unfortunately, however, the rumor mill was ignited at the BBC when Sir Allenby was overheard calling Ellan Quigley "a bloody bitch," on the telephone.

Holly Woodson learned a valuable but costly lesson from falling in love with a married man. In a dark seedy section of London, a quack of an abortionist had turned butcher, leaving her childless for life—a heavy price to carry for a young woman who loved children.

She had learned from this experience that men would take advantage of her if she let them, but she possessed the power of the pen. All she had to do to get her story was bat her sensuous green eyes and press some breast, and mighty men ran their egotistical mouths and would tell everything.

Holly followed the map for Giron and listened to the Havana news bulletins on the Range Rover's radio. "By Jove," she remarked to Sam, "I have a sterling contact in the village of San Blas on the way that will be a great source."

"Who's that?" Sam asked.

"Remember Lieutenant Relondo Silas? He's the garrison commander in San Blas now."

"You're kidding? Do you think the bloody bloke will ever speak to you again after what you put him through?"

"Probably not," she replied, thinking back to that night of drinking daiquiris at El Floridita when her flirtatious eyes caught Lieutenant Silas standing at the bar in his dress uniform. *What a handsome target*, she thought. *He has the looks of Clark Gable and holds himself like Prince Phillip.* "Lieutenant, buy this thirsty lady a drink, would you, please?"

"If I only had the money, I would buy you the El Floridita, señorita! But are you not with the BBC?"

"How did you know that?"

"I asked the bartender."

"Are you stationed in Havana?"

"No, I'm the adjutant at the garrison in Santiago de Cuba and have been attending a promotion party at the Castillo."

"Should I ask if the bartender dislikes the way the Revolution is going Socialist as much as you do?"

"It is not permissible to discuss politics with foreign journalists, I'm sorry," Silas replied politely, bowing his head and smiling, revealing a mouth full of white, straight teeth.

"Do you think the revolution is turning Communist?" she persisted.

"I'm sorry."

"I do understand your reluctance to discuss political issues in public," Holly winked. "We can go some secluded place and our conversation will be off the record," she smiled, now challenged to draw in her target.

"I'm forbidden on or off the record to discuss the Revolution's politics with journalists."

"Yes, of course. As they say, loose lips sink ships."

"I don't understand."

"Oh that's just an old saying in the U.K. during the war," Holly replied, before taking a sip of her daiquiri and puckering her lips, blowing the lieutenant a kiss. "How long are you going to be in Havana? Or is that a classified military secret, too, my very handsome lieutenant?"

Long enough to get into your panties, Silas thought as he glanced down at the cleavage nestled in her blouse. "Until next Tuesday, señorita. I would like very much to take you to dinner at the *Tocororo* tomorrow night, perhaps, if you are free."

"Nice of you, but sorry. Unfortunately I have a commitment for tomorrow evening."

What a dandy story, Holly imagined: *Cuban Officer's View of Castro's Socialistic Movement. At the same time I'll get him to tell me the latest troop strength at Santiago de Cuba. Yes indeed. This bloke's in double jeopardy,* she thought, reaching for a cigarette. "But for this evening, now that might just be arranged if you are in the mood for the show at the Tropicana, and maybe dancing and a drink afterwards."

Holly smiled as the Range Rover bumped along recalling that night at the world's most flamboyant nightclub. The beautiful near-naked showgirls had danced with glowing chandeliers atop their heads in the paradise under the stars. Afterwards they drank rum and smoked cigarettes in the Bar Los Jardines until closing. Then she slipped her horny lieutenant up to her eighth floor corner suite in the Hotel Nacional where they made mad passionate love until daylight.

Within twenty-four hours a series of BBC broadcasts hit the airways, quoting the lieutenant frequently but accurately from the tapes she had secretly recorded in bed. Axial Hanson was ecstatic with Holly's first success in the CIA's anti-Castro propaganda campaign.

Holly still felt guilty about Lieutenant Silas' court-martial. She had tried to get permission to cover it but was denied by the Army. She had thought later about getting in touch with Silas to apologize, but learned from the Cuban University Directorate, Major Cubelas: "Silas has been sent to the remote garrison at San Blas in the Zapata Swamp, just one step above being sent to the political prison on the Isle of Pines."

I wonder if Relondo will give me an interview or even speak to me now, she was thinking when they were stopped for an Army roadblock outside Real Campiña, still some thirty miles from the Bay of Pigs. "We're with the BBC. Fidel has given us authorization to cover the battle," Holly said as she got out and took off her scarf, letting her shoulder length hair fall free.

"The *Commandante* has ordered the road closed to all traffic," the sergeant sternly replied.

"Got a light, Sarge?" Holly beckoned, pressing against the non-com's arm and offering him a cigarette. "Let us through and I will buy you a *cerveza* when I return in a day or two."

The sergeant shook his head and smiled and no matter how hard she tried they were stuck. Holly and her crew spent the next two nights camped in the Range Rover, waiting. On Wednesday morning reports of the battle of San Blas filtered in from the wounded being evacuated to Havana, and the roadblock finally opened at nine in the morning.

Thirty minutes later the vehicle came to a quick stop in the Plaza de Armas after snaking its way through the wreckage of the convoy that littered the highway. The film crew immediately set up their camera and was filming the shelled-out remains of Our Lady of the Assumption and the village. Holly strolled into the Bar Habana looking for Lieutenant Silas and a cold beer. "Gonzo! What in the bloody hell are you doing here?"

"Señorita Woodson! You are so lovely—I cannot believe my eyes. Welcome to my Bar Habana. Castro arrested Don Carlos, the owner, whom I have been told is locked up in the sugar mill. Are you still living at the Hotel Nacional?"

"Yes, and I will have a cerveza. Is this by chance the same Don Carlos who used to gamble at the casino?"

"Yes, he owns this building."

"Poor man—what happened to your jaw, Gonzo?"

"A big ugly Americano soldier hit me."

"Are you sure he was an American? How many were here? Are there any casualties?" Holly asked the man she knew, if asked the time, would tell her how to build a clock.

"Just the one they called *El Grande*, but he hit me very hard. He was the bastard who killed Jose Onis. Sorry, no *cerveza*, Señorita. I have only the local cane liquor or coffee."

"Is the coffee fresh?" Holly asked, looking out the window. "This San Blas is it not a bloody pity? Did they arrest Don Carlos here at the bar?"

"No, at his villa and Castro says he's a counter-revolutionist. I was here the whole time in the cellar and was lucky the shells missed me and my son."

"The commander of the garrison, Lieutenant Silas? Do you know where in the bloody hell he is?"

Gonzo poured his customer's coffee, "*Si*. He's a very brave officer, the lieutenant."

"Is Silas okay?"

"I think so. He left for Giron yesterday with Fidel to join the fighting, but I think most of the fighting is over with."

"If you had to guess, where would the lieutenant be now?"

"I heard from a sergeant that Fidel has set up his headquarters at the Central Australian and that they are holding the Don prisoner there. He said he saw the lieutenant and he was okay. They have the only telephone in the area at the sugar mill. You would be foolish to go there—it is very dangerous, Señorita."

"Jolly good, Gonzo. Tell me the way."

"First right off the Giron highway. There is, or was, a sign, but be very careful."

"I will need a place for me and my camera crew to stay when we get back. What's in your cellar?"

"It is not a place for you, Señorita. There is are no beds, only coffins."

"My God—coffins for whom, may I ask?"

"*Si*, Señorita Woodson, our padre left town and we are waiting for him to return to bury our dead before they begin to smell."

Holly looked up when a pickup truck pulled up outside and Luis Benes got out. He tipped his hat and sat down at the bar. "This is no place for a very pretty foreigner to be," he said, undressing Holly Woodson's image in the bar mirror as Gonzo poured his midmorning drink.

Holly smiled at the well-spoken and intellectual half-breed whose appearance was appealing to the young woman with an attraction to older men after having been raised by her father. Their eyes locked and lingered until their thoughts were interrupted when Eduardo came running in screaming, "Papa! Papa! Manuel has

157

murdered Father Lopez—chopped off his head with a machete. He killed San Lazaro, too!"

"*What?*"

"Father Lopez's head has been cut off! I saw Manuel leave the hut with the machete, honest to God," the wide-eyed teenager gestured with his hand in a mock beheadal. "Lazaro was stabbed in the back."

"*Bullshit!*" Luis said, downing his drinking without looking up.

"*Si*, Señor Luis—in the swamp, at San Lazaro's hut, I swear. They left their suitcases," Eduardo replied, holding up a baseball glove and keeping a straight face that he was lying about having seen Manuel commit the double murders. "Papa, can I keep this?"

"Gonzo, you have a fool and a liar for a son," Luis said, motioning for another drink.

"No, Luis, the Garcia kids left on Monday with the padre in a skiff just before the shelling."

"You really think anyone would believe that young kid killed Father Lopez and San Lazaro, do you?"

"Eduardo said he saw the murders—why would my son lie—look he has the kid's glove," Gonzo smirked.

"What would be his motive?"

"He knew that the priest would testify that his papa helped the invaders. Let's go see for ourselves."

"If it is true, which I doubt, I must get word to Castro's police. If I go the hell out into that swamp and your boy's lying—I will kick his ass," Luis snarled, tilting his head back and polishing off his drink.

"My God, what in the bloody hell are you people talking about might I ask?"

"I'm sorry, Señorita Woodson, may I present my amigo, Señor Luis Benes from the Hacienda del Azucar. Luis, Señorita Woodson is with the BBC in Havana."

"It is my great pleasure to meet you," Luis said, bowing and kissing her hand. "So, Señorita, this is why you travel to such a dangerous place? To tell the world that the Yankees have destroyed San Blas? Look at the mess they have made. If you want a real story, come go with us to investigate the priest murdered by Don Carlos' son, Manuel."

"Sorry, but I have a bloody war to cover. Not that a boy murdering his priest is not a good story, I do say. I'm just on the way to the Central Australian to find Lieutenant Silas and to arrange an interview with the Don. Should I ask him if his son murdered the priest, Señor—what is your last name?"

"Benes—B E N E S—as you like, Señorita," Luis replied, taking her hand and kissing it again. "This skinny kid, Eduardo here, is our witness that saw Manuel cut off the Padre's head with a machete…"

"Really now? Why would a boy murder his priest and not be home with his mum, may I ask?"

"She died last December. And to answer your other question, well, just come along and I will tell you the story. I overheard Don Carlos plotting with the CIA for the invasion over a month ago."

"*Si!* Señorita Woodson—Don Carlos is a CIA spy, that is why," Gonzo shouted waving his hand for his son to stop when he saw Eduardo pulling a pair of Maria's panties out of the glove and laughing.

"Thank you very much. Another time if you don't mind," Holly said, looking at Luis' strong muscular body and feeling a hot-flash run up her thighs while Gonzo looked for his keys.

Eduardo double-checked his pocket for the five thousand pesos he had taken off the dead padre's body. *Now I've really fucked Manuel up and gotten rich at the same time,* he thought. *I'm going back to Havana and organize my own street gang I'll call the Serpents. I'll show these country bastards around here what a bad ass I am.*

Chapter Seventeen

Havana

Wednesday, April 19, 1961

There was a cool evening breeze blowing across the veranda of the stately colonial mansion on Embassy Row in the affluent district of Miramar. Roscena Valdovinos was having a glass of sherry with her husband, Gilberto Valdovinos Gonzalez, the Colombian ambassador to Cuba.

The ambassador was drinking a *pisco doble* and smoking an H. Upman cigar and watching his lovely wife as she brushed her black hair, laced with traces of gray, from her face. "They will be okay," he said, noticing her radiant face was absent the smile that warmed every room she had ever entered. She flinched when the gunfire erupted in the center of Havana.

When they first met in the spring of 1936, Roscena could never have imagined that someday she would be married to the Colombian Ambassador and living in Havana. How amazingly handsome he had looked when she first saw the student of law at Madrid University. She remembered like yesterday the tall aristocratic youth wearing an open-collared white shirt and smoking one of the finest Havana's.

"Do you remember that spring evening we met at the café *Canas y Barro* in the plaza near the center of the campus?" she asked, snapped back into the present by another burst of gunfire.

"How could I ever forget?"

Roscena placed her hand on her husband's leg and smiled sadly. "How wonderful Madrid was that spring before Franco's civil war destroyed it," she said, with tears forming in her eyes.

"We were lucky to have escaped to Portugal," the ambassador added, sensing his wife was about to cry. "It's only Castro's soldiers celebrating their victory at the Bay of Pigs."

"Yes," Roscena nodded, her husband's words bringing back the hellish memories of being caught in the battle for Madrid with all the death and destruction.

They both had tried to erase the horrors of their escape from Madrid to Campo Maior, the Portuguese village with whitewashed houses on the Spanish border. It had been a living hell witnessing dictator Antonio Salazar's soldiers surround the village square and march thousands of exhausted, starving Republicans back to the border to be executed by Franco's army. An elderly woman known only as Ana had hidden them for two days in a ceramic olive oil tank before they escaped to the safety of the Colombian mission in Lisbon. Until this day, the smell of olive oil still sickened Roscena when she returned to visit.

Gilberto noticed his wife's shoulders shaking with the harsh realization that Don Carlos and his children were caught in the battle for Giron.

"Don't cry, my darling," he said, handing her his handkerchief, knowing how much his childless wife loved her niece and nephews. "I know you're greatly concerned for their safety."

"Yes," she replied softly as though Castro's DGI were listening. "You must get in touch with Carlos *now*," she pleaded, wiping away tears, "and get them safely to Havana."

The ambassador took a sip of his drink. "Okay, I will call the Cuban foreign secretary first thing tomorrow morning and get a report…"

"You're wasting time!" snapped Roscena, then adding firmly, "Giron is to-tally destroyed just a few miles from the Casa de Azucar, and I'm worried sick about them. You must do something *tonight*, Gilberto, *please!*"

"Stop worrying, Roscena. If only Carlos had a telephone. Tomorrow I will go to the foreign secretary at eight o'clock and demand an answer. Then, if neces-sary, I will go down to Giron myself."

"No, don't! Going to Giron is too dangerous. Have you forgotten how it was trying to escape Madrid? Send one of your attachés, *but send them tonight.*"

"Carlos is okay, so don't worry about him, Roscena. He'll not have any prob-lems because he is well known and respected all over Cuba," Gilberto said shift-ing in his chair, hoping to mask his concerns for his brother-in-law's safety. He looked toward Havana where he knew the DGI were arresting thousands of dissidents at this very moment. *I warned Carlos that his name was on Major Valdés' list.*

"Respected by everyone except Fidel Castro and his henchmen," Roscena re-plied. "We cannot just sit here like dummies and pretend that it's not happening."

* * *

The engine in Luis Benes' new Chevy dieseled after having been driven hard over the back roads from the Hacienda del Azucar to Cienfuegos. He parked outside the *Centro de Teléfonos* and rushed inside with just ten minutes to place his calls to Havana before the telephone office closed for the night.

In Havana the ambassador and his wife had retired for the evening when Mario's knock interrupted Gilberto brushing his teeth. "It's Señor Luis calling from Cienfuegos. It's urgent."

"I'll take it in my study," Gilberto whispered to his secretary, not wanting to alarm his wife. "Hello, Luis, what are you doing in Cienfuegos?"

"Calling you for Don Carlos to see if the children have arrived.

"No! When did they leave?"

"They left Monday afternoon with Father Lopez."

"What? My God, they're not here yet, but if they are with Father Lopez they should be okay, I think. Is Don Carlos..."

"Ambassador, Father Lopez has been..."

"Where is Don Carlos?" Gilberto interrupted.

"Don Carlos has been arrested."

"Arrested? Why in the hell didn't you tell me that to start with?"

"I tried..."

"Shut up, and just answer my question for once. Who arrested Carlos?"

"Castro's soldiers," *you asshole*. "They came to the Casa de Azucar, tied him up, and took him to the sugar mill Tuesday afternoon. Then after lunch today they took the prisoners to Havana, but I don't think that Don Carlos was with them."

"You should have called me immediately when it happened. What in the hell were you thinking about, you idiot?"

"Look! There's a war going on down here. Don Carlos is going nowhere. He is still being held prisoner at the Central Australian as far as I know."

"Okay, now you listen to me for once. Go confirm that and get back with me first thing in the morning. What has happened at the hacienda?"

"Oh, nothing much. Just that Raul Castro and his men have taken over the villa, using it as their headquarters and drinking the Don's select cognac," Luis replied sarcastically. "And they shot Manuel's dog, Blanco."

"For God's sakes, Luis. Shot the boy's little white dog?"

"In the head."

"Stay out of Raul's way then. Those damn Communists."

"How are you going to get Don Carlos released?"

"That's not your concern, so just make sure he's there and I'll arrange his release tomorrow by filing a protest with Castro's foreign secretary. I'll go to Giron in my official car, if necessary. When did you say Father Lopez and the children left San Blas?"

"I tried to tell you before you called me an idiot that Father Lopez has been found murdered."

"*What?* What in the hell are you saying, man? I thought you said the children left with him for Havana."

163

"Yes, I did, but the priest has been murdered in the swamp. Beheaded with a machete."

"Where *are* the children?"

"There's no sign of the children. Their suitcases were found with the Padre's body in the swamp."

"Do you think they have been kidnapped or…or murdered, maybe eaten by crocks?"

"How the hell would I know?"

"God, let's see. Let's see, just a second…" *Roscena must not hear me*, he thought, shutting his study door. "I will have to attend to this now. You go directly back to the hacienda and take care of the harvest. And stay out of Raul's way. I will organize a search for the children immediately and get Don Carlos released in the morning. You just get the cane harvested."

"I will try, but it will not be an easy job. All of the macheteros are drunk on *aguardiente*. It's almost impossible to get them back to the fields since Raul has promised them that he is dividing the Hacienda del Azucar among them when he leaves."

"*Damn it!* Do as you are told for once, Luis! Your job is to get the sugar cane harvested, so get those black bastards back in the fields even if you have to shoot them or I will fire your ass."

"Si, Señor Ambassador," Luis shouted into the phone before slamming down the receiver and bursting out in laughter. *Fuck you Señor Ambassador! Who is that lijo de pufa Colombiano to order me around?* he thought. *I'm the Don now, not the ambassador's Negrito. I have the deed to the Hacienda del Azucar in the drawer at the Casa de Azucar and the checkbook in my truck.*

Luis stood there for a moment, his hands trembling, trying to contemplate his next move. He glanced up at the clock. The office would close in two minutes. He snatched up the receiver. "Operator…"

"Sorry, we're closed."

"No, this call is very important. I need to speak to the Director of General Intelligence in Havana."

To Luis' surprise the call went directly through to the desk sergeant in Havana. "Señor, I would like to report a murder by the son of Don Carlos Garcia who was arrested by Fidel and taken to the Central Australian for spying for the CIA at Giron."

"Hold it. What's your name?"

"Let me speak to the person in charge…"

"This is Major Valdés speaking. Who am I speaking with?"

"I am an informer for the revolution, Major. Don Carlos Garcia's son, Manuel, murdered Father Lopez, the village priest in San Blas yesterday. Don Carlos has been arrested by Fidel and is being held at the Central Australian for aiding the CIA in the invasion of Giron. I know this because he conspired with his brother-in-law, the ambassador from Colombia, who is also a spy for the American CIA."

"Don Carlos is already under arrest, but why would his son murder a priest?"

"Father Lopez knew that Don Carlos was working for the CIA and was going to report Carlos Garcia to the DGI. The old priest told me this at confession. You listen to me, Major. The boy is fifteen and I have a witness, Señor Eduardo Martinez from San Blas."

"Okay, I'll have my agents pick him up for questioning. Where is he now?"

"Traveling on the train to the Colombian embassy in Havana. Don Carlos' sister is married to the ambassador. As I told you, the Colombian bastard is also a spy for the CIA."

"Give me your name and address, señor."

"I am an informant for the Revolution. It's the truth, so check it out. *Viva la Revolucion!*" Luis shouted, hanging up.

It was another hour before sunrise and Don Carlos had spent the past two nights sleeping on the hard concrete floor in the oily maintenance shop of the Central Australian. He had been given only water and a small helping of black beans and rice each evening by his captors. *How much longer will they keep me here before Gilberto gets me released?* he wondered, his guts knotted from hunger and worry. *I will get even by personally shooting the lijo de pufa that*

165

killed Blanco. God, I hope the children are safe in Havana and Luis has gotten the macheteros back to the fields.

It was deadly quiet in the idle sugar mill in the aftermath of the Battle of Giron. Carlos had slept little, especially the first night when the final assault on Giron was in progress with all the shelling. Now it seemed from behind the locked steel door that the Cuban Army had advanced and forgotten him.

He heard the distant sounds of Lieutenant Silas walking with two soldiers from the mill's administrative office where only a few hours before Fidel Castro had commanded his field headquarters. The commander of the San Blas garrison was under orders to stand guard over the only telephone in the region. The twenty-three year old lieutenant, like his Cuban regulars, loved, yet feared their *Commandante.*

Lieutenant Silas had commanded the garrison at San Blas since January. The humiliation of his court-martial for talking to the foreign press and being reassigned to such a lowly post as San Blas was a great dishonor to his family. Also weighing heavily on his troubled mind was having his garrison captured in their nightshirts by the exiles, which could land him back before the court-martial board.

Relondo Silas was awake most of the night hating Holly Woodson for what she had done to him but also aching for the woman he had fallen in love with. He had finally fallen asleep after thanking God for sparing him execution or long imprisonment on the Isle of Pines.

As a child, Relondo Silas had dreamed of becoming a priest, and at this moment being a priest would be the most wonderful thing in the world. He said a silent confession for his angry verbal assault on Holly yesterday when she arrived at the mill requesting to interview Don Carlos.

What nerve that woman has, he thought, approaching the maintenance shop. In *Genesis,* Adam was expelled from the Garden of Eden for eating the forbidden fruit Eve offered him. Samson lost his strength, his sight, and his life because Delilah betrayed him. *Oh God, help me with my weakness and keep Holly Woodson forever from my mind. Amen.*

In his tunic, the lieutenant had two fine H. Upman cigars, which were a gift from Raul when he departed to establish his headquarters in the Casa de Azucar. The lieutenant looked back over his shoulder at the soldier carrying a pot of steaming black coffee and two cups.

Lieutenant Silas knew his prisoner only casually, having seen him at Our Lady of the Assumption masses and in the Bar Habana drinking alone. The two men had once chatted briefly in the plaza when Silas had admired the Don's new Oldsmobile.

Finally they come, Don Carlos thought, hearing the approaching footsteps. *The mill workers are going back to work and they will release me.* He heard the key turning in the lock and shaded his eyes when the light flicked on. The lieutenant was handing him a coffee cup.

"Good morning, lieutenant," Don Carlos said cheerfully upon seeing a familiar face.

"Coffee?" the lieutenant asked.

Don Carlos started to speak then stopped as the aroma of the coffee filled the oily air. "Don Carlos Garcia Rangel, I am hereby ordered to inform you that you have been found guilty of espionage and are condemned to death for crimes against the Revolution. You will be executed today at sunrise by my firing squad."

Don Carlos jerked up straight like a man stuck in the ass with a hot poker. He searched the lieutenant's eyes for an explanation as his executioner stood in a stiff military brace, staring at the wall.

"What did you say?" Don Carlos whispered, glancing over at the soldiers for an answer. "How can this be?" he asked, his voice building. "I have not had a trial or legal counsel, and for what crime?"

"Don Carlos, I'm sorry," the lieutenant replied, looking the condemned man in the eyes. "It was ordered by the military tribunal of Raul Castro and approved last night by the *Commandante* himself. I'm only following orders. You have until sunrise in about an hour. I tried to find your priest, but Father Lopez must have been killed when the shelling destroyed your church."

"Father Lopez dead? Our Lady of the Assumption destroyed?"

"Completely."

"No! Father Lopez left with my…" the Don's voice trailing off when he realized that the children might be placed in a state orphanage if they did not reach Roscena.

"I'm sorry, Don Carlos."

"I must be granted the civility of seeing a priest! I still have my last rites with God, don't I?" the Don shouted, crossing himself.

"I agree completely, but we have not a priest or the time…"

"This cannot be, lieutenant! A man cannot be executed in Cuba without a fair trial and without having his priest grant him last rites! What are the charges?" Don Carlos asked, lunging for the door.

The lieutenant jerked back as the soldiers grabbed him. "I told you that you have been convicted of espionage for being an agent of the CIA."

"I have had nothing to do with any damn CIA…"

"It has been ordered," the lieutenant interrupted. "I'm only following my orders. I'm sorry I have nothing but coffee for your last meal. Please, enjoy this cigar before I return for you at sunrise."

Don Carlos Garcia took the cigar, watching the lieutenant strike a match. "If you have any final request besides seeing a priest, I will try to accommodate you."

Don Carlos took a long draw feeling the effect of the nicotine. He replied firmly, "Yes, there is one, lieutenant."

"Name it," Lieutenant Silas replied, pouring more coffee with a trembling hand.

"Please bring me pen and paper. I want to write a letter to my children. Can I trust you to have it delivered?"

"I will send it at once. You have my word of honor as an officer of the Cuban Army. I will mail it myself."

"I'm grateful, lieutenant. I appreciate your kindness."

"I am sorry to tell you…" the lieutenant began.

"It is okay," Don Carlos interrupted. "You have your orders."

"What I was going to say…" The lieutenant stopped himself from telling the condemned man that the secret police had called him from Havana and were looking for Manuel. *Let him die in peace.* "I will have the stationery sent right away."

As the soldiers' steps faded away and softly echoed in the emptiness of the room, Don Carlos began to write.

April 20, 1961

Dear Maria, Manuel, and Alfredo,

I have lived a privileged life in which my most cherished possession has been my children. The joy and pride that you bring me cannot be written into words.

My misfortunes have fallen fate to our times under Fidel Castro. In an hour I will be executed without a trial by his soldiers for crimes against the Revolution. I do not know the person or persons who have falsely accused me. May God forgive them.

It is now my time to join your mother in heaven, and we shall both be watching over you. I can only say that it is God's will that this terrible injustice has taken place. I will miss you more than the written word can ever tell. Having been born into the Garcia family, you shall survive; you shall prevail and go on to live happy and successful lives.

My last instruction is for you to leave Cuba at once and find refuge in the United States. If Castro will kill me, he could very well place you in an orphanage run by the Communists. And besides, Cuba under Castro holds no future for anyone. In the States you can receive a proper education that will prepare you for a good life. When Castro is dead, you can return to Cuba. Manuel, as my oldest son, you are heir to the Hacienda del Azucar that I love so much.

My final request is to make sure, if at all possible, to have my remains buried by your mother's side in our family cemetery at the Casa de Azucar.

Take guidance from Aunt Roscena and Luis Benes, your uncle, whom I have left in charge of operations until you return, Manuel. God will look after you.

All my love,
Papa

Holly Woodson was waiting outside Central Australian at daybreak to film Castro's field headquarters as the sun came up. She had only begun her quest for an interview with Don Carlos after being thrown out of the administration building Wednesday afternoon. *Relondo, you poor darling. I have the powers of a lioness over her cub when it comes to controlling you, ole chap.* Today she would unbutton the top buttons of her blouse and smile sadly. There was no doubt she would get through to interview Don Carlos by noon.

Watching her film crew set up their camera for an early morning shot of the Cuban headquarters, Holly suddenly realized that there was something very newsworthy happening in the adjacent field. "Catch those torches over there, will you, Sam?"

In the camera lens, Sam could see a soldier holding a flashlight for his burial detail. The soldiers were up to their chests in the rich red earth. "*Rapido! Rapido!*" they faintly heard the sergeant saying.

"Get down," Holly whispered, crouching behind a parked truck.

Fifteen minutes later they watched Don Carlos being marched into the field with the hot stub of the cigar clinched in his teeth. He stood bare headed before the open grave, taking a deep final draw before snuffing the stub with his boot.

The sun was cast in a halo of haze on the eastern horizon, and there was that gentle breeze of the early Cuban morning that Don Carlos loved so much. It carried away the smoke as he exhaled.

"Sam, are we getting this?" Holly whispered.

The lieutenant stepped forward with a blindfold, and there was no fear in the condemned man's eyes when he refused. Making the sign of the cross, the Don bowed his head and prayed. *Merciful Father, may my children arrive safely to Havana. I have made peace with my brother, Luis, and now it is time to give thanks for such a rich and wonderful life.* He opened his eyes as the bolts of the soldiers' rifles locked into place.

The prisoner stood erect and took a deep breath. "Do you have any last words, Don Carlos?" called the lieutenant, who stood adjacent to the firing squad some twenty paces away.

"May the gentle winds of Cuba cleanse your sins, my amigos, and may God spare your souls from hell."

"God rest your soul, Don Carlos," replied the lieutenant, nodding and giving his men the order, *"Squad! Ready! Aim! Fire!"*

"Jesus, Sam," Holly whispered, seeing the muzzle blast fold Don Carlos' body at the waist like an accordion and thrust it backwards into his grave. The sweet breeze of the early Cuban morning that Don Carlos loved turned sour with the pungent smell of spent powder that blew in Holly's face.

She regained her composure as the report of the rifles died away and the cameraman focused in on her. In her crisp, precise English, Holly began her commentary of the ghastly execution without hesitation, as though she was reading from a script. She ended with these somber words: "Don Carlos Garcia Rangel's execution has left Cuba with three more orphans. When will this carnage end, and what will happen to all the thousands of orphans on this island of impoverished millions?"

The news of Don Carlos' execution spread like wildfire, first to the battlefield in Giron where the foreign journalists were swarming, then on to Havana within hours. By the next day, Holly Woodson's face was on newsreels and television sets around the world. In less than twenty-four hours she had been catapulted from an obscure, unknown reporter to the BBC's first female war correspondent, bringing upon herself international acclaim.

* * *

In Cienfuegos, Luis Benes had checked into the Hotel Jagua, gone to the lobby bar, and gotten drunk off aged rum. The next morning, with a thunderous hangover, he stayed in bed until noon and stared up at the ceiling, laughing to himself. He began talking to a gathering of circling houseflies that came in with the breeze blowing through the open windows. "After fifty years, justice has prevailed," he shouted, getting up.

It was early afternoon when he arrived back at the Casa de Azucar. Angered by the large gathering of macheteros behind the villa, he jumped out of his truck. "Why are you not in the fields?" he shouted.

The beat of the African drums died, stopping Luis in his tracks. *Oh my God, Carlos must be dead.*

The drums started again as Luis leaned on the hood of the Chevy and removed his hat. He crossed himself and watched the chanting worshipers paying respect to Don Carlos' spirit. *They hated him in life and now fear him in death. May God rest your soul, brother.*

Luis gathered his composure knowing he had to play his hand very delicately or precious time would be lost in getting the macheteros back to the fields. He watched the superstition etched on their black chanting faces as the priest prayed to the beat of the drums that abruptly stopped when he approached. "What is wrong, Jose?" Luis asked the gray-haired priest.

The grandson of a plantation slave was looking at him with big white eyes that dramatically contrasted with the white robe he was wearing. His collar was decorated with red and white plastic beads. He motioned Luis to join him at the altar beneath the shade of a ceiba tree, piled high with offerings to the saints to ward off the evil of Don Carlos' spirit. Jose gathered the macheteros into a tight curious circle. "They have killed Don Carlos, Señor Luis."

"*What?*"

"They shot him at the sugar mill this morning...early."

"Oh my God," Luis said as he crossed himself and watched the whites of their eyes widen with fear.

On a signal from the priest, a solo drum began beating.

"What do we now do?" Jose, the second-generation worker asked, glancing up at Luis.

"We must all get back to work or we will lose the harvest and anger Don Carlos' spirit," Luis replied sternly. "Jose, get some men to dig Don Carlos' grave next to the one you dug for his wife last Christmas. Don Carlos' spirit will smile on you when he's buried next to his wife. Where is Gerardo?"

"Gerardo is cooking for the men who took over the big house."

"Then I will go to Central Australian to find Don Carlos' body and bring it back for burial. It will please his spirit, and no harm will come to us."

"I then prepare for the spirit's arrival," the priest said, looking up and saying to his people, "Go back to the fields and harvest Don Carlos' cane before his spirit casts a curse with a million miseries."

The priest raised a hand, and the African drums began to beat to the chant of the departing macheteros trailing off to the yet un-harvested cane. The priest was left with his drummer to appease the Don's spirits.

* * *

Fidel Castro was back in Havana, arriving triumphantly with his *La Brigada* prisoners. Cheering crowds of thousands poured into the streets when he arrived at his apartment. "Get me Major Valdés pronto!" he shouted to his aide. "This BBC television reporter is making a martyr out of Don Carlos and his children, and she must be stopped at once!"

Within ten minutes, the DGI director arrived winded at the dictator's door. "I am at your service," Valdés said, saluting.

"You must have your men pick up Don Carlos Garcia's children. The last thing we need is for them to be martyred by the press so we appear to the world as murderers. We will put them in the system; make them a model of how we take care of our orphans. Do you understand, Major?"

"Yes, *Commandante*. I have already issued the order to have them picked up. The oldest son, Manuel, is accused of murdering the parish priest to keep him from reporting his father for espionage. He will be arrested and stand trial for murder. I will see to his arrest personally. Is there anything else?"

"Yes, I also want Señorita Woodson apprehended and deported immediately."

Chapter Eighteen

Noon, Real Campiña

Thursday, April 20, 1961

At Real Campiña, the Giron highway meets the Havana railway, and Father O'Brien had the same sick feeling in his guts as the day he was arrested by the Belfast police. When he heard that Giron had been invaded, the twenty-seven-year-old Irishman had gone into hiding, fearing arrest by Castro's secret police. A fugitive now, his only chance for survival was to shed his cleric collar and flee to Havana. *God will see me safely to the United States, I pray.*

He looked more like a linebacker than a priest except he stood only five-foot-eight, with wide shoulders and a thick chest. The freckled-skin redhead knew it was almost impossible to hide on this tropical island of mixed races as he prepared to flee.

O'Brien had visited the United States initially to meet the Cardinal of Chicago under the guise of soliciting funds for a Belfast orphanage. He had been introduced to Chicago's most generous philanthropist, Sam Giancana's wife Ange, and returned to Northern Ireland not only with money but also with plastic explosives that the Irish Republican Army used to bomb the Belfast police station in January of 1958.

Patrick O'Brien got his passport and pondered his next move, while asking himself, *how in this world did I end up in Real Campiña in the first place?*

His story began with the Vatican losing Eastern Europe to the Communists at the beginning of the Cold War. The Soviet Union had stripped the church of its power to influence and control the governments of Eastern Europe. In Cuba when he took over, Fidel Castro made it clear to Bishop Masvidal in Havana that he would tolerate the church only if it stayed out of his way.

The Church of Rome received this message and decided to co-exist with Castro's government. Pope John XXIII was determined not to give up easily, as the church had done in Eastern Europe. Losing all of Latin America to the Communists was not an option, so the Catholic Federation resistance movement was organized in clandestine opposition to keep Bishop Masvidal in Havana informed.

In 1958, Father O'Brien had been arrested and sentenced to ten years in a British prison for conspiring with the IRA after British intelligence agents traced the explosives that killed four Belfast policemen to the Chicago Mafia. To distance the Church from the bombing and suppress the tension between the Protestants and the Catholics, Patrick O'Brien was exiled from Northern Ireland to serve the Vatican in Havana. This arrangement was negotiated with the British Foreign Secretary by the U.S. State Department after receiving political pressure from the Cardinal of Chicago and the Mafia.

Father O'Brien had served as a courier between Havana, New Orleans, and Chicago to launder the Syndicates' drug money under the disguise of his priest's robe. The cash was converted to bonds and transferred to the Finibank in Switzerland under the watchful eye of Sam Giancana in Chicago and Carlos Marcello's lieutenant, Anthony Alfonso, in New Orleans. After Castro shut down the mob's Havana operations in 1960, Father O'Brien had been reassigned to Real Campiña as a spy for Bishop Masvidal. As one of a handful of foreign priests who served as organizers for the resistance, he trained the local clergy in the surrounding villages in anti-Castro propaganda and surveillance techniques.

At this moment, Father O'Brien feared for his life. An hour ago word of Don Carlos' execution and Father Lopez's death had reached him by way of the underground Giron highway. He was certain the old priest had been tortured and killed by the police for his resistance activities, after having exposed O'Brien's identity.

The priest flinched hearing a loud knock at the side entrance to the church. Dressed in khakis, he peeked out the window and saw three pathetic-looking children standing at his back entry. "Oh Lord, what now?" he asked as he went to open the door, crossing himself, and quickly ushered them inside.

"Are you Father O'Brien?" Maria asked, expecting to see a priest in his Roman collar.

"I am he—ye speak English, do you? And who are ye? How did ye get here, for pity sake?"

"On the bus from Covadonga where we had to spend two nights at the hotel before the bus started running again. We are the Garcias. I am Maria. These are my brothers, Manuel and Alfredo. We live on the Hacienda del Azucar in Giron. Father Lopez said that you would help us escape to Havana."

"Ye father is Don Carlos, is he?"

"Yes. We are on our way to our aunt's in Havana where it will be safe from the fighting."

"Come in and stay quiet." *Dear God, these poor children don't know that their father has been executed,* the priest thought ushering the children into his chambers. "What happened to Father Lopez? I heard the poor old padre is dead."

Maria and Manuel's eyes collided. "Yes, he is. But he told us you would help us get to Havana."

"I am trying to get there myself, lassie. Did anyone follow ye here?"

A loud knock at the door was the priest's answer. "Down here quickly," he ordered, opening a trapdoor under the table in the corner of the very dark room. "It's Castro's police. Do as I say now and keep quiet," O'Brien whispered in his Irish brogue, forcing the children down into the chamber that had been built to hide him. He quickly slipped in on top of them, easing down the trapdoor.

177

"Open up! It's the police!" came the order, followed by the crashing of the door as it was kicked open. "Father O'Brien, you're under arrest!"

Alfredo began whimpering, as Maria clasped her hand over his mouth.

"He's not here," the first voice said. "Must have escaped out the back door."

"It's siesta time," the second voice answered. "Let's go eat. A redheaded priest will be easy to find."

"Okay," replied the first voice walking out of the church, "but we must find the boy who murdered the priest."

"Father, what did he say?" Manuel whispered.

"Quiet, lad, I think they've departed," O'Brien ordered, easing up the trap-door and helping Maria out. "Now, we must go straightaway to the train station. In twenty minutes the Cienfuegos Express leaves for Havana."

"Father O'Brien, did...did I hear the police say they were going to arrest me?" Manuel insisted, before seeing his sister shake her head.

"We have no time to dally, lad, just follow closely and do as I say," O'Brien replied as they quietly walked out into the deserted back alley to the avenue that ran through the center of Real Campiña. To Maria the station looked a hundred miles away as she watched the Havana train slowly pull into the station.

"We must make a break for it when I say. I'll carry the lad, and when I say 'run,' run like ye being chased by the devil and get on that train. Understand me? If the police nab one of ye the rest of ye get on the train without delay. *Do not stop for anyone!*"

"We don't have tickets, Father."

"Just get on the train. I'll see to the tickets, Maria."

The train had been at the station now for nearly ten minutes. Father O'Brien gave the order as they sprinted across the way, with Alfredo clinging to the priest's back. Manuel sprinted ahead and across the broad tree-lined avenue looking back at Maria falling behind. The train sounded a loud, harsh blast followed by the sharp hiss of the airbrakes as it began to slowly roll. The creaky sounds of the carriages over the rails grew louder as Manuel jumped on board, grabbing Alfredo from Father O'Brien.

"Faster! Maria! Run faster!" Manuel screamed, as Alfredo cried hysterically at the sight of his sister disappearing down the platform.

* * *

In his Havana office, the Colombian Ambassador took the call from the Director of the DGI. "No, Don Carlos Garcia's son, Manuel, is not here. Why do you ask if he is fifteen?"

"Ambassador, my officers have reported the suspect traveling on the Cienfuegos Express to Havana. You're sure he's not in your embassy?" the major asked. "He is wanted for the murder of Father Lopez, a priest in San Blas."

"That is ludicrous."

"Ambassador, you had better cooperate with my investigators or else you will be deported for harboring enemies of the Revolution. I am sending my officers over to search your place."

"Sir, you are talking to the Colombian ambassador. How dare you threaten me? This embassy is the sovereign property of my government and no one can enter its mission without my permission."

"Ambassador let me remind you that your brother-in-law is being held for espionage, and it has been reported that you're also an American spy."

"Despicable lies!" the ambassador shouted, slamming down the phone.

Within the hour the Colombian ambassador was leaving for a meeting with the Cuban Foreign Secretary to demand Don Carlos' release and an apology. Still livid over Major Valdés' accusations, he called his driver and told him to bring the car around to the front gate. Within minutes, the driver appeared and waited while the ambassador spoke to the guards. "When my niece and nephews arrive make sure you protect them, even if you have to use deadly force. If I don't find the children this morning, my wife will have a nervous breakdown."

Telling Manuel that Blanco was dead was going to be difficult, but telling Roscena he had failed to get Don Carlos released from jail would be unthinkable. He *had* to get Carlos released today so he could tell his son about his dog when he arrived. *Manuel killing the priest is bullshit*, the ambassador was thinking when he heard Mario's anguished cries coming from the courtyard. "Wait! Ambassador, wait! I've just heard that Don Carlos Garcia has been executed by Castro!"

"What? Who told you that?"

"On the television. I have just seen it on the Miami station."

The ambassador rocked back on his heels and stood frozen in the driveway, his face turning the color of paste.

"Ambassador? Are you okay?"

"I'm okay, Mario. Go quickly and get Señora Roscena and bring her to my office at once. Say nothing and send coffee up from the kitchen. Damn you to hell, Fidel, you murderer!"

Roscena was descending as Mario rushed up the spiral staircase. The secretary stopped and retreated back to the landing, waiting for her to pass. From the ghostly look on her face he knew that she had already heard of her brother's execution. Mario bowed respectfully when she passed, seeing Gilberto standing in the entry hall waiting.

"I have just heard the news from Miami," Roscena said softly, falling into her husband's arms. They embraced for a long moment and then retreated into the privacy of the ambassador's office as Mario shut the door quietly behind them.

* * *

In downtown Havana, a Soviet truck snaked its way down the crowded streets blaring Fidel Castro's war bulletin from mounted speakers: *"The mercenary invasion has been totally crushed."* The news brought the sounds of gunfire along with the chants of *"Death to the mercenaries! Traitors to the wall!"*

The *Cienfuegos Express* creaked into Havana's *Central de Ferrocarril Station* a half-hour behind schedule. A dozen of Major Valdés' plain-clothed agents pushed their way through the crowd, their eyes searching the cars for any sign of Father O'Brien and the children as the train slowed along the platform. Before the diesel engine jerked to an abrupt stop, the officers swarmed on board.

Ten minutes later they reassembled. "Major," the DGI inspector sighed, "the suspects were not on this train."

"Where the hell are they? The boy is wanted for murder."

180

"This passenger says he saw a man with children fitting our description get off the train when it stopped on the outskirts of the city. But he's not sure if it was them."

"Damn it! Take two of your best officers and set up surveillance on the Colombian Embassy. They will show up sooner or later. Arrest them before they get inside, even if you have to shoot them. Also, put out an all-points bulletin to pick up the priest. The redheaded bastard shouldn't be hard to find."

"I will place men at the cathedral also. We will capture all of them, Major."

"You had damn well better," Valdés replied, dreading the thought of reporting to Fidel Castro that he had come up empty-handed.

Two miles back down the track and an hour earlier, in the suburb of Mirador de Lawton, the eastbound train from Pinar del Rio had brought the *Cienfuegos Express* to an unscheduled stop after it was switched off the main line closed for construction. Father O'Brien grabbed Alfredo and ordered the children off the train while it was still rolling. They disappeared into the tree line where they were greeted by the polluted stench of the Rio Hondo.

The priest stopped to catch his breath. "If I am seen with ye," he whispered, "the devils will arrest us, so we must split up now."

"Father, how can I ever thank you for pulling me on the train?" Maria asked, hugging him tightly.

"Don't thank me, thank God. Now stay on this path close to the river and follow the current toward Havana. You'll reach the highway soon, then ye catch a taxi. Do ye know the address of the embassy?"

"Yes."

"Okay, don't get out of the cab at the embassy gate. Understand? The police will be watching it. Do ye understand me, Maria?"

"What do we do? Please, go with us!"

"No. Have the taxi drop ye off before ye get there and telephone your aunt," Father O'Brien replied before running into the dark without saying goodbye.

After almost being left by the train in Real Campiña, Maria thanked God that Father O'Brien had run to the end of the train and jerked her on board just in the nick of time. "God help us now," she prayed, trying to conquer her fear of negoti- ating Havana alone in the dark with the police looking for them. *Is this just a nightmare?* she kept asking herself as they followed the path. Maria Garcia could feel her spirits sliding into a cavern of despair known only to refugees of war.

"Walk faster, Manuel," she ordered, herding her brothers along the river. *Dear God, what else could possibly happen?* she was thinking when the sounds of the busy highway were heard up ahead.

Manuel looked back, flashing her a reassuring smile. *When we arrive at Aunt Roscena's everything will be fine, and my papa will tell the police to go to hell if they try to get me,* he thought, climbing the bank to the broad thoroughfare. "Do you think Papa will really bring Blanco?"

"Of course. Hopefully tomorrow," Maria replied, and seeing the welcome light of an empty taxi approaching, she waved her hand in the air.

"Where are you going, señorita?"

"146 #515, Miramar, please."

"Do you have any money?"

"Yes," Maria replied as she pushed her brothers in the cab ahead of her. When Alfredo fell asleep in her lap, Manuel whispered, "Maria, did you hear the police at the church call me a murderer?"

His sister put her finger to his lips and shook her head. "Quiet, Papa will take care of it."

The rows of mansions on the grand avenue in Miramar were passing by, all looking like the Colombian embassy to Manuel. "Where do we go to call Aunt Roscena?" he whispered, as Alfredo awakened whining for a bathroom.

"This is as close as we should get. Stop here, driver," Maria ordered handing the driver the fare and getting the boys out.

"Where is Aunt Roscena's casa?"

"Just ahead. Keep walking, Manuel," Maria said, her heart sinking when she saw the car parked across the street turn off its headlights as two men jumped out and ran toward them.

"Run!" Manuel yelled, hearing his sister screaming for help as they ran across the street just as the embassy gates flung open and the Columbian guards stepped out with their weapons drawn.

"Stop or I'll shoot!" the DGI inspector shouted behind them as the guard fired his machine pistol into the air. "Turn the children over. The boy's under arrest for murder," the inspector ordered, drawing up short and flashing his badge.

"Stand back from our gate or *you* two will be the dead ones," the mission guard replied as Maria came inside.

"I'm the niece of Señora Roscena Valdovinos Garcia, and these are my brothers."

"Si, señorita. We were expecting you. Go quickly inside the embassy."

"You ignorant Colombian bastards, don't you understand Spanish?" the first agent shouted. "These children are wanted by Fidel."

"Stand back or I will shoot both of you!" the guard shouted back, waving his machine pistol in the Cuban's faces.

Mario ran out of his office shouting, "Ambassador! Come quickly. Señora Roscena's niece and nephews are all safely inside the compound."

Roscena and the ambassador came running as he held the door open. "Bring them in here, Mario!" Roscena ordered, "and have the staff ready the guest-rooms."

The children washed their filthy hands and faces and sat down at a table spread for the starving when everyone started talking at once.

"How did you get here, Maria?" Roscena asked.

"Papa took us to Father Lopez in San Blas the night of the invasion. We got stranded for two nights in Covadonga until the bus took us to Real Campiña where we caught the train with Father O'Brien, an Irish priest. He saved my life, Aunt Roscena, by pulling me on the train. Have you heard from Papa?"

"No," Roscena replied softly. *Good, the children don't know yet,* she thought, glancing at her husband, who slightly shook his head as if to say, *we'll tell them tomorrow.*

"They destroyed our church, Aunt Roscena," Manuel said, spewing rice onto the table. "I saw it! The shells from the cannons blew off the belfry. *Ka-boom!* I hope it killed the giant *Americano* who was inside it."

Roscena gave Manuel a motherly hug. "My God. What a horrible experience. Did you say *Americano?*"

*"*An American giant with a machine gun. He killed a soldier named Jose Onis. Ta-da-ta-dat! I heard the gunshots and I have been in a war..."

Alfredo began sobbing, "I—want—my—Pa-pa."

"Come, Alfredo. You're such a little big man, eat your supper," the ambassador said, taking a napkin and wiping away the boy's tears.

"Father Lopez is killed," the little boy blurted out catching the wrath of his siblings' glares.

"Yes, we know," the ambassador said in a fatherly voice.

"You do?"

"Yes, Father Lopez was killed in the fighting," Maria interrupted, taking her youngest brother's shoulder and gripping it firmly, whispering, "Shut up, Alfredo, or I will skin you."

"Don't think about it, my big man," the ambassador replied, lifting Alfredo up and placing him onto his lap. "Father Lopez was a man of God and he is now in heaven with the angels."

"You are all exhausted. Hot baths for everyone and then off to bed," Aunt Roscena ordered, kissing each one on the forehead.

Ambassador Valdovinos and his wife were awake until past midnight trying to decide the appropriate way to tell the children of their father's death. Finally it was decided that Don Carlos' death must be dealt with in a straightforward manner.

The next morning, the couple took a long painful walk to meet the children on the veranda for breakfast. It was a beautiful sunny morning and the children looked rested as Manuel came running, sloshing orange juice on the tile floor. "When Papa gets here with Blanco can I go to the beach?"

"Watch it! You're making a mess," his sister scolded.

"Come with us children. Bring your orange juice and sit with me out of the sun," Aunt Roscena said, smiling sadly. "You tell them, darling, I can't."

"What is it?" Maria asked, seeing the tears forming in her aunt's eyes.

The ambassador took a deep breath before delivering the most difficult message of his life. "Children, your father is dead," he said quietly, putting his hands in his pockets and rattling his loose change.

Maria Garcia wailed uncontrollably and fell into her aunt's arms with Alfredo clinging to her back. Roscena broke into sobs. "Maria, my poor Maria," she kept saying.

Manuel stood for a moment and looked up into the ambassador's bloodshot eyes. "Did Castro kill my Papa?" he asked, biting his lower lip.

"Yes. Your father was executed by the Revolution. I...I don't know what to tell you. He was such a wonderful man."

Young Manuel Garcia stood steady, still looking up at the ambassador, his voice that of a man. "I will kill Fidel Castro, just like I killed..." the boy said stopping in mid-sentence glaring at his sister, who was crying and shaking her head.

"Uncle Gilberto, please take me home to get Blanco."

Tears welled in the ambassador's eyes as he dropped to the boy's side, his voice cracking. "Manuel," he said in a whisper, "I'm sorry, but Castro's soldiers killed Blanco too..."

"Take me to the cowards that did it and I will kill all of them with my machete!" the boy shouted, crossing himself before he turned and ran to the veranda railing and burst into tears. Suddenly the boy's hatred for the giant *Americano* vanished as Uncle Gilberto placed his hand on his shoulder.

An hour later, Carlos Garcia Rangel's letter to his children was brought to the veranda on a silver tray. "Sorry to interrupt, Ambassador," Mario said, "but a letter has come for you, Señora. It was hand delivered by a Cuban lieutenant who would not give me his name."

Roscena's hands shook uncontrollably when she tried to open it, and the ambassador took it from her. "Please read it to us darling," she said.

The ambassador opened the letter and began to read with a voice as clear as the morning sky. When he had finished, he said in a firm and fatherly manner, "Children, you must now get ready to go to America."

The ambassador shook his head, knowing it would not be an easy task since Castro's secret police had the embassy surrounded, determined not to let the Garcia orphans escape to the free world.

* * *

Holly Woodson was among the masses detained at the magistrate's court awaiting their fate. In the Plaza outside, she could hear chants of *Paredón! Paredón! To the wall! To the wall!* Then she flinched with the discharge of the firing squad's rifles bringing roars of approval from the crowd.

Under immediate protest from the British embassy, she was placed under house arrest in her suite at the Hotel Nacional until her deportation to the United States on Eastern Airlines' Monday morning flight.

Father O'Brien, with help from the Catholic underground, escaped on a trawler out into international waters that night. He was picked up by the CIA in a high-powered speedboat and taken to JM/WAVE, the newly formed secret CIA station south of Miami. After two days of debriefing by Axial Hanson on the University of Miami campus he was given a choice of applying for political asylum in Panama or becoming an agent of the Central Intelligence Agency.

It was a simple decision, and on April 24th Father O'Brien arrived at Guy Banister's Camp Street detective office in New Orleans, the CIA's front for covert Cuban exile operations. The priest was given a warm welcoming lunch at Antoine's by his old boss, Mafia lieutenant Anthony Alfonso and his banker, Tommy Frazier, the president of Whitney National Bank.

Chapter Nineteen

Miami

April 24, 1961

The Operation Pedro Pan chartered Southern Airways DC-3 prepared for takeoff from Havana's *Rancho Boyeros* airport with sixty-four children on board. Flight 1077 was sponsored by the Catholic diocese of Miami and was cleared to taxi, its mission to evacuate the children made orphans by Castro's firing squads. Maria crossed herself before gripping young Alfredo's hand and uttering a silent prayer that she wouldn't start crying all over again.

Manuel sat on the edge of his seat peering out the window and fidgeting with excitement as the engines revved and the plane began to roll. A few moments later the boy watched the runway flashing by on his maiden flight and smiled reassuringly at his sister when the plane lumbered into the air. "Maria, when I am older I will return to kill Fidel for killing our Papa," he said watching a tear trickling down his sister's cheek as she watched the Havana harbor fade into the morning haze.

Thirty minutes later Eastern Airlines Flight 277 lifted off for Miami with Holly Woodson seated in the first class cabin drinking a bloody Mary. The de-

187

ported journalist looked down and saw her beloved Hotel Nacional fading in the distance. *Don't worry, my love, I shall return*, she thought, recalling the many fond memories she had in residence over the past three years. Once the sting was out of her coverage of Don Carlos' execution, she hoped to get her work visa reinstated as a journalist. *Castro is a publicity junkie and his bloody Revolution lives off the press, both good and bad*, she thought. *So Fidel, ole chap, as Churchill once said, this is going to be a very long fight.*

Holly was looking forward to the afternoon news conference where she would be reporting as a guest on the CBS news in their coverage of the arrival of the Cuban orphans. Axial Hanson was meeting her at customs, before going on to the University of Miami campus to rehearse. She opened her portable typewriter and began composing the script describing the brutal and appalling fate of the hundreds of orphans still left on the island. When she finished, her story was so sad that it brought tears to her eyes as she stared down into the deep blue waters of the Florida Straits.

The nattily attired gentleman had just finished his coffee when Holly saw her case officer motioning for her to follow him when she walked out of customs with her luggage. A taxi was waiting, and Axial Hanson opened the door and rushed her inside. Twenty minutes later they were in his campus office when Axial closed the door and said, "Give me your piece on the orphans."

Holly handed him the speech and watched as a distressed look covered Hanson's face. "Wow, that's quite emotional," he said with a sigh. "I'll have to turn it over to the *Miami Herald* for release under a pen name."

"Like hell you will, Axial! I've been told I was going on the air live with *The CBS Evening News*."

"Look, Holly, any more coverage of the orphans and you will really piss Castro off. You'll run the risk of blowing your cover and alienating the Castro government so that you will *never* be allowed to return to Havana."

"You have a valid point, Axial, but, it tears my heart out not to be with those kids," Holly said with tears welling up in her eyes as her voice broke. "Very well, what's my next assignment then?" she managed to say wiping her eyes with a Kleenex and digging in her purse for a cigarette.

Axial rose and gently placed his hand on her shoulder as he lit her cigarette. "How about taking some time off in New Orleans, doing your own thing for a while? I've made arrangements with Sir Allenby for a leave of absence from the BBC."

Holly's mouth curled into a weak smile as she exhaled. "The Big Easy? I do say, New Orleans in the spring is a real jazz lover's dream. But what do I do there?"

"Drink a cool Hurricane in the courtyard at Pat O'Brien's in the French Quarter. Listen to some jazz—just take it easy."

"Seriously, Axial. I don't have anything to wear."

"Don't worry. Buy some outfits and put it on your expense account," Axial chuckled, gathering up his briefcase and handing her a photograph. "I was just kidding, you're not really going on a vacation, so listen up. You have exactly forty minutes to catch your flight. When you get to the New Orleans airport, here's your target."

"What a handsome bloke. Who is this chap?"

"Let's get going. I'll brief you on the way. I'll have my secretary call the FAA and cancel his flight to Costa Rica so he can't take off."

***

Thirty miles south of Miami that morning the Southern Flight 1077 was on its final approach to the Homestead Air Force Base when the tower gave it permission to land. Thanks to Uncle Gilberto, Don Carlos' last instructions to his children were completed when the ambassador smuggled the children out of the embassy in his limo and took them to a private mass held by Bishop Masvidal in the Iglesia del Sagrado Corazon de Jesus. Afterwards they were given fake birth certificates and spent the night in the Bishop's private residence before being mingled with the other orphans to be deported.

"Thank God," Maria sighed when the captain announced they were about to land. The Garcias clapped along with their fellow orphans and chaperones when the plane touched down in their new homeland. A few minutes later they disembarked into the Florida sunshine before filing into a hangar filled with rows of perfectly aligned folding chairs and Red Cross workers assisting the nuns and priests. The orphans scurried through the blinding flashbulbs and the army of reporters as smiling airmen in starched fatigues flirted with Maria as they handed out Coca-Colas. *America the Beautiful* was playing in the background and the only thing missing to Manuel was Blanco.

"Are you the Garcias?" a priest inquired of Maria.

"Yes we are."

"What did he say?" Manuel asked as he followed his sister to seats on the front row.

"You are going to have to learn English, Manuel," Maria replied as a hush fell over the hangar when the base color guard marched in to the band playing the *Stars and Stripes Forever*.

A graying cleric appeared on the podium accompanied by an Air Force chaplain and the base commander. The Cardinal of New York seemed very distressed waving to the television camera that was part of the CIA propaganda ploy to be used against the Cuban dictator. He began by saying, "Children, God bless you and God bless America for receiving you. America is your new home, so thank the Americans for their kind deeds."

Then the bishop of Miami took over in Spanish. "Today you will be going through in-processing with U.S. immigration officers. You will all receive medical exams, and don't worry about the shots. They only sting a little and will keep you healthy. I have appealed to the generous Americans to give you all new homes. The Americans have been very helpful, and all of you will be finding new homes very soon. Life will start anew, so try not to worry about the loss of your parents and loved ones. Forget about the past and look to the future. When possible, we will try to keep brothers and sisters with the same foster parents, but I must warn you now that this will not always be possible. With God's help, we will try."

Maria grasped her brothers' hands and bit her lip. *Please, God, please, keep us together.*

In a modest row cottage on Joseph Street, Charles and Lena Fontenot were sitting down to their red beans and rice on TV trays to watch the evening news.

190

"Good evening, this is the CBS Evening News," Walter Cronkite opened in his customary manner. "I'm reporting tonight from Homestead Air Force Base south of Miami where the Cardinal of New York has come to welcome sixty-four Cuban war orphans whose parents were executed by Fidel Castro."

The camera panned first to the Cardinal and then to the audience before focusing in on the Garcia orphans when the anchorman's voice turned unusually grim. "In Cuba there has been a display of human brutality unknown to the modern world since the days of Adolph Hitler's Nazi Germany. These are only a handful of the orphans resulting from Castro's execution squads. Tonight we have the orphans of the late Don Carlos Garcia Rangel, whose execution was filmed by the BBC after the failed Bay of Pigs invasion. The atrocity has shocked the free world."

The camera broke away to replay Holly's footage of Don Carlos' bullet-riddled body falling into the grave.

The broadcast returned to the Garcias who had no clue they were being filmed. "These are the children of Don Carlos Garcia Rangel. Their mother died a year ago of cancer. A few short weeks ago they lived in the Casa de Azucar, an elegant villa on the family's vast sugar plantation near the Bay of Pigs. When the village priest who was escorting them to Havana was killed in the battle, they miraculously escaped and made their way alone to the Colombian embassy. Without the Colombian ambassador's appeal to Bishop Masvidal in Havana and the Cardinal of New York, their evacuation to freedom would have never taken place. We can only speculate what their fate would have been at the hands of the Communist Revolution."

The camera panned around the hangar, focusing once again on the Garcias as Cronkite continued. "The Garcia children are being placed in foster homes in the United States thanks to Operation Pedro Pan of the diocese of Miami. CBS News has been informed that an exiled Cuban physician and his wife, now living in Miami, have accepted Maria and the youngest brother, Alfredo, leaving twelve-year-old Manuel yet without a home. America's hearts go out to the Garcia children and especially to Manuel, along with the rest of the Cuban orphans assembled here. I am confident that the generosity of the American people will be forthcoming as always in this most tragic situation."

Lena Fontenot burst into tears at the sight of Manuel Garcia on her television screen. The resemblance of Manuel to her dead son, Charlie, was shocking, even to her husband Charles, who reached over and hugged his wife. "Now, now, sugar," he said softly as he held her and fought back his tears.

"Charles," Lena sobbed, "please, please call Father Gautier. Tell him...tell him we have a home for that young Cuban boy. He can have Charlie's room and all his toys, clothes, and everything. Please, for God's sakes, can't we all have a new life together? Please, Charles."

Charles Fontenot's hands trembled as he dialed Father Gautier's number at the Holy Name of Jesus Church on St. Charles Avenue. The priest had buried Charlie less than two weeks ago after he electrocuted himself by putting on the headset of his short-wave radio in the bathtub. His grieving father could feel tears of joy at the thought of having a new foster son to take to the LSU football games. *If only I had never bought Charlie that damn war surplus radio for his thirteenth birthday,* the baker was thinking when the priest's comforting voice came on the line.

In the New Orleans airport just a few miles from the Fontenot's home in the Garden District, Tex Morris waited for his flight to Central America. Tex was sipping Jack Daniels and Coke and watching the television behind the bar when Walter Cronkite came on the screen and his voice faded. "Bartender, will you turn it up?" Tex asked, as the camera zoomed in on the Garcia orphans followed by the BBC footage of Don Carlos' execution. He listened intently to the BBC reporter's account of the shocking event.

"Well, I'll be damned," Tex muttered, recalling how bravely Manuel Garcia had protected his sister and brother inside the San Blas church.

The lieutenant suddenly felt the urge to nudge the strangers seated next to him and say, "Hey partner, I know those kids!" Tex wanted to stand up and shout that the Bay of Pigs had been a fucking disaster. He wanted to tell the crowd that he had fought with *La Brigada* in the battle of San Blas and how stupid it was that Max had gotten killed. He wanted to tell the world that his commander-in-chief was a yellow-bellied chicken-shit for leaving his brave Guats to die on the beaches of Giron.

Orders are orders and my lips are sealed, Tex thought, feeling a surge of adrenaline as he watched Manuel's face fade into the Oldsmobile jingle showcasing a shiny new black Ninety-Eight. Tex sipped his drink and stared blankly at the screen, suddenly realizing that the black Olds he had shot up on the San Blas highway was somehow connected to all of this.

He remembered stopping on his way back to Blue Beach and finding no bloodstains on the seats before tracking the driver's footprints into the cane field toward the tower. *My God,* he realized, *the driver of that Olds was the same guy who Cronkite just showed being executed, and those are his kids in Miami that I nearly murdered!*

The hair on Tex's neck bristled at how close he had come to blasting the car with his BAR as it streaked toward San Blas that night. "Damn it! I can't believe it!"

"Believe what, lieutenant?" asked a seductive British voice standing behind him making Tex jump like he had been kicked in the ass with a cowboy boot.

"Who...who are you?" Tex stammered, spinning around on his stool to find himself staring at the cleavage escaping from Holly Woodson's black lace bra.

"Excuse me, ole chap. I'm up here," Holly purred as Tex slowly stood and shook her outstretched hand. "My name is Holly Woodson of the BBC."

"I'm sorry but you've got me mixed up with someone else Miss, uh...Woodson," Tex stuttered thinking—*Jesus, those knockers must be 38-Ds.* He then glanced at the television, stepping back from the bar.

"Come now, Lieutenant Morris. I know who you are, and that's okay. I filmed that piece at the Central Australian for the BBC last week."

Who the hell is this chick? Is she trying to mess me over or what? Get me to admit I went ashore with the 4th at Giron? Watch it Tex, ole buddy, or you'll get your ass court-martialed for running your mouth to the press.

Tex was reaching inside his jacket for his wallet when he heard the announcement. "Lasca Flight 247 for San Jose, Costa Rica has been canceled. All passengers please go immediately to the Lasca ticket counter for rebooking."

"Aw man! That's my flight, lady. Nice to meet you, but I gotta bug-out now," Tex groaned, throwing down a ten dollar bill on the bar.

"Not so bloody fast, lieutenant. Your flight was cancelled. Relax, let's have a drink. I just left Miami, where I was briefed on your mission at the Bay of Pigs. My handler got your story straightaway from Gray, and some bloke named Walter something-or-other. What a terrific story yours is, I must say, and very brave…"

Tex glanced around nervously, picking up his change. "Let's step over there," he said, motioning toward an empty table in the corner. "How about showing me some ID."

Holly produced her BBC press credentials, along with her passport. "Relax, ole chap, we're working for the same people."

"You're the reporter who filmed that execution?"

"Precisely. I filmed that piece at the sugar mill. And why did you sock my mate Gonzo in the jaw at the Bar Habana? Don't you know it's unbecoming of an officer and a gentlemen to sock little blokes and then run out on your bar tab, *El Grande*?"

"Who the hell are you, really? I don't know any Gonzo. Who sent you and what in the hell do you want with me? Hey, I've got to bug out of here lady."

"Steady now, ole chap. No one sent me. Destiny, I say, made our paths cross today. Strange, isn't it? Buy me a drink, Tex, and I will tell you how rotten Lieutenant Silas really felt about executing that chap, Don Carlos, even if it is making him a bloody Cuban hero, thanks to me and the BBC. It's to your credit the Garcia children on the telly are not dead tonight."

Tex was watching Holly's perfectly formed moist lips spill out her words while imagining how wonderful it would feel to have those luscious lips to give him a blowjob. "All right, I haven't got anything else to do. Let's get the hell out of here, and you're not writing about me in the press. Is that damn well understood?"

"Fair enough, ole chap. Let's, as you Yanks say, blow this joint…"

"Okay, but let me check my flight first. We'll talk down in the Quarter, unless I can get a flight tonight."

"Have you been to Pat O'Brien's?"

"Are you shitten me, I'm from Texas!"

"Let's go queue for your flight change then. I've got reservations at the Jung Hotel and I need to drop off my luggage or I will lose my room. The dear ole Jung—not the Roosevelt, is it? But it's all I can afford off the dole."

"Roger that. Now, let's get the hell out of Dodge," Tex exclaimed as his jaw slackened watching Holly straighten her skirt.

The red neon sign hanging on the side of the Jung cast a flashing glow on her tits sliding to and fro with the smoothness of the glider on Grandma Morris' front porch. *By the numbers,* the lieutenant was thinking, listening to Holly's groans harmonizing with the slow drone of the ceiling fan as Fats sang, "*I found my thrill on Blueberry Hill,*" on the clock radio. The sweat dripped off the end of his nose to the sound of their sweaty bellies keeping rhythm with the beat of the song.

He liked having her long legs driving him deeper with each powerful thrust as Fats Domino finished the song and the news came on. The lieutenant never missed a stroke as he reached over and turned off the radio leaving the sounds of their sweaty bellies still slapping together: "Faster! Faster! I s-a-y! Don't stop! Don't you dare stop, you bloody bastard!"

Tex watched the sweat raining off his face, pooling on her breasts before trickling onto the bed, "I'm drowning you, baby. Wanna get on top for a spell?"

"What's wrong? Those Hurricanes take the lead out your pistol, first lieu...?"

"Hell no! Now shut up and get your fine ass on top for a while, and that's an order," Tex gasped.

"My dear lieu, you are out of uniform," Holly giggled, locking her legs tightly. "I do say, if you want a different throw at this, let's go Fido."

"On top, you hot bitch, and make damn sure the fact I needed a breather doesn't hit *The Army Times.*"

"Naughty boy, you. Okay, you get your way. Yes, my...oh my. My Yes! Oh yes! This is...this is delightful, I say!"

Tex watched the play of the red flashing light casting her shadow off the cracked ceiling when her head suddenly thrust back and he knew Holly Woodson was nearing her climax. "Oh God, *now,*" she screamed before collapsing with a great sigh on his chest.

Tex reached over and turned the radio back on in time to hear the announcer saying he was about to play a new Ray Charles song—*I Can't Stop Loving You.* He took her in his arms and kissed her when Holly took her hand and wiped the perspiration off his face. "How did it feel?" she asked, leaning over and lighting a cigarette.

"Not bad for round two."

"No, I mean going ashore at Giron. Weren't you terrified being under enemy fire for the first time in your…?"

"I don't know what in the hell you are talking about. Roger?"

"Come now, Tex. Tell me how you felt after you shot Jose Onis…"

"Who the hell is Jose Onis?"

"Okay, if you don't want to talk about it—*don't*," Holly pouted, bouncing out of bed and running into the bathroom.

Tex got up and poured a stiff bourbon before hearing the commode flush. "What did this guy Walter look like?" he asked when Holly came back into the room, lifting her cigarette out of the ashtray.

"Gimpy little creep, Elliot was," Holly replied getting back in bed. Tex lay back down feeling very perplexed when she leaned over him. Swaying her breasts in his face, she stuck her nipple in his mouth and said with a laugh, "Naughty boy, you. Still don't trust me after all of that?"

"Something real strange about you being at the airport has got me bugged. That shit-head Elliot got you trailing me and asking all this bullshit about Cuba?"

"Don't feel so bloody important," Holly giggled. "Why in the hell would Elliot want you trailed?" she added, putting her arms around him and laying her head on his shoulder.

"Screw it. I don't know."

"I'm jolly game for doing that," she laughed, going to her knees and applying hot moist lips to cock his pistol for round three.

The wakeup call rang harshly at six the next morning sending Tex into the shower. "Do we have time to pop down to the French Market for beignets and coffee, love?" Holly yawned, stretching her long legs out from under the sheet, and rolling onto her side to turn on the radio.

Tex began dressing, saying with a laugh, "Sorry gal, I gotta bug out of here. Gotta catch a plane."

Holly smiled up at him. "Why not stay here with me for a few days?"

"Another time—got some business to attend to down yonder."

"By the name of Teresa Ortiz, no less."

Tex slammed his towel on the bed. "What the hell are you talking about now? Who the hell are you, Goddamn it?"

"Steady, ole chap, just joshing you. Now come down here and give me a quickie or I will get insanely jealous," Holly beckoned, lying back and spreading her legs.

Twenty minutes later Tex stood in the door, and heard Holly Woodson's cheerful, "Cheerio. You have my card, love. Do stay in touch."

"Don't you worry, gal, I got you on file," Tex replied, closing the door.

Wow! What a stud, that one, Holly thought as she showered. *What do I tell Hanson? Is Lieutenant Morris a risk to national security by leaking the CIA's role at the Bay of Pigs? Yes or No?*

* * *

Three hours later, Tex passed through customs at the Juan Santa Maria Airport and out into a pleasant breeze. It was eleven in the morning and the San Jose air felt cool and refreshing, a welcome change from the humidity of New Orleans. On the flight down, he had drunk a Bacardi the stewardess poured off the serving cart that warmed his belly and made him dream about the bizarre night he had spent at the Jung. Tex Morris had that intimate feeling a young soldier gets deep in his groin after screwing his brains out—he wanted to run out in the street and howl like a dog.

He had just arrived but already liked Costa Rica immensely, watching the lush green of the surrounding hills covered with flowering poinsettias on the ride into San Jose. He tipped the *taxista* an extra ten *colones* and stood momentarily so he could get a good look at the Key Largo Bar and the adjacent Morazan Park.

The joint is just like Teresa described it, he thought as he picked up his bag and crossed the street and disappeared inside the Key Largo. The bar was dead except for the barman who was taking inventory and an old woman who stopped mopping and looked up from the dance floor surrounded with tables, their chairs turned on top.

"*Buenos Dias, señor,*" the barman called out. "*Somos cerrados hasta seis esta noche.*"

"*La Señorita Ortiz ani esta? Me llamo Tex Morris.*"

"*Un momento, señor,*" the barman replied while turning his back and picking up the intercom. He hung up, gesturing with his hand to the top of the stairs as Tex smiled to the old woman who quickly returned to her mopping.

He was halfway up the stairs when the door flung open. "Tex! I thought I would never hear from you again." Teresa shrieked at the man now running up the steps to sweep her off her feet.

"Don't lie to me, Señorita Ortiz. You knew I'd drag my sorry ass up. How've you been, gal, since you ran out on me in San Felipe?" he asked, putting her down in the middle of a large spacious room.

"*So,* you got my note, sweetheart. What are you doing here?"

"I just figured I would drop down and surprise you before I shipped out."

"Oh, you are so handsome, Tex, and you made it back alive from Cuba, thank God. Why didn't you call me, *sin verguenza?*"

"Because you ran out on me, and who in the hell said I'd been to Cuba?"

"I have my way of knowing such things. I once worked for the Company in Guatemala in an establishment you named the *Casa de Teresa* in my honor, remember that, John Wayne?"

"How the hell could I forget? You're mighty right. I'll never forget the night you showed up down there and threw me out of your room, gal. I've missed the hell out of you!"

"*La Brigada,* it is terrible, leaving the poor Guats to die and get captured by Castro. Was it awful?"

"I only know what I've seen on TV."

"Oh, shut up and kiss me, and kiss me again, you animal. Are you just going to stand there and not make love to me, Duke?" Teresa whispered, unbuttoning his shirt and rubbing his chest as they slipped down to the couch. "Wait, Tex! Lock the door first."

* * *

Holly finished her café au lait and beignets at the open-air Café du Monde in the French Market before strolling through Jackson Square. She quickened her pace as she crossed Canal Street and entered the Jung Hotel.

From her room she dialed her case officer's secure line at his Buena Vista apartment in Miami. "You were quite right, Axial. If ever there was a man with a keen eye for a fancy skirt, it's Lieutenant William G. Morris. What a show dog, that one."

"Could you get him to talk about the Bay of Pigs or Guatemala?"

"Not a wee peep."

"Not going ashore or anything? Did you give it your best shot?"

"Many shots indeed!" Holly laughed before the wailing jazz of a funeral procession passing by the hotel caused her to pause. "Morris left for San Jose this morning. Is there anything else?"

"Yes," Hanson replied. "There are a couple of things we need done as long as you're down in the Big Easy, but hang ten, I don't have time to discuss it now."

Axial Hanson hung up the telephone and lit a cigarette, leaving his last one still burning in the ashtray next to his train ticket to Washington. The man who prided himself in being Mr. Coup gazed out the window at the Buena Vista swimming pool and picked up a top-secret document off the table. "To hell with you, Kirkpatrick. You sold the Company down the river, you turncoat son-of-a bitch," Hanson swore, throwing down the photocopy marked TOP SECRET EYES OF THE PRESIDENT ONLY document on the table. He glared at it for a while and finally read the title in a whisper, "DRAFT—The Inspector General's Survey of the Cuban Operation, to be dated October 1961 and not issued without the consent of the DCI and the President." ·

Hanson was thinking about Lyman Kirkpatrick who he had considered a friend since the OSS days and Company man. Back in 1952 he had gone to see him in the hospital after he had been stricken with polio, ending his chances of promotion to the Deputy Director of Plans leaving him no other option but to assume the Inspector General post or take a medical retirement. Axial picked up the report again and reread the summary of the IG's inquiry that was about to be released to the President of the United States.

- "The president's cancellation of the D-Day air strike was not the chief cause of failure." *Bullshit! After we lost air superiority we were sitting ducks. Bissell begged the president for the D-Day strikes.*
- "The operation was predicated on the belief, held by CIA Deputy Director of plans Richard Bissell, that the invasion would, like a *deus ex machina,* produce a shock inside Cuba and trigger an uprising against Castro." *Are you shitting me, Kirk? We were supposed to land at Trinidad where there were six thousand political prisoners to be armed and allowed to escape into the Escambry Mountains, for God's sake.*
- "Agency handlers treated the Cuban exile politicians like puppets." *Congratulations, you got that right, Kirk. We didn't select the Cubans, Washington politicians did and they were a royal pain in the ass.*
- "What was supposed to be a covert operation became a major overt military project due to multiple security leaks." *Well sure. The president read the March 17th New York Times articles published well beforehand telling anyone who could read that the invasion was on its way.*
- "CIA officials misled the White House into believing that success was still likely." *Fuck Kirkpatrick! Dulles told Kennedy that without the support of American air power after the invasion was moved to the Bay of Pigs there was only a twenty percent chance of success.*

Hanson took his lighter and burned each page of the secret document he had received from his co-conspirators back at Langley. *Dulles, Bissell, and the General are finished for sure,* he thought, *and my ass will be next after this report gets released. That son-of-a-bitch Kennedy is well on his way to making good his threat to destroy the CIA.*

An hour later, Hanson was in his sleeper on the overnight train to Washington's Union Station. To the singing of rails, his clandestine frame of mind for a coup d'etat turned into a self-analysis of his planned actions against the president. He felt his failure to act would have a great impact on the future national security goals of the United States. He had, in his own patriotic mind, done the right thing by forming the White Hand with two senior officers of the CIA. The White Hand Black Hand partnership was a play on words to the Black Hand—or Chicago Mafia. Axial snuffed out his cigarette and turned off the lights as his thoughts turned to the times he had laid his life on the line for his country. Axial Hanson was too tired now to try and count.

Before he allowed the swaying coach to rock him to sleep, Mr. Coup recited the premise for a successful covert operation: *Is the mission in the best interest of the United States? Can it be accomplished? Will secrecy be maintained?*

Yes is the answer to all three, Axial Hanson yawned, feeling free of all moral restrictions and legal technicalities of the pros and cons of executing his White Hand assassination plot. The only thing he had left to do was to recruit the fourth member of the secret cell. Hanson knew just the man to help pull off the biggest coup of his career as he drifted off into a sound sleep.

Chapter Twenty

Boston

November 29, 1961

The slate grayness of the cold November sky reminded Walter of the afternoon he buried his father four years ago to the day. Standing at his mother's grave, he read Winston Porter Elliot's name chiseled on the granite headstone and suddenly realized he was alone. *Maybe no one knew about her passing,* he thought, feeling embarrassed that no one had shown up for her graveside service.

He stared down at the bronze casket blanketed with a spray of white roses sent by Mr. and Mrs. Dulles and waited for the rector to begin the service. Mildred Cole had called to express Mr. Dulles' condolences and inform him that the DCI was meeting with President Kennedy in the morning and would be unable to attend the funeral. Miss Cole had sounded very sympathetic and upset when Walter had told her the flowers were beautiful.

It's Dulles' final day as Director of the CIA, Walter thought, *and it's a damn shame I'm not able to be with him.* He felt a surge of deep resentment that neither his mentor nor anyone else from the Company came to pay their respects to the widow of one of its WWII OSS heroes.

These thoughts were colder than the wind whipping the Episcopal rector's white robe against his legs as he recited the 23rd Psalm. When the rector finished the scripture reading, he went on to speak of Margaret Chamberlain Elliot's belief in God and the hereafter. At the end of the service a lone train whistle sounded in the distance. "The sound of that train makes me think your mother is heaven bound, Walter," the rector said smiling at him. "Now will you join me in reciting the Lord's Prayer."

What a wonderful comforting feeling: Mother on the train bound for heaven, Walter was thinking, recalling the swaying north bound *Metroliner* racing over the rails from Washington's Union Station. The distant, morbid whistle kept him awake as the train streaked through the night bringing him home for his last Thanksgiving before the estate was to be auctioned off by the bank in early December. *It's such a pity that Mother couldn't live her remaining years in her birthplace,* Walter had thought on entering the foyer that night to the warm smile and hug from the frail woman. *At least she died peacefully in her sleep knowing I was home with her.*

Walter shook the hands of the few friends in attendance and then found himself standing alone at the grave after the mourners had quietly retreated from the cold. Attorney Ashton shuffled over and shook Walter's hand, passing on his somber condolences. "I'm awfully sorry about your mother, Walter. Sometimes it's for the best."

"Thank you for being here. In a way it *is* a blessing that she was spared the foreclosure."

"Yes, it really was. You're going to remain in Boston for a few days, aren't you?"

"Yes sir, until next Sunday."

"Good. Come to my office at nine tomorrow and I'll read her will and we can discuss the details of the bankruptcy proceedings."

"Nine o'clock tomorrow, yes sir. Thank you once again for coming."

The old attorney slowly walked across the cemetery, taking care not to fall on the frozen earth. Walter watched him go, remembering fondly the times when he was a strong and robust man laughing with Walter's parents on their sailing yacht,

Silver Service. Taking a white rose off the spray, Walter tucked it in his lapel and kneeled down to kiss his mother's casket.

He then turned to the rector, who was the only one remaining besides the funeral director and the workers. Walter had up until this moment held his emotions in control. Shaking the rector's cold hand made it difficult to fight back tears as the permanence of her death sank in with the Rector saying, "She was a wonderful woman who loved you deeply, Walter."

Walter thanked him for the beautiful service and his kind words and took a seat on a concrete bench to watch the gravediggers fill in the grave.

The CIA was the only thing Walter Elliott had left. Dulles was going to get canned, and he wasn't certain where he stood with the Company after being the DCI's fair-haired boy for so long. This was especially true now that Kennedy had made Dulles the scapegoat for the Bay of Pigs. Walter smiled weakly, recalling the words of the Great White Case Officer, riddling so elegantly in the aftermath of the Bay of Pigs: "Junior, I am getting you out of the limelight in my twilight so you won't get burned in my firing fight. I am hiding you in the most secretive and secure position of all for your own well-being, I reckon," he added with a chuckle as he lit his pipe and winked.

"And where might that be, sir?"

"In the 'Bank' for covert operations where you will help prepare the $260 million budget to keep our eighteen hundred officers going, amongst other things, I reckon. The Bank *is* the very heart of the CIA. Use your time there wisely and keep a low profile. Let time pass and don't become restless."

The young officer had accepted Dulles' advice and taken things a day at a time. His new staff position gave him important contacts within the Directorate of Administration preparing the covert action budget. It was definitely a demotion after working for the DCI, and he had seriously considered quitting at first and going to graduate school. Walter Elliot had no choice but to stay in the CIA until his trust fund became available at age thirty-three.

With the budget approval process, Walter became intrigued with the money trail. He had learned from the Bank that where there is money there lies the power. The covert action funding of $260 million was only a drop in the bucket compared to the controller's total budget of hundreds of millions of dollars. Only the president and the chairmen of the House and Senate Appropriations Committees had an estimate of the exact amount with the director and a handful of senior officers knowing how it was spent. When the OMB auditors came to investigate, it was reported that there was absolutely no accountability to congress or the White House.

After the workmen put the finishing touches on the dark earth with their spades, Walter walked over to the grave. *Mother, I have buried my past with you today, I am glad to say. I swear on your grave that I will rise to the top, and someday Walter Stewart Elliot III will become the Director of the CIA.* He stood there until the snow turned the earth white saying his final good by. *This is the beginning of a new chapter in my life. You are at peace now, Mother—may God rest your soul.*

Returning to his father's old black Cadillac, Walter started the engine and was shivering waiting for the car to warm up. Suddenly, the passenger door was jerked open and a man jumped in without saying a word. "Axial! You scared the shit out of me."

"Sorry I missed the funeral, Walt. The snow hit D.C. and my shuttle was delayed. I'm awful sorry about your mother, son."

"Thanks, Axial, but you shouldn't have come," Walter replied to the senior officer whom he had not seen since the war room after the Bay of Pigs.

Axial Hanson had disappeared from Langley and obviously escaped up until now from being axed by President Kennedy. Back at Langley his lingering reputation as *the* renegade Mr. Coup from the remaining few OSS old guard was built into a legend. "Where have you been, for God's sake?" Walter asked, before noticing Hanson's telltale tan, a sure bet the senior officer was stationed at JM/WAVE in Miami.

Hanson combed the snow out of his sun-bleached hair and rubbed his muscular legs warming up his hands. "I've forgotten how miserably cold these New England winters can get. Remember that time you fell out of the C-54 down in Guatemala, Walt?"

"Don't remind me. You shouldn't have come all this way."

"Wouldn't have missed it out of respect for my old colleague's widow and for you, my man. The director has a meeting with President Kennedy and requested that I represent him and Mrs. Dulles. So, for God's sake, don't tell him I was late."

"Well, thank you for coming."

"Forget it. Are you okay, son? You look pale."

"Sure, fine. Just a little cold. You never told me that you were a friend of my old man."

"We covert spooks are all blood brothers in one way or the other. CIA, OSS, what the hell. It's all the same intelligence fraternity. But you and I have something special too: Skull and Bones and Yale, you know?"

"Sure thing. Sure we do."

"Okay. Then let's get this Caddy rolling and find some coffee someplace where we can chat. I've just left Langley and there's something big I'm going to share with you under the secrecy of the 'Bones,' brother Walter, understand?"

* * *

Walter was waiting in Mr. Ashton's law office the next morning and was reading the *New York Times* that was lying on the coffee table. The front-page headline read that Kennedy had forced Allen Dulles' resignation and had appointed John A. McCone as his replacement. After meeting with Hanson in a roadside diner last night, this was old news.

The events of the last twenty-four hours were beyond his wildest comprehension and left Walter Elliott with a sick feeling in his guts. The very thought that he had been tapped by Hanson to be part of the conspiracy had not fully sunk in yet. *Am I going to be a Benedict Arnold or a Nathan Hale?* he wondered, feeling his heart flutter.

He could clearly picture the statue of Captain Nathan Hale standing on the campus at Yale, his hands bound behind his back before being hanged by the British as a spy. His perception of being a Nathan Hale rather than the traitor Benedict Arnold was weighing heavily on Walter Elliot's mind. Hanson's words kept coming back again and again. "Walter, I have something to tell you within the shrouded secrecy of our brotherhood."

"You have my word," Walter shrugged.

"You swear to commit suicide rather than to disclose your co-conspirators, two of whose names you will never know or never have the need to know?"

"*Jesus!*" Walter whispered when Hanson grabbed his right hand in a strong grip while at the same time reaching into his coat pocket and withdrawing a handsome Parker fountain pen. "Merry Christmas, Walt. Your present has a cyanide pill hidden in the top."

Every word of their conversation remained as vile this morning as the coffee in Maxi's Diner on the seedy Boston street did last night. Darkness had fallen and the snow was blowing horizontally against the foggy windows when Hanson made his pitch. "As you know, Dulles and General Cabell, along with Richard Bissell, are the fall guys for Kennedy screwing up the Bay of Pigs."

"Axial, it's not your place…"

"Don't interrupt me. Kirkpatrick gave the new director, McCone, a copy of his Inspector General report before either Dulles or Bissell had a chance to review it, prior to McCone being sworn in as the new DCI. Kirkpatrick and McCone are definitely part of Kennedy's witch-hunt to destroy the agency, and I'm damn well not going to sit on my ass and let them."

"Why would they?" Walter asked, glancing nervously around him.

"Kirkpatrick is an envious bastard who's sore about losing out to Bissell for the Deputy Director of Plans job after he was stricken with polio a few years back. He's using his IG survey to suck up to the Kennedys in hopes of getting the DDP job now that Bissell has been canned. His report blames the total failure of the Bay of Pigs on the Directorate for Plans. Bissell, in particular, has been accused of dereliction of duty for not advising Kennedy of the possibility of failure, if you can believe that crap."

"Have you read the IG's report?"

"Every Goddamn lying word of it…twice! It never mentions that Kennedy moved the invasion site from Trinidad to the Bay of Pigs at the last minute or called off the air strikes."

"How did you get a copy?"

"I got ways to get any and every Goddamn thing there is at Langley."

"What's the status of General Taylor's board of inquiry?"

"Hell, that's even worse, Walt. The general is bucking for the Chairmanship of the Joint Chiefs. He and Bobby Kennedy, along with Admiral Burke and Dulles, comprise the investigating board. They didn't even have a court reporter present to record the witnesses' testimonies. Bobby took notes on a yellow tablet and afterwards dictated his version of the story to cover JFK's ass. Gray Lynch told me that shit personally, along with others."

"What a waste, getting these incredibly competent officers canned over presidential politics. Why are you telling me all of this?"

"Just relax. I haven't got to the good part yet. National Security Action Memoranda Numbers 55, 56, 57 for starters," Hanson continued, "issued by the president on June 28th of this year."

"I'm out of the loop now. What's that all about?"

"What's that all about? That fucking Kennedy has redefined and transferred the executive branch's responsibility for executing unconventional warfare in Southeast Asia from the CIA to the Pentagon in retaliation for his screwing up the Bay of Pigs, for a starter, not to mention his détente of selling out to the Soviets."

"Are you kidding? With our involvement in Vietnam? What the hell does the Pentagon know about unconventional warfare?"

"That's not the point. The point is that this is his first step in following through on his promise to break the CIA into a thousand pieces; to wipe our ass out, period."

"There's nothing that can be done about it?"

Hanson leaned forward, whispering his words one at a time. "There is a select group of three of us in the Company that feel it is in the critical interest of the security of the United States Government to eliminate the President."

"Jesus Christ! Do you realize what you just said?"

"Where will the Kennedys stop, Walt? The president *is*, as we speak, smashing the CIA into a thousand pieces to cover his ass politically. Now, Walter Elliot, whether or not you like it, you are now the sworn fourth partner in the White Hand. Remember what the King of Hearts said to the Hatter when he was called to testify?" Hanson asked, imitating Dulles.

"Sure," Walter replied. "And don't be nervous, or I'll have you executed on the spot."

"Very good, Walter. Very good. Now after hearing it all, if you want out, it's too late, son, because I'll have to kill you."

"I wish you wouldn't squeeze so, said the dormouse, who was sitting next to Alice. I can hardly breathe," Walter replied from a following line with Hanson's words sending a cold chill up his spine. He looked at the former OSS Jed, recalling his reputation for having killed hundreds of Germans while serving with the French underground. "What's our next move?"

"Your job is twofold, son. *First*, we need money to operate and pay our agents, and you have access to money at the Bank. *Second*, we need an insider who can get close to Bobby Kennedy, Director McCone, and the White House to keep me apprised of their every move, including every time they take a crap."

"I'm assigned to the Bank, how can I..." Walter's voice trailed off.

"Look, son, I will be your handler from JM/WAVE. I've been at this game for a helluva long time so don't worry. I will arrange all of the details. Just do as you are instructed and everything will be hunky-dory."

Walter had lain awake most of last night mulling over the dubious honor of being selected as a member of the White Hand cell within the CIA that Hanson had forced upon him. While he waited for Mr. Ashton, he didn't know whether to scream with exultation or flee in fear at the very thought of being an integral part of the assassination conspiracy.

There was a fine line between patriotism and treason he had reasoned. It was President Kennedy and not Walter Stewart Elliot III, he concluded, who had crossed the line. Kennedy's blatant abuse of the Oval Office to fulfill political ambitions went against the oath they both had taken to uphold the Constitution of the United States. *He*, Walter Stewart Elliot III, had sworn to uphold the Constitution and in his own mind he was doing just that by reluctantly conceding to become a member of the White Hand. After much debate, Hanson had been convincing in his arguments that the checks and balances of government were about to fail. If the democracy was to be preserved then, under the secrecy of the "S&B," Walter Elliott must do his part as an officer of the CIA.

Walter was still wrestling with his confused emotions, when Mr. Ashton came into the reception room. "Well, Walter, I see you have a new boss back in Washington. Know this fellow McCone?"

"Not personally, sir. He was the chairman of the Atomic Energy Commission under Eisenhower."

"I'm sure the president has made a good choice."

"*Sure he did.* McCone has no previous intelligence experience, is an outsider to the intelligence community, and is a devout Catholic, according to the *Times.*"

"Really? I'm surprised the president didn't appoint his brother Bobby then."

Walter shrugged, following his lawyer into his office thinking: *Bobby would sure as hell have a hand in everything that goes on to salvage the president's reputation. Kennedy's no fool. If he appoints his brother as the new director he would have no plausible way of denying if future CIA operations get screwed up.*

Walter declined coffee and then said to his lawyer behind closed doors, "Bobby Kennedy will remain at the Justice Department, but I will assure you that he will be assuming the informal role of special advisor to the president on CIA affairs. But don't quote me on that. Off the record, the Kennedys are more determined now than ever to avenge the Bay of Pigs fiasco somehow."

* * *

It was a beautiful fall afternoon in Washington, when Robert Kennedy convened a joint meeting of Pentagon and CIA officers in the White House cabinet room. "Gentlemen, our new operation against the Communist regime in Havana shall be code-named 'MONGOOSE,' a name arbitrarily picked for a ferret killing the snake in Cuba. Its sole mission is the elimination of Fidel Castro. It will operate out of our secret CIA station outside of Miami."

Axial Hanson looked across the table at Richard Bissell and was thinking how wrong he had been about the President firing the architect of the Bay of Pigs. *Should I reconsider my White Hand conspiracy,* he asked himself as the meeting was adjourned. He took his notes on his job in the implementation of MON-

GOOSE and put them in his briefcase. Item one on the list was to arrange for Holly Woodson to return to Havana to get close to Fidel.

The next afternoon, Holly had flown in from New Orleans and walked in Hanson's JM/WAVE office. "Holly, you are going to be briefed on Task Force W, the CIA component of Operation MONGOOSE which you will be taking part in. It will take four or five weeks for me to put it all together. MONGOOSE is designed to create a revolt inside Cuba, and your job is to counter Castro's propaganda as soon as you have been reinstated as a BBC correspondent to Havana. I'm still working on that."

"MONGOOSE? What a silly name," Holly replied. *Who is the ferret and who is the snake?* she wondered. *Kennedy or Fidel?*

"Silly or not, the Kennedys are dead serious. Now, my job is to convince Bissell that we need you in Havana, *and* I hope to hell I can get you a work visa. The Cubans are still sensitive to your execution clip of that Cuban guy."

"Does this mean I'm finished in New Orleans?"

"Not yet, these things take time," Hanson replied when there was a knock at the door. Hanson got up and answered it. "Hey Bob, come on in. Holly, meet Bob Planky. He's assigned to monitor the Cuban exiles' terrorist activities in Havana."

Holly glanced up and smiled at the handsome man with the perfectly bronzed physique of a surf bum. He leaned his tall, muscular body against the door, running his hand through his black curly hair while molesting her with intense dark eyes.

Bob Planky had just returned from spending a month with his wife and two young daughters in Huntington Beach, California where he led a double life as a petroleum engineer for Standard Oil traveling the world exploring for oil. His civilian job cover gave the highly decorated Korean War vet an excuse to stay away from home for months as an officer of the CIA's clandestine service.

When Hanson excused himself, Bob Planky quickly asked in his deep baritone voice that resounded around the small room like a foghorn, "You're quite a looker, Holly. Whatcha say we go to the O Club after work for drinks to get acquainted?"

"Yes, yes, I would like that very much," Holly replied, swooning like an English schoolgirl being asked out on her first date. "Are you married, Bob?"

"Sexy lady, do I look like the marrying kind?"

Chapter Twenty-One

Langley

January 1, 1963

Walter Elliot was spending New Years day in his Georgetown living room now being converted into a library to store the volumes of books he had salvaged from his family's Boston estate. The mortgage payments for the 18th-century townhouse had overextended his budget, creating a concern for the young man who never before in his life had to worry about money. He looked at the stack of unpaid bills on the desk and shook his head in disgust.

Glancing up at his great-grandfather's portrait hanging over the fireplace mantel, he admired the founder of the Elliot Silver Company after reading *The Affluent Society* by Harvard economist John Kenneth Galbraith. The book had been a gift from former Yale economist Richard Bissell for 'the sterling job' Walter had done in the war room during the Bay of Pigs and he had just now gotten around to reading it.

Galbraith's book contrasting the affluent few and the impoverished masses in American society struck home. Walter had once been one of the affluent few and he hated being one of the impoverished after the collapse of Elliot Silver. He was having difficulties making ends meet on his meager nine thousand dollar salary as a GS-7. His check barely covered his basic necessities, much less the monthly eight hundred dollar mortgage payment that required dipping into his savings account each month to keep the wolves away. *With wealth there is power,* he thought, glancing back at the portrait of his wealthy grandfather, remembering how important it was to have real money. He leaned back in his Queen Anne chair and watched the glowing fire, counting the days until his trust fund became available at age thirty-three.

Reading the book brought back his fondness for Richard Bissell, the senior officer Attorney General Robert Kennedy fired as chief of Operation MONGOOSE. Axial Hanson had told Walter about the meeting in the cabinet room when Bobby confronted Bissell with the failure of Task Force W. "Dick, you're sitting on your ass and not doing anything about getting rid of Castro and his regime! Bissell! The president's confidence in you has evaporated, especially after you failed to…uh…rectify the Bay of Pigs by assassinating Castro. The 1964 elections are breathing down our necks and Castro's embarrassment to the administration must be fixed."

Mr. Bissell was a good man. Too bad he got canned by the Kennedys, Walter thought. He recalled how awkward everyone felt at the awards ceremony at the White House when President Kennedy presented Bissell the Medal of Freedom after having fired him.

Nineteen sixty-two had been the fastest year in Walter's life. Hanson's visit after his mother's funeral became a constant replay in his mind as he submerged himself in his new job in the Bank. He was relieved that the White Hand had not once contacted him as he went about his duties, duplicating his father's reputation for getting things done. The agency's efficiency reports rated his performance "exceptional, at the highest level of proficiency."

Walter threw himself into his job with the same zeal that had impressed Dulles and Bissell at the beginning of his career. He worked ninety- or, if necessary, one hundred-hour weeks until he was assigned the total responsibility of preparing the covert operations' $260 million budget for the next fiscal year. He now reported directly to the deputy comptroller, the CIA's third most powerful man.

In the process, Walter became mesmerized by the clandestine service's money laundering schemes with organized crime to provide 'off the books' sources of income. The CIA's covert operations were financed through multiple dummy corporations hidden in a labyrinth of secret bank accounts scattered around the globe, and there was an awful lot of money that seemed to fall out of the sky with no apparent source. *The knowledge I'll gain from this assignment will be of great value in the future*, he was thinking as he got up and threw another log on the fire.

Walter felt bored looking out at the falling snow. The National Museum of History was closed for the holiday and watching Southern Cal play Wisconsin in the Rose Bowl or Ole Miss versus Arkansas in the Sugar Bowl was not on his list of things to do since he didn't own a television or have any plans to buy one.

He threw the clipping from the December 28, 1961 *Washington Post* Bissell had sent with his book into the fire as he placed it on the bookshelf. The flames consumed JFK's picture in the Miami Orange Bowl with the survivors of *La Brigada* 2506, and Walter couldn't help but think of the $53 million ransom in pharmaceuticals and farm machinery the president had paid Fidel Castro for the exiles' release.

What a farce, he thought, searching for a book on Caesar, Alexander the Great, Napoleon or another great power broker when the phone rang. *Oh, shit. I hope that's not Mr. Coup calling about the White Hand,* he cringed, reaching for the phone.

Calls at his home made Walter's heartbeat become irregular. It was at times like this that he struggled with the Hale versus Arnold analogy—the fine line between patriotism and treason—that always sent Walter on a guilt trip. He had spent hours wrestling with the issue and had on several occasions considered going to the Inspector General to spill his guts. He had quickly dismissed the idea, remembering that Hanson had two other accomplices and that he might die in some unexplained accident, like using his electric razor in the shower.

Walter felt his heart palpitations subside when the call turned out to be a wrong number. He then considered calling and wishing Desmond FitzGerald a Happy New Year, before thinking better of it. Des was at his country home in Plains, Virginia watching bowl games, and it would be impolite to bother him.

215

The former Wall Street lawyer had just returned to Langley from the head of the Far East division. Walter had originally met Mr. FitzGerald while serving as Dulles' special assistant and was very impressed with the former Army officer who had served with the Chinese in Indo China during World War II. Like Hanson, FitzGerald was turning into another contemporary CIA legend.

Walter greatly admired Des' whimsical ways as he went around quoting phrases from *Alice's Adventures in Wonderland* as a metaphor for his clandestine acts. It helped to keep others off balance to gain an upper hand while driving colleagues crazy. Everyone, that is, except Walter, who had committed large parts of the book to memory while working as Director Dulles' assistant. The two men would have frequent lunches in the Langley cafeteria and enter into friendly *Alice in Wonderland* sparring competitions as their fellow workers looked on in disgust.

* * *

After Bobby Kennedy pulled the plug on Operation MONGOOSE, he held a meeting with the president in the Oval Office on January 25, 1963 where Bobby informed his brother, "This joint MONGOOSE/Pentagon/CIA effort has accomplished little more than, uh, blowing up a few telephone poles in Cuba. I've shut it down."

"What are your plans to get rid of Fidel then?"

"A solo mission by the CIA, with only one person in charge. This ultra secret cell will be designated the Special Affairs Staff and I will be the person in charge."

"Special Affairs Staff—gotta nice ring to it."

"It's so damn secretive, Jack, that your own CIA director, John McCone, doesn't know of its existence."

"Sounds like we're finally getting somewhere. No Pentagon or DCI are involved to screw things up this time, right? Who have you chosen to run the S.A.S. from the CIA side of the house?"

"He's waiting outside. Uh, would you like to meet him?"

"Bring him in please."

"Hello, Desmond, so you're Bobby's S.A.S. Director, are you?" the President asked, smiling warmly while shaking FitzGerald's hand.

"Yes, Mr. President. Given the right staff—Fidel Castro can be considered a dead man," replied FitzGerald who was overwhelmed with being this closely associated with the White House.

"Whatever staff you need to run S.A.S., uh, get them Fitz," Bobby interceded. "The president just wants Castro dead before the '64 elections."

The handsome professional covert operator replied with a sparkle in his eyes, "Okay. I'll need a good administrative assistant. Mildred Cole, Allen Dulles' former secretary, is whom I had in mind. I'll need the brightest young mind at Langley— Dulles' former special assistant, Walter Elliot. You know, gentlemen, Elliot had nothing to do with planning the Bay of Pigs. He's been wasting away for over a year now working for the deputy comptroller on budgets and such. And I'll also need Gray Lynch to keep running our Cuban covert operations out of JM/WAVE."

Bobby Kennedy crossed his arms and looked at the dark haired man with a Roman nose. "I don't know about, uh, Lynch. I didn't like his attitude at General Taylor's Bay of Pigs inquiry…uh…and I am not sure he can be trusted."

"Don't worry. He's the right man, I assure you," FitzGerald replied, feeling skeptical of the President's brother who knew nothing about intelligence.

"Anyone else?"

"Yes, as a matter-of-fact I would like BBC Correspondent Holly Woodson to serve as our agent in Havana. Bissell was unable to get her a Cuban visa and that is the main reason for Operation MONGOOSE's failure, in my opinion. I will assure you, Mr. President, if anyone can get an audience with Fidel, Miss Woodson sure as hell can."

"Now we're getting somewhere," the president replied, sounding optimistic for the first time. "We need a good-looking dish like that inside Havana—I'd be interested in meeting with the lady myself."

Bobby shook his head and grinned at his brother. "Sorry, Jack, no time for that sort of thing. Whatever you say, Fitz, you got it."

That afternoon Walter Elliot was taking a break and eating a candy bar in the art-filled hallway in the Langley headquarters. He was gazing at a colorful piece by Thomas Downing and admiring the contrast of the center modules blues and reds marshaling nicely with the overlying depth of the painting. He glanced up when he saw Desmond FitzGerald confidently coming down the hall. He stopped and asked in *Wonderland* code, "'A mad tea party?' asked the Hatter…"

"Tomorrow at noon?"

"There's plenty of room," Desmond replied with a smile, anxious to have lunch at the Alibi Club to inform Walter of his pending transfer from the Bank to become his special S.A.S assistant.

The next day the newly appointed S.A.S. chief drove Walter to the Alibi Club. For once Walter noticed their conversation had nothing to do with *Alice in Wonderland* or the CIA. There was no talk of the Far East or Fidel Castro, which Walter thought was very strange when he asked himself: *Is Fitz a member of the White Hand—God forbid, and could he possibly be one of the two other co-conspirators?*

President Kennedy was working in the Oval Office a few blocks down Pennsylvania Avenue as the two men got out of the car and entered the Alibi Club. Inside, the cozy old-world charm of the elite men's club was always a nostalgic occasion to Walter, bringing back memories of his lunch as the guest of Allen Dulles.

The men were seated and drinks were ordered. "Now, Walter, this will be the most remembered lunch of your career," FitzGerald said, holding out his glass and reciting from *Alice*:

"*Tweedledum and Tweedledee*
    Agreed to have a battle;
        For Tweedledum said Tweedledee
            Had spoiled his nice new rattle."

Walter responded, "'*I know what you're thinking about,*' said Tweedledum; '*but it isn't so, nohow.*'"

"What do you think I am talking about, Walt?"

"The Kennedys are after Castro and you're now the monstrous crow, *Which frightened both the heroes so, They quite forgot about their quarrel.* Which means the whole Castro problem has been forgotten by the President?" Walter asked.

"'*Contrariwise,*' continued Tweedledee, '*if it was so, it might be; and if it were so, it would be; but as it isn't, it ain't. That's logic.*' So you are wrong, Walter, but a splendid try. Damn, you're a smart young man," FitzGerald replied with a laugh.

"Thank you, sir. So please don't keep me in the tar barrel and tell me what's up."

"Top, Top Secret." FitzGerald said, looking around him. You, my young friend, have just been selected, with the president's approval; to be my assistant in an ultra-secret cell within the Company that Bobby Kennedy has put me in charge of. *Ultra top secret*—all I know about the job is that I have to hate Castro."

"Really?" Walter replied, relieved to learn that FitzGerald was not involved with the White Hand conspiracy.

"Yes, the mission of the S.A.S.—the cryptonym for the Special Affairs Staff, is to eliminate Castro before the 1964 presidential election and you are my man."

"Thank you very much, sir," Walter replied, finding it difficult to act inspired. *Here I am, a stone's throw from the White House and caught in the middle of the White Hand's plot to assassinate the president and the S.A.S. plot on Fidel Castro. What a frigging paradox,* Walter Elliot thought, shaking his new boss' hand—a hand that was very warm, yet very cold.

Chapter Twenty-Two

Dallas

February 21, 1963

Walter boarded a CIA flight waiting to take off for JM/WAVE from the "Roost." Axial Hanson's unannounced appearance last night in the deli down the street from Walter's Georgetown townhouse went off without either man saying a word. The older man sat down by him at the counter and drank his coffee, using the opportunity to make a drop ordering Walter to requisition a $250,000 wire transfer to a bank account in Port-au-Prince, Haiti in the name of George De-Mohrenschildt. *What was the money to be used fo*r—was the question Walter was asking himself as his plane took off for Miami.

Walter had learned from his banking experience that there were no internal controls over the covert funds. Officers of a certain grade in the clandestine service could order money wired anywhere in the world without any questions being asked. The two hundred fifty grand transferred to the wealthy Count De-Mohrenschildt, an exiled Russian living in Dallas, was just another transfer.

Walter's curiosity had made him wonder earlier in his career where the un-budgeted funds that seemed to fall out of the sky came from. Then one day he noticed that all large covert cash deposits came from banks in cities where the Mafia had a strong presence: Chicago, New York, Miami and New Orleans seemed to always be at the top of the list. He had figured it out—*we're getting a percentage of the Mafia's drug profits, you dunce!*

Walter was reading *The Washington Post* and not giving the Haitian wire transfer another thought in his excitement over being on TDY to Miami to escape the winter. JM/WAVE was the largest CIA station in the world, with over four hundred officers supervising approximately two thousand Cuban contact agents. Its budget alone was $50 million, and Walter could recite the exact amount of each budget line item if he were asked.

Two hours later he checked into the BOQ at Richmond Field, a World War II Navy blimp base located ten miles south of Miami that was under lease to the CIA from the University of Miami. Walter then went directly to the chief of station's office and was ushered into a small conference room.

Holly Woodson, dressed in a revealing white sundress and red high heels, was seated in the conference room adjoining the Cuban Task Force Special Operations Division office. A muscular man in his mid-thirties remained seated when Walter introduced himself.

"So you're the kid Hanson thinks hung the moon?" Bob Planky snarled when he nearly crushed Walter's hand with his iron grip.

"Nice to meet you, sir," Walter replied, too preoccupied with the outline of Holly's erect nipples in the cold air conditioning to pay any attention to Planky's sly remark.

"Have you guys met before?" Axial Hanson asked as he walked in during introductions with Walter looking surprised to see that he had beaten him down from D.C.

"Only…only by Miss Woodson's fast reputation," Walter stammered, "Or, what I— what I meant to say is 'vast' reputation as a BBC journalist."

Walter's face reddened when Planky let out a horselaugh. "You know how to win friends and influence people, Elliot, you dumb-ass."

"Okay, let's get down to business now," Hanson began. "Mr. FitzGerald asked that I organize the *new* Cuban Task Force hit team. Holly, you're going to be the S.A.S. main contact in Havana, our deep cover agent working for the BBC. Elliot is Fitz's right-hand man at Langley. Planky is 'control' working out of JM/WAVE, and he will be coordinating covert operations by our ad hoc anti-Castro agents inside Cuba. The mission, lady and gentlemen, is to eliminate Fidel Castro and his government on or before November of 1963…"

"Mr. FitzGerald and the attorney general also sent me down here to make a reassessment of our covert actions in Cuba after the MONGOOSE flap," Walter interrupted, looking over at Holly with a sheepish grin.

Planky glanced up at the ceiling in disgust. "What the hell's that got to do with this meeting, Elliot? Didn't you hear what the man just said, boy? We're going to assassinate fucking Fidel Castro!"

"Let's hold it down now," Hanson intervened. "That's hunky-dory, Walter, my boy, and you will get the chance to prepare your report for Fitz. Later on I'll introduce you to Planky's boss here at SOD, Gray Lynch. Gray's one of the toughest paramilitary guys we've got."

"You've got that right," Planky added. "Gray even wears a Catholic Virgin de Cobre medallion around his neck for good luck. The medallion is a custom of the Cuban exiles, and so far it's kept him alive against the thousands of Cuban bullets that he's ducked."

"So you're saying we've *already* been running covert raids against Cuba after the Bay of Pigs?" Walter asked as he scribbled a note on his pad sneaking another glance at Holly's breasts.

"Where the *fuck* have you been, kid?" Planky asked, slamming his pencil on the table and shaking his head.

"You better believe it!" Axial laughed. "We've conducted over four hundred raids to date since the Bay of Pigs. Lynch and Planky here are doing a helluva fine job blowing up sugar mills, sawmills, utility facilities, and the list goes on and on. In the process, there have been hundreds of Cuban military and a number of civilian casualties. Lynch, on the other hand, has lost only one of his agents, who drowned in a storm in the Gulf Stream. Of course, that is classified top-secret, but you need to know, Holly, so you can hopefully get interviews with Castro."

222

Walter caught a rim of Holly's brown nipple when she leaned over to retrieve Planky's pencil that had rolled off the table. She flashed him a seductive smile replying, "Oh, you don't worry, Axial. I will if I get to Havana…"

Bob Planky's voice shot across the table, "Look, Elliot. Lay off Holly's tits and pay attention. This is serious stuff. *Goddamn*, Axial, where did you find this kid?"

"*Lookit*, Mr. Planky," Walter snapped, feeling his face flush, "that's enough of the insults, and I'll have you know I'm twenty-five years old."

"Well, act like it, then kid."

What the hell is this— some kind of test? Walter thought, feeling humiliated by this Planky jerk. He gasped, feeling a shortness of breath that only intensified his self-consciousness at being in the presence of the sexiest woman alive. *She can't possibly be attracted to me*, he thought when he heard Hanson say, "Well, that's about it for the day."

"Would you gents like to join me at the O Club for Happy Hour?" Holly asked. "I'll introduce you to Gray Lynch and by the way, Bob, maybe you guys can kiss and make up."

Planky blew Walter a kiss, saying with a lisp, "Holly, you're telling me that Walter's queer."

"Oh will you stop it, Bob," Holly laughed, slapping Planky playfully on the shoulder. "Gray is usually at the club about this time of day so I say, tallyho. I'll roll you blokes for the first round," she added, straightening her dress and running her hands down her curves with the slightest wiggle of her hips.

"Helluva good idea. Let's hit it," Hanson grinned, raising his eyebrows and smiling at Walter, who was preoccupied by Holly's ass as she walked out the door.

"I'm sorry, Holly," Walter mumbled, realizing he had to make an excuse to get back to the BOQ to take his heart medication. "I've got to get some stuff cabled to Mr. FitzGerald ASAP if you guys will give me a rain check."

"So you don't drink, Wonder Boy?" Planky asked, flashing Walter a limp-wristed gesture that made the others break out in hysterical laughter.

Back at the BOQ Walter Elliot took his medicine and lay down to allow time for his heart rate to stabilize. He got up after an hour and looked at himself in the bathroom mirror: *Jesus Christ, Walter! You looked like a complete fool today. Being bullied by that fucking Planky is bad enough, but you acted like some moonstruck high school nerd when it came to Holly— you dumb ass.*

Walter missed seeing Axial Hanson again during his three-week stay at JM/WAVE. Working with Holly filled his mind with infatuation and lust for a woman he knew he could never have. Happy Hours at the club made things worse while watching Holly in a crowd of men rolling dice for drinks of tonic and gin. He despised that sarcastic son-of-a-bitch Bob Planky who guarded her like a hawk.

During the planning sessions, Walter got sick of listening to Bob Planky boast about what a great covert operator he was. Each day it became more difficult to take the senior officer's unwarranted ridicule. The boring sessions allowed Walter time for his mind to wander off into outer space—*Is Hanson setting me up for some kind of sick joke with his White Hand conspiracy plot?*

On leaving JM/WAVE, Walter got his answer by returning Hanson's page from a pay phone at the Miami airport on his way back to Washington. "Meet me on President's Day, February 22, in Dallas for a secret meeting at the old St. Francis Hotel located at 1321 Commerce Street. Go by the bank and pick up my cash and make sure you cover your tracks by staying at the Holiday Inn under your alias…"

"I don't have an alias."

"Sure you do, Stuart Walters." Hanson said with a laugh, hanging up.

Stuart Walters, not bad for an alias, he thought, boarding the plane for Washington and thinking; *Thank God I'm away from Planky. I hope I never have to see that son-of-a-bitch again.*

The next morning, Walter Elliot took the Delta 'red-eye-special' flight from Washington National after spending a sleepless night anticipating what lay ahead for him in Dallas. In his attaché case he had one hundred thousand dollars in circulated hundred dollar biils that Hanson had ordered from the Langley Bank.

Mr. Coup sure has balls of steel, Walter was thinking as the plane landed at Love Field and he was walking out of the terminal to the taxi stand.

Thirty minutes later Stuart Walters registered at the downtown Holiday Inn and lay down to catch a nap when the phone rang. "Mr. Walters, meet me at the Museum of Art at Fair Park at four o'clock – the American West Exhibit. Bring your attaché case," the familiar voice ordered before the line went dead.

After ordering room service for lunch, Elliot brushed his teeth and walked down to the lobby. Ten minutes later the cab passed the sign entering Fair Park and the Cotton Bowl and stopped in front of the Museum of Art. Walter went inside the museum and reluctantly checked his attaché case at the reception desk before finding his way to the American West Exhibit in a deserted wing.

He found Axial Hanson seated on the bench in the middle of the dark hall with his back to him. When Hanson heard Walter's approaching footsteps echoing off the walls, he stood and walked over and examined a painting of a cowboy branding a steer on the lone prairie.

When Walter joined him, Axial pointed up to the painting and said with a chuckled, "Walter, my boy, Bob Planky burned your ass at JM/WAVE, didn't he?"

"That bastard is an *asshole*," replied Elliot as the two men slowly moved around the exhibit in silence reviewing the paintings until Hanson stopped and looked Walter square in the eyes. "Don't take it personally, Planky's a tough guy. Having a license to kill is an awesome assignment and a job he does extremely well." Axial said with a consoling pat on the back.

The two men sat down on the hard wooden bench in the middle of the gallery. "Jesus Christ! Planky's not the hit man is he?" Elliot gasped, hearing his words fading away unanswered while at the same time feeling his heart jump out of sync.

He took a very deep breath and held it. Walter Elliot had a sickening feeling in his guts that his mission for the White Hand was over. *Oh God! Planky is going to blow me away now that I have delivered the money,* he thought, glancing over his shoulder. At any minute he expected to see a High Standard .22 silencer pointed his way as he fought to regain his composure when the museum's closing was announced. Finally, he heard himself saying, "Yes sir, Axial. What's next?"

"Let's get out of here Walt and take a walk in the park. Here, give me your claim check and your attaché key and follow me out after I take a leak," Axial replied, handing Walter his briefcase check in exchange.

"My plane ticket is in my case, so don't run off with it."

There was a light unseasonably warm southwesterly wind kissing the two men in the face as they casually strolled through Fair Park in the late afternoon. Axial Hanson took a seat on a park bench overlooking Leonhardt Lagoon and lit a cigarette. "Let me tell you the secret for a perfect coup d'etat," he began, in the voice that reminded Walter of his political science professor at Yale as they watched a pair of squirrels scampering down from the tree.

"Walter, the perfect coup d'etat is a covert action by a few co-conspirators using limited force to overthrow a government without conforming to the constitutional election process or the governing laws of a nation. *Pure and simple*," he added with a twinkle in his eyes. "To be successful at a coup, you must have precise planning by the sponsors—the White/Black Hand partnership–and the protection of other collaborators–the Praetorian Guard, you might say."

"As in the Roman emperor's imperial bodyguard? Are you kidding? Who the hell in the Secret Service or FBI do you think is stupid enough to assassinate the President, Axial?"

"Let me finish, please. After the coup has taken place there must be a diversionary cover-up and a ratification of the coup by the new government. And finally, there must be mass misinformation by the media to calm the people's nerves."

Walter ran his hands through his hair and gazed up at the dark front blowing in from the north. After hearing what Hanson had just said, he was relieved that his heart was no longer tearing a hole in his chest.

"Now, to answer your question regarding the Praetorian Guard, Walter," Hanson said with an amused grin, "there has never been any love lost between the 35th President and the Director of the FBI. Hoover has stayed in power all these years by keeping close surveillance on the politicians' involvement with prostitutes, kickbacks, you name it. Hoover's got their number. In JFK's case, there is a long dossier that includes fraternizing with a female Nazi spy during the war, and stealing the 1960 election from Dick Nixon. *And,* don't forget Hoover's private lunch with the President when he first got in office advising J.F.K. to back off his eminent relationship with Giancana's girlfriend while he's in the White House."

Walter felt the wind shifting out of the north as the sunny sky turned to haze. "What about the Secret Service? There is no way..."

"Don't be so naïve, Walt! Within the Praetorian Guard there are a number of anti-Communist extremists who have served their country with great distinction in the OSS who detest the President's sexual escapades and his détente with the Russians, not to mention selling out the Cubans at the Bay of Pigs. The same can be said for certain generals and admirals at the Pentagon."

The cold wind swirled the leaves around Walter Elliot's feet as he zipped up his jacket. "L.B.J. is a hawk alright, the generals don't call him 'Senator Defense' just for the hell of it, do they?"

"You are precisely correct, Walt."

"Okay, that makes sense. The Vice President, you might say, sure as hell hates the Kennedys."

"Especially after L.B.J. got wind that they are going to drop him from the 1964 ticket to make room for Bobby to run."

"Axial that was an interesting comment. I just overheard Bobby say the other day at the S.A.S. that the Senate Rules Committee is starting an investigation on L.B.J.'s old protégé and former Senate Majority leader secretary, Bobby Baker. Something about Baker getting kickbacks for Johnson from the life insurance company that wrote his policy after he had his heart attack."

"*Very good,* Mr. Walters," Hanson laughed, lighting another cigarette off the butt of his Chesterfield. "The Senate Rules Committee *is* secretly investigating Johnson and Baker as we speak! L.B.J. has always been known as a ruthless SOB, and it's common knowledge that he stole the election for the Senate seat in the first place. Johnson has everything to gain and nothing to lose in achieving his lifelong dream of becoming the 36th President of the United States."

"What about the misinformation, the cover-up? How the hell do you fool the press?"

Hanson stood and picked up Walter's briefcase. "Lest I forget," he said, unlocking the case and handing Walter his plane ticket back to Washington. "Now, getting misinformation to the press is the easiest part. Coups create instant panic—politicians, public servants and the press hate panic. I have a plan to feed misinformation to the press for instant ratification of President Johnson's new administration. I want the American people to feel secure."

Hanson's low monotone was swept away in the stiff wind as he leaned closer. "Now, Walter, it is time to finalize our White Hand involvement in this thing with our Black Hand partners. You will meet a man tomorrow at the St. Frances named Jack Ruby. He is a long-time, trusted lieutenant of Sam Giancana, and the little sawed-off son-of-a-bitch runs this frigging town. Ruby will arrange and coordinate the hit teams and make the payoff with this," Axial said, holding up the briefcase. "Ruby practically lives in the Dallas Police Department Headquarters..."

"*Stop!* Don't tell me all this shit, Axial."

"Sorry, my boy, there is now, as we spooks say, 'the need for you to know' just in case something happens to ole Nine-fingers before the assassination date. If that's the case, then you, Stuart Walters, become the leader of the White Hand coup d'etat."

Walter's face turned gray watching Axial as he limped down the path and vanished in the dusk. The sun disappeared into the approaching storm, leaving Elliot alone searching his soul as he watched the squirrels scamper up the tree and disappear into the safety of their hole. In the emptiness of Fair Park, Walter Elliot wondered if he was going to be able to catch a cab back to the Holiday Inn.

Chapter Twenty-Three

New Orleans

April 20, 1963

It seemed like only yesterday to Holly Woodson that she had been living the good life at the Hotel Nacional, drinking frozen daiquiris and rumbaing away the hot Cuban nights on the El Floridita dance floor. The lunch crowd was arriving at Commander's Palace as the jazz trio struck up Fats Domino's *Blueberry Hill*, bringing a weak smile to the journalist's lovely face. *Oh what a wonderful night it had been at the old Jung Hotel,* she was thinking, when she remembered she had not heard a word from Tex Morris since he sent her a telegram from Bangkok while he was on R&R.

The British expatriate gazed out at the bright spring sunshine transforming the courtyard of the Victorian mansion into a Garden of Eden when she realized that it had been two years since she arrived in the Crescent City. The Bay of Pigs seemed to be all but forgotten by everyone except Holly Woodson who longed to return to Havana. Maybe her case officer would be bringing her good news this time, she was thinking, as she waited in the Garden Room for Axial Hanson's arrival. The songs lyrics, *"I found my thrill on blueberry hill,"* took her back to the April afternoon when she received Hanson's call from Miami. "Holly, there is good news and bad news," he had said.

"Give me the bad news straightaway—is Lieutenant Morris in trouble with the CIA?" she asked, gazing out of her Jung Hotel window at the distant triple spires of St Louis Cathedral in the French Quarters.

"Not unless we catch him spouting off at the mouth. Now, the good news is that you've been assigned by the BBC to cover New Orleans until things cool off in Havana. Act surprised when London gives you a ring."

At that moment in their conversation, Holly still remembered having a warm fuzzy feeling knowing Hanson's plan of entrapment for Lieutenant Morris for his involvement in the Bay of Pigs had failed. "*What* the bloody hell's the bad news then, Axial?"

Holly's waiter refilled her champagne glass, and watching the bubbles floating to the top reminded her of how corny Hanson's mimicking of a redneck had sounded when he said, "Well, Miss Holly, as we say down South, I do declare, the bad news is that you've gotta cover them Freedom Riders and the Ku Klux Klan in New Orleans."

"The devil you say—why not Birmingham?"

She could still hear Hanson's laugh crackling over the line. "Because covering the Civil Rights thing for the BBC will serve as cover for my other operation. Report to Guy Banister and Associates on the morning of Thursday, April 27th to get your marching orders."

"Well, I must say the news could have been worse. New Orleans is a hell of a lot better than Birmingham."

"You're mighty right about that. Now, Banister is located in the Newman Building at 544 Camp Street, catty-corner to Lafayette Square. There's an Irish priest named Father Patrick O'Brien who is working there. He was assigned to the Cuban Bishop before the Bay of Pigs. If you're not Catholic, working with O'Brien—be careful or you will be."

Holly's voice tightened. "A bloody Irishman, the hell you say?"

"Yes, but it's actually Banister's Cuban Revolutionary Council or Front that's your target, Holly."

"This is bloody awful news! How long do I have to work with the jerk?"

"Long enough to get to know the 'Big Easy' and lots of its quirky citizens. Not to mention Clay Shaw, the Director of the International Trade Mart. Shaw is just one of many, so remember that name—Clay Shaw."

"Who is this fellow?"

"Shaw is one of our former operatives who got busted by the Italian press for being a member of the Board of *Centro Mondiale Commerciale,* a front we used to transfer funds for political-espionage to get the Fascist government a majority against the Communists. Shaw is highly regarded in the New Orleans social circles and he knows every king and queen, duke and duchess, earl and prince and princess in Europe. We sent him to Rome because he had a close tie with the Italian royal family."

"Where do you expect me to stay, Axial? This hotel's a bloody fire trap."

"I've taken care of you, lady, so just calm down. You have a third floor furnished apartment in the Quarter with a private entrance to the courtyard on Dauphine Street. It's hunky-dory and you're going to love it. Now let's get down to business. Tomorrow check Continental bus Number 4212 arriving at 4:32 in the afternoon from Miami and use your alias, Patricia Isbell, to retrieve O'Brien's file. I'm mailing you a briefing on Banister's C.R.C. operation. Oh, before I forget it, you need to pick up your key in Pat Isbell's name at the Lafayette Street Post Office."

Holly smiled at the waiter refilling her champagne glass. She remembered reading the *Times-Picayune's* article on the Jackson-bound Freedom Rider bus being fire-bombed at the Mississippi line before she opened Father O'Brien's file that April afternoon. After carefully examining the priest's mug shot, Holly recalled how appalled she was at the priest's IRA connections, not to mention the Mafia and his assignment with the Cuban Federation as a Vatican spy in Havana. *What a bloody rotten assignment this one is—trailing this IRA bastard who's probably a pedophile,* she had thought when she finished.

The next morning Holly placed O'Brien's file in the secret compartment of her attaché case and walked down Canal Street to find Banister's office. After taking a wrong turn on St. Charles Avenue, she entered the Masonic Temple that just happened to be the home of the New Orleans FBI and CIA Offices to ask for directions. "You's just abouts done got there, lady," said the old janitor with a friendly smile, pointing her in the right direction.

Holly thanked the man and was relieved to find the Lafayette Street Post Office Building looming like the Rock of Gibraltar just ahead of her in this seedy section of the New Orleans business district. She remembered posting a letter to her father inviting him to come over before it got too hot. After a short wait, she was given a key to box 701-43255 in Pat Isbell's name, and upon leaving noticed the Post Office was also the headquarters of the Office of Naval Intelligence and the United States Secret Service.

Holly crossed the street to the small gray-granite building and climbed the stairs to the second floor. She straightened her dress and entered the offices of Guy Banister Associates, Inc, Investigators. Instantly an immaculately dressed man in a blue business suit sporting a small rosebud in his lapel appeared and introduced himself. "Good morning, Miss Woodson, my name is Guy Banister. Welcome to New Orleans. From now on, please remember to use the Camp Street entrance to the building."

Holly could feel the cold eyes of the former special agent in charge of the Chicago office of the FBI undressing her as they talked. "How clever, Mr. Banister, easy way to get your clients in or out of your office undetected, I take it."

The ruddy-faced retired deputy superintendent of the New Orleans police department glanced across the street to the Post Office and nodded his head. "Very observant of you, Miss Woodson. Now, let me show you the bullpen and I apologize for our crowded accommodations. You'll be spending most of your time out in the surrounding parish to get your stories," Banister said, leading Holly down a narrow hall to a large room filled with a beat-up assortment of desks and chairs.

Holly was immediately taken aback by a man who appeared dressed for a masquerade party sitting with his binoculars trained on the entrance to the Post Office Building. Banister cleared his throat, "David Ferrie, meet Miss Woodson, she is a freelance reporter covering the Civil Rights movement and the N-double A-CP. Holly's hired us to assist her in finding leads—the BBC, don't you see, is her sponsor."

The former commercial airlines pilot turned legendary CIA gunrunner for the anti-Castro Cuban movement looked at Holly with a furious grin on his face.

Holly had cast a quizzical eye on the reddish handcrafted wig Ferrie was wearing. She watched as he adjusted his red bowtie and took off his crumpled white tux jacket and placed it on the back of the chair revealing dark perspiration stains under his armpits. Without saying a word, he meticulously licked his fingers and smoothed his blackened half-mooned mascara-painted eyebrows, punctuating his dark beady eyes that were prancing around in his head like a lunatic's before he finally spoke.

"Lady Woodson, so you're one of those foreign liberals coming down here to stir up trouble with our colored brethren for those Kennedy bastards, are you, your royal highness?" asked Ferrie flashing his furious grin. Releasing a nervous high-pitched cackle, he glanced over at Banister for approval.

Holly Woodson, for once in her life, found herself speechless. *Who is this weirdo?* she was thinking of the man suffering from alopecia, a rare disease that leaves the body hairless, when she heard Banister snarl, "Cut it out David. Miss Woodson is a cash paying client."

"Sorry, your Lordship."

"Pay no attention to Ferrie," Banister said with a sigh. "His only redeeming feature is that he has a way of finding leads in New Orleans. Any story you need, he'll get it, right, David?"

"At your service, Lady Woodson," Ferrie replied, still flashing his furious grin. He bowed and motioned to the priest reading the *Times-Picayune* and drinking his morning coffee. "Father O'Brien is really your man, my Lady."

The Irishman stood and smiled politely. *Dear God, it's the BBC reporter who filmed Don Carlos' execution! I detest having to work with this snobbish British bitch,* the priest was thinking as he extended his hand and looked at Ferrie who was grinning back at him.

"Your Ladyship, the padre is very busy helping me with the Cuban exiles. *But,* I'll bet your Ladyship a quad if you give him a blow job he'll stir-up more Negro trouble than those goddamned Kennedy brothers can shake a stick at."

"*David*—That's by-God enough," Banister shouted, watching Holly's face light up as she shook hands with O'Brien.

Holly then looked at her new colleagues and said with a sinister laugh, "Gentlemen, it *is* my pleasure to be working with such interesting people. Now, if you will excuse me, I must skedaddle and get settled in my new flat. I'll see you bright and early Monday morning, Father O'Brien. We'll go over to the *Times-Picayune* and get acquainted with the editors. Cheerio to you, Mr. Banister and you to, Mr. Fairy."

As she left the building, Holly thought to herself. *What in the hell did I do to deserve this? What a rotten bunch of losers: one sawed-off little IRA prick and the world's biggest bigot, that Ferrie faggot.*

Holly Woodson snapped back to reality when the waiter asked, "Would you like to order an appetizer while you are waiting for your guest?"

"No thank you," Holly replied, lighting a cigarette and glancing at twelve thirty on her wristwatch. The champagne was making her feel horny after living a near-celibacy existence since her Tex Morris encounter. After being branded a Civil Rights activist and blacklisted on the city's clannish social register, it had been difficult to get socially connected in New Orleans. With the exception of an occasional one-nighter with an out-of-towner, Holly had established a monogamous relationship with a homosexual liberal arts professor at Tulane University— perfect cover for getting invited to parties at her neighbor Clay Shaw's house. So far she was relieved not to have been exposed in the *Times-Picayune* gossip column as a member of the socially accepted homosexual community.

It is sad that Axial is not younger and my boss, was a fleeting thought crossing Holly's mind as she waited. It quickly faded with memories of her disastrous affair with her professor at Oxford. *Getting involved with Hanson would turn into another bloody nightmare,* she was thinking, *I wish to hell Axial would get here, I'm starving. Something big must be coming down from Langley for Hanson to expose himself.*

Axial Hanson took a cab from the Pontchartrain Hotel on St Charles Avenue and was wearing a gray wig with matching mustache. If it were not for his slightly exaggerated limp, he would have been just another grandfatherly figure when he dropped down at Holly's table and propped his cane against the wall. "Grandfather, you fooled the bloody hell out of me wearing that one. Why the bloody disguise, ole chap?"

Hanson nodded for the waiter to pour him a glass of champagne. "Here's looking at you kid," he said with a laugh. "We've got a lot to talk about and little time to do it. Your last report on Banister's C.R.C. didn't explain why our Dallas-New Orleans-Miami arms shipments stopped after Ferrie raided the Schlumberger Corporation's ammo dump at the blimp base in Houma. Our munitions stockpile at JM/WAVE for the Cuban raids are being seriously depleted."

Holly shrugged, returning Hanson's toast. "Jesus Christ, you came all the way to New Orleans to discuss stealing the Company's armaments you gave the French O.A.S. to assassinate Charles DeGaulle, Mr. Coup? Come now, Grandfather, it's really just a holiday in the Big Easy to buy my lunch, isn't it?"

"No, actually it's a helluva lot more important than that," Hanson chuckled, handing Holly a sheet of paper out of the breast pocket of his coat. "Here, read this carefully, and then give it back."

Holly examined the subject's mug shot before reading a photocopy of Commission Document 321 – TOP SECRET: "Chronology of Lee Harvey Oswald in Russia and Return to US."

Oswald, Lee Harvey: (Alias Lee Osborne). White Caucasian age 23. Height 5' 11": weight 155 pounds. Born New Orleans, Louisiana, 18 Oct 39. U.S. Citizen. Tenth-grade education N.O. Public Schools. Fatherless at birth, raised by mother, influenced by uncle, Anthony Alfonso, lieutenant to New Orleans Mafia boss, Carlos Marcello. As teenager served in the Civil Air Patrol with CIA operative David Ferrie, known homosexual and Mafia pilot used to fly drugs and arms to Cuba and Central America. Long-time acquaintance of Jack Ruby, underling of Chicago Mafioso Sam Giancana now living in Dallas, Texas with close ties to Marcello in N.O.

Military service: Enlisted in U.S. Marine Corp 24 Oct 56. Completed boot camp San Diego, 18 Jan 57 qualifying as "sharpshooter" with M-1 rifle on a marksman/sharpshooter/expert rating. Graduated from Naval Air Technical Training and Aircraft Control and Warning Operator course. Secret security clearance issued 28 Jan 57. Completed Russian language test on 25 February 59 and assigned to MACS-1 Marine Air Group, 1st Marine Air Wing, Atsugi, Japan, for deployment at top-secret intelligence base on Asabikawa, northern Japan.

Honorable Discharge 11 Sep 59 to accept agency intelligence assignment for Office of Soviet Analysis Scientific & Weapons Research. Traveled to Soviet Union 16 Oct 59 under cover of student visa to attend Patrice Lumumba Friendship U. in Moscow. Request U.S. Embassy on 3 Nov 59 to revoke U.S. citizenship to get clearance to work under cover in Soviet aircraft plant as sheet metal worker.

Married Marina Prusakova, Russian citizen, on 30 Apr 61, niece of KGB Colonel Yuriy Prusakova, member of Communist Party assigned to Ministry of Internal Affairs in Leningrad as KGB officer.

Returned to Fort Worth, Texas on 14 June 62 with wife and daughter, June Lee, born 15 Feb 62. Sponsored by George DeMohrenschildt, Russian born petroleum engineer and agency operative of Russian nobility with close ties to the Texas oil industry.

Contacted 26 June 62 by Dallas FBI office, recruited as informant to infiltrate growing Russian-speaking community in Dallas-Fort Worth area.

Recruited by Guy Banister, covert action branch, to organize New Orleans branch of Fair Play for Cuba Committee, F.P.C.C. (pro-Castro organization competing with anti-Castro Cuban Revolutionary Council, C.R.C. for domestic support of Cuban government). Assigned to Guy Banister and Associates Investigators, 544 Camp Street as undercover agent inside F.P.C.C. Arrival in N.O. on or about 24 April 63.

Holly handed the document back to Hanson.

"Now, Holly, your most important mission to date is to keep close tabs on Oswald. Spend as much time with him as possible when he arrives back in New Orleans. Keep it on the QT and don't get Banister pissed that you're interfering with Oswald's infiltration of the pro-Castro Fair Play for Cuba Committee."

"Do you mean get intimately involved?" Holly blushed.

"No, that won't be necessary, Oswald is a happily married man," Hanson replied, taking a sip of his champagne. "By the way, congratulations on the excellent job you have done in keeping me informed on the anti-Castro training operations up on Lake Pontchartrain that Ferrie is running. Dave's a weird bastard, but very good at what he does. We almost lost him during the Bay of Pigs when he got stabbed in the stomach flying out of Cuba."

Holly nodded in agreement, "Sorry about the JM/WAVE arms interruption, ole chap. The FBI is running an investigation on the C.R.C. for violating the Neutrality Act. That's why the bloody Schlumberger thing went screwy. I must say the right hand does not know what the bloody hell..."

Hanson held up his hands. "Yeah, those overzealous Justice Department bastards! I'll handle that with Langley as soon as I get back. Now Holly, what about Clay Shaw? You're an insider in his social circles, right?"

"Check, boss. Shaw and Ferrie, my God, those two have some perverted lifestyle..."

"Hunky-dory. Now before Oswald arrives back in New Orleans, I want you to keep even closer tabs on them. When he gets here, keep me informed on how he's doing. Remember, Ferrie was Lee's teenage idol when he was involved with the Civil Air Patrol."

"That's no problem. Shaw uses his alias Clay Bertrand when he's hanging with Ferrie at Cosimo's in the Quarter picking up fresh meat to bring home. I can sit in my bloody flat across the street and see them coming and going at all hours. Would you like to drop by Dauphine Street after lunch and see for yourself?"

Axial shook his head. "I'll leave that up to you," Hanson replied, glancing around the room. "Now listen. This is the real reason for my visit. Meet me at JM/WAVE when I call for the final briefing on your next assignment."

"I'm really going back to Cuba this time, am I?"

Axial lit a Chesterfield and let the smoke curl out of the side of his mouth before changing the subject. "Holly, this new Voter Registration Act couldn't have been timed better for your civil rights cover, could it? You and Father O'Brien have been getting some nice press in the *New York Times* and the *Washington Post* on all of Dr. King's bullshit."

"Thank you, but I certainly don't consider Dr. King's voter registration bullshit. It is time..."

"Well, that's a matter of opinion. But I'm leaving dealing with Dr. King up to J. Edgar and the FBI. So remember, be careful with Shaw and Ferrie, don't blow your cover."

***

At the Buena Vista Apartments in Miami, Hanson received a call from the alias, Pat Isbell. "Lee Oswald has just arrived in New Orleans on the bus this afternoon from Dallas and is staying with his aunt Lillian Murret at her home at 757 French Street. He met Shaw and Ferrie for a drink at Cosimo's."

Hanson thanked Holly and entered 02:30, April 24, 1963 in his log.

Hanson received Pat Isbell's airmail letter postmarked May 11, 1963 from New Orleans on May the 13th. "Lee was in Banister's office today for a long closed-door meeting with the boss." Her letter went on to say that Banister had gotten Lee a job at the William B. Reily Co., Inc., a coffee company located only a few blocks from the office at 640 Magazine Street.

Hanson's face came with a weak smile as he reread the final paragraph of Holly's letter out loud: "Lee appears in grand spirits after getting the new job and has rented an apartment for $65 dollars a month at 4905 Magazine Street. He almost burst with pride telling me that Ruth Paine, a friend of theirs from Dallas, was driving Marina and the baby over tomorrow."

Hanson entered the date in his log and burned the letter.

Pat Isbell's voice had a sense of urgency when Axial answered her call on the afternoon of July 19th. "Oswald has been sacked from his job at the Reily Company. He was in Banister's office laughing about it this afternoon."

"What was Guy's reaction?"

"Positive, very positive. Guy told him not to worry about his rent. The Fair Play for Cuba Committee Lee has been organizing since April was now officially open for business. Lee left the office with leaflets and met Shaw at Cosimo's for a drink."

Hanson had just returned from his morning swim in the Buena Vista pool on the morning of August 10th when the phone rang. "Lots of excitement over here, chief. Lee was arrested yesterday after getting into a fight with three Cuban C.R.C. exiles outside our building while passing out Fair Play for Cuba pamphlets and spent the night in jail. Banister is going down this morning to spring him."

The next afternoon, Axial's phone rang again, "Sorry to bother you, Axial, but you should be watching Lee on the evening news broadcast passing out literature in front of the International Trade Mart. The commentator said he will be on the radio tomorrow night."

Hanson thanked Holly and made the entry in his log. He made a mental note to be sure to tune in on William Stuckey's "Latin Listening Post" radio broadcast from New Orleans on the JM/WAVE short-wave radio.

***

On September 22nd, Holly got approval from Hanson to rent an Impala to trail Lee Oswald back to Dallas. Ruth Paine, a close associate of Russian Count George DeMohrenschildt, was moving the Oswald family back in her station wagon.

During the following week spent in Dallas, Holly trailed Oswald to three meetings with Jack Ruby at his Carousel Nightclub where he spent time with David Ferrie. She also confirmed that Mr. and Mrs. Oswald were still keeping close company with the DeMohrenschildts, a very odd social arrangement due to the disparity in their personal incomes.

On the morning of September 25th Holly followed Ferrie in the black Impala as he drove Lee Oswald back to New Orleans. In the late afternoon she watched him board Continental Trailways bus Number 5121 bound for Houston after having purchased a ticket for Mexico City. She went directly to Banister's office and called Hanson at JM/WAVE.

"Oswald is on the bus for Mexico City."

"Hunky-dory, Holly. Pack up quickly and catch the first flight tomorrow morning for Miami. We've got to get you registered for the fall semester at the *Universidad de la Habana*," he said before hanging up and lighting another cigarette, leaving one still burning in the ashtray.

239

Chapter Twenty-Four

CIA Headquarters

Friday, November 22, 1963

CIA Director John McCone returned to Langley after having a leisurely lunch at the Alibi Club in Washington. The moment he walked into his plush seventh-floor director's suite his secretary thrust the telephone in his hand. "It's the National Security Agency," Anne Cantrell whispered, retrieving a steno pad from her desk drawer before returning to find the color draining from her boss' face.

The DCI was listening intently to the caller while slowly sliding down in his chair at the conference table. Anne watched as he said goodbye and placed the red receiver carefully in the cradle. McCone stared blankly at the landscape painting on the wall for a moment before releasing a great sigh, "Oh, my God!"

"What's wrong?" Anne asked, looking at her boss flanked on either side by the American and CIA flags as he run his fingers through his neatly trimmed gray hair. He covered his face, before saying, "The president has been shot in Dallas."

"Oh no! Is…is he dead?"

"Yes, the president is dead," McCone replied matter-of-factly rushing to switch on the television, as Anne watched her telephone light up like a Christmas tree. "Get Des on the phone for me please."

Anne dialed the secure line to the basement to the Special Affairs Staff vault. "Mildred, get Mr. FitzGerald for the DCI. Okay—then try and contact him immediately and have him call Mr. McCone, it's a national emergency."

Des FitzGerald had just finished hosting a luncheon at the City Tavern Club in Georgetown when his secretary had the maitre d' summon him to the phone. "Mr. FitzGerald, call the DCI. It's urgent."

FitzGerald dialed the Director's direct number and McCone answered. "Fitz, the president's been shot in Dallas!"

"I hope it has nothing to do with the Cubans," the S.A.S. chief replied in the autocratic voice of a former partner in the Wall Street law firm of Hotchkiss Spencer.

The Director cringed at the word "Cubans," adding to his indecisiveness on what to say or do next. McCone suddenly had a sick feeling that FitzGerald's top-secret Special Affairs Staff might just have had something to do the president's death.

"What do you mean? Is Fidel Castro involved?"

"Yeah, well, we'll see. I'm returning to Langley now," FitzGerald replied, leaving the restaurant and walking to his car with his head down and for the first time wondering if he had fallen pray to a "dangle" or double agent. He was trying to muster his great ability to stand back in a time of crisis and view things as normal.

On the drive back to Langley, swirling leaves twirled on the George Washington Parkway as the S.A.S. chief found himself reciting from the final chapter of *Alice in Wonderland.*

"Long has paled that sunny sky;
Echoes fade and memories die,
Autumn frosts have slain July."

Speeding past the rapids of the Potomac River, FitzGerald floored his mud-colored Chevy Corvair and cursed his college roommate who he had entrusted to

invest his fortune of $2 million. Through poor investments, his fortune had dwin-
dled down to almost nothing forcing Fitz to sell his beloved black Jaguar. Life
was not going well for the S.A.S. director as he glanced out the window at the
white rapids and continued with a sigh:

> *"Ever drifting down the stream,*
> *Lingering in the golden gleam-*
> *Life, what is it but a dream?"*

His thoughts turned to yesterday's S.A.S. meeting when Bobby Kennedy
gave the orders for the latest attempt on Fidel Castro's life. "A poison pen, how
clever. So, this is it. Uh…what the hell are we waiting for, Des? Get it done
tomorrow," Bobby had said slapping FitzGerald on the back. "What, by the
way…uh…do we call our agent AMLASH's mission?"

"Operation PAPER MATE what else?" FitzGerald remembered telling the
attorney general. *How ironic it is that twenty-four hours later Bobby's brother is
dead instead of Fidel Castro. My God! This could mean WWIII,* he thought taking
the Langley exit of the parkway.

It is too late to contact AMLASH, he thought knowing that the Cuban agent
had already left Paris for Havana. It had been his highly unorthodox decision as a
senior CIA official to meet with a foreign agent to arrange the assassination plot.
With Bobby Kennedy's prodding's, FitzGerald had taken it upon himself to meet
Rolando Cubelas on October the 29th to personally arrange Castro's hit. FitzGerald was having second thoughts for having gone against the advice of his senior
counterintelligence advisors that Cubelas might be a double agent.

The S.A.S. chief cleared security at the CIA gate and wheeled into the private
parking lot. As he rushed in, he glanced at the quotation from the New Testament
that Mr. Dulles had insisted be chiseled into the granite wall in the lobby of the
CIA headquarters when it was built: "And ye shall know the truth…"

*If the truth were known, the Cubans and Russians are the assassins and this
will be Armageddon,* he thought as he cleared security and took the elevator down
to the basement. He entered in the security code known only by three agency
employees and Bobby Kennedy and waited ten seconds before the thick carbon

steel door slowly swung open. Mildred Cole raised her heavily stenciled eyebrows and handed her boss the phone. "It's the DCI on the line, chief. He's frantic."

"Hello, Mr. Director. I've just arrived. I've got to call the attorney general and then I'll get back to you," FitzGerald said with an intense sense of urgency hanging up.

Pacing around the vault, FitzGerald kept saying over and over to himself, *and ye shall know the truth,* when suddenly the hair on his neck rose up like quills on a porcupine. In the afternoon's chaos, he had almost forgotten that Rolando Cubelas had left Paris last night with the Paper Mate ballpoint pen and by now had arrived back in Havana. *My God,* he thought, glancing at 1:55 EST on his watch. *Operation PAPER MATE has already been launched!*

"Get the attorney general, Mildred. He's at Hickory Hill having lunch," FitzGerald ordered, pacing the floor as the seasoned CIA secretary dialed Robert Kennedy's residence over the secure telephone line.

Mildred bit her lip, wondering what words of condolence her boss could find for the occasion when the call went through. "Mr. Kennedy please. It's urgent. Mr. FitzGerald is calling."

"Damn it!" FitzGerald said, seeing Mildred put her hand over the receiver while she waited. "I should have been more forceful in advising the president that his obsession to assassinate Castro would blow back on him."

"Don't blame yourself," Mildred replied with a sigh. "This all started long before your watch. It really began with the Bay of Pigs fiasco. If anyone is to be blamed, it's the president and Bobby for keeping on with this thing. They were both emphatic about killing Fidel."

"Yes, I warned them that Castro had threatened to retaliate if they kept after him. He's no dummy, you know."

"Well, if you ask me, the attorney general has been reading far too many Ian Fleming novels... Mr. FitzGerald is on the line, Mr. Kennedy. One moment, please."

Robert Kennedy's voice came over the line in a very hoarse whisper, like a baseball fan whose team had just lost in the final game of the World Series. To

FitzGerald he sounded as if he could break down at any moment. "Hello, Bobby. I'm awfully sorry…Yes, we are at battle stations here at the Special Affairs Staff."

"I'll be at home until late afternoon before meeting McNamara at the Pentagon. We'll be going to Andrews to meet Air Force One."

"Okay, Bobby. I'm surely sorry. I'll be in the vault. My condolences to you and the president's family. Have you spoken with the First Lady yet?"

"No, not yet. Uh…was the president an isolated target or are there more of us?"

"Don't know, but take every precaution. You've got security?"

"Damn right I have."

"Bobby," FitzGerald began in a subdued voice, "I know this is a terrible time to have to discuss it, but we must act immediately to abort Operation PAPER MATE. If we kill Castro now the Russians will think we have retaliated. Khrushchev very well could start World War III. Okay? We could easily start a nuclear war, for God's sake."

There was a long silence on Kennedy's end of the line. "Correct, Fitz. Uh…abort it immediately. Have any word if there are leads on the assassins?"

"No, not yet... Oh, wait a sec. Miss Cole just handed me a message from the situation room. Seems the FBI just made an arrest. Apparently he acted alone and there's no conspiracy."

"Who was it?"

"Lee Harvey Oswald."

"Who the hell's Oswald?"

"He's one of Axial Hanson's agents in New Orleans. They have him jailed in Dallas."

"What the hell do you mean 'Hanson's agent'?"

"Part of JM/WAVE. Oswald infiltrated the Free Play for Cuba Committee for Hanson's covert operation—a mole in the pro-Castro group keeping tabs on the F.P.C.C."

"You aren't making any sense, Des."

"That's all I know about it."

"No, it sounds like there's something funny going on within the military or CIA. Uh…who sent that message?"

"The White House situation room. No, Bobby, if anything, it's apparently a double-cross by this Oswald asshole."

"Fitz, you get down to Dallas then and…uh…interrogate this Oswald personally," Bobby ordered. "There's something phony going on here, and I damn well want to know about it."

"I will, Bobby. Right after I brief Johnson tomorrow morning, I'll fly down to Dallas first thing. In the meantime, to prevent panic, we must make it appear as if Oswald acted solo for now…until we get to the bottom of this thing."

"Have the son-of-a-bitch flown up to D.C. That would be the best thing."

"I'll talk to Hoover."

"What about L.B.J.? Do you think he had anything to do with this?" Bobby asked.

"*Jesus Christ*! He's the vice president of the United States!"

"Wrong, the president, and he hates Kennedys. You…uh…don't suppose that it leaked that Jack was going to dump Lyndon from the '64 ticket?"

"God, don't even talk about it," Desmond replied.

"Uh, well let's make damn sure nothing happens to Castro for the time being. And cover your ass…uh…until you can interrogate Oswald. We'll…uh…get to Castro later. How are you going to cover our tracks on this?"

"The DCI is on the line now. I'll get John to do it for us."

"Hell, Des, have you gone fucking crazy!" Bobby yelled into the phone. "McCone doesn't know his ass from first base about any of this! The S.A.S. is ultra secret."

"That's precisely my point," argued the former lawyer. "Mac knows absolutely nothing about the S.A.S. I'll write the briefing that he'll give to L.B.J. tomorrow morning. Don't you worry. I'll take care of it. He's our messenger. Don't you worry, Bobby. It's taken care of. I will schedule our briefing for Johnson well ahead of Hoover's."

"Yeah, Des. Uh…Hoover and Johnson are asshole buddies you know, so be careful. I don't trust either one of the son-of-a-bitches further than I can throw them."

"I'm working on it now."

"Lyndon Johnson—President! I can't goddamn believe it! Jesus Christ. L.B.J., the crooked son-of-a-bitch, could have gotten Hoover to use the FBI…" Bobby said, his voice cracking.

"Stop it, Bobby. I'm awfully sorry about all this. Again, my condolences to the family. I've got the boss holding the other line," Des said, exchanging phones. "Yes, Mr. Director, I…"

"Did you get the attorney general, Fitz? Who's next? What can you tell me? It's either the KGB or Castro," McCone said, catching his breath.

"Just got a report from the situation room at the White House that there's no conspiracy and only one person is involved, Mr. McCone, so just stay calm," FitzGerald replied. "We have things under control. I suggest you contact L.B.J. in Dallas immediately—sorry, I meant to say the President—and tell him we're at full alert here at headquarters and we're on top of things. Tell him you want to give him a briefing at 9 a.m. in the morning to update our intelligence report on the president's assassination. Make damn sure we get a meeting with the president before Hoover and the FBI."

"What in God's name can I tell the president?"

"Don't you worry about that. I'll prepare the briefing and go with you. Now, just stay calm, Mr. Director. The last thing we need is the appearance of panic."

"Okay," replied McCone, lowering the phone gently into its cradle like it was fine crystal, masking his frustration. He remembered all too well the near-nuclear Armageddon that the Kennedys had created in October of 1962 with the Cuban missile crisis. It had been McCone's first crisis after taking office after Allen Dulles' dismissal.

Thinking back on it, I think I'm being used, thought the tall, reserved engineer who had made millions as a shipbuilder and was now approaching his second anniversary as the director of the world's largest intelligence agency. At this moment, Kennedy's assassination made the missile crisis seem very distant history. "Anne, get President Johnson on the phone, please. I have to do *something*."

The DCI went into his bathroom and shut the door. *Should I go down to the vault to see what those guys are doing? No, the vault is off-limits by orders of the president—the dead president. I can't just sit here and do nothing,* he thought, flushing the toilet. *I'm just a figurehead on a helmless schooner adrift in a sea of deceit. Bobby runs the show. When the big flap hits, the less I know about it the better.*

McCone returned to his desk thinking, *why did this have to happen on my watch?* It all started with the Bay of Pigs, which created the Cuban missile crisis. Kennedy panicked when the U-2 flights discovered Soviet missiles being secretly installed in Cuba, just ninety miles from Miami. *Those babies could have rained nukes on millions of Americans except for one thing—they had no guidance systems.*

For thirteen days and nights the Kennedy's played chess with the fate of the world as the President debated whether or not to risk World War III. *By God,* McCone concluded, *the president and his brother created a helluva mess back then but compared to this, it was nothing.*

"Vice President Johnson is on Air Force One on his way back to Washington," Anne said interrupting his thoughts. "I'm having a terrible time getting through."

"President—keep trying." *What did they expect with JM/WAVE raining holy terror on the Cubans with ad hoc exiles they had no control over? Hundreds of bombings, and no telling how many failed attempts on Castro himself. What the hell did Kennedy expect but for the Russians to turn Cuba into an armed citadel and provide Castro with the latest in conventional weapons and over forty thousand Soviet troops? No wonder Khrushchev sent nuclear missiles down there.*

"Any luck yet with the president, Anne?"

"No sir."

"Just keep trying," the CIA Director said before returning to this thoughts. *To get out of the mess, Kennedy deceived the American people into believing that he had bluffed Khrushchev into withdrawing his missiles. That's bullshit; he had to make a secret deal with the Russians. He had to secretly remove our missiles on the Turkish border to close the deal with the Soviets. Kennedy never even told his Cabinet much less the American people. Just wanted to look like a hero. Jesus*

Christ, Jack almost obliterated the human race over his political ego— risking nuclear war to maintain his political image.

"Anne, stop what you're doing and get the chief of counterintelligence up here on the double," the DCI ordered, thinking it was time to start his own internal investigation of Kennedy's assassination as he leaned back in his chair and waited.

"Mr. Angleton is still at lunch. His office is trying to locate him now."

McCone's watch showed 2:30. He shook his head in disgust knowing Angleton was probably still at the bar drinking his lunch.

Downstairs at the vault Walter Elliot punched in his security code, which was authenticated by Mildred Cole. His heart had not yet recovered after the run from the parking lot. Des FitzGerald glanced up at him when he rushed into the vault. "Where in the hell you have been, Walt? Get JM/WAVE on the line. No, on second thought, we'll go over their heads and call, Holly Woodson, at the Hotel Nacional in Havana. Time's running out on us."

"Right away, sir. Who do you think did it? KGB? Mafia?" Walter calmly asked, feeling things out with his boss who had given up his Park Avenue apartment and membership in the prestigious Piping Rock Club to work for the CIA.

"The FBI arrested Lee Harvey Oswald in Dallas."

"Lee Harvey Oswald? No way, sir, he is in New Orleans working as a mole in the Fair Play for Cuba Committee. There seems to be something wrong—very wrong—with his arrest, sir."

"Cut the BS. Are you getting through to Havana?"

"Not yet, sir. But, my God, Lee Harvey Oswald could not have been involved. He's one of Hanson's agents."

The autocratic and cutting side of the S.A.S. chief exploded, "Get on with it, Goddamn it, Walt. Time is of the essence."

God, what have I done? Walter's conscience was now asking as his thoughts shot back to Harvey's Restaurant in downtown D.C. where politicians deal among lobbyist while discretely fondling their mistresses in the dark. Axial Hanson had calmly ordered grilled salmon with rice and a salad with blue cheese on the side when Walter asked him, "How have you been, Axial? I haven't seen you for a while."

"You bet, TDY to Saigon, and that's classified," Hanson replied glancing at 1:29 on his watch and visualizing the president's open limousine making an unscheduled right turn off the Main Street parade route onto Houston Street. Half a block later it would slow to 10 miles per hour to make a 120-degree turn onto Elm Street, passing in front of the Texas School Book Depository Building where Lee Oswald was having lunch. Moving down the slight hill through Dealey Plaza to the triple underpass onto the Stemmons Freeway, the three two-man assassin teams were waiting as the President's limo approached.

At this moment, the Dallas central police radio was recording only the sounds of a motorcycle engine for the next four minutes after one of the escort officer's mikes in the motorcade was keyed.

The radiotelephone in the pursuing press car became inoperative at 12:31, seconds after one of the journalists called in the assassination to the press. It was 1:32 Eastern time in Washington, D.C., when the telephone system for the city went silent for the next hour.

Walter glanced at 1:34 on his watch when the news of the president's assassination spread through Harvey's Restaurant like a tidal wave. The expression on Axial Hanson's face never changed as Walter Elliot chewed on a breadstick and watched the chief of the White Hand calmly butter his roll.

"Mission accomplished, Walt," Hanson whispered, lowering his eyes and reciting from *Ecclesiastes Chapter 3*: "To every thing there is a season. A time to kill, and a time to heal: a time to break down, and a time to build up."

The reciting of the scripture shocked Walter to the core. *That's not like Hanson at all. Does he mean there are others on his hit list?* he thought as Hanson raised his hand to the waiter. "I'll get the check. Are you okay?" Axial asked, seeing that Walter was holding his chest.

"Let's get the hell out of here…"

"Okay, get back to Langley and keep close tabs on what's said at the S.A.S. We're just one step away from having pulled this thing off. I've got to run and catch my flight to Chicago. I'll be registered at the Nickerbocker Hotel under

Alex Hudson, and by the way, I've been permanently reassigned to the Saigon Chief of Station—so don't call me, I'll call you."

Just one step away from pulling this thing off, were Axial's words that kept repeating themselves in Walter's head as he redialed Havana. *So far so good here at the S.A.S. Our Oswald bait has been taken hook, line, and sinker by FitzGerald, but something has gone terribly wrong. A Dallas cop was supposed to have killed Oswald at the Book Depository under the guise of self-defense. Now Jack Ruby has his ass in a jam with Giancana for letting Oswald get arrested.*

Mr. FitzGerald was now standing at Walter's desk dialing the FBI director's hotline, reserved for national emergencies. Mr. Hoover had just gotten to his office after returning that morning from Dallas where he and Richard Nixon were houseguests of oil baron Clint Murchison.

"Mr. Hoover, this is Desmond FitzGerald at Langley. What can you tell me about this Oswald your agents just picked up in Dallas? Come now, Mr. Hoover. This sure as hell isn't time for any interagency politics, is it? Have Oswald flown to Washington. We want to interrogate him. Look, the president of the United States is dead, and if you're not going to fly him up here I'm going to fly down there and personally interrogate him. No, look that's an order from your boss, the attorney general. Does Bobby Kennedy have to tell you personally? What do you mean you take orders only from Lyndon Johnson now?"

What the hell is going on? FitzGerald asked himself, slamming down the phone. *Oswald is going to talk, by God! Maybe Bobby Kennedy was right; there is something fishy going on with the FBI.* FitzGerald glanced at his watch—*My God! I've got to stop AMLASH!*

"Walter, you got Woodson yet? We're running out of time."

"No sir. She's not answering. What's the flap?" Walter asked while redialing.

"*Goddamn it.* We have to abort PAPER MATE or start WWIII."

"*I realize* that, sir. What's up with Hoover?"

"Just shut up and get through to fucking Havana!"

Mildred Cole raised one eyebrow, drawing out her words, "Please, gentlemen. Will you stop it?" she asked.

"I'm sorry, Mildred," FitzGerald replied with a weak smile of apology.

This is more than I can take, Mildred Cole was thinking as she scribbled notes trying to look busy. *The CIA's gone too far. Spying was an honorable and noble job back in the good ole days when Mr. Dulles ran things. Now I'm working for the Hyannis Port Mafia. The Kennedys betrayed the nation with self-serving egomania and now the president's paid the price.*

"Mildred, *A secret, kept from all the rest. Between yourself and me...*"

"Mr. FitzGerald! *Please!* This is *not* the time for reciting Alice..."

"Yes, I know, but the question still remains in my mind. Did Castro kill Kennedy before Kennedy killed Fidel?" the boss asked before pausing, "I should have tried harder to persuade the president there would be blowback if he kept after him. Remember, just a few days ago Castro said 'if United States leaders are aiding in terrorist plans to eliminate Cuban leaders, they themselves will not be safe.'"

"For God's sake, *stop it!*" Mildred snapped. "Don't make it so hard on yourself. I've been around the Kennedys from the beginning of this Castro fiasco and they brought it all upon themselves, in my opinion. If the president had listened to Mr. Dulles and given air support to *La Brigada* in the Bay of Pigs, Castro would have long ago been history. Then they almost started World War III with the missile crisis. Bobby turning on the mob with the Justice Department's organized crime investigation, now that was *really stupid*. Fidel Castro had nothing to do with the assassination; it has everything to do with the Mafia. Oh, I'm sorry for running on like this—I'm out of bounds, Mr. D."

The S.A.S. chief patted his loyal secretary on the shoulder. "I just heard more of the truth about the Cuban affair than I've heard spoken since returning from the Far East."

Mildred smiled weakly at her boss who she knew had fought with the Chinese during World War II in Indochina and was not one to panic. He had just returned from serving as CIA chief of the Far East mission, where he organized the Hmong tribesmen in Laos to fight against the Pathet Lao Communists. *Mr. FitzGerald is a great patriot and an honorable man*, she thought in admiration.

Laos was someone else's problem for the senior CIA officer who was how holding himself responsible for starting World War III. FitzGerald, who never panicked, felt his guts tighten as he asked his assistant, "Can't we get through to Holly, Walt?"

"No sir. She's not answering at the BBC bureau either," Walter replied, now feeling the pressure to get through to prevent a nuclear war with the Russians.

"Goddamn it then!" FitzGerald swore. "Breach security and send a cable straight to our AMLASH back-up agent in Havana."

"Expose our agent at in the *Ministerio de Agricultura*, sir?"

"Damn right—we have no choice. Send this top priority, 'For your eyes only,' Contact AMLASH. Abort PAPER MATE immediately. Now send a *second* message to the Captain of the *La Cuenta* that is tied up at the Havana wharf. Abort PAPER MATE prior to 1600 hours and terminate cover agent in case of mole."

"*My God*, kill our agent in Havana, Mr. FitzGerald?" Mildred gasped, "For God's sake, which one? You don't mean Woodson?"

FitzGerald ignored his secretary. "You got that Walter? We can't take any chances. After Oswald, I don't know who can be trusted or if there's been an assassination conspiracy or not. There could be forces besides Castro and the KGB involved, AMLASH could be a ..."

"And don't forget the Mafia, boss...?"

"I know that Mildred—get me what you have on Oswald."

Ten minutes later FitzGerald turned to Mildred Cole after he finished reading Commission Document 321 – TOP SECRET: "Chronology of Lee Harvey Oswald in Russia and Return to U.S." which he noted had been updated by Axial Hanson the day before. "Take this memo for the director's signature. I have to brief President Johnson with him at nine in the morning, so make this Ultra Secret, for the eyes of the President and DCI only."

"Yes sir. I'm ready."

"Lee Harvey Oswald confirmed visit to Soviet and Cuban embassies in Mexico City on 28 September 1963. Confirmed meeting with Soviet vice-consul who is known KGB expert in assassination and sabotage. Also visited Cubans. Report is not final. Oswald is indeed part of foreign conspiracy, and might be killed before he has time to be interrogated by U.S. authorities."

"You're kidding? Oswald in the Dallas jail?" Miss Mildred laughed. "You're not really sending *this* to the President of the United States, are you?"

"I said it very clearly, I think," Desmond FitzGerald replied sarcastically. "Oswald has just evidently switched sides, or there's a third party involved that I don't know about. Hurry now. Get it typed and hand carry it up to Anne Cantrell. Our next job is to leak a story on Oswald's connection to Castro's government to the press—CBS, *The Times*, etc. Use standard operating protocol, but get it in the media."

Chapter Twenty-Five

Havana

November 22, 1963

After lunch, Captain Relondo Silas left the Hotel Regis and walked back to his office in the *Ministerio de Agricultura* where he served as the meat-rationing liaison for the Cuban and Russian military. He lit a cigar as he strolled down the broad, tree-lined *Prado* Boulevard that ran from the capital in the center of old Havana to the *Castillo la Punta* by the harbor. Captain Silas was having second thoughts—*has Luis Benes got the guts to execute Fidel Castro in a few hours?*

The Captain stopped along the way at his favorite bench to smoke and let his lunch digest. During the minutes alone he reflected back on his role in the assassination conspiracy that began with the BBC television coverage of Don Carlos Garcia's execution over two-and-a-half-years ago.

The world television coverage made Captain Silas a Cuban hero when Castro labeled the BBC and the western press "the tongue of Satan, poisoning world opinion" for their reporting of the event. The publicity as the executioner brought a promotion to captain along with a high-profile position in the *Ministerio de Agricultura*. Captain Silas' knowledge of the military strength of all Cuban and

Russian units made him a vital CIA intelligence source. Today, as always, he felt relieved after the daily strength and unit locations contained in the meat rationing reports had been secretly transmitted to JM/WAVE.

Captain Silas flashed a broad smile at a beautiful woman passing by and thought of Holly Woodson, whose footage of the execution had made him famous. After numerous confessions to his priest, he had forgiven Holly for the press releases that had gotten him court-martialed and banished to remote San Blas four years ago.

The Cuban officer was proud of being a third-generation graduate of the Cuban Military Academy. However, as a youth he had a burning desire to enter the priesthood, but Cuban priests came from Spain and his destiny remained with the family tradition of wearing the uniform.

Over the years, Don Carlos Garcia's execution had weighed heavily on the officers' conscience, tormenting him with haunting nightmares of watching Luis Benes exhuming the Don's body from its grave at Australian Central a few days after the Bay of Pigs. Equally haunting was the nightly recurrence of the muzzle flash of his men's rifles that made the executioner jerk awake screaming, drenching wet with sweat. This was only one of many demons that possessed Relondo Silas—thousands of innocent Cubans had been executed in mock trials. In his nightmarish hell he heard the screams of the crowds—*"Paredón! To the wall!"*— which was taking an emotional toll through loss of sleep.

After Silas was posted to the *Ministerio de Agricultura*, Holly Woodson had slipped seductively back into his life one afternoon out of nowhere as he strolled along the *Prado.* "Will you please forgive me, Captain?" she asked, taking his hand and pressing her soft breast against his arm as they walked along.

Like Samson, Silas had unwillingly fallen for the enchantment of Delilah. This time, however, he had not tried to fight his emotions—Holly was just too beautiful and too good in bed. The Captain had fallen deeply in love with the foreign agent whose sexual promiscuousness, along with his disenchantment with the Communist regime, had turned him into an unwilling traitor to his beloved nation.

Upon her return to Havana, Holly had once again been challenged to recruit Silas after having used him as a source in her propaganda on the Revolution's Communist movement. This time she traveled on a student visa to attend the *Universidad de la Habana* to study Spanish. Writing a series of articles in the student newspaper flattering Fidel as the leader who freed Cuba from Yankee imperialism, Holly had gotten her press visa reinstated. At the same time Captain Silas' position at the *ministerio* made him a priority mark to become a spy for Axial Hanson at JM/WAVE and FitzGerald at the S.A.S as the back up for AMLASH.

The CIA knew that Castro's Revolution thrived off the foreign news media after *New York Times* reporter, Hebert Mathews, had given Fidel the coverage to place him in power in the first place. Holly's BBC coverage now required censoring before being released but allowed her to roam freely throughout the island to get her stories. The American agent had been instructed by her handlers to intentionally slant her articles to support the Revolution's propaganda—a clandestine ploy to get her closer to Castro by using the Havana press to denounce the raids that Gray Lynch was running out of JM/WAVE.

Upon entering the *Ministerio de Agricultura,* Captain Silas nervously evaluated the personal risk he was taking as a member of the S.A.S. assassination plot. With Castro dead in a few hours, there would be free elections and he would use his family's political and military connections to become the youngest major in the Cuban Army. He would then be in a position to ask Holly Woodson to marry him.

When Silas unlocked his office, he noticed that Castro's photo was slightly off-center, signaling an urgent message had been received from the Americans. He straightened the picture, which had been tilted by an electronic sensor from the incoming cable. The explosive device built in the closet floor by the young West German Western Union technician named Hans Wolf was now disarmed.

Captain Silas locked his office door before unlocking his closet and lifting up the trap door. He admired how the CIA had been able to plant such sophisticated communication equipment in the heart of the building by splicing into the Western Union cable to Miami. It took Silas only a few seconds to decode the cable from the S.A.S. at Langley and swallow it in a panic. *Where in the hell is Cubelas?* Silas asked himself, realizing he had less than forty-five minutes to get down to the docks, find the Captain of the *La Cuenta*, and locate Luis Benes.

* * *

During the walk to his apartment, Luis Benes reflected back to the day he buried Don Carlos Garcia beside his wife in the family cemetery on the Hacienda del Azucar. He had exhumed his half-brother's bullet-riddled body as a means of getting his workers back to the fields. While loading the corpse into his pickup, he had expected trouble from Lieutenant Silas who was watching from the door of Central Australian's administrative building.

Unable to locate Father Lopez in San Blas, Luis had driven to Giron and asked the young priest to say mass, at Carlos' reburial while Raul Castro drank with Che inside the Casa de Azucar. Afterwards he went to his villa, showered and dressed in a white linen countryman's shirt, before returning to the kitchen where Gerardo was preparing dinner.

"Luis, stop," Gerardo whispered grabbing his arm when he saw him heading to the library. "Are you crazy? They will kill you if you go in there."

"I hope not," Luis replied as he calmly walked down the corridor toward the cigar smoke and drunken laughter. To officially become master of the Hacienda del Azucar he would have to join the Revolution.

No Cuban was more experienced in growing and harvesting sugar cane than Luis Benes. If he convinced Raul Castro of this he could hopefully live out his life in the luxury of the Casa de Azucar. *It's a long shot*, he thought, *but dreams are what life is made of.*

He walked in on the short, thin Raul Castro with his feet propped on Don Carlos' desk drinking with Che Guevara, The two men were smoking cigars and had just opened a new bottle of Bacardi Select. The empty bottle Luis had shared with his brother a few days before was lying on the floor.

"Who the hell are you?" Che shouted, jumping to his feet.

"Good afternoon, señors, my name is Luis Benes. I'm the superintendent of the Hacienda del Azucar. *Viva la Revolucion*! Please pardon me, but now that you have taken over the hacienda from the tyrant, Don Carlos, I want to join you."

"Who is this man?" Che asked, his eyes darting at Raul.

"Didn't you hear? He said he's the superintendent of the hacienda," Fidel's brother replied with a sarcastic chuckle.

"Should we throw him out or have him shot for barging in on us?"

"Shot? Should we shoot you, Señor Superintendent?"

"It would be a very grave error on your part, señor," Luis said. "Without a good harvest this year Cuba's economy will be wrecked and the Revolution will fail, and you know that. You can ill afford to have another crop failure of five million metric tons. Shoot me if you like, amigo, but if you do, you will be shooting yourselves in the foot. Bullets are cheap. My knowledge of how to increase sugar production in this country is of great value to the Revolution."

"Oh, a smart ass, this superintendent. Guards!" Che shouted, as the door was flung open and soldiers rushed in.

"*Paredon* with this smart ass," the Argentine Doctor ordered, spitting out a chunk of his well-chomped cigar into the puddle of dog's blood.

"No, Che, wait," Raul shouted, "Let's not be too hasty. This man is making sense if he knows what he is talking about. Remember, if the sugar crop fails, so fails the Revolution. The sugar crop is the Cuban economy; it means everything to our survival. I rather like this superintendent with balls. He can be of vital importance to us if he, in fact, knows how to increase the sugar harvest to over five million metric tons and makes me look good to Fidel..." Raul rambled on while Luis stood watching, his ponytail bouncing up and down like the tail of a prancing stallion.

Che leaned back in his chair. "I don't know, Raul. Cuba is *azucar*, *but* does this man know how to solve the problem?"

"Okay, Señor Superintendent, what are your credentials? Do you have a degree in agriculture from an American university like LSU, or are you an economist from the University of Chicago?"

"No, Señor Raul, Luis Benes is only self-educated from reading the books in this library," the superintendent said, pointing at the hundreds of volumes lining the shelves on the walls. "Go ask Gerardo the cook. For years he smuggled the books out for me each night one by one so I could study by lamplight without Don Carlos' knowledge. I have also been forty seasons to the fields for the plantings..."

"Very interesting, the Don wouldn't let you read his stinking books," Che interrupted. "It is typical of the rich bastards to keep their people illiterate. Only four percent of the Cuban people know how to read, you know."

"Yes, and all of that will change with the Revolution. Every Cuban will be able to get a free education and health care. I'm impressed so far, Superintendent, do join us for a drink and tell me how to improve the sugar harvest," Raul said, motioning to a chair.

"With pleasure," Luis replied, lifting a clean brandy glass off the bar. "We must start, señors, by increasing our annual sugar production to at least six million metric tons. This will not be easy to accomplish with the American sugar embargo and having to sell our sugar only to the Eastern Bloc nations. This production problem cannot be corrected without reversing the stupid decisions some asshole made in Havana to cut back on the cane planting and turn fertile land into raising cattle. We have also had many of our technicians go to the U.S., and there is a shortage of spare parts for the machinery because of the damn Yankee embargo."

"Hold it! Now you are sounding like an economist..."

"*Si*, Che. I read the discarded *Bohemia* daily from Don Carlos' trash along with the National Sugar Association's journals that he throws away each month. I also discuss the sugar market with the bastard, and I must tell you, most of Carlos' ideas that made him the president of the NSA came from me if the truth were known."

Raul lit a fresh cigar. "It all started in the summer of 1960 when the American government passed the sugar bill legislation that eliminated our quota for the American market to protect their international monopolies for their big sugar interest..."

Che pounded on the desk. "And Fidel retaliated by nationalizing the American electric companies, telephone companies, mills and all the United States industry…"

"That is all history now, señors. The fact remains; I predict that the 1963 harvest will be less than 4.8 million tons, a disaster. *Now*, I have a plan that will compensate for all these problems that the Americans have caused us, if you are willing to listen."

It was almost midnight when Che stumbled off to bed leaving Raul and Luis to finish off the second bottle of rum. "Okay Luis, you will come to Havana and I will introduce you to Fidel and recommend that he appoint you *Don Azucar*," Raul yawned when he saw the sun coming up.

Luis was now walking through the *Plaza de San Francisco* in the heart of old Havana and past the *Iglesia de San Francisco* across from the Havana cruise ship terminal. He glanced up at his apartment on the second floor of a teal-colored building with dark green shutters and a sloping tile roof. The cobblestone plaza was quiet except for the foghorns of Russian cruise ships when they occasionally docked at the terminal.

Luis had lived well since arriving in Havana, buying expensive tailored suits and dining out each night at expensive restaurants and nightclubs. With a clear conscience, he had emptied the hacienda's checking account into his own account—the equivalent of some sixty thousand U.S. dollars. It was just as much his money as anyone's, especially now that the Hacienda del Azucar belonged to the Revolution and Carlos was dead. He also received a nice salary from his prestigious position in the agricultural ministry that supplemented his lavish lifestyle.

He paused briefly by the three-tiered fountain in the plaza and thought of returning to the Plaza de Armas in San Blas someday soon. He recalled sitting in the Bar Habana and watching Don Carlos stand with Manuel on the steps of the church that fatal Sunday in April that seemed like an eternity ago to him now.

Luis was inside his apartment boiling water for his coffee when he took out the deed to the hacienda and examined it carefully. It was the only thing that he would take with him to Miami after he poisoned Castro. Then, in a few months, he could return to the Casa de Azucar, and maybe by next year at this time he would be living there with his bride, if Holly Woodson would marry him. With that thought, he got up and placed the deed safely under his mattress.

The assassin felt sweat running down his flanks, having never killed a man with his bare hands before. Killing Don Carlos was easy; one phone call to the DGI was all it took. This assassination saga all started the night he found Captain Silas perched at the El Floridita bar drinking frozen daiquiris with Holly Woodson.

"*El Don de Azucar*," she purred when he walked by, taking Luis by surprise.

"Oh, Señorita Woodson. I have not seen you since the Bar Habana in San Blas during the invasion, remember?"

"At Gonzo's bar. Of course I remember you."

"Good evening, Señor Benes," Captain Silas said, extending his hand. "Will you please join us for a drink?"

"With pleasure, Captain. I have not had the pleasure of meeting you officially. I saw you from a distance at San Blas in the old days and I will look forward to seeing more of you now that both of us are assigned to the ministry."

"Do join us," Holly's voice beckoned. *God, look at that man's sexy body*, she thought when he sat down next to her.

"Gladly, if I am not intruding."

"No, of course not. Shall we roll for the first round?"

"Relondo, stop it, Señor Benes is our guest."

"If the Captain would like to roll, I know the game of Horse," Luis laughed.

"You are my guest, so roll to me, señor."

Four kings and a jack tumbled neatly out of the leather cup and bounced nicely and well behaved on the bar. "Four kings, all day long, Captain."

The captain smiled disparagingly and looked fondly at the lady who was smiling back at the man who had just rolled the quad kings. Rattling the cup, he rolled an ace high.

"Only trash," the Captain sighed, ordering a fresh round. "Do you take salt, Señor Benes?"

"Yes, thank you. And thank you for bringing me luck, señorita," Luis replied, feeling her warm hand firmly and intentionally rest on his thigh.

On the following Friday after an evening of heavy drinking at El Floridita and the barman shouting, "last call," Holly giggled as she slid off her bar stool while exposing a lot of thigh. "Come along you two drunks. The night's still young."

"Where to?" Luis asked as the threesome stumbled outside into an awaiting taxi.

"Hotel Nacional, driver," Holly replied, sliding in between them.

While Relondo was looking down on the lights of the cars speeding along the Malecon, Holly put a forty-five record of *El Cuarto de Tula* on her hi-fi. She rubbed her breast up against Luis while pouring three stiff Bacardi Ron 8 Años into brandy snifters for her guests.

"Dance with me, Luis, you sexy man," Holly giggled, holding her hands over her head and moving her hips provocatively to the beat of the bongos as she rumbaed around the room.

"Go on, Luis, dance with the lady," Silas insisted, loosening his tie and kicking off his shoes, feeling an erection watching Holly's moves.

Luis stood and took off his coat. His baritone voice joined in with the heavily sexed lyrics of the Cuban favorite, *Cuarto de Tula* as they danced.

Holly glanced over at Silas and smiled seductively, knowing her ploy to recruit Luis was working out as they had planned. She began singing her version of the song. "There's a real commotion going on in the Hotel Nacional. It's Holly's bedroom. It's gone up in flames. Call Relondo and Luis. Call the fire brigade. I think Holly wants them to put out her fire."

Holly and Luis danced belly to belly, and after the record stopped she put it on again and turned off the lights. "Come and drink," the Captain beckoned as she snuggled her sweating body between the men on the sofa.

"Call the fire brigade to come quickly. Look! I'm on fire," Holly sniggered, wiping her face.

"Let's put out your fire, then," the Captain said, nibbling playfully on the lady's neck.

"To Holly's fire," Luis replied with surprise as she put her arms around him and thrust her flickering tongue deep into his mouth.

The Captain watched with voyeuristic delight as Holly's heavy breathing and passionate moans drowned out the sounds of the traffic on the seaside boulevard below. He hesitated, not knowing if he should participate, watching Luis' dark hand slowly move up the smooth white flesh of her leg until it rested high on her inner thigh. "Oh my God," Holly softly whimpered.

The Captain unzipped his fly as he watched the dark hand disappear into her panties and began slowly sliding them down.

"Oh Luis," she whispered, "Oh, God, Luis, please! Please make love to me."

Relondo felt his breaths coming hot and heavy as he placed his drink on the table and slowly unbuttoned the back of her blouse. He bent over and kissed her neck while Luis unhooked her bra, running his hands under her firm breast. "How very nice," he said before pushing her back against the couch and slowly teasing her erect nipples with his tongue.

"Harder," she moaned, lifting her buttocks off the sofa as Relondo removed her skirt, leaving her in high heels thrust high into the air.

Luis' face disappeared between her thighs bringing hushed cries of desire until suddenly Holly was pushing both her men away. She was panting and standing naked in the weak light as she finished her drink before leading them by their hands toward her bedroom. "Come quickly, Holly's on fire. My, God, look at you, Luis, you show dog, you," she laughed closing the door behind them.

On Friday nights the ménage à trois became a regular thing after rolling dice for daiquiris at El Floridita. Sandwiched between the dark skin of the strong mulatto and the handsome, muscular body of the captain half his age, her lily-white body was silhouetted against the Havana skyline in the thrusting, twisted entanglements of naked flesh. Afterward they would lie exhausted and fall asleep, until they awoke and Holly's bedroom in the corner suite of the Hotel Nacional would again catch on fire all over again with human desire.

Holly Woodson knew she was getting good at sexpionage with her seduction of Luis Benes into their S.A.S. conspiracy plot. She was constantly dropping subtle reminders of his loss of the Hacienda del Azucar in the El Floridita turned Rick's Café Americana. The only thing missing from a scene from the movie *Casablanca* was Sam playing—*As Time Goes By.* Holly had fallen in love with the mulatto while remaining devoted to the captain's cause, bringing great praise at JM/WAVE for a sterling job.

On Halloween night, former Major Rolando Cubelas, who in 1959 as a student revolutionary shot and killed Batista's chief of military intelligence and had later run the University Revolutionary Directorate, joined the threesome at the bar. Raul Castro had demoted Cubelas for going soft on the Catholic Church and had stripped him of his military rank, automobile, and lavish lifestyle. If he had not been such a loyal supporter of Fidel, he would have been imprisoned on the Isle of Pines. His loss of faith in Fidel had left him with the burning desire to plot a coup.

Now there were four players of the game of Horse seated at the El Floridita Bar along with Russian officers and embassy personnel.

Late that evening, after heavy drinking, Cubelas turned to Luis and whispered, "Did you ever think that we could visit you at the Hacienda del Azucar if Castro was dead?"

"The Hacienda del Azucar belongs to the Revolution now."

"Not if Castro is dead and we have a new government."

"Yes, you have been screwed, just like I was, Luis. What a great loss you have suffered by losing the Hacienda del Azucar," Cubelas said with a sigh, as all eyes were on Luis, who was sipping his sixth drink.

"Yes, I know," Luis replied soberly.

"It would be very easy for you to kill Castro. You have almost daily access to him and he trusts you."

"It would be impossible for me to do that, Holly."

"Not at all," Cubelas replied, emphasizing his words. "Now listen carefully to me. You, and only you, can become Cuba's modern Jose Marti, changing our country's history forever."

"Jose Marti was executed. To hell with that!"

"You will never get caught, and when Castro is dead the Revolution is dead, and with its death Cuba will have free elections and be a free country once again. I will see to it that you will then get the legal title to your Hacienda del Azucar as your reward."

"Luis, if not for Cuba, do it for me, love," Holly said with the persuasiveness of Eve handing Adam the apple.

* * *

The hurricane season had passed, and the November sky over Old Havana was filled with millions of twinkling stars. Rolando Cubelas had flown in late that afternoon from meeting with a CIA officer in a hotel in Paris. He dropped off his luggage, took a shower, and went to the El Floridita, where AMLASH found his co-conspirators in a very serious mood.

"Did you bring it?" Captain Silas asked.

"I have it," Cubelas whispered, reaching into his jacket pocket.

"Good. Give the pen to me. Luis, tomorrow is your day to play Jose Marti to liberate Cuba from the Communists," Captain Silas replied, taking a sip of his daiquiri and slipping the pen into Luis' shirt pocket.

"Good luck."

"I will need it, Holly." Luis sighed, crossing himself and holding up his glass.

That was last night, and now it was nearing the appointed hour. Luis felt like his chest was in a vise, and each tick of the clock clamped it tighter. His breaths came short and frequent, like a fish out of water. Only an hour remained before his four o'clock meeting with Castro in the *Ministro de Agricultura* to announce the plan for planting the spring crop. The dictator would be signing, on national television, the Agrarian Spring 1964 Declaration that mandated full participation by the Cuban people in the spring planting.

The sun was shining brightly through his open apartment window as Havana awakened from its noon siesta. The foghorn blast of the departing ship made his cup rattle in its saucer as if he was a man suddenly stricken with palsy. Luis lit his cigar and began reading the morning *Revolucion*. *This is my day in history*, he thought glancing at November 22, 1963, on the paper's masthead.

Luis put the paper aside and examined the Paper Mate pen for the hundredth time. *I hope this damn thing really works*, he thought, clicking the pen rigged with a needle so fine that the lethal Blackleaf 40 injection would go unnoticed. A simple jab of the spring-loaded pen into Castro's arm while he was signing the

265

declaration should be simple. The nicotine-based insecticide would have no immediate effect; Castro would feel nothing. Luis would have time to return to his apartment, get the deed to the Hacienda del Azucar and board *La Cuenta*, which was chartered by the CIA's Zenith Technical Enterprises in Miami.

The boat would take him across the Florida Straits to its homeport at JM/WAVE and to freedom in the United States, where he would hire a hit man to track down and murder nephew Manuel Garcia. After Castro's death there would be free elections, and he would return triumphant and unchallenged to reclaim the Hacienda del Azucar and have a big wedding like Roscena and the Ambassador.

There was a soft knock on his door, and Luis jumped up, spilling his coffee. "Who's there?" he whispered, cracking the door, surprised to see that Captain Silas had company.

"It's Silas, let us in. This is Captain Planky, the skipper of the fishing boat."

Luis opened the door for the men and glanced up and down the narrow hall to make sure they were not being followed. He shut the door quickly, locking it before motioning his guests to be seated at the table and closing the shutters. "Why did you bring the skipper here, Relondo? This is dangerous."

"Do you have the pen?"

"Of course," Luis replied, taking it out of his pocket and laying it on the table, his hand shaking.

"There has been a change in our plans," Silas said quietly, watching Luis' face light up as though the weight of the world had been lifted off his chest.

"Unfortunately for you, there has been a very big change of plans," Bob Planky said in his deep voice while jerking from his jacket pocket a .22-caliber silencer that spit a single slug of lead into Luis Benes' forehead. His target uttered not a sound as he slumped down, his head falling with a thump on the table.

Captain Silas jumped back, throwing up his hands, "God, no! Please don't shoot me, Planky. I'm one of your agents!"

The assassin pointed the pistol at Silas' head. "It's your lucky day, Captain, you're not on my list. If you ever tell who did this, you damn well will be," Planky snarled, grabbing the pen and putting it into his pocket before making sure his victim was dead.

Silas held onto the chair to steady himself and stared blankly at the body. "What have you done?"

"Shut up and make it look like a robbery," Planky ordered, emptying out drawers. "Goddamn, get with it man!"

"Oh my God. I can't believe you killed him," Silas mumbled, turning over the bed, as the aged brown envelope fell unnoticed on the floor. "Planky, let's get the hell out of here now."

The *La Cuenta* sailed within the hour for Miami with Rolando Cubelas not Luis Benes on board.

* * *

It was a small room with very tall ceilings and to "Manny Garcia" it still seemed to belong to Charlie whose name was seldom mentioned when Mama Lena and Charles talked. Still at times when they thought that he was asleep, he heard them whispering about Charlie who had been dead for two years. Manny liked his room in the modest white row cottage on Joseph Street in the otherwise affluent University District of New Orleans, even if there was no comparison to his room in the Casa de Azucar with a view of the Bay of Pigs.

It was a cool November morning, and as Manny dressed for school he wondered who was getting dressed in his room in the Casa de Azucar. *When I'm older I'm going to go back, find out, and kill Castro, if someone has not already done so*, he thought as he reached down and patted Zoë on the head. "Good girl," he smiled to the black and white English setter whose large sad eyes were covered by a black Zoro mask of hair. *She misses Charlie*, he thought. "Zoë, you're a good doggy, you skittish bitch, not brave and bold like Blanco, but I still love you doggy."

The boy smelled the bacon frying in the kitchen and realized he was lucky to have found a foster home on this quiet tree-lined street. *Gerardo's bacon couldn't hold a candle to Mama Lena's*; he was thinking when he heard her calling. "Breakfast, Sonny! Hurry on now, child. Don't be late for school."

"Yes, ma'am," the ninth grader replied, tying his highly prized high-topped sneakers before heading for the kitchen.

"You get out of school next week for the Thanksgiving holiday. You didn't have Thanksgiving in Cuba, did you, Sonny?"

"No ma'am. We had Christmas and New Year's. Castro stopped Christmas."

"Well, I do declare."

"You're a better cook than Gerardo, Mama Lena."

"Oh Manny! How nice of you to say so. Maybe Christmas we can have your sister and brother come up from Miami to visit. But heavens, I don't know where everybody would sleep in this little old house."

"I'll sleep on the floor! Maria can have my bed!"

"Now, now, don't get your hopes up. It's a long train ride all the way from Miami and must cost a small fortune, I guess."

"Yes ma'am," Manuel replied, taking a bite of bacon and putting tomato ketchup on his scrambled eggs. "Can we ask Papa Charles *cuanto cuesta los billetes?*"

"Whatcha say, Sonny?"

"Sorry," the boy giggled. "Tickets cost, how much, I meant to say."

"Your English is gettin' pretty good, so hurry on now. It's time you get your smiling face on down to school before those teachers rap your knuckles for being late, ya hear me now? We'll check with Charles when he gets home from the bakery on how much the train tickets from Miami would run."

It was after lunch at the Eleanor McMain Public School across the street from the exclusive Ursuline Academy, the oldest girls school in America. Manuel was in his fifth-period social studies class but was thinking about Ursuline student Carlena Alfonso rather than paying attention. They would meet after school and he would carry her books home—his plans were abruptly interrupted by Mr. Gourgues' crackly voice being piped into the room over the PA system: "Children, I have *terrible* news. President Kennedy has been shot in Dallas and is dead."

The room fell deathly silent, the announcement sending a shock wave of disbelief through the students who dearly loved the first Roman Catholic president of the United States. Miss Fry burst into tears, crossing herself, as did many of her students who were sobbing uncontrollably. The teacher was trying hard to console them when Mr. Gourgues' voice came back on the PA system calling for the children to go to the school auditorium for a memorial.

Manny Garcia bit his lower lip. *Kennedy's the president who turned his back on the brave La Brigada who tried to liberate Cuba. Kennedy is the reason the Bay of Pigs invasion failed. He's the reason that Papa and Blanco are dead now. He's the reason that I'm living in a row cottage in New Orleans and not on my grand Hacienda del Azucar with Maria and Alfredo and going to school in Havana.*

Manny Garcia did not feel any sorrow for the man who had destroyed his world as his mind flashed back to Havana. Castro was probably celebrating over the death of the man who had tried many times to assassinate him. The people in the streets were celebrating Kennedy's death after being victimized by the CIA's terrorist bombings. But the boy realized that this was America, not Cuba, and he was glad school was being dismissed so he could see his new girl friend, Carlena Alfonso.

Manny walked across the street and waited outside the Ursuline Academy. Inside the Our Lady of Prompt Succor Chapel he could hear the mass being held for the president. He would have to ask the tall dark-haired beauty with big green eyes whose rich father worked for Mr. Marcello if she was feeling sad while they shared a Coca Cola at the corner drugstore. Suddenly, Manny Garcia felt the strong hands of a man massaging his shoulders. Looking up, he smiled, "Father O'Brien! What are you doing here?"

Chapter Twenty-Six

Varadero Beach Resort, Cuba

Noon, Friday, November 22, 1963

Holly Woodson was trying to think of the title she would use for Fidel Castro's last interview: *Fidel's Finally, A Dead Dictator's Memories, Castro's Epitaph,* or *A Closure to Communism in Cuba.* In a few hours, Luis Benes' poisonous pen would prick Castro's arm and silence the tyrant for eternity. Holly's interview would be read and reread, editorialized, and published in newspapers and magazines around the world. *This is the interview that will be written into the history books*, she thought as she imagined her picture on the cover of *Life Magazine.*

The Cuban dictator had excused himself from the table to take an urgent telephone call from Ramiro Valdés, head of the DGI. Holly's heart was at her throat. *My God, they might have discovered our assassination plot,* she was thinking as she lit her cigarette and waited.

The journalist glanced at her watch. It was 1:47 P.M. and Fidel had been gone for nearly twenty minutes as her fear turned into panic. *Our assassination plot has been unveiled*, she thought as she prepared to bolt from the table.

She was reaching for her purse when she saw Castro returning, his face clouded with despair. "It's bad news. The American president has been shot in Dallas."

Holly's mouth dropped open. "Is the president dead?" she asked, relieved that Operation PAPER MATE remained undetected.

"I don't know," Castro replied, pacing the floor and puffing heavily on his cigar as he always did when he was agitated. "All American radio and television stations are off the air."

Then the Miami NBC radio affiliate resumed its broadcast: "The thirty-fifth president of the United States, John Fitzgerald Kennedy, is dead." Castro shook his head slowly and sank back down in the chair across the table. "Well, there's the end of your mission of peace. Everything has changed. I'll tell you one thing: at least Kennedy was an enemy to whom we had become accustomed."

Holly's mind went blank. *I can't believe this is really happening. Here I am interviewing the target of the president who had just been assassinated*, she thought, regaining her professional composure. "Maximum Leader, it has been reported that President Kennedy has plotted with the Mafia to kill you. How do you feel now that he is the one dead?"

Castro leaned forward, looking very worried. "The assassination could affect millions of lives in all parts of the world, especially in Cuba. Just let it be said that the American president's death now commands the respect of the world's leaders. It is unfortunate that President Kennedy was naive to the Revolution's efforts to improve the standard of living of the Cuban people. Who is this Lyndon Johnson and what authority does he have over the Central Intelligence Agency?"

"I have never met Lyndon Johnson. Will you try to have a positive dialogue with the new administration?"

Castro's attention was distracted by the television being brought in and tuned to the Miami CBS station. Walter Cronkite was giving the latest news bulletin. "Ladies and gentlemen," he said, "we have just been informed that the FBI and Secret Service have arrested a suspect in the president's assassination. Lee Harvey Oswald, a known Marxist member of the Fair Play for Cuba Committee of New Orleans, was arrested moments ago in a downtown Dallas movie theater. We take you now to our CBS affiliate in Dallas…"

271

"*What?*" Castro shouted. "Oswald? We've never heard of him. Is it not possible that a plot against President Kennedy existed in the CIA or the American mob?"

Hearing Lee Harvey Oswald's name roll off Cronkite's lips sent Holly's mind into a tailspin. *What kind of CIA plot is this? For some reason they have made a bloody patsy out of my chap Oswald. When Luis assassinates Fidel in a few hours there will be hell to pay with the Russians. I must contact Relondo immediately to authenticate Paper Mate with JM/WAVE as a go or no go.*

Holly looked around to make sure his aides were listening before capitalizing on Cronkite's statement. "Beware, Maximum Leader. Listen to that. The Americans have now associated your government with the assassination. The Yanks could jolly well be setting you up for another invasion."

"I'm no fool, señorita. The Americans have unsheathed their daggers. I must go now. At four this afternoon Luis Benes and I will speak on national television from the *Ministro de Agricultura* about the Agrarian Spring Declaration. You will be there for your BBC coverage of my speech, yes?"

"Yes, Maximum Leader," Holly smiled, thanking him for the interview.

Castro turned around and stopped when he was halfway out of the restaurant. "I will also tell the Cuban people this Oswald story is all a CIA lie."

Holly smiled and waved to the departing dictator before turning off her tape recorder. *Cheerio, ole chap. I will make the world a witness to your fate, Fidel. So sad, ole chap. Pity dying of natural causes at such a young age; that is, if this bloody mission doesn't blow up in our faces.*

At 3:30, Holly entered the *Ministro de Agricultura* alone to find Luis' secretary scurrying around in a panic asking if anyone had seen him. The journalistic feeling that something had gone terribly wrong with Operation PAPER MATE was confirmed five minutes before airtime when a hushed cry swept through the ministry. Luis Benes had been found murdered in his apartment. Holly panicked, trying hard to control her emotions: *My God, there's been a double-cross. The DGI must have discovered our plot and assassinated Kennedy. I've got to get the hell out of here and warn JM/WAVE.*

Holly Woodson found herself running up the stairs toward Captain Silas' office on the third floor. She stopped, realizing that Silas could have been arrested and it was best that she not be seen with him. *Only three people could be involved and Luis is dead*, she thought as she walked down to the ground level. *Relondo or Cubelas are either double agents or it was the CIA that ordered Luis' hit. If I had my passport I would go straight away to the bloody airport before the CIA or DGI kills me.*

She heard the staff applauding as Castro entered from a side door of the building, dressed in a fresh set of heavily starched fatigues. Castro was under extremely heavy security with Major Valdés ordering the doors locked and guarded. It was impossible to leave now; Holly was trapped as she took a seat searching the crowd for Silas.

Under the heated lights, the camera rolled for the next two hours as Castro ranted and raved about the Kennedy and Luis Benes deaths as a CIA plot to invade Cuba. When he was finished, the perspiration-drenched dictator approached Holly. "Go with Major Valdés to investigate the crime scene and then write an article on Señor Benes' murder for the morning paper."

Holly complimented Castro on his speech before leaving. At least for the moment the DGI was unaware that she was an agent, she was thinking when it hit her: *My God, they will let me write their bloody story and then kill me.*

Twenty minutes later Holly found herself standing in Luis' ransacked apartment where the DGI investigators were popping flashbulbs and gathering evidence. *Thank God, Luis' body has already been removed*, Holly was thinking as she took notes and tried her hardest to keep from crying while discretely searching for any sign of the brown envelope.

Back in her suite at the Hotel Nacional, Holly's hands shook uncontrollably as she poured a stiff whiskey and waited for Relondo to call. *I've got to get hold of myself,* she thought as she peered down at the northwesterly gale sending breakers crashing against the seawall. As she watched the white sheets of spray smashing onto the boulevard below, she felt her emotions being flooded with sorrow, horror, and fear for her life. "Damn it! Why in the bloody hell did I get Luis mixed up in all of this?" she sobbed.

She dried her eyes and addressed the damning task at hand: to write the truth about her lover's murder without knowing all the facts. She had to turn the story into gray propaganda; this was Castro's orders. Holly Woodson realized the real truth of having to write half-truths about Luis' death violated every principle of her journalistic training.

If Relondo had not been arrested he would tell her the truth at dinner. She glanced at the desk clock slowly ticking away the hour and began to write about Luis Benes' murder in a race against her nine o'clock deadline.

While she struggled with the opening paragraph, Holly's thoughts shot back to her surveillance of Lee Harvey Oswald in New Orleans. She smiled weakly, thinking of what a great assignment the "Big Easy" had been, starting with her one-night fling with Tex Morris at the Jung Hotel. For a fleeting moment she wondering if Tex had gotten her letter that she was back in Havana.

Castro's comments that afternoon about the Mafia suddenly rang true. Holly had forgotten about trailing Oswald into Guy Banister's office one afternoon in the company of a silver-haired man in a tailored suit. *My God. It had to have been Johnny Roselli I saw Lee talking with because they got out of Marcello's limousine.*

Holly was now sure of one thing if nothing else: Oswald was not a KBG or Castro agent, nor was he a Communist. He might look like a Commie, smell like a Commie, and act like a Commie, and that's why he's been arrested. *He's the CIA's patsy, poor bloke. If anything, Oswald is a young CIA zealot; I've read his CIA file to prove it. This had nothing to do with Luis' death, or does it?*

Oh no! Time is running out! Holly thought putting a fresh sheet of paper in her Remington portable. She began pounding on the keys, her words appearing on the paper as if a brush had been magically dipped into her brain. In no time she jerked out the last page of a four-page draft.

She lit a cigarette and glanced at 8:30—time had run out. She hurriedly made the final corrections in pen before freshening her makeup and calling for her car and driver. Grabbing her purse, she ran down the hall to the elevator and looked for Silas in the lobby bar before getting into her car.

Ten minutes later she instructed her driver to wait as she scampered into the *Revolucion's* newsroom. It was a minute before nine. The last second deadline for the Saturday edition had been met when she handed the article to the censor. She dug in her purse for a cigarette wondering if she was next on the hit list now that she finished her story.

Holly took a long drag, exhaling out her nose as she watched the censor editing her work. Had she left anything out? Luis Benes' death was not a robbery but an assassination by the CIA, her story reported, and she dared not mention any DGI involvement. By laying the blame on the CIA, Holly hoped she had temporarily preserved her cover until she could get out of Havana.

Major Valdés walked in and did not speak. She watched as he read each page of her article carefully. *I've gotten myself in a mess, this one,* and the more she thought about it, she realized the bloody truth had been written. *Luis Benes' murder was a CIA hit and I'm next on their list, I can feel it.*

Holly let out a sigh of relief at the sound of the censor's stamp of approval and the scratching of his signature releasing the story to the API and UPI news services. She was quickly out the door, realizing Valdés was behind her.

"El Floridita, and make sure we're not followed," she ordered her driver grinding out her cigarette and searched in her purse for another. She kept glancing over her shoulder to see if the DGI was trailing her and hoping Captain Silas was still alive.

Entering El Floridita, Holly moved gracefully in her skin-tight dress emphasizing the movements of her hips as she walked past a group of drunken Russian officers at the bar who were discussing Kennedy's death. She spotted Silas and crumpled into his arms, releasing her emotions on his shoulder. "Thank God you're alive."

"You look exhausted. Dry your tears," the Captain said as he reached for his handkerchief. "We're in public. Where have you been?" he whispered.

"I am exhausted, darling. It was awful, having to go to Luis' apartment with the DGI. I had to go to the scene of the crime and the flat had been ransacked. Then, having to write and rewrite the story for Fidel, it was bloody hell."

"Was there blood everywhere?"

"No, none come to think of it."

"How long did it take you?" he asked, lighting her cigarette.

"An eternity, but I made the deadline. Now tell me the truth, Relondo. Who made the hit? It had to be either you or Cubelas or the CIA—Cubelas shot the…"

Silas' dark eyes flashed with anger. "Don't insult me, Holly. The DGI did it. Neither of us are double agents. What time do you want to eat?" the Captain asked, ordering daiquiris.

"Luis was murdered at approximately three o'clock this afternoon. They found the body at a little before four when he was a no-show at the *Ministerio*. I was there, and you should have seen his staff's anger. Bloody terrible, this damn thing is."

"Yes, he was our friend, but let's not talk about it now."

"Yes, but only four of us knew. You…you didn't take Luis out, did you, Relondo?"

"*Hell no!* And this is not the place to talk about it, Holly," her Captain bristled, his face reddened with anger. "Let's finish this round and have dinner."

"Yes, shall we, my darling?" she said softly with tears smearing her mascara. "Relondo, I am sorry, darling. I know it could never have been you. It's just the reporter in me. I am scared to bloody death. This thing has turned nasty—*very* nasty indeed. I'm so very sorry I insulted you."

"It's okay. Luis once told me a very deep secret that he…"

"That he loved me," Holly interrupted, "and we were going to get married and live at the Casa de Azucar? Yes, he told me many times, and I loved him too."

The captain's face turned to granite, and then he turned away.

Holly covered her mouth, saying, "What I meant to say is that we all loved each other, darling, the three of us. Oh how wonderful and beautiful it was," she sighed, getting a fresh Kleenex.

Silas stared down at his drink. *I can't believe the bitch just said that.*

"He had the deed to the Hacienda del Azucar hidden under his mattress and he wanted to marry me. I looked around the flat the best I could but with the investigators there I couldn't find it."

"*The deed?* He has it really?"

"Yes, Relondo. I want you to go there early tomorrow morning and look for it. I have the key to the flat, but not the building. Will you, please, my darling?"

"You have a *key* to Luis' apartment?"

Holly Woodson looked away then placed her hands on Relondo's shoulders, looking deeply into his angry eyes. "Yes, Relondo. I went there, and often. Don't be angry, *please*. Just do it, darling, before I leave for London tomorrow. Get the deed and please come with me. I will get you political asylum in the U.K. Castro will not be in power forever and then we can return and turn the hacienda into an orphanage, you and I. *Oh God!* Don't turn around, Major Valdés is seated at the bar watching us."

Chapter Twenty-Seven

Havana

Saturday, November 23, 1963

It was before sunrise on this clear, cool November morning, and the north-westerly wind had died down on the deserted streets of old Havana. Captain Silas had a sleepless night after being told that the woman he loved was really in love with a dead man. He had tried comforting her but what he needed most was for her to comfort him. He would never have gone along with her plan to seduce Luis in a ménage à trois if it meant losing her. After their terrible fight he had stayed awake all night reminding himself that she was just a spy doing a spy's work, but it still hurt. He had finally dressed and set out to fulfill her pleading request to return the deed before she left.

He trudged along the cobblestones of *Calle Oficios*, his steps echoing off the dark buildings, capturing his conscience in a tomb of gloom after lying to Holly at the El Floridita last night. He stared straight ahead with the same hollowness and helplessness he had seen in Luis Benes' eyes the split second before the bullet popped a nice, neat hole in his forehead. "I cannot take this anymore," he said to no one.

I could not have stopped Planky if I had wanted to, he thought. The skipper just did it—shot him quickly, without warning—but I was his accompanist. *Killing Luis Benes is much worse than executing Don Carlos nearly three years ago—this is cold-blooded murder.*

The musk of Holly's perfume was still lingering on his face, as he wiped his mouth. *God*, he dreaded telling her the truth after failing to convince her last night that it was the DGI. Holly was too smart a reporter to believe him and when he returned with the deed, he would confess that it was a CIA hit even if Planky killed him. *If Holly flies to England this morning, she will be lost forever. And maybe that would be best for both of us*, he thought sadly.

Arriving in the deserted Plaza de San Francisco there was still no morning breeze off the ocean and it was deathly quiet. He glanced up at Luis Benes' dark apartment while the gushing waters of the Fountain of the Lions in the plaza seemed to be saying, *"Silas come and wash Luis Benes' blood from your hands. Come and wash Luis Benes' blood from your hands...blood from your hands."*

The heavy wooden doors of the *Iglesia de San Francisco* stood open, and with the first traces of daylight, the crown of St. Helen holding the Sacred Cross of Jerusalem was barely visible atop the forty-meter bell tower. Captain Silas entered the church abandoned by the Catholics after the English held Protestant worship there in 1762 during their brief occupation. The entrance to Luis' apartment was in view and he was having second thoughts. *Why am I risking my life to get a piece of worthless paper for a woman who has always used me? What if the DGI has me under surveillance?*

Dear God, please forgive me for being an accomplice to my friend's death, Silas prayed as he walked down the altarless church and glanced up into the dark main nave. He stood for a moment, crossed himself before kneeling, and prayed in earnest. *Our most heavenly creator of the universe, the maker of all men, good and evil, I pray for the lost soul of Luis Benes and for your Holy forgiveness for my part in murdering him. I acted on instructions from the CIA, as a soldier takes orders. I pray that it was your Divine intervention that the taking of his life was in*

279

*the best interest of Cuba. God, I pray for your forgiveness in the name of the Holy
Spirit and the Virgin Mary. Amen.*

With his amen came six chimes on the grandfather clock hidden deep in the
darkness as Silas arose, crossed himself, and stood in the church entrance. It was
not long before the door across the way slowly opened with the departure of the
old light keeper leaving for his morning shift at the Morro Castle lighthouse
guarding the entrance to Havana Harbor. The front door of Luis' apartment
building was now open.

Silas quickly crossed the plaza and he entered the apartment with his flashlight. Within a few minute the beam of the light fell on the deed on the floor under
the bed. He stuck the brown envelope inside his jacket and quietly left.

A few short blocks down the street he was lured into the Casa del Café by the
strong aroma of freshly brewed coffee. Sipping from a paper cup, he strolled out
into the center of the Plaza de Armas and stood beneath the statue of Manuel de
Cespedes. He slowly opened the faded brown envelope and read the deed to the
Hacienda del Azucar, dated 1763 when the sad realization that Holly had chosen
this piece of faded parchment and an older man tore at his heart.

Relondo Silas felt it strange, however, that he had no hatred for Luis Benes: a
man who stole his woman but paid the price after being duped by the American
spy. It seemed so senseless now for Planky to have killed him when all the CIA
had to do was to abort the mission.

Captain Silas sat down on the bench and tried to rationalize the last twenty-
four hours. *First, I murdered Don Carlos on Castro's orders, now Luis for the
CIA. There are no good men left in this fight against Fidel, only opportunists,
murderers, and foreign CIA cowards in Washington. I am a professional soldier
trained to follow orders. But damn it,* he thought, *I should have been a priest.
Priests don't have to murder people in cold blood.*

Relondo suddenly realized that if the CIA killed Luis, they were probably
planning on killing him too. If not, they would expose him to Castro and he would
be a traitor to his country and be executed by a firing squad just like Don Carlos
had been.

The captain cringed at the sounds before reflecting back on the Battle for San Blas. He was captured in his nightshirt and locked in his barracks by an *Americano* and a handful of exiles. He was terrified by the shelling while, at the same time, cursing Holly for her self-serving newspaper articles that had him posted to San Blas in the first place. He could hear Don Carlos' voice now, as clear as the morning sky which seemed to say it all: *"May the gentle winds of Cuba cleanse your sins, my friend, and may God spare your soul from hell."*

"May God spare my soul," the captain said aloud, watching the sun turn into an orange glow in the east and feeling good about delivering Don Carlos' letter to his children at the embassy after his death.

The passing front had left the sky a deep blue giving it the appearance of a painted prop on a theater stage. Seated on a park bench, the captain suddenly felt the urge to take his pistol and shoot it full of holes when his eye caught the lifeless face of the father of Cuba's War of Independence standing on the pedestal above him. *Cespedes was a patriot, a poet, and a planter who gave his life to free Cuba. God, what a hero. Why could I not have been remembered for doing something good and decent instead of being filmed by Holly Woodson executing an innocent man?*

A deep darkness fell over Relondo Silas remembering the many nights the three of them had strolled under the Plaza de Armas faded filigreed lamps. Gazing up into the face of the bronze statue, thoughts of his pistol in its highly polished holster reentered his tormented mind. The only honorable thing left to do was for the captain to blow his brains out. But first he had to go the Hotel Nacional and confess to Holly that he had no way of knowing that Planky would shoot Luis between the eyes. Relondo prayed she would forgive him, and if not, he would kill her too.

Relondo stuck the deed to the Hacienda del Azucar back into his jacket, feeling the frustration of Holly's betrayal over a worthless deed and his closest friend. He rose and started his long walk to the Hotel Nacional when he heard Major Valdés getting out of his car, calling, "Captain Silas, come with me, you're wanted for questioning in the death of Luis Benes."

Relondo froze, glancing up at the noise of the British Airways Constellation taking off overhead.

I've made it! Holly Woodson sighed from the plane above as she began to cry at seeing the symmetrical lines of headstones in the *Cementerio Colon* and all of Havana passing beneath her. She had read the morning *Revolucion* as she waited to board the British Airways flight for Bermuda with Luis Benes' picture on the front page. The article told of the arrangements for his state funeral with Fidel Castro's eulogy that afternoon in the cemetery below.

She dried her eyes before reading the article in *The Revolucion* denying the Castro regime's connection to Lee Harvey Oswald and the Kennedy assassination as blatant CIA propaganda that threatened the Cuban people with another invasion.

Four hours later, when she arrived in Bermuda to change planes, she bought a copy of the *International Herald Tribune* to see if her article on the DGI's investigation into Luis Benes' death and the CIA assassination plot to sabotage Cuba's 1964 sugar crop had hit the British press. *Nothing.*

There was suddenly a feeling, a very sickening feeling; the same emptiness felt the night Holly Woodson told Clive Langford she was pregnant at Lady Margaret Hall. *The CIA is going to kill me for writing about Luis' murder!*

Holly raced to the nearest pay phone and called London. "Hello, Father. Is there anything over the wire about a Cuban official named Luis Benes being murdered in Havana?"

"Not that I have seen and I check everything. What is wrong, Holly?"

"Send a car to Heathrow—British Airways flight Number 47 arriving at seven o'clock to meet me tonight. I'm on the lam, so for God's sake, don't you come along."

Sir Allenby had been in his study editing a BBC documentary on the dead American President's Irish heritage when he received the call. Hearing the fear in his daughter's voice riveting into his ear. "Tell me, Holly, what in the bloody hell is this all about?"

"Just book me a flight to some out of the way place in the name of Jane Austin until we can talk," Holly replied, hanging up.

"Holly—wait." Allenby shouted when the line went dead. *My God! What in the bloody hell have I done to my daughter?*

Five hours later a driver was at Heathrow Airport holding a sign for Miss Austin. "I have an important meeting, so go straight away to the Park Lane Hotel, 105 Piccadilly," she told him after he handed her a large brown envelope marked "confidential." As the cab crept through the traffic on its way into central London, Holly read her father's note:

> Dear Holly,
>
> Your plane ticket to Barcelona out of Gatwick is enclosed for Sunday evening at 9 o'clock. I called ahead to my contact at the British Consulate to meet you at customs with your visa. Jeremy Thrasher is a very tall man with a peculiar shaped head. You can't miss him.
>
> Proceed to San Bastion, a quaint fishing village sixty or so kilometers down the coast towards Portugal, where you will find the Villa de Playa on the far end of town. I met the owner, Don Juan Horrillo, years ago in Madrid while covering the Spanish Civil War and he owes me his life. Send me a telegram immediately upon your arrival. I beg your forgiveness for getting you into this bloody mess—I was dead wrong in trying to have you live Harold's life.
>
> Love,
> Daddy

What a wonderful man, Holly thought thanking the driver. She put on her sunglasses and a scarf before hurrying into the Park Lane Hotel and registering under her alias for the night.

It was past seven on Sunday night and Holly Woodson was in a taxi on the way to Victoria Station to catch the train to Gatwick Airport. She suddenly broke into tears at the thoughts of leaving behind her lovers—one dead and the other holding the deed to the House of Sugar, she prayed.

The cabdriver, seeing his lovely passenger's despair in his rearview, turned up the classical music on his radio and did not know what to say when a news bulletin was announced: "The BBC interrupts this program to bring you a breaking news bulletin on the assassination of President John F. Kennedy. Lee Harvey Oswald has just been shot to death in the Dallas, Texas police station. The shooting took place at 11:21 AM Dallas time and was witnessed by millions of Americans on live television as Oswald was being taken for arraignment to the Federal Magistrate's chambers as the lone assassin in President Kennedy's murder. Mr. Jack Ruby, a Dallas nightclub owner, is now in custody for the shooting of Oswald. We will keep you informed on further events in Dallas."

"*Oh my God!* Step on it driver, I cannot afford to miss my train." Holly cried out, realizing now that tailing Lee Harvey Oswald to Dallas had confirmed her fate as the next victim of the CIA's cover up of the assassination of the President of the United States.

***

On the Friday afternoon of Kennedy's assassination, Axial Hanson flew into Midway Airport in Chicago arriving at 6 P.M. He took a taxi downtown to the Ambassador East Hotel on North State, the hangout for Frank Sinatra and his Rat Pack along with the National Commission. Wearing a pair of dark glasses and a black wig, he cased the hotel lobby while having coffee in the legendary Pump Room before calling the front desk to see if Mr. John Rawlston from Las Vegas was registered.

"Who may I say is calling?" the desk clerk asked.

"Hudson, Alex Hudson."

The clerk excused himself and returned in a few moments. "Do you want me to ring Mr. Rawlston's room, sir?"

"No thanks. I'll check back later. Just give him the message that Alex Hudson is back in town."

Hanson took a cab to the Nickerbocker Hotel; a small boutique property located a short distance from the nightlife on Rush Street, where he rewarded himself with a prostitute, before taking a shower and a nap.

Two hours later he was back at the Ambassador East entering the hotel through the staff entrance and taking the service elevator to the top floor where Sam Giancana's bodyguards met him. "Alex Hudson for Mr. Rawlston," he said to them.

The doors of the Presidential Suite swung open with the eruption of a standing ovation from the Mafia boss Sam Giancana and his closest lieutenants. "Nine-fingers! Welcome back to Chicago, partner. We done pulled it off! Now get in here and let me fix you a drink, you beautiful White Handed son-of-a-bitch."

Johnny Roselli ran over and stuck a glass of champagne in Hanson's hand while a peroxide blond in a low-cut dress took his overcoat.

"Babe, you and them other broads get the hell out of here for a while, *capisce?*" Giancana ordered. "Us guys gotta talk."

Axial Hanson flashed a broad smile with his toast: "To Bobby Kennedy. He needs no eulogy. The president speaks for him."

When the laughter and cheering died down, his voice turned serious. "Congratulations to the Black Hand. It's a pleasure to work with professionals who can get the job done. Now all we have to do, gentlemen, is keep a low profile until Earl Warren has finished his investigation."

"Who d'fuck is Earl Warren?" Trafficante shouted across the room.

"The Chief Justice of the Supreme Court, bozo," Giancana laughed. "Hey, Nine-fingers, how the hell did you know about that?"

"Sam, my friend, I'm the White Hand, remember?" Hanson replied, knowing that the new President of the United States had just appointed the 'Great White Case Officer' as a member of the Warren Commission. Allen Dulles was now the official point man responsible for coordinating all evidence in the investigation of any wrong doing by the intelligence communities of the United States Government.

"Now, Sam, if you gentlemen will excuse me, I can be reached in Saigon having a drink at the Hotel Continental's On the Shelf Bar if you need me."

Giancana held up his glass. "Thanks again, Nine-fingers. And here's to Bobby Kennedy—a big headache is coming from us guys in the Chicago Outfit, the New Orleans Combine, and the New York Mob…"

"Here's to the National Commission!" Hanson added with the self-satisfaction that he had orchestrated the coup d'etat for the overthrow of the Government of the United States to add to his list.

***

In Odessa, Texas, Lara Jane Morris was having the worst Thanksgiving of her life. She stared out of the dining room window of her new ranch home on the outskirts of town hoping at any moment to see her son's Ford convertible coming up the driveway. She looked at her husband, tears streaming down her cheeks, as he bowed his head and said Thanksgiving grace: "Dear Lord, bless this food to the nourishment of our bodies and please, oh Lord, bring our Billy safely back from wherever over yonder across the pond Billy's serving in the Army at. Amen."

"Now, Momma, pass the gravy and don't you cry," Leon said, looking up. "Why Billy's over there somewhere having C-rations for Thanksgiving and I'll bet you a hundred dollars our boy's doing just fine."

"But Leon, baby, we haven't heard from Billy since before Labor Day. That's nearly three months ago, and it's just not like him not to write."

"I know, but all we can do is wait and see what Lyndon can find out next week for us. You know if anybody can find out where Billy's at, it's the President of the United States. Lyndon promised me he'd get right on it come Monday morning and send one of his very best aides, fellow with the CIA called Walter Elliot, over to that Laos place." Leon Morris sighed as he poured giblet gravy over his turkey and dressing.

Until the sequel,

House of Deception: Laos and the Secret Opium War

The *House of Deception* is a startling account of the CIA Secret War in Laos for control of the Golden Triangle opium supply to prop up the governments of the United States' corrupt allies in Southeast Asia. It is the story of the State Department's overthrow of the South Vietnam government and the Johnson Administration's use of covert deception by the CIA to orchestrate the Tonkin Gulf Resolution that led to Congress declaring war on North Vietnam. It is a story of the heroin addiction of thousands of American GIs who were sent to fight and die in the rice paddies and jungles of Southeast Asia—the genesis of America's current "War on Drugs" that we are still fighting today.

The novel unveils the State Department betrayal of its Hmong allies abandoned to the horrors of the Communist chemical-biological genocide in the aftermath of the United States withdrawal from Laos in 1975. It is the untold account of high-ranking members of the intelligence community, operating under the cloak of patriotism, obtaining vast personal fortunes by dealing with the Mafia in international armaments and narcotics to fund the Contras in the Nicaraguan Civil War.

The novel begins with Walter Elliot being sent to Laos to find Lieutenant Tex Morris who is missing in action while training General Vang Pao's Hmong mercenaries to fight the Pathet Lao Communists. Axial Hanson and Bob Planky have been assigned to Saigon to orchestrate the Kennedy Administration's assassination of President Ngo Dinh Diem. Walter, suffering from a defective heart, lives in constant fear that the Warren Commission investigation into the assassination of the President will reveal his role in the White Hand conspiracy.

Holly Woodson has gone into hiding on the Spanish *Costa del Sol* after realizing that she will be killed for her knowledge that Lee Harvey Oswald was not the 'lone gunman.' While she mourns Luis Benes' death, she becomes aware that Captain Relondo Silas has been picked up by the DGI for questioning in Benes' murder.

In New Orleans, the orphan Manny Garcia becomes a high school baseball star getting into serious trouble with the local Mafia's daughter. Maria is a student at the University of Miami when Cuban intelligence agent Eduardo Martinez infiltrates the U.S., seeking revenge for the beating he received by Don Carlos at the Bar Habana as a teenager.

The deed to the *Hacienda del Azucar* becomes lost in time awaiting the demise of Fidel Castro's Communist government and the return of the *House of Sugar* into the hands Manuel Garcia.

Printed in the United States
851200002B